One of the Boys

One of the Boys

VICTORIA ZELLER

LQ

Montclair | Amsterdam | Hoboken

This is an Arthur A. Levine Book
Published by Levine Querido

www.levinequerido.com · info@levinequerido.com
Levine Querido is distributed by Chronicle Books, LLC
Copyright © 2025 by Victoria Zeller
Selection on page 121 from "FUCKMYLIFE666"
written by Laura Jane Grace, © Total Treble Music (BMI),
administered by Rough Trade Publishing (BMI).
Selection on page 183 from "Buffalo," by Spencer Hall, *SB Nation*
and Vox Media, LLC.
All rights reserved.

Library of Congress Control Number: 2024942334
ISBN 978-1-64614-502-7
Printed and bound in China

Published in May 2025
First Printing

*For the girls like me that taped their wrists,
fastened their chinstraps,
and hid their hearts.*

PART I

September

"My art occurs over the course of 1.3 seconds . . . This 1.3 second field goal operation—from the snap to the hold to the kick—is a performance."

—Justin Tucker, Commencement speech for the University of Texas College of Fine Arts, 2014

One

My last shift at Lucky's could've gone better.

I slept through a half-dozen alarms and woke up just as my shift was supposed to start, which, *great*. I rushed through my morning ritual—a delicate dance of scalding hot water, razors, and cheap concealer—in the resulting panic, which led to predictable disaster when I sliced my chin open. By the time I stopped the bleeding and got my makeup done, I'd officially given up on punctuality. I didn't even bother speeding on the highway to make up lost time.

When I strolled into the kitchen at Lucky's an hour late for my shift, Natalie was nuclear. Even her moles were glaring at me. "Where were you, Grace?"

Usually, I would've lied and said I was held up in traffic or something. But since I planned on never seeing her again in my life if I could help it, I just shrugged. "I slept in. Won't happen again, I promise."

She didn't appreciate the joke. I was staring down the barrel of Mad Nat one last time, then. *Wonderful.*

It was a busy morning by Lucky's standards, the other servers and I all flying around the place like professional athletes. Our regular clientele was a mix of fussy old people, townies, and the odd trucker or two blown in off the 90, but, unfortunately, it was Labor Day weekend. Since Lucky's was right by Buffalo Niagara International, we were swamped by groggy tourists who just got off their red-eyes and couldn't seem to grasp that Niagara Falls wasn't spitting distance from their terminal.

My tables were a mixed bag: a very polite family from India that tipped well, a trucker who wouldn't stop staring at my flat chest, a handful of regulars who joked about the hustle and bustle. By the time I reached my first cigarette break (I didn't smoke, but I told Natalie I did for those sweet, sweet breaks), I felt like I'd done light cardio.

Pros of working at Lucky's: it gave me something to do, it was far enough away from Pageland that I never saw people I recognized, most of my coworkers were nice enough, and the tips were okay when people thought I was a girl.

Cons of working at Lucky's: Mad Nat ran the place like the Navy, it was a pain in the ass to drive all the way out to the airport every shift, and the tips weren't as good when customers didn't know what to make of me.

A millisecond after I reentered the diner, Natalie pounced. "Seventeen," she barked. "Go."

I took a moment to slip back into Server Mode before venturing out onto the floor. Table Seventeen was by these big bay windows that gave you a *wonderful* scenic view of the parking lot, so it was always in demand. A party of one had claimed it: a thirties-ish Black dude in a polo and a visor. He'd turned the table into an improvised workstation, complete with two (two!) legal pads and a laptop.

He gave me a strained smile when I asked him what he wanted to drink. "Just some coffee," he said. "That's all I need, actually."

"That's it?"

He nodded, his eyes going back to his laptop screen. He tapped his trackpad impatiently. "I'm a good tipper, I promise. Just keep my cup full. Lord knows I need it."

When I came back with his coffee, it hit me: Seventeen must've been a football coach. If you're wearing a matching polo and visor, you're either a coach or a professional golfer, and this dude was *not* built like Tiger Woods. I didn't recognize the logo on his polo; an out-of-towner, maybe? A nosy glance told me that he was watching game film on his laptop, but glare from the window made deciphering the details impossible.

"You sure you don't need anything else?" I asked him during refill number four, now officially concerned. Lucky's coffee was garbage—*always* burnt—but he sucked it down without cream or sugar. "Food? Water? Our coffee's not *that* good."

He didn't bother to look up from the notetaking he was doing on his legal pad. Coaches rarely mean to be rude; they're just so busy they forget how to be human sometimes. "Maybe that wouldn't be a bad idea. Food, I mean. What's good here?"

I'd developed rehearsed answers over the summer, but I was in a very fuck-it, burn-it-all-down mood. "Not much," I said, shrugging. "The omelettes are decent, but we don't season the home fries, like, at *all*. The chicken souvlaki's pretty solid, actually, but only when they order the good feta."

The corners of his mouth twitched. "That was . . . honest."

"It's my last day," I explained, wiping off my sweaty palms on my apron. "Three hours to go."

He laughed, deep and warm, and I found myself warming up to the guy. "Home stretch!"

He ordered two eggs and toast, and when I set the plate in front of him ten minutes later, I decided to go for it. "You a football coach?"

He spun his pen between his fingers and gave me a Look. "I am, actually. Jerome Metellus, University of Wisconsin–Saxon Valley."

I knew what that Look meant. I was pretty visibly trans—sturdy and broad—so he'd probably assumed I was some artsy kid that was allergic to sports. "That's an FCS school, right?"

He looked amused. "New to FBS, actually. We play Buffalo tomorrow, so I'm doing some scouting today. Going to a few scrimmages, talking to recruits."

Right, it was scrimmage week. It'd been surprisingly easy for me to forget the rhythm of football's endless offseason. "Where you headed?"

"Out to some town called Pageland," Jerome said. "Public school there's having a scrimmage. Then, uh, St. Sebastian's, it's called, to meet this one linebacker named *Cleavers*. You ever heard a name like that in your life?"

God, keeping my poker face was *impossible*, but I tried my best. "That's where I go, actually. Pageland, obviously. I'm *not* a private school kid."

He laughed at that. "You know ball?"

It was such a ridiculous question I had to bite back a smirk. "A little," I said. "My brother used to play."

Smoothest lie I've ever told. Definitely.

"Great! You can be my Upstate New York sherpa, then."

"*Western* New York," I corrected him reflexively. "Say the U-word to the wrong people around here, you'll get yelled at. There's a difference."

He snorted. "Good to know. Got any Ahmed Nassar intel? Bad grades? Character concerns?" He clicked his pen. "You know him at all? I just wanna know if it's even worth my time."

Yeah, I *definitely* knew Ahmed. I spent junior year partying in his backyard, sure, but I'd also played soccer with him before he hit his growth spurt in seventh grade and practically doubled in size overnight. He started playing left tackle the next year, and it wasn't long after that that colleges started sniffing around. By the start of our senior year, he was a four-star prospect on FightSong, ranked the eleventh-best tackle in the country. Schools from the Big Ten to the SEC were all over him.

"He's out of your league," I told him, figuring he'd appreciate the honesty. "He's basically Superman. Class president, in APs, all that stuff. Good guy, too."

He sighed. "I figured. Still, there's lots of players to watch. Cleavers looks like the real deal. And your kicker's supposed to be a real gem, too."

Oh.

Maybe I should've expected that.

If Jerome noticed me flinch, he didn't say anything. I gave him a vacant look. "Really? I don't think we have anyone special. I dunno, I don't follow it closely."

He glanced at his notes before looking back at me, brows furrowed. "Dang, my information must be wrong. I thought Jordan Woodhouse kicked at your school."

My hand traveled absent-mindedly to my nametag. *Grace. Grace.* "Not anymore," I said, turning to leave. "Pretty sure Woodhouse quit."

I took my time looping back around to Jerome, letting our conversation wilt and die. He was just a recruiter doing his job, and I refused to let it faze me. Maybe he'd get lucky and that linebacker from St. Sebastian's would work out, keep this from being a wasted trip. Either way, it wasn't my business. By the time I checked on him again, he'd packed up his notebooks.

"I'll take the check," he said. "I'm all set."

He paid cash, making a big show of fishing two twenties out of his wallet and leaving them under his coffee cup as his tip. "Thanks for the service, Grace," he said, his eyes finding my nametag. If my name in contrast to my voice or appearance tripped him up, he didn't show it. "I appreciate it. Don't work too hard, alright?"

I thanked him, gathered up his dishes, and hustled them back to the kitchen. My hands were shaking. I needed another "cigarette" break.

Before—Last November

Your last name's Woodhouse, so most people call you Woody. You play football. You're in the middle of a game right now.

"Woody!" comes the call from Coach Rutkowski. "*Woody!*"

Your team, Pageland High, is trailing Bellarmine Jesuit 19 to 17. Your offense stalled out just two yards away from the end zone. There are three seconds on the clock. Your coach is about to tell you it's your job to win the game.

You jog over to him, try to keep yourself loose. "Here, Coach."

He looks down at you skeptically. He's never trusted you, even with how well you've kicked this year. "You ready?"

"I got this," you say, rolling your shoulders. "One hundred percent."

You jog onto the field with the rest of the field goal unit while the Pageland crowd makes some noise. Even though tonight's game is out in Brockport—a solid hour-and-a-half drive away—*everyone* showed up. This is the deepest playoff run the Druids have had in decades. It's a big deal.

One tiny kick and you're through to State Semifinals. Piece of cake.

Dray, an old friend, grabs you as he trots off the field with the offense. He slaps your helmet, brings you close. "You got this, Woody. You're a beast!"

You slap his helmet back. "You know it, bro."

You're arrogant. You're good, and you know it. FightSong ranks you as the eighteenth-best junior kicker in the country, but you might be even better than that. This kick will help you climb even higher.

"Alright, boys," you say in the huddle. "We make this op perfect, we go home, we *fucking* celebrate."

Ahmed grins like a maniac and cracks his knuckles. "Party at my place."

A senior lineman laughs. "Yeah, Ock, we know."

As you break the huddle, Truck—the long snapper, and one of your best friends when he isn't being weird—grabs you by the shoulder. "Focus, alright? We still have to pull this off."

He's been kind of a bitch lately. "Just snap the ball, Trucky," you say, shrugging off his hand. "Leave the hard part to me."

He stares at you for a moment, then he shakes his head. He says nothing.

Ash, the holder, taps your helmet. "Don't worry about him, bro. Get in your zone."

You line up next to Ash, take a deep breath, and pace out three steps back, then two to your left. You've made big kicks before (like the forty-eight-yarder in Week One that put you on the map), but you've never had to make a game-winner. This one'll be cake: nineteen yards out, neutral field. In a few years, you'll be playing in front of tens of thousands of fans at a Big Ten school and this'll look like a joke to you.

That's when you notice something.

One of Bellarmine's linebackers, this tall dude wearing twenty-nine, is dancing. He waves his arms over his head, thrashes them around, does everything short of the funky chicken to try and get your attention. A field goal operation is rehearsed to the millisecond: every movement from Truck's snap to Ash's hold to your kick have to be perfect. No mistakes. No lapses in concentration.

Two-Nine's trying to get in your head. It's pathetic, really. Big bad Bellarmine's going out *sad*.

Ash calls for the snap and Truck puts the ball right in his hands. Ash's hold is perfect. They're both perfect.

You're the one who blows it.

You're a beat too late on your first approach step, and it throws everything else out of whack. Your plant foot is too far back, your stance is too open, your follow-through is clipped. As soon as it leaves your foot, your heart sinks. You pulled it.

The ball hits the left upright with a horrible *clang*, a sound you'll never forget. The uprights shake and groan as the ball careens wide left. The referees take a beat, almost like they're as shocked as you are, before waving their arms in confirmation.

The announcer cries: *"The kick is no good!"*

While Bellarmine's players start losing their minds and your teammates look around in disbelief, you feel that horrible sensation behind your eyes. You blink hard. You will *not* cry in public. You *won't*.

"Woody—"

Before Truck can finish his thought, you shove him away from you. *Hard.* "Don't touch me," you hiss, even though he never touched you. "Learn how to fucking snap!"

While the rest of the team steps in to try and calm you down, your mind is blank. You can't hear them. Mentally, you're gone. You want to be somewhere far away from here; somewhere dark, somewhere alone.

Two

"You know the guy who painted rectangle people?"

I glared at my reflection in the bathroom mirror while Riley pondered the question on the other end of our video call. "Uh, you mean Picasso?"

"Yeah, Picasso," I replied, leaning closer to the mirror, scrutinizing my upper lip. Had I hit it with enough concealer? "I look like one of Picasso's idiot rectangle people. That's what my whole body looks like right now."

Even though I'd spent months mentally preparing for my grand reinstatement into Pageland High's social scene, I still woke up scared shitless on the first day of senior year. I ended up calling Riley, one of my best friends, hoping some of her easy confidence would rub off on me. It didn't seem to be working.

"You're not even *slightly* rectangular," she said, rolling her eyes.

I took a step back from the mirror and heaved a deep breath. I tried to find some things about myself I didn't hate, which is what people on the internet said to do. I was proud of my hair: muddy reddish-brown, frizzy and wild from the years I'd gone since my last trim. I never minded the freckles that ran from cheekbone to cheekbone, which Grandma used to say gave me "character." My eyes were alright, I guess. Precisely once, Zoe called them *pretty*. I savored that compliment for months, like a little kid carefully rationing the last few pieces of her Halloween candy deep into December.

My shoulders were *wide*. They were always the first thing I noticed about my body, forever sticking out like they had blaring sirens attached. I was still pretty muscular, too, even though a summer away from football and a few months of estradiol had softened me somewhat. I had a face that Zoe used to call *handsome*, all sharp features and jawbone. A face that looked a lot like Dad's.

I closed my eyes and swore under my breath, cursing the night Dad took a waitress home eighteen years ago and set the clown car that is my life in motion.

"Picasso's the guy who cut his ear off, right?" I asked. Weighing my options felt like the responsible thing to do. "If I cut my ear off, do I get to skip school?"

"Grace Woodhouse," Riley said, her voice severe like she was giving a lecture. "Even I know that was Van Gogh. And you need to *stop hiding*. Who was a dick to you when you came out in June?"

I didn't say anything.

"Go on now, make a list. I'll wait!"

"No one was a dick *to my face*," I protested. "But that doesn't mean it's gonna be all sunshine and rainbows, you know."

Coming out *had* gone better than I thought it would, all in all. I'd locked my Instagram, done a big heartfelt post with a few photos, all the stuff you're supposed to do. It'd gotten a lot of attention in Pageland circles, all of it positive. A stream of congratulatory texts and DMs trickled in for a week afterward, mostly from girls I was friendly with from classes. Zoe sent me a single heart emoji, which somehow felt like both way too much and not nearly enough. Even my old friends from the football team seemed to be mostly cool about it, or at least the ones who'd bothered to reach out and say something did.

All anyone ever told me was that it was *so* surprising that *I*, of all people, was trans. There were a billion reasons why people thought that, and pretty much all of them made me feel like shit.

"You worried about seeing Zoe again or something?"

"*No*," I said, admittedly too quickly. I wasn't in the mood to wander into that particular minefield anytime soon. "It's fine. It'll be fine."

"Ooh-*kay*," she said, not sounding convinced. "Still, I'm gonna pick you up. It's the first day of school, Mom's gotta walk you to the door."

"I am *older* than you."

"Whatever! I'm scooping you and Tab, you ungrateful bitch. Want anything from Tim's?"

I told her I just wanted coffee (with cream and sugar, obviously, I'm not a psycho), and a moment later, my phone *beep*ed as Riley hung up. I was alone again.

I hastily threw on mascara and turned over what Riley said in my head a few times. She was right; I *had* been hiding. I took a summer job at Lucky's because it was out of town, I avoided all the big summer parties like the plague. Being a guy, as much as I'd hated it, was easy: there was a script, and if you followed it, you wouldn't have any problems. But now I had to figure *all* this out—Grace, the real me, whatever you wanna call it—as I went along.

I dug through my makeup bag, found my favorite lipstick—this bright red thing I found at Sephora that really popped against my ghostly skin—and ran my hand through a tangle of hair one last time. *Sure*, I thought. *I could buy that that's a girl in the mirror.*

"Morning," my dad grunted in my general direction as I slipped out the front door. In his left hand he juggled a coffee thermos and a lunch bag; in his right, a garden hose. With his hands occupied, his glasses slid treacherously down his nose. "I see Riley's giving you a ride."

I glanced at the street to find Riley's pickup parked in the shade of a tree. She promptly flipped me off. "She probably thinks I'm gonna run off and join the circus if she doesn't escort me herself."

"Well, that's nice of her." He released the trigger on his fancy hose nozzle, the spray of water vanishing, and pushed his glasses back up. Dad took his garden *seriously*; if he wasn't leaving the house for work at the crack of dawn, it usually had to do with the garden. "You, uh, ready for school and everything?"

"Think so."

That was a pretty typical conversation for us. It'd been just me and him since my mom ditched us when I was two, so we had the system down to a science. Even though Dad's job was 1) union and 2) pretty great—a fact he drilled into me young, which was why I got in trouble in seventh grade history class for calling George Pullman a bitch—he worked overtime a lot. He'd trusted me to look after myself for ages, and we'd always used the same language: *Do you need anything? Is there anything I need to know about? I need you to do this for me.*

It wasn't better or worse than any other father–daughter relationship, I guess. I'd always had a long leash to do whatever I wanted, and if I ever needed anything he came through like clockwork. When I told him I needed a car if I wanted a summer job, Lorraine appeared in the driveway a few days later. When I told him back in April that I needed to transition, he nodded, said he respected me, and asked what I needed from him.

I mean, he wasn't exactly a wizard in the feelingsball department, but you take what you can get.

"Working late tonight?"

Dad scratched at his scruffy beard while he mulled it over. "Dunno yet. I'll text you later about dinner. Capisce?"

I sighed. He wasn't much of a cook anyway. "Capisce."

◆

Tab agreed to take the middle seat without even putting up a fight, which is how I knew she was worried about me.

"Look at you!" she cried, giving me a one-armed hug. "You're *glowing*, Grace!"

"S'just sunburn. Some of us have to deal with that kinda thing, you know."

Her brow furrowed. "I sunburn, dummy. Being Bori doesn't give me Superman ultraviolet powers."

Feeling enlightened ever since I told her I liked Bad Bunny and she responded by sending me a dozen essays about Puerto Rican independence, I had the confidence to say: "I know! I just meant you're not Irish!"

"Or Dutch," Riley chipped in.

She rolled her eyes and passed me my drink. "Just take the compliment, Woodhouse."

I grumbled a *thank you* and sipped my coffee, praying the sugary caffeine would magically fix me. "Sick necklace, by the way."

Tab smiled and fingered the steel pentagram charm. It had intricate runes etched into the metal, a ruby centerpiece. Tab had announced a couple months ago that she was entering her goth era, and it looked like she was committed. "Badass, right?"

"She put it on in the car so her mom didn't see it," Riley noted breezily, drumming her callused fingers on the steering wheel.

"Shut up! You are literally *so* annoying."

"It's cute, Tab. Riley, leave her alone."

Riley had bought her ancient pickup, Scarlett, for a few hundred bucks back in May and spent the summer fixing it up in her driveway. She'd done an admirable job, but Scarlett's one flaw was that she didn't have a back seat, just a bench seat you could squeeze three butts into if you felt ambitious. Since Tab couldn't drive and my car—following Riley's lead, I'd named her Lorraine—only had AC when she felt like it, our three butts ended up squeezed into that seat a lot.

The bench seat was why Riley had to lean around Tab to flip me off for the second time that morning, her shock of green hair *whooshing* along with her.

I sighed. "I feel so loved and supported by you, Ri."

"You should! I'm a *great* friend! Why do you think the other girls voted me captain?"

"*Co*-captain," Tab corrected her. "I'm telling Imani you said that."

"Yeah? When are you getting voted co-captain of the theater club, loser?"

I stared out the window and kept quiet while the girls sniped at each other. I didn't remember quite when the play-fighting started—whether it was immediately after the three of us got grouped together in trig last year or when we started hanging out outside of class—but we'd been communicating via good-natured roasts ever since. Normally, it put me at ease. That morning, though? I was wound up so tight I barely even heard them bicker.

By the time Riley pulled Scarlett into the Pageland High parking lot, Tab knew something was up. She gave my knee a reassuring pat. "It'll be okay, Grace. We've got your back, okay? Promise."

I tried to give her a brave smile. Key word: tried.

When you come out as trans, most people pretend nothing's different.

They might not get it, they might not *want* to get it, or they're terrified acknowledging it will drag them into a conversation they don't want to have. Those people simply choose not to see you: they'll look over your shoulder, mumble a *hello* if they have to, and keep it moving. There are also the confused glances, the Looks that linger just a second too long, the wide-eyed stares you manage to catch in the corner of your eye.

Only a few brave souls dared to approach me directly on the first day, and they all had questions.

Chill senior girl I kinda knew from last year's English class: "Oh, hey, I saw your coming out post! How'd you come up with your new name?"

Junior girl I only knew from her constant cat video retweets: "You're really inspiring, you know that? And, like, if you *ever* need makeup tips or anything, let me know!"

Weepy junior guy who did something for the school yearbook: "So, like, are you just *really* gay?"

Senior girl who did National Honor Society with Zoe: "I know it's none of my business, but is this why you guys broke up?"

After suffering through four periods of *that* (mixed with typical first-day-of-school drudgery), I was more than ready for lunch with the girls. When I spotted Tab waving me over to a relatively secluded corner table in East Cafeteria—a coveted spot, one we'd been hoping to snag—I breathed a sigh of relief.

"So, everyone," Tab said, patting my shoulder, "this is Grace."

"She's alright," Riley said. "Be nice to her. I'm talking to *you*, Jamie."

It was a motley crew: some of them Riley's people, some Tab's, some in-between. I already knew Imani Westbrook, thankfully; she was Riley's co-captain on the soccer team. Tab sat with her theater friends: Robin, who was playing absent-mindedly with a tarot deck, and Jade, who had an Instagram account just for her houseplants. Jamie Navarro, who sat across from me, flashed me a toothy grin when I waved *hi*. I recognized him from his moderately popular skateboarding TikToks and the Stoner Pigpen–style weed cloud that always seemed to follow him around. And also, you know, for being the only other trans kid in our grade. "It's an exclusive club, Grace. Welcome."

I tried my best to return his smile. "It's an honor."

Tab and her theater friends started talking about some indie band I'd never heard of, and when the rest of the table joined in, I let myself fade into the background. I hadn't felt this much like a token new kid in years. The great thing about football was the built-in friend group: you could show up on your first day of school and know fifty guys already. You never had to go it alone, never had to make new friends if you didn't want to. I'd always hung out with them in classes, lunch, everything in between. It was *easy*.

After a few minutes, I felt a soft kick against my shin. I looked up to find Jamie, concern breaking through his perma-chill stoner visage. "Hanging in there?"

"It's . . . tough."

"It is," he agreed, taking a moment to munch thoughtfully on a kettle chip. Even though both Riley and Tab were friendly with the guy, I'd never talked to him before. I'd never talked to *any* person like me before. "Forget to bring something to eat?"

Somehow, I only just realized that I had. I nodded, feeling dumb.

"You like pears?"

Before I could answer, he reached into a paper bag and, with a clean flick of the wrist, sent a pear skittering across the table. I snatched it just before it could fall off the edge onto the cafeteria floor. "Sick catch."

I turned the pear over in my hand a few times, oddly touched by the whole thing. "Thanks, man."

He shrugged, like, *no big deal*, and went right back to his chips like nothing ever happened.

The first few bites I took settled in my anxious stomach like cement. I cleared my throat, trying to distract myself. "So, uh..." God, this was stupid. It'd never been hard for me to be outgoing when I was a boy, when I played the part of a cocky football player. So why couldn't I string together a full sentence for Jamie Navarro? "Are we still the only ones?"

"The only out trans kids, you mean?" He took a moment to ponder that. "We're the only seniors I know of. There's gotta be some underclassmen, though. I know of at least two closeted freshmen."

"How do you know freshmen?"

"Support group," he said, like no further explanation was needed. "Like I said, might be more. 'Course, there *used* to be Dee, but she graduated last year. I dunno if you knew her, or..."

As far as I knew, Dee was the first trans girl Pageland High had ever seen; she came out before her senior year, just like I did. She was effortlessly feminine in that way that trans girls were supposed to be, the way I wasn't. Even once I figured myself out, I was way too intimidated to talk to her. What could we possibly have in common?

And now, as good as it felt to be surrounded by friendly faces, it was hard not to dwell on every single way that I *didn't* fit in with Tab's theater gays, or even Riley's soccer jocks. I wasn't lucky enough to be the right kind of queer.

"Never met her," I sighed. "Wish I had."

"She was badass," Jamie said, smiling a little. "But, you know, you'll do great too. You always seemed cool for a jock."

Three

A wave of relief crashed over me at the final bell. One day down, a hundred-something more to go.

I kept my head down in the hallway on the way to my locker. I felt restless; mentally tired, but physically jittery. Idle. Useless. Going home right at the bell in September just felt *wrong* when the football team was about to dig into a Tuesday practice. Maybe I needed to go on a run, burn off some of this energy.

Just as I started mentally planning out my route, a familiar voice cut through the after-school din. "Woodhouse! I was looking for you."

My head snapped up to see Kaeden Park-Campbell, of all people, standing in front of me. The guy was unassuming: five-five, skinny, arms covered in blotchy football bruises. From his position at strong safety, though, the dude was an absolute menace, throwing his body around with no regard for his health. I'd seen him make players six inches taller and fifty pounds heavier than him cry.

"Kaeden," I greeted him, unable to suppress a grin. I noticed heavy bags under his eyes. "Junior been keeping you up?"

He ran a hand through his hair. "You know, I don't even have him half the time. Mikayla and I split it up evenly. But he's five months old now. You know what sleep regression is?"

I shook my head.

He exhaled. "Don't learn."

I laughed at his expense, but started to get nervous. Kaeden and I were friendly enough that he'd liked my coming out post (I'd expected him to, given that he had two moms), but he'd never been my closest friend. If he wanted to *talk*—not just say hi—it wasn't because he'd wanted to tell me about his son's sleep schedule.

"Look," he said, sounding embarrassed, "you heard I'm replacing you at kicker, right?"

That made me perk up. "Really? I figured Rut would poach someone from the soccer team."

"Oh, he tried. Held open tryouts for a few of the boys and everything, but none of them were any good. So"—he pointed at his chest—"it's my job. Like everything else."

Kaeden was cursed by two things: 1) he was smart, and 2) he was quick to volunteer when an extra body was needed. Offense, defense, special teams, wherever. He'd become the designated utility man of the team, a steady hand who could be trusted not to mess anything up. Add *kicker* to his already lengthy list of responsibilities.

"How's it been going?"

He sighed. "I mean, I'm *okay*. I just haven't had the time, you know? I don't get the reps at kicker 'cause they need me everywhere else. I was, uh, actually wondering if you could help me?"

A choked laugh escaped my throat. "How?"

"Just a little extra work after practice. I'd go to Rhoads"—the special teams coach—"but he's old, you know? I feel bad asking him to do extra work." He winced, which is how I realized I was making a face. "You don't have to, obviously. Totally get why you wouldn't want to."

If it was anyone else, I would've said no, turned on my heel, and marched home without a second thought. But Kaeden had the most jobs on the team, a schedule full of honors classes, *and* a goddamn baby at home. I didn't know how the poor guy was still standing, let alone learning how to kick a football.

"What exactly do you have in mind?" I asked hesitantly.

He smiled. "When can you start?"

I pulled Lorraine into the Pageland High parking lot around six that afternoon, very pointedly ignoring the knot my insides had tied themselves into.

I ran through another inventory of the practice materials I'd scrounged up, pawing through the old mesh equipment bag in my passenger seat. Some part of me hoped I'd forgotten something, given myself an excuse to head back home, but I hadn't gotten lucky: there were the few footballs I had laying around, there was my kicking stand. My old cleats—highlighter-orange Nikes, made for soccer—taunted me from the top of the pile.

I glanced up at the field to find Kaeden, as expected, in a ratty T-shirt and gym shorts on the sideline. What I *didn't* expect to see were the three other guys with him. *Crap.* I hadn't dressed for a crowd; I'd just thrown on a tank top and athletic shorts. Getting feminine workout clothes had been an early-transition priority, but they still weren't a natural fit. I felt my stupid boxy body below the material with every move I made.

I closed my eyes and took a deep breath. *Teach Kaeden how to kick, suck it up, it's the right thing to do.*

I was halfway to the field when Ahmed Nassar glanced over his shoulder and called out: "Here comes Coach!"

I bit back a smile as the boys cheered, keeping my eyes glued to the ground. After what felt like an eternity, I crossed the track that circled the field and tossed my equipment bag to the ground in a heap. "Ta-da!"

Ahmed was the first to greet me, grinning like an absolute dork. "My *queen*," he said, extending his hand for a dap. "How's it going?"

I'd forgotten how big he was. I mean, I knew it logically—he was listed at six-three, two eighty last year—but it looked like he might've grown another inch over the summer. For how dangerous he was on the field, he couldn't have been less serious off of it; he was constantly making dumb jokes, throwing parties, and always, *always* smiling. It was hard to remember that he might play in the NFL someday.

"I'm alright," I said, remembering his question. "Hanging in there."

He clapped my shoulder. "Good shit."

Next up was Dray, a wide grin on his face. Since the last time I saw him, he'd switched up his hair again: he'd let his twists grow out, bleaching the ends blond. "About time, Grace."

I'm not the biggest hugger in the world, but I couldn't resist the pull. "It's good to see you, dude."

Dray had been my first real football friend, back when we were both freshmen running backs on the JV team. A few weeks into the season, our sophomore kicker tore his hamstring, and they stuck me—the kid who used to play soccer—in as the emergency kicker. Dray eventually switched positions himself, becoming one of the best receivers in Western New York.

When he came out as gay two years ago, I was embarrassed and confused and extremely *fifteen* about it. For a few months, I barely spoke to him out of an emotion that I could now see was jealousy. So stupid. Add that to the list of things I regretted.

The day I came out as trans, the very first text I got was from him. Well, the first two texts.

The first: *Grace Woodhouse!*

The second: *Feel better now?*

"Good to see you too," he said, patting my back as he pulled away from the hug. "Glad you're here."

Prez, who lingered off to the side, looked considerably less comfortable. He'd been Dray's closest friend for a few years, but the two of us had never been particularly close. He waved shyly. "Grace."

"Zachary."

That broke the ice, just like I hoped it would. "Just 'cause you're not on the team anymore doesn't mean you get to call me that," he said, rolling his eyes. "You sound like my mom."

Prez was as stereotypically Quarterback as they came: tall, blond, easy to get along with. Handsome in a *Riverdale* extra kinda way. I found myself thinking back to a party at Ahmed's last spring, one where everyone was ranking the hotness of celebrities on a one-to-ten scale. Prez had deemed me "sus" for thinking Kristen Stewart was hot, since "only lesbians" thought that. Which, yeah, funny in retrospect, but . . . did it have anything to do with why he didn't seem thrilled to see me? I mean, he was best friends with Dray, but just because you're cool with gay people doesn't mean trans people get a pass.

I decided not to linger on it. He'd shown up, after all, and he didn't have to.

Lastly, of course, was Kaeden, who I realized with a start was holding his son. I didn't *immediately* drop everything and demand to see him, but it took a lot of effort. Kaeden saw the look on my face and smiled. "You wanna hold KJ?" He held up the little dude dramatically as Dray hummed "Circle of Life," which cracked everyone up. "He's chill. He won't puke on you or anything."

I gingerly took the baby from Kaeden, holding KJ under the arms. He was pretty damn cute by baby standards, with his little mop of black curls and his tiny Buffalo Bills onesie. "Hey, buddy. What's up?"

KJ reached out his tiny hands and brushed my hair, which he seemed to find fascinating. I couldn't help but giggle. "Where'd he come from? Didn't you guys just get out of practice?"

"KJ loves ball," Dray said. "He's the next Kyler Murray."

"You can't just say that 'cause he's Black and Korean, bro," Ahmed replied, shaking his head. "That's a cancelable offense."

"That's not why I said it! I picked Kyler 'cause he's *short!*"

"My grandma dropped him off," Kaeden clarified. "He's not used to spending all this time away from me or his mom, you know? I figured he'd wanna see me ASAP."

"Aww!" KJ grabbed two fistfuls of my hair and babbled happily. "Did you miss your dad?"

Then he pulled *hard* and squealed in delight.

Kaeden looked mortified while the rest of the guys laughed at my expense. "Sorry, he *really* likes pulling hair. I should've warned you."

"It's—*ow*—it's okay!" I held him further away from me, depriving him of torturing me further. "You're a little menace, aren't you?"

KJ giggled and kicked his legs in reply. *Confirmed menace.*

"Alright, I'm calling it. Feelingsball's over." Ahmed held out his arms expectantly. "Gimme the criminal. Go coach his daddy up."

I hesitated and glanced at Kaeden, who nodded like it was the obvious thing to do. "You don't trust me?" Ahmed asked incredulously. "I'll have you know I'm excellent with kids. You know I got three little nieces."

"He's better at changing diapers than I am," Kaeden admitted sheepishly.

Once I handed KJ off to Ahmed, who started fussing over him like he was a goddamn prince, Kaeden and I lugged our equipment towards the near goalposts. I set up the kicking stand at the ten-yard line, the distance of an extra point attempt, and had him kick without any coaching to get a sense of what I was working with.

The results weren't encouraging. His steps back and to the left were all choppy and uneven; his approach was a mess. When he finally made contact with the ball, he punched it low and to the left, accompanied by copious mumbled swearing.

"Okay," I said, sucking in a breath through my teeth, trying to figure out where to begin. "Let's start with your steps."

I modeled the process for him, taking three even steps back followed by two sidesteps to the left. I walked him through his approach steps in slow motion and showed him where his plant foot was supposed to end up relative to the ball. It'd be easier if I changed into my cleats—Converse don't exactly bite into field turf—but I was afraid of the feelings they might dredge back up. Last year still hurt. I wasn't ready to poke the hornet's nest yet.

"Don't worry about kicking right now," I told him. "Work on those steps. Take it slow."

While Kaeden ran through a dozen reps, the boys settled into a spot on the turf maybe ten yards behind us. "Looking good, Kaeden!" Prez called. "You're in your Tyler Bass era!"

"I thought this was a private lesson, K," I said while Kaeden slowly counted out his steps again. "You got fans?"

"Sorry," he said sheepishly, not taking his eyes off the turf. "I mentioned it in the captains' groupchat. They invited themselves."

I put my hands on my hips and theatrically looked over the four of them. "*These* are the captains of the *Section VI favorite* Pageland Druids? We're doomed."

"C'mon now," Ahmed said. KJ sat contently on his knee, his big brown eyes trained on his father. "You know we're keeping the boys in line."

"How's the squad looking? Is this really 'Pageland's best team ever?'"

That was what every Section VI football preview seemed to think, anyway. Consensus was that the Druids would roll over their section schedule and into the state championship in Syracuse, which no Pageland team had ever made before. Given that we were a botched field goal away from State Semis last year, I could believe it.

Dray sat up straight and cleared his throat. "We're just gonna play our game, give a hundred and ten percent, and leave it all out there on the field," he said in flawless Football Speak. "We're taking it one week at a time. Right now, we're focused on Seabass."

Prez rolled his eyes as Dray cackled at his own joke. "We're gonna wreck the section. Our only real competition is Wake East, *maybe* Bennett."

"Good stuff." I glanced sideways at Kaeden. "Gonna need a kicker for all that, right? Think we're ready to put laces on leather again?"

He sighed, rolling out his shoulders. "Guess so."

Kaeden's second kick wasn't *perfect*, but it looked a hell of a lot better than his first. His steps looked solid, and even though his trajectory was a little low, his kick sailed comfortably between the uprights. The guys whooped in celebration as I slapped Kaeden on the back. "Hell yeah, dude!"

"Ugly," he noted, suppressing a grin, "but it got there."

"It's a good start. If you just make your extra points consistently, it'll put us ahead of half the schools in the state."

"Woody's right," Prez said. "Keep working at it, dude. You got this!"

We stayed at it for another ten minutes or so, just long enough for Kaeden to knock a few more kicks through the uprights. Even though he held his own, I wasn't surprised to see him hit a wall quickly; there was only so much progress you could make in one afternoon. I told him to call it a day, and he left to go chase down the balls he'd scattered behind the goalposts.

"Can you still kick, Grace?" Ahmed asked suddenly.

I shrugged, trying my hardest to act like I hadn't been wondering the exact same thing. I hadn't kicked a football since that night in November; the pain of the loss had kept me away from practicing over the winter, and by the time the pain began to fade, I realized I was a girl, and football was gone forever. "Probably not."

"Come on," Prez said, gesturing towards me with a half-eaten protein bar. "I know you can still hit 'em from deep."

Dray nudged him with his elbow. "Leave her alone, Zach. She don't wanna kick, she don't have to kick."

Kaeden came trudging back towards us, delicately balancing an armful of footballs. "Could be a good learning experience," he said with a shrug. "To watch a pro, you know."

"I was never a *pro*!"

"Says the kid who visited Penn State on a recruiting trip last year," Ahmed said, waving a hand dismissively. "You got schmoozed by *James Franklin*. When'd you get so humble?"

It's not like I was ever really *that* good. FightSong said I was the eighteenth-best junior kicker in the country, sure, but there are so few decent high school kickers that people think the best ones are wizards. I was the Paul Bunyan of Section VI last year, with preposterous rumors spreading far and wide about my kicking exploits. *I heard Woodhouse can kick right AND left-footed. I heard Woodhouse hit from seventy yards out in practice. I heard Woodhouse has never missed.*

That kicker—the one they told myths about—wasn't real. *That* kicker wouldn't have missed a chip shot with the season on the line.

"Can't do it, guys," I said, finally unclenching my jaw. I hadn't even realized I'd been grinding my teeth. "Sorry."

"S'alright," Dray said, holding his hands up. "Don't sweat it."

While Kaeden and I loaded up my equipment bag and the other captains started to drift off, he gave me a tight smile. "I appreciate it, Woodhouse. Do you, uh, mind meeting up again? So we can work on kickoff?"

I shrugged and tried to act like I wasn't stoked, like this wasn't the first time all day I hadn't felt like an alien. "Yeah, I think I'm down for that."

Four

I got halfway to my car before my ex-girlfriend almost ran me over.

It was my fault, really, since I had my eyes on the ground and my head on a different planet. I barely even registered the silhouette of a sedan before the horn blared.

"Jeez!" I held up my one free hand—*my bad*—and kept my head down, praying the pavement would open up and swallow me whole.

Then I heard the person in the car gasp. "Hey! Wait!"

There was Zoe Ferragamo behind the wheel, eyes wide. I hadn't seen her in months, but she hadn't changed a bit: there was the same anxious blush in her cheeks, the wide-rimmed glasses, the long brown hair in a braid. The same put-together rich girl that spent her junior year dating a sullen jock that didn't exist anymore.

I couldn't imagine what she saw when she looked at me.

For a moment, we were deer caught in each other's headlights, both terrified to move a muscle. Finally, I remembered how to be human. "You, uh, got a car?"

She blushed harder, pushed her glasses up her nose. "It was a birthday present from Mom and Dad," she said quickly, clearly embarrassed. "You know how they are, always extra."

"Of course." It was a Kia, so new it sparkled. If I hadn't already been self-conscious about Lorraine's dented sides and backseat patched with duct tape, I sure was now. "What are you doing here this late?"

"Student council stuff," she said, knowing that was all the explanation I needed. "Planning Friday's pep rally."

"On the first day of school? Jeez."

"The grind never stops!" she said cheerfully. I guess for her, the girl who wanted to be valedictorian and change the world and all that, the grind never did. "What are you doing here?"

"Teaching Kaeden Park-Campbell how to kick," I said stiffly, adjusting the weight of the equipment bag on my shoulder. Once again, I was conscious of my clothes, my not-quite-right body, the fact that I wasn't wearing makeup. "Making sure my old teammates aren't totally hopeless."

"That's nice of you."

"Guess so." I glanced back at the field to see Kaeden strapping his kid into a baby carrier. "Really, *I* needed it. Today's been . . . a lot."

"Gosh, I can't even imagine."

My mouth felt dry. I kept my eyes on the field. "Mmhmm."

"Sooooo," she said slowly, taking a deep breath. "We haven't really talked since . . . well, you know." *You know*, in this case, meaning *since we broke up three months ago.* "How have you been?"

I don't know if it was because I was exhausted, lonely, or some combination of the two, but I migrated to the driver's side window and told her about my summer job at Lucky's. "The tip money was clutch," I said. "I have way more expenses now."

"I bet." Her smile was small, wistful. "Mom and Dad, they've been, you know, asking about you."

A whole new wave of anxiety crashed over me. Zoe's parents had *loved* me. Like, invites-to-family-functions, you're-part-of-the-family, we-think-you're-gonna-marry-our-daughter-someday kinda love. "Oh." The smallness of my own voice surprised me. "Do they know?"

"Yeah." She looked away, her face turning red. "I–I didn't say anything right away. I waited for you to come out, but I wanted them to hear it from me." She shook her head. "Sorry. *Sorry.* That's weird to bring up. I'm being weird."

"It's okay," I assured her, but I didn't really know how to feel. When I told her I was trans and we mutually agreed to break up, she didn't have much to say at all, and the only time I'd heard from her since was that single solitary heart emoji the day I came out. I had no idea what that meant, where we stood anymore.

It was really, *really* out of the ordinary for Zoe Ferragamo to say too *little* instead of too much.

Finally, I forced a smile. "I'll, uh, see you around?"

"Wait!" she said suddenly, her voice cracking, which made her face turn an even deeper shade of red. I couldn't help but smirk; she was definitely still her old self. "I've just been . . . thinking about you. Hoping you're okay. Hoping everything's going well."

I gave her an honest shrug. "It's a process."

She pursed her lips and nodded. "Take care of yourself, yeah?"

That night, around eleven, I decided I couldn't sit still for another second.

On autopilot, I peeled myself out of bed, marched outside, and grabbed my equipment bag out of Lorraine's trunk. I pulled my kicking net out of the backyard shed and laced up my old cleats, the fluorescent orange gleaming in the moonlight. In the blink of an eye, I was standing in front of the net, my instep grazing a football held upright by my kicking stand.

Three steps back, two steps left.

That's when my autopilot switched off. I realized all at once how funny I must've looked; this clocky trans girl in pajama shorts and soccer cleats. I shivered, the late summer air chilly after sunset.

I used to do this all the time. Kicking was one of the few things that always grounded me, helped me get out my energy in a productive way. I never had a hobby, not like Tab with her art or Riley with cars. This was all I had. The day last fall when I first realized the word *transgender* might apply to some of the feelings I'd been having for years, I kicked into this net for hours.

Three steps back, two steps left.

Realizing I was trans—or, I guess, admitting to myself that I was trans—only made everything harder. When I didn't have a name for the constant fucked-up feeling in the bottom of my stomach, it was easier to ignore. By spring, I knew there was no way I could pretend to be a boy long enough to get a college scholarship out of my right leg. Football had to go.

My eyes drifted back down towards the ball, to my cleated foot. Football was gone, sure, but maybe I could still make this work, just for me.

I closed my eyes, sucked in a breath through my teeth, and bounced on my toes. Then I took three steps back, two steps left.

When I sent my first kick into the net, my heart ached in a euphoric, intoxicating way. Feeling a burst of energy, I set the ball back up and pounded another kick into the net, rocking it back a bit and making its metal frame creak in approval. I did it again: three steps, two steps, *boom*. Three steps, two steps, *boom*. The outside world disappeared: all that was left was the ball, the net, and my steps.

I don't know how many balls I kicked—dozens, easily—before a phone notification jolted me out of my trance. It was stupid—something from the ESPN app—but I unlocked my phone and opened Instagram, pulling up Zoe's page for the first time since the breakup. There she was, rowing a canoe at summer debate camp. Frozen yogurt with the girls. Her best friend's deck decorated in string lights. If you scrolled down for a while, there I was. Old Me, I mean. *Him*. The last post that included me was junior prom, all fake smiles in my tux. The further I scrolled, the shorter my hair got and the happier I looked.

I threw my phone across the yard.

Three steps back, two steps left. I rocketed the ball into the net so hard it toppled backward with one last metallic creak. I was *angry*. I was *good* at this.

It wasn't fair that I didn't get to do it anymore.

Before—Last September

You and your girlfriend have a system.

You leave your house around midnight, once your dad is sound asleep. If you're feeling bold, you hop on your bike—there's a place to hide it in the bushes—but you usually walk. It's only a couple of miles across the tracks to South Pageland anyway, where the houses get big and the streets get lights. From there, it's a quick turn down Silver Maple Place, where her house is surrounded by a dozen others just like it. You head into the backyard through a gate (you have the code memorized) and then *very carefully* climb up a wooden trellis and through Zoe's window, where the two of you are free to do what horny teenagers do.

Sometimes, she makes the trip to you. But you're the man of this relationship, and if anyone should be walking halfway across town in the middle of the night, it's you. You're the very picture of chivalry.

When the silent alarm sent to your watch wakes you up at five in the morning, it takes you a second to remember where exactly you are. Zoe's room is . . . not like yours. It's bigger, tidier, decorated with posters of musicians: BTS, Taylor Swift, Carly Rae Jepsen. There's a vanity pushed against one wall. Everything smells like cinnamon candles.

"Mmmph," comes Zoe's mumbled voice, feeling the rumble of your alarm. In the faint orange glow of the streetlights coming in through

Zoe's window, you can see her face. Her curls spread out over her pillow like she's a damn mermaid or something. The light finds those gorgeous eyes of hers and you just *melt*.

You kiss her through the morning breath, which is kinda gross, but she's so beautiful you can't help it. Once the kiss breaks off, she sticks out her tongue at you. "Your mouth tastes like death."

"So does yours!"

You've been together for six months, and this is probably, like, a forever thing. This has to be what it feels like to love someone. How could you ever give something like this up?

After a few lazy minutes of cuddling, your watch *brr*s at you again. "Okay," she mumbles. "Up. Go."

It takes a herculean effort to force yourself out from under her covers, but it all gets easier once you're moving. You pull on your sneakers, get in a good stretch, and steel yourself. You're not afraid of heights—you're not afraid of anything—but falling out of Zoe's window isn't on your bucket list. You hook your leg up and over the windowsill, pausing when you're temporarily blinded by the nearest streetlight. You blink, trying to find your vision again.

"Wait!"

You turn, and Zoe's staring at you in the low light. You ask her what's wrong, but she's on her feet, walking toward you with a hand over her mouth. With her other hand, she grabs your chin and tilts it to your right. That's when you figure it out. "Oh my *gosh*."

You ask her how bad it is. She responds by turning on her overhead light and leading you to her vanity.

There's three of them. The first two could be hideable; they're fainter, reddish, down by your collarbone. A shirt with a collar would do the trick. The last one, though, is a monster. It's an inch north of the other two, and it's unmistakable: a big, solid, purple blotch. You could tell it was a hickey from a quarter mile away.

"Jesus," you mumble. "Did you use a plunger?"

She grabs two big handfuls of her hair and closes her eyes. "Crap. *Crap!*"

"I'll just stay home from school," you say, trying to head off a full-blown freakout. "I'll have Dad call me in sick so it doesn't count as a skip."

"No way. You aren't missing school over *this*! I'll... I'll figure something out. Just..."

She paces, making sure not to tread too heavily. With Zoe, there's always a freakout, then there's always a plan. After a minute, she freezes, then marches back to you and grabs your arm. "Sit," she says, leading you to the chair in front of her vanity.

While Zoe rummages through her makeup bag, you suddenly feel queasy. "Wait. Are you—"

"Yes," she says, not taking her eyes off her little pouch.

"But—" Your voice catches in your throat. "I can't... you know..."

She glares at you.

"It's *makeup*," you say weakly, "and I'm a *dude*."

"Oh my gosh," she mutters under her breath. "It's *concealer*, not a full beat. The whole point is that no one will notice. You're not the first boy who's ever had to cover up a hickey, you know."

"But—"

"Now's not the time for you have some fucking masculinity crisis, Jordan!" she says, just loud enough that both of you flinch. Her serious face, the one that comes out when she's stressed, vanishes. "I'm sorry. You just need to let me work, okay? We need to get you out of here. *Now*."

You nod, then say the first thing that *actually* popped into your head when she went for her makeup bag. "I'm paler than you. Is that a problem?"

"If I was doing your full face, it might be," she says, spinning your chair towards her. She unscrews a tiny tube to reveal a little brush covered in skin-tone goo, then leans on the chair between your legs with her knee. Your heart's hammering. "We should be fine, though. Tilt your head up."

Neither of you say a word while she works. It's you, and it's her, and she's dabbing goo on your neck. It's *totally* not a big deal. Like she said, you're not the first guy this has happened to. Really, as you're sitting there, you take some pride in it. Some guys might've refused outright, but the fact that you didn't just proves how secure you are. Plus, you know, this is all happening because you made out with your girlfriend last night. That's a bulletproof way to shut down any shit you could get for wearing makeup.

There's this weird tingle you feel at the back of your neck, though, and this soft *buzz* on your skin where she's working. You feel warm and safe and *alive*, and you don't know why.

Maybe it's because your girlfriend is hovering over you. It's probably that.

Zoe finishes up by patting your skin with this weird foam egg—you're too intimidated to ask what it does—and then takes a step back. "Not bad. Have a look."

She spins your chair back towards the mirror, and there *he* is. The stranger in the mirror. You try your best to ignore . . . *all* of that and focus on her handiwork. It's pretty magical, you concede. Someone would have to be looking for it to spot it, even if the tones don't quite match.

"Pretty cool, right?" she says.

You admit it's pretty cool. She bends down, gives you a quick kiss, and then points at the window. "Now get out of here before my parents wake up."

Five

Back in August, two weeks before the start of senior year, I'd had to meet with Principal Keller.

Part of the official process of Coming Out, apparently, was Dad and I sweating our asses off in Keller's poorly air-conditioned office while she droned on for hours. She gave us a detailed overview of district policies about bathrooms, how teachers would be instructed to handle my name and pronouns, stuff like that. "Our goal here, Ms. Woodhouse," Keller said, her smile all gums, "is to help you find your *new normal*."

The way she'd said *New Normal* stuck with me, like it was simple, easy, even inevitable. Like my New Normal could seamlessly slot in with everyone else's Old Normal. Based on my first two days of senior year, I was ready to call bullshit.

Take my class with Zoe, for instance.

On the first day of physics, I performed New Normal flawlessly: I set myself up in the corner, kept my head down, and said nothing. Mr. Lundqvist was a grouchy hardass nobody liked, so my only goal for the class was survival. On the second day, though, a minute after the bell rang, Zoe streaked into the room in a frenzy and breathlessly explained that she got put into this class last minute and she was *so* sorry for being late, and–

"Thank you, Ms. Ferragamo," Lundqvist replied curtly. One of the stoners sitting in the corner opposite me cackled. "Could you find a seat now so we can get started?"

Her face went even redder. "Sorry," she repeated, and then scanned the room for friendly faces. She eventually sat with a group of girls she knew—she knew *everyone*—but not before she saw me. She gave me a tight smile, which I couldn't help but return.

I was surprised to see her here at all. Zoe was one of those kids that school came naturally to, one who stacked APs and extracurriculars high like it was nothing. I'd been friends with lots of kids like that: Ahmed and Dray were both top ten in the class, and Kaeden wasn't far behind them, either. Tab could improvise an English essay last minute and get a 90 on it without breaking a sweat.

If school is like this for you, then I truly, sincerely hate you.

I wasn't *terrible* in school or anything—I mostly clocked in around the low 80s when I really tried—but I'd never been able to make myself care about any of it. When they herded the juniors into the auditorium last year for our first You Have To Think About College Soon assembly, I didn't take it seriously. I was gonna go to whatever school offered me a football scholarship and had the sickest campus; I couldn't imagine a world where anything else mattered.

So where did that leave me now?

When the bell finally rang and I started packing my bag, I glanced up to find Zoe shyly approaching my desk. "How stupid did I look barging into class like that?"

If anyone else had asked me that question, I would've assured them it was no big deal. But this was Zoe, and it'd been far too long since I'd roasted her. "You looked like a complete and total dork," I said, smirking. "*I'm so sorry for being late, Mr. Lundqvist, I—*"

"Shut *up*! I do *not* sound like that?"

"When you're nervous, you do." I zipped my backpack shut and popped to my feet, but Zoe didn't seem to be in a hurry to get going. "Why are you in a normal class, anyway?"

"AP Physics and AP Econ are both third period, so one had to be sacrificed."

I faux-shuddered. "How could you *possibly* choose between the two of them?"

"They're not *that* bad."

"Of course you would say that, you *like* school." I pointed at her Canisius University shirt. "You're literally wearing a school!"

"I'm twinning!" she said, sounding offended. "With Leah!"

Honestly, I'd totally forgotten about Twin Day. The first week of school at Pageland was also a mini-Spirit Week, since it always coincided with the football team's season opener against St. Sebastian's, the despised Catholic school across town. Even though we almost always won the game, the rivalry was red-hot. People took Seabass Week *very* seriously.

It made perfect sense that Zoe and Leah were twinning, though. They'd been best friends for years, probably spent the summer sketching out the floor plan for the tiny dorm they planned to share at Canisius next year. Must've felt nice, having your future planned out so far in advance. I didn't even have a plan for tomorrow.

"You know," I said, "you couldn't have picked a worse week to rep a Catholic school."

She rolled her eyes. "Should I skip out on mass this week, too? Really stick it to St. Sebastian's?"

"Nah, you should go. Maybe Catholic God will send us some good luck."

I was beyond relieved that we were joking again, that it wasn't horrifically awkward to be in the same room as her. It was better than spending our senior year tiptoeing around each other, that's for sure. I mean, I still liked Zoe. I wanted us to be friendly.

So, of course, I had to go and make things weird again.

"Hey, so, there's actually something I've been meaning to talk to you about."

Maybe I shouldn't have phrased it like that, because Zoe's eyes were wide as softballs. "It's nothing bad!" I assured her. "There's just... there's a lot of old pictures of me on your Instagram, and–"

She turned a shade of red I'd only ever seen once or twice the entire time we dated. "I'm *so* sorry. I didn't even—I completely forgot, I didn't even realize—I'll take them down. I'm sorry."

I held up my hands in surrender. "It's okay! Just—"

"I should've already done it. Ugh, I'm such a bitch. You probably don't even *want* to be talking to me right now, I shouldn't have—"

"*Zoe.* It's fine. I'm not mad at you or anything, okay? We're cool."

She finally took a breath, nodding a moment later. "Okay. I'm glad we're cool," she said, trying her best to smile. "C'mon, we're gonna be late for seventh period."

I rolled my eyes. "Can't be late for AP Basketweaving."

TRIG 11R SUPPORT GROUP

Today 11:32 AM

TAB: should we update the gc name now that we aren't in trig anymore

RILEY: Nah our origin story is important

We were forged in the fires of sine cosine and tangent

@Grace I'm watching you rn btw. You look bored

GRACE: excuse me???? where tf are you stalker

RILEY: Got the seat by the door in Econ. You're in the room right across from me lol

Last row. Bills shirt on. Phone in your lap. In your lane. Thriving. Etc

TAB: lmfao?

GRACE: by "thriving" you mean everybody in english is afraid to breath my direction or else theyll catch The Transgenderism

then yeah im thriving. AND im bored out of my fucking mind

> *i swear every august im like: oh i kinda miss school! then im in class for one single day and i would rather eat dirt than be here for another millisecond*
>
> *being alive is so humiliating*
>
> **TAB:** breathe*
>
> **GRACE:** pls go play in traffic

Thursday was when the boys asked me.

Since I probably said ten words all day at school (including my lunch period, when I was *supposed* to be a little more relaxed), I was stoked for Kaeden's third lesson. I had him practice his kickoff steps again while Dray and Prez patrolled the end zone on kick-shagging duty. Ahmed's babysitting service was up and running on the sideline, the big guy doting on KJ while he tried in vain to pull tufts of plastic turf out of the ground.

After we put in a solid half hour of work, Kaeden was ready to call it. "Coach Woodhouse put your daddy through the ringer again," Ahmed said in KJ's ear. "She's gonna get him to the league."

"Fat fucking chance," Kaeden grumbled, pouring water over his head. Even though he *was* improving, he didn't seem to believe it. Leave it to Kaeden, who was good at everything he put his mind to, to be a huge self-doubter.

"Hey, man, it'll be fine," Dray said, jogging towards us with Prez in tow. "Who cares if you're not perfect? You're getting better!"

"I just hope it's enough," Kaeden replied flatly.

"Cut the feelingsball, man," Prez said. "You got this."

"Plus," I added, "I'm a *great* coach. You'll kill it."

"Don't jinx me," Kaeden groaned. "Someone knock on wood."

While the captains laughed over some team in-joke—one about *knocking* and *wood*, because football players are nothing if not predictable—I packed up my gear in silence, threw the bag over my shoulder, and prepared to slip away unnoticed like I had the last two days. I was halfway to the fence when Ahmed called out to me.

"Woodhouse! Got anything planned tonight?"

I almost laughed. "You joking?"

His face fell. "What do you mean?"

Was he serious? Did he think I had some secret social life I'd been hiding? "I don't really . . . do anything."

"See, now you're putting me in my *feelings*, Grace," Ahmed said. "A Druid never flies alone. Even if she's a former Druid."

"Druids fly?"

He held up his hands in mock surrender. "Alright! Alright. You can get out of here if you want. We were gonna hoop, though, if you're down."

I blinked. "What?"

Dray produced a basketball from his backpack. "If you play, that means we can leave Zach's trash ass on the sideline."

"*Hey!*"

I laughed, but it ended up sounding more like I was choking. "You want me to ball in skinny jeans?" *And tucked*, I mentally added, though I'd never say that aloud to anyone, much less a bunch of boys. Since Thursday practice was just a short walkthrough and the guys were done a little after four, I hadn't bothered to run home and change. I barely even noticed until just now.

"When'd you get so damn precious?" Dray asked, laughing. Even his normally well-dressed self was wearing basketball shorts and a cut-off Pageland Football shirt, the unofficial post-practice uniform. I was *seriously* overdressed for pickup ball. "C'mon, Grace. Remember how we used to run kids back in the day?"

I smiled at the distant memory: freshman year gym class, Dray and I teaming up for a two-on-two tournament. He drew up plays for us to run and everything. "You've clearly never had to worry about sweating makeup off."

Ahmed raised an eyebrow. "You put on that mascara and lose your jumper, Woodhouse?"

I felt my nostrils flare. "Oh, it's on, you big bitch."

And then we were across the parking lot and over on the court before I could decide if it was a good idea or not. Dray and I paired up against Ahmed and Kaeden (Prez sat out, babysitting KJ), and since Dray was the much better shooter, it was my job to compete for rebounds with a six-four offensive lineman with SEC football in his future. The game devolved into Dray and Kaeden chucking up wild threes while Prez chirped us all from the bleachers. I managed to pull down a few rebounds and feed Dray for open buckets, but I mostly threw elbows at Ahmed and tried to keep things interesting.

Thanks almost entirely to Dray, we held a 10-7 lead late, needing one more bucket to win. He dribbled the ball outside the key, Kaeden right at his shoulder. I dabbed at my sweaty forehead with a napkin that I kept in my pocket, fighting a losing battle against my foundation. "Come on, Dray. Wrap it up."

He looked up, grinning like a maniac, and called out something I hadn't heard in years. "Tango! Tango!"

I had to stop myself from laughing. *Tango* had been our play call for a pick and roll back in freshman year. I moved to the key and set a pick on Kaeden, which let Dray drive hard to the basket to his right. Ahmed and Kaeden both went to defend Dray, which meant that when he passed to me, I had a wide-open shot. Nothing but net.

"*Bang!*" came the call from Prez, doing his best Mike Breen impression.

Ahmed collapsed in mock agony while Dray lost his mind, crushing me in a hug. "I *told* y'all! I told y'all not to mess with us!"

Kaeden just shook his head. "Of *course* I lost. I had this idiot as my teammate."

"I had a million boards, little man!" Ahmed wailed from the blacktop. "You gotta hit your shots!"

My stomach tied itself in a knot, watching the boys like this. It was nice of them to go out of their way to include me, but they were delaying the inevitable. They all still fit together, and I didn't fit in anywhere anymore. It wouldn't be long before we stopped hanging out, when the occasional *hey we should hang out sometime* texts dried up. *Hi*s in the hall were doomed to become perfunctory Boy Nods.

"This was fun," I said, ripping the Band-Aid off, "but I should get going."

"Actually, uh—" Dray looked around at the other guys. "We wanted to—yo, Ahmed, get your ass off the ground!—we wanted to say something. Real talk."

"Uh—"

"I called a captains-only meeting yesterday after practice," Ahmed said as Kaeden pulled him to his feet. "We got to talking. About the team. About the season."

"Okay?"

Ahmed looked at Prez, who sheepishly rubbed the back of his neck. "We're just a little worried," the quarterback said. "We've got high expectations, and I think we can meet them. We're good. *Real* good. But we aren't as good as we could be."

I squinted at him. "Uh-huh?"

"All hands gotta be on deck," Ahmed said. "You feel me?"

When I saw the look on Dray's face, I put it all together.

"Look, guys," I said, feeling my stomach lurch, "there are *lots* of reasons why I can't play anymore. I'm not as strong as I used to be. Most of the guys would be weird about it."

"I dunno about that," Dray said with a shrug. "Like, first few team workouts in June after you came out—I'm not gonna lie, some of them were a little shook. They probably just need to talk to you, be around you, you know?"

"Everyone knows you," Prez added. "We've all played with you before."

"But—" I exhaled hard, something between a cough and a disbelieving laugh. "What happened to me teaching Kaeden how to kick?"

He grinned sheepishly. "You're a good coach, but we all know I'm not gonna improve much more. Why settle for me when we can get the best kicker in New York State back?"

I opened my mouth to say something like: *I haven't kicked in a year, you can't possibly know how hard this would be for me, what the fuck are you guys thinking?* Of course, nothing came out.

"Look," Ahmed said, holding up his hands in surrender, "it's no pressure from us. But if you *wanna* come back, just know we've got you. We've talked to other seniors about it, and they're all cool. You know Coach Rhoads would go to the mat for you. If we all made a big show of supporting you, we could get Rut on board for sure."

Finally, I managed to say: "I don't know, guys. This is a *lot*."

"Just think it over," Dray said. He gave me a friendly punch to the shoulder, a bright smile. "You deserve to be a part of this thing if you want to be."

Six

Fuck Seabass Day felt so different on the other side.

The hallways were still green, sure. My pre-calc teacher, Mr. Ryland, still blared the school's fight song over his speakers before first period. There was the same yearly assembly where Principal Keller reminded everyone of the district's strict policies on alcohol, since the night after a Seabass game was always good for a party big enough that someone's mom would freak out and call the cops. I sat behind a soccer boy in the auditorium who rolled his eyes and drank something clear out of a plastic water bottle. It was *not* water.

Ninth period was replaced by a pep rally, as was tradition. Tab and I sat near a pack of stoners that surreptitiously vaped and cracked jokes about how gay football was, but their voices were drowned out by applause when the players took the floor. Band kids banged out the fight song, cheerleaders soared through the air, and Prez did his best All-American Boy impression when he took the mic. "*Go Druids!*" rattled off the windows in the gym louder than I'd ever heard it.

When you've sweated through a summer of two-a-days with your teammates, when the captains regale underclassmen with tales of Seabass blowouts past, when they lead you in singing "Seabass Eats Ass" through warmups in practice? Fuck Seabass Day is special.

From my spot in the bleachers with the stoners, though? It felt like just another day. It felt like nothing at all.

I shuffled home after school and crawled into bed, hoping I'd be able to get in a quick nap before Riley picked me up for the game. Of course, that'd been optimistic. I shut my eyes and tried not to endlessly dwell on the offer the captains had made me, which went about as well as you'd expect.

I'd never been *angry* about being trans. Sure, things would be simpler if I was a cis, but there wasn't shit I could do about it. Nothing about this would ever be easy, because I wasn't delicate, or sweet, or pretty, or whatever. I was just Me, and that would have to be enough.

In that moment, though? I *really* wished I didn't have to be Me.

The teams had just finished warmups when Riley, Tab, and I finally arrived.

Riley's teammates on the soccer team had claimed the very top right corner of the packed student section, saving us spots on the blisteringly hot metal bleachers. The few of them I knew well smiled and waved, and before long they were chatting about their third game of the season tomorrow against Lockport.

I tried not to feel jealous. Soccer was my first love; I was a solid midfielder for my club team back in middle school, and I still kept up with the Premier League. I only made the switch to football before freshman year. If things had gone differently—*very* differently, the way I wish they had in retrospect—I might have been teammates with Riley.

I shook my head, trying to physically chase the thought away, and shifted my focus to the field. The Druids, dressed in emerald from head to toe, looked loose and confident. Ahmed and his fellow linemen sucked down water on the sideline, Dray and Prez talked strategy while the offensive coordinator gestured at his clipboard, and Coach Rutkowski paced the sideline, barking at anyone who wandered into his path. *Same old Druids.*

In their away uniforms—white with red trim to go with their heinous orange helmets—Seabass looked like a troupe of clowns that played football on the side. They usually had a standout player or two—like Kendall Cleavers, that linebacker the coach I met at Lucky's had mentioned—but never a good team, since the bigger Catholic schools in the county hoovered up most of the studs. That didn't stop Seabass from taking it just as seriously as we did, though; the visitor's bleachers were packed, full of sentient orange polo shirts with too much money.

"So, you used to kick the ball, right?" Tab asked. Even though everyone else wore green, she'd abided by the Official Goth Dress Code and seemed to be paying the price. She'd already sweat through her black band T-shirt, I'd had to lend her a scrunchie, and her eyeliner looked like it was melting. "Who does that now?"

I pointed down at Kaeden, who was getting an earful from Coach Rhoads, my old mentor. Seeing him talk to another kicker was *freaky*.

"Is he any good at it?"

After a second, I said: "Well, he's getting better."

"*And now, the captains of your Pageland Druids!*" came the tinny voice of Mr. Ryland over the PA system. "*Number thirteen, Aundray Fulton. Number seventy-one, Ahmed Nassar. Number nineteen, Kaeden Park-Campbell Sr. And number nine, Zach Przezdziecki!*"

While the four of them locked arms and walked to midfield for the coin toss, Tab asked: "So after you kick the ball, who goes and gets it?"

I gave her a blank look.

"I mean, do you have to go fetch the ball yourself?"

Riley scoffed. "God, no, kickers don't have to do that."

"That's a little rude, isn't it? They boot the ball, someone *else* chases it down?"

After I explained that referees hunted down the ball after field goals, she nodded thoughtfully. "Do kickers thank them, at least?"

"Oh, of course," Riley said. "Kickers always send fruit baskets to the refs who work their games. That's one of football's unspoken rules. Garo Yepremian started it back in the seventies."

Tab looked *very* confused for a second before Riley finally broke and started cackling. I rolled my eyes and reached around Tab to shove her shoulder. "Dude, you suck!"

"Wait," Tab said, frowning, "is the fruit basket thing real or not?"

While Riley burst into another round of laughter, Mr. Ryland informed us that Pageland won the coin toss and elected to receive. I cheered along with the crowd, laughed at Riley's stupid joke, and tried to relax. Millions of teenage girls across the country spent their Friday nights in the bleachers with their friends, and I could be one, too.

In the first quarter, both teams withered in the oppressive heat.

It was regularly-check-to-make-sure-your-cleats-aren't-melting weather, and the sluggish play on the field showed it better than any thermometer could. Seabass went nowhere. Prez and his receivers were out of sync. Coach Rutkowski paced the sideline like a caged tiger for the entire quarter while the Druids and the Arrows exchanged punts.

Finally, early in the second quarter, Prez connected with Dray a few times to move the offense down the field. After a few stymied runs, though, they were stranded at fourth and goal from the eight-yard line. As soon as I saw Rut call a timeout, I hissed: "Shit."

Tab flashed me a quizzical look. "They might have to go for it," I explained.

"Is that a bad thing?"

I racked my brain for a Tab-friendly explanation. "So, football has checkpoints. You have four tries—downs, they're called—to move forward ten yards. If you can't, the other team takes the ball. Okay?"

Tab shrugged. "Sure. Okay. Checkpoints."

"When you get to fourth down, you usually punt the ball way downfield or attempt a field goal. It's less risky. But if you don't trust your kicker, you can gamble and try to get to the checkpoint on fourth down."

"And they don't trust Kaeden?"

Seeing the offense jog back onto the field answered her question for me. "Not enough, I guess."

Prez took the shotgun snap and rolled to his right, where he had three receivers bunched in trips. Dray, lined up the slot, cooked a poor cornerback with a whip route so disgusting my ankles felt sympathy pain. Prez put the ball right on the numbers.

"Touchdown, Druids!"

While the student section lost their minds and the marching band played the fight song, I felt . . . *something*. Something jealous, something empty. "Let's go!" Riley screamed, passing out emphatic high fives to everyone in her zip code. "First of many!"

I tried to match her energy on the high five, but I kept my eyes on the field. There was Dray, hitting a decent griddy in the back of the end zone before Prez embraced him in the biggest, bro-iest hug of all time. You only scored the first touchdown of the year once, after all.

Whatever that taste in my mouth was—that *something*—I had to ignore it.

While I was sweating through a ten-minute wait in line for the concession stand at halftime, I glanced up to find Jerome Metellus—the coach from Lucky's—chatting with another polo shirt in the shade.

I immediately looked away, hoping he'd get the message, but he *waved*—seriously!—and made his way over to me a moment later. Of *course* I'd had the bad luck of bumping into the most sociable football coach in the world.

"Back in Buffalo again?" I asked him, crossing my arms. "You'd *better* sign that linebacker at this rate."

He chuckled. "Things with Cleavers look pretty good. He's a priority for us."

I'd looked him up, naturally: his job title at Saxon Valley was Linebackers Coach/Special Teams, but college coaches also have to recruit. In between working million-hour weeks and coaching his own guys back home, he was obligated to befriend teenagers in his spare time. Very normal system, very normal sport.

"So I spoke to Coach Rutkowski last week," he said sheepishly, "and I asked him where his old kicker was."

Oh. "Mmhmm?"

"He didn't say much of anything," he continued. "Then Coach Rhoads tells me something *interesting* that I hadn't heard before, and he mentions the name *Grace*. Then I put two and two together."

I put my hands up in mock surrender. "You caught me."

"I just . . ." Metellus set his jaw and adjusted his visor. "I wanted to apologize for bringing all that up before. And . . . the old name and stuff. I don't know much about your situation, but I know that's not cool."

"It's not like you knew," I said, shrugging. "It's whatever."

He nodded. "Right. And, uh–you could *really* play, you know that? Watched some of your tape from last year. Great mechanics. You could've done some damage."

My mouth went dry. "Yeah. Well."

"I just . . . I wanted to say something. Take care, now."

I watched him begin the long trudge back to the visitors' stands where he and the rest of the scouts were sitting. I didn't know what to make of him. Trusting a college football coach is a little like trusting a tiger, but he seemed nice enough.

"Come on, Zach!" Riley cried, cupping her hands around her mouth. "Put 'em away!"

I'd already shouted until my head hurt and my throat felt raw. "They've sat in Cover 3 all day!" I rasped. "Hit the seams!"

My old teammates clung to a 20–16 lead with just three minutes left. The Druids and Arrows managed two touchdowns apiece in the third quarter—Seabass made both of their two-point conversions and we were just one for three, narrowing our lead to four points—but neither side was playing well. Given our sky-high expectations, this definitely qualified as a disappointment for the Druids. Still, all we had to do was punch the ball into the end zone to ice the game, escape with a W, then regroup for the start of league play. A win was a win.

Of course, Prez chucked a pass that flew five feet over Dray's head along the sideline on first down. The student section groaned. *"Jeez,"* Imani Westbrook hissed. "What's gotten into him today?"

It's not like Prez was an all-state quarterback on his best days, but he really had been struggling today. "They need to kill the clock," I said, watching Dray say something in Prez's ear in the huddle. "Let's pound the rock here."

The next play was a handoff to Scotty Bowen, a junior running back with long blond hair trailing out the back of his helmet. I involuntarily fist pumped as he followed Ahmed for a decent gain. *"Nate Bowen on the carry for seven yards. Third down and three."*

"Just give it to Scotty again," Riley said. I nodded along vigorously.

Tab's eyebrows bunched together. "Wait. Mr. Ryland called him *Nate.*"

"He's Scotty," I said, so fixated on the game I barely heard her.

"Why?"

"He looks like a Scotty," I said, waving her off. "Priorities."

Unfortunately, Rut listened to Riley and me, and Scotty got thumped by Kendall Cleavers just past the line of scrimmage. *Crap.* Now it was fourth down, maybe two yards to go.

Oh, *no.*

"Number nineteen, Kaeden Park-Campbell Sr., is on for the field goal."

While Kaeden and the rest of the field goal unit took the field, Tab turned to me. "If he makes this, do we win?"

I gritted my teeth as the team huddled up. "Probably. We'd have a seven-point lead. Seabass *could* score again, but they wouldn't have much time to do it."

Seabass called their last timeout to stop the clock with a little over a minute left, meaning Kaeden had plenty of time to get in his own head. "Not good," I said under my breath.

When Tab cocked an eyebrow, I told her: "The last thing a kicker should ever do is think."

The huddle broke. Ash, the holder, got into his usual crouch. Kaeden crossed himself and pointed to the sky. Three steps back, two steps left, just like I taught him. Ash barked for the snap. I held my breath.

The second the ball came off his foot, I heard Coach Rhoads holler: "*Block!*"

The trajectory on his kick was low enough that the ball hit a Seabass defender's outstretched arm and caromed skyward, where it hung in the air for an endless, agonizing moment.

It dropped right into the waiting arms of Kendall Cleavers.

"HIT HIM!" Riley and a million other people around me screamed.

Unfortunately, Cleavers could scoot, and most of the guys on the field for Pageland were linemen, big and slow. Ash got swallowed up by a block while Cleavers booked it hard down the far sideline. Kaeden, the only Druid with a chance in hell at catching him, took flight. He managed to close in on Cleavers near the fifty-yard line, but the linebacker cut back towards the center of the field at the last second and left Kaeden diving at air. From the bench to the bleachers, the visitor's side of the field *roared*.

When Cleavers crossed the goal line with the football, his teammates mobbed him. The only sound on our sideline was Rutkowski cursing up a storm after he threw his clipboard.

The soccer girls and I didn't say a word when Seabass kicked off. We watched the offense go on one last doomed drive that ended in Dray being dragged down by Arrows around midfield. The referee blew the final whistle, Seabass players hit their coach with a Gatorade bath, and all my old teammates could do was watch.

"*The final,*" called Mr. Ryland, "is St. Sebastian's 22, Pageland 20."

Tab, who hadn't made a peep since the blocked field goal, gave me a wary look. "Are you good?"

It wasn't until then that I realized I was breathing shallowly, or that my hands balled into fists. I smoothed out my shirt and took a deep breath while my old teammates forced themselves into a miserable line for the post-game handshake.

"I'll be fine," I mumbled. "It's just a game. It's just a stupid game."

Seven

On our miserable trudge back to the parking lot, Tab suggested we get food.

I was *way* too worked up to be hungry, but still, it gave Riley and me something tangible to latch onto in our Seabass-induced despair. While the girls argued over the specifics of our order in the Popeyes drive-thru, I half-heartedly tossed in the occasional suggestion and replayed the blocked kick over and over again in my head.

"Here," Riley grunted, depositing the steaming hot bag in my lap. Unlike me, she seemed to be rallying. "You're being awfully quiet, Grace."

What I wanted more than anything was to forget about all of it: the loss to St. Sebastian's, the offer the captains put on the table yesterday, the entire concept of football. I wanted to laugh at my friends' jokes, eat an irresponsible amount of fast food, and pretend to be a normal girl, even if it was just for one night.

"Sorry," I said, shaking my head. *Change the subject. Be normal.* "Where do you guys wanna eat?"

The unbearable heat of the day had faded after sunset, so we decided to picnic under the streetlights in Riley's truck bed. We parked in a quiet section of a nearby Wegmans lot and migrated outside, passing around orange paper boxes, distributing sides. Tab goaded Riley into trying one of her ghost pepper wings, and when Riley's eyes went wide and she scrambled for her sweet tea, I laughed harder than I had in weeks. For a moment, weight left my shoulders, my head cleared, and I could delude myself into believing everything really *was* fine.

As if on cue, Dray's voice sliced through the noise: *You deserve to be a part of this thing if you want to be.*

"Fuck," I whispered through clenched teeth. I didn't trust myself to keep a straight face, so I leaned back against the truck's cabin, gazed up into the sky. Thanks to the light pollution, I couldn't see more than a few scattered stars.

I wondered what the boys were doing tonight, how they were coping with everything. I tried to remember the games we lost last season, but they felt distant to me. Inaccessible. Like I'd barely been there at all.

But I *had* been there. For three years, I'd been there. And then I left without a lick of closure.

"Grace?" The voice belonged to Tab, sitting across from me against the tailgate. "You good?"

"Yes," I replied automatically, but when my brain caught back up to my mouth, I coughed out a weak laugh. "Obviously not, no."

From there, the dam broke, and I relayed the events of Thursday as quickly and emotionlessly as I could, keeping my eyes on the sky so my voice wouldn't break. Neither of them interrupted me, thankfully, though I heard Tab gasp once or twice. Once the words were out, nausea settled in my stomach. Why had I said anything at all?

Tab was the first to break the silence: "*Shit.*"

I sighed, returning my gaze to the truck bed. Tab looked concerned, but from her perch on top of the left wheel well, Riley seemed . . . excited? "Shit," I agreed.

"You guys are *surprised*?" Riley asked, sounding shocked. She took a sip from her drink, clearly still dealing with ghost pepper aftermath. "It's a no-brainer, Grace. I mean, you were great. No one around has a kicker that's half as good as you. 'Course they want you back."

"Yeah, but..." My voice trailed off. "I dunno. I don't really think the guys are *just* thinking about winning state or whatever. I've known most of them for years, you know? They want me to be a part of it. And... that feels nice."

"You think Ahmed Nassar is, like, a steadfast trans ally?" Tab asked dryly.

"You don't know Ock," I shot back. I knew why she said that; from a distance, he must've looked like the most stereotypical jock on Earth. "I've been friends with him since we were nine. We played soccer together. He's always been good to me."

"Maybe that had something to do with the fact that he thought you were, you know, a douchebag like him?"

"Hey," Riley snapped, "*chill.*"

"Grace, you don't owe those guys *anything*," Tab said, raising her voice. I'd seen her get righteously angry before, but I'd never seen it aimed in my direction. "You know that, right? You're *yourself* now. You've got us! Why would you go back?"

That landed like a punch to the gut. I bit back the thing I *wanted* to say—that I didn't fit in anywhere else, that I didn't have anything *but* football—and hugged my legs to my chest. My eyes felt heavy, and I couldn't stand crying in front of people. "None of this is about you," I said into my knees. "It's not."

"Then what's it about?" she asked, incredulous. "You *got out*, girl!"

"It's not *prison*," Riley said, rolling her eyes. "It's *team sports.*"

"And I was good at it," I said, my voice hollow. "I suck at everything else I've ever tried. I'm not—I'm not like you, Tab. I don't have hobbies. Remember when I tried to bake bread over the summer?"

Riley snorted. "I remember you had to throw out the loaf pan."

"Girl, who *cares* about bread?" Tab said exasperatedly. "The team isn't your problem anymore. Don't let them walk all over you! They can pick the wings off butterflies and get concussions without you, you know!"

"You're being ridiculous," Riley said, crossing her arms. "She never even said she wanted to do it, anyway. She just defended her teammates. I would've done the same—"

"I *do* want to do it, though."

The silence that filled the air was cut only by the soft *whir* of the streetlights.

Riley dropped me off last.

"Tell me what I'm doing is a bad idea."

She hesitated. "I can't do that."

I groaned theatrically. "Come *on*."

"Really, though," she said, "Why not? There's *tons* of female kickers in high school football. Even college! There was Sarah Fuller for Vanderbilt a few years ago! Katie Hnida, for, err—"

"New Mexico," I filled in. "But it's not the same thing, Ri. You know that."

She gave me a conciliatory nod, opened her mouth to say something, then stopped. "Screw it, I'm just gonna say this now. Imani and I were talking, and . . . we were gonna offer you the chance to practice with the soccer team. Our team. If you wanted it."

I stared at her, confused. "But . . . I'm, y'know . . . and I haven't played soccer in *years*, and—"

"I know, I know. We wouldn't ask you to play in games or anything—you wouldn't be good enough anyway, honey, sorry—but, like, as a team manager or something. Scrimmage with us, help Coach set up drills, that kinda thing. I knew it would be hard for you to go from being on a team to being . . . not *alone*, but, well, you know. It's different. Tab doesn't get it 'cause she's not an athlete."

"Yeah," I said, exhaling hard.

"I just . . . I wanted you to know the offer stands."

I let the idea wash over me. I imagined running on a soccer pitch again, feeling the euphoria of sending a pass that threaded the needle between two defenders. I'd be with the girls for once, and I knew that most of them would be happy to have me. It's exactly what I wanted in an ideal world: one where I was cis, or one where I spent my awkward middle school years on hormone blockers, one where *I* arrived sooner.

But that wasn't the Me I was stuck with. Whether I liked it or not, I left soccer four years ago and realized I was trans at sixteen. Nothing I could do about any of that.

I spent years with that group of guys in the football locker room, and I'd known most of them for longer than that. We'd been building towards this season for years, in every dog-ass-hot two-a-day practice we'd suffered through and every loss we'd taken. The thought of saying *no* now—when they needed me more than ever—felt like a betrayal. And I couldn't let my last memory with them be a missed kick that ended the season and a stupid fight over nothing.

"That means a lot, Ri," I said shakily. "Like, more than I can put into words. But I gotta finish what I started."

"I get it." She smiled at me. "I'm proud of you for this."

"Why?"

She scoffed. "This is a *big deal*, you know, whether you like it or not. It's a lot of pressure. I'm ... not sure if I would be up to it, to be honest."

"Yeah," I mumbled. "I guess."

She nudged my shoulder. "It's okay, though. You're great. You'll do great."

"Yeah," I said, again, like a malfunctioning robot.

"And don't, umm ..." She cleared her throat. "Don't think too hard about what Tab said. She's just worried about you, in her own dramatic theater kid-ass way."

I clenched my jaw and exhaled hard through my nose. I was, in fact, thinking hard about it. She'd been half right, at least: I *did* feel a sense of obligation to the boys. She just couldn't imagine a world where that wasn't necessarily a bad thing.

"Plus, I've got your back if anyone messes with you," she said, smiling wickedly. "Okay. Thank god the mushy shit's outta the way.

You're all set with gear for Monday, right? Got a few sports bras that fit well?"

I blinked. "Umm."

"Oh my god, *tell me* you have a sports bra!"

"I barely have *nipples*, dude," I said, my cheeks going red. "I've been on hormones for, like, two seconds."

She looked at my chest *just* long enough that I felt compelled to cross my arms. "I don't have boobs either, you know," she said. "I'm built like Flat Stanley, and I don't even *know* how many sports bras I own. Trust me, you're gonna need some. Let's go shopping tomorrow."

I nodded, grateful that I wouldn't have to do this on my own. "Thanks, Ri. I don't care what everyone says, you know. You *are* nice."

"Don't tell anyone. It'd ruin my reputation."

AHMED, DRAY, PREZ & KAEDEN

Saturday 10:57 AM

GRACE: *and were actually gonna be able to pull this off?*

AHMED: *Of course. Have a little faith in us*

DRAY: *Fr we a bunch of honors students plus zach we can plan a breakfast*

PREZ: *Bitch!!!*

AHMED: *Rut's coming to breakfast. Rhoads knows the plan + is on board. Kaeden reserved the table. We're on*

*Ahmed named the conversation **"The Rutty Trap"***

GRACE: *wait thats not right. the whole point of the parent trap is that the lindsey lohans are tricking BOTH their parents. we're just tricking rut*

AHMED: *Shhhhhhh*

GRACE: *ive been out for three months and you're already silencing me you really DO think im a woman* ♥

Eight

Around a greasy table at Thessaloniki the next morning, the bright lights of the diner made the captains look like zombies.

I'd decided to walk to breakfast to try and work off some of my anxious energy, persevering even when I glanced out my bedroom window to find rain coming down in sheets. I wasn't *super* late, but I also wasn't surprised when I pushed open Thessaloniki's heavy front door to find the boys already seated in the back.

"We shoulda knew you were different," Ahmed said when I sat down next to him, tucking my umbrella under my seat. He cracked a weak smile. "I don't know a single straight dude who owns an umbrella."

I rolled my eyes. "Fellas, is it gay to stay dry when it rains?"

"Nah, Ock actually might be onto something," Dray said, sounding amused. A moment later, he pulled an umbrella of his own out from under the table.

Naturally, that made *all* of us crack up, and the laughter helped the block of ice in my stomach melt a little bit. "You guys holding up okay?"

"Better than yesterday, I think," Prez replied, and the others nodded along with him. "We're done with feelingsball. We're on to Kenmore West."

So: *feelingsball*. It came from our old JV coach, this ancient maniac who retired after our freshman year. He had a lethal arsenal of one-liners, decades upon decades of Football Speak built up in his bones. One of his favorite things to bark whenever someone got upset, made a bad play, or carried on too long: "It's called *football*, not *feelingsball*, son."

It started as an in-joke among the guys: if you talk about your crush on a girl, that's feelingsball. Hugging your mom? Feelingsball. Showing emotion of any kind? Feelingsball. Like any in-joke, it wasn't long before it snowballed, lodging itself in all of our vocabularies permanently.

Dealing with the emotional hangover of an agonizing loss? Feelingsball. Being so anxious about rejoining the team that you can't sit still? *Definitely* feelingsball.

"Everything's still on schedule, right?" I asked. "Rhoady's coming through?"

As if on cue, Coach Rhoads strode in, hand raised in a wave. He looked like your typical white grandpa: thinning gray hair, skin like leather from too many summers and not enough sunscreen, and an accent thick from a lifetime of coaching ball in the Carolinas. He walked with a wooden cane that he thrust around theatrically when there was a point to be made.

We hadn't spoken since June, and I didn't realize until now just how much I'd missed him.

"You sumbitches really pulled it off," he said dryly, sliding into an open chair across from me. He was trying *very* hard not to smile. "Grace Woodhouse, back in the fold. Heist of the century."

"Good to see you, Coach."

He chuckled. "After the week we just had, trust me, it's better to see *you*. How you been?"

I caught him up on what I'd been up to—stressing I wasn't hopelessly out of shape thanks to regular runs and the old rowing machine in my basement—while he nodded and *hmm*ed. "We can go over how we get you up to speed later," he said. "Let's not put the cart before the horse. We still have Coach to reckon with."

When a tall figure I knew well materialized in the foyer a few minutes later, I inhaled hard and tried not to panic, distracting myself with my phone. A moment later, though, there he was: Coach Rutkowski, as yoked as ever, regarding the table with his usual grimace. Given the insane workout videos he posted on Instagram, there were constant rumors on the team that he juiced, which wouldn't surprise me in the least. We used to call him Polish Hulk behind his back. "Well," he said, looking pointedly at me, "this is unexpected."

"Sit down, Coach," said Ahmed, as serious as I'd ever seen him. "We need to talk."

He gave Rutkowski a modified version of the pitch he'd given me on Thursday, peppering in the obvious fact that the Druids would be 1-0 with the "best kicker in the state" (Ahmed's assertion, not mine) on the team. "That's not even factoring in kickoffs and everything else," Prez added when Ahmed was finished. "Think about how much field position we're giving up right now. It's a no-brainer, Coach."

Coach Rut nodded thoughtfully. "Well, then"—he paused to take a long sip of coffee—"whatever you're gonna say, say it."

Ahmed opened his mouth, but Rut shook his head. "Not you." He turned his gaze to me. "Him. I wanna hear it from him."

I should've known it was coming, but *him* still stung me like a slap in the face. "*Her*, Coach," Dray corrected. "*Her*."

"Right. Let's hear what she has to say."

I sat forward, still reeling a bit. "I want to help the team win, Coach," I said, my voice wobbly. "I can still do that."

"Did you help us win last year in the playoffs?"

The guys roared in disapproval while I sank back into my chair, feeling monumentally stupid for ever believing this was a good idea.

"The way I see it is," Rut continued, "everyone knows kickers are head cases. *She* looked like I punched her in the face after I used the wrong word a minute ago. What do you think other players are gonna say? There's already a million ways to get in a kicker's head, this gives them a billion more."

"We'll fight for her," Ahmed said, sounding like he couldn't believe what Rut was saying. "Woodhouse is our teammate, Coach. What don't you get about that?"

"Setting aside . . ." He gestured to me with his mug. ". . . her situation, do you think she demonstrated she was a good teammate when she picked a fight with Nguyen after the Bellarmine game? How about that little meltdown in the locker room afterwards? Christ, he's *lucky* we even gave him the option of signing up again."

"I know I messed up last year, Coach," I said, my voice cracking. I *really* didn't like to think about that night. "I want a chance to make things right."

"Listen to the kid, Coach," Rhoads intoned, speaking for the first time.

Rut sighed. "I didn't—"

"As a coach—as a *teacher*—you're supposed to be guiding these young folks. Helping them become better people, shaping their character. I won't have you turning Woodhouse away on account of your stubbornness. You ought to be *grateful* that you're getting a second chance with this fine student-athlete here.

"And you *do* need her," Rhoads continued, "if you wanna win state. Her absence is losing us yards in a game decided by inches. Not that that should have anything to do with it, but it's the damn truth."

"Forreal," Ahmed said.

A round of brilliantly timed coffee refills cut Rut off from immediately retorting. He took a deep breath, shook his head. "I just don't know if what we need right now is another distraction."

"You think I'm a distraction, Coach?" Dray asked, his voice sharpened steel. "Cause I'm gay?"

"That's different and you know it, Fulton. Apples to oranges."

"You make an exception for me 'cause I run a 4.6 forty," Dray snapped. "You stay making exceptions for some people and coming down hard on others. Grace won't be a distraction. She's a *kicker*."

"I wanna keep my head down and kick," I said. "No headaches, I promise."

Rut's gaze passed from Prez to Ahmed to Kaeden, who all glared daggers right back. Finally, he threw his hands up. "Okay, Woodhouse. You know the deal, get your physical into the nurse's office and be ready for practice on Monday. Expect conditioning, you've missed a *lot* of time. But don't expect any special treatment. You're just like any other mid-season sign-up, yeah? You've gotta earn your spot." He pointed a finger at Rhoads. "This is your responsibility, Howard. You're in charge of logistics on this—you're gonna figure out the locker room situation, all that. If—*when*—this all goes sideways on us, it's your ass."

Rut drained the rest of his coffee, rose to his feet, and nodded curtly. "Great talk. See you boys tomorrow."

Rhoads snorted and shook his head while Rut strode out of Thessaloniki without another word. "Don't worry about it, kid. The other assistants and I'll handle him tomorrow. You just focus on yourself, okay?"

With Rut gone, the reality of what had just happened started to dawn on me. "I can't believe we're doing this," I said, feeling light-headed.

Ahmed saluted. "It's an honor, *Madame Kicker*."

That broke the tension, thankfully, and the whole table seemed to exhale at once. I hurled a sugar packet at him. "You better cut that shit out *right* now."

Once everything calmed back down and our food arrived, I met Dray's eyes and tried to give him a look that said *hey, thanks for having my back*. He smiled, held his right fist over his heart, and mouthed "*Gotchu.*"

I arrived home an hour later to find my dad on his hands and knees in the garden.

"Isn't it a little wet to be working out here?" I asked him. Even though the rain let up an hour ago, the ground was still drenched. His well-loved flannel work shirt was soaked up to the elbows in mud.

He rose to his feet, wiped off his hands on his pants, and shrugged. "There's work that needs to be done. Join me?"

Dad's garden was small, but it'd always been impressive. Maybe a quarter of the real estate was taken up by his vegetable garden (I'd grown up on tomato sandwiches thanks to that) but the rest was all flowers: hydrangeas, black-eyed susans, asters, lots of stuff. The plants changed year to year, but the garden had been like this for as long as I could remember: filled with bright colors, carefully trimmed and weeded and cared for.

For all the afternoons I spent in the garden with Dad growing up, I never once asked him *why*. He was an electrician, about as stereotypically Dad as you get: he watched History Channel, he had opinions about Scotch, he was bad at feelingsball. Obviously, it had something to do with Grandma, whose flower garden had colonized her entire front yard by the time she passed. Still, he never talked about what any of these plants meant to him. I could never bring myself to ask him about it directly; it felt too personal, too big of a question. Knowing Dad, he probably wouldn't have the words anyway.

After I ran inside to change, Dad put me to work. I got *filthy* pulling weeds, soaking my sweatpants through at the knees. Afterwards, I helped him trim the pansies. We barely said more than a few words to each other the entire time, which was comforting, in a weird kinda way. Like the two of us knew each other well enough that we didn't need words. Other than, you know, all the times when it felt like I barely knew the guy at all.

Once Dad called it a day and started taking off his gloves, I said: "Hey, wait."

He made eye contact and nodded. *Go ahead.*

"The friends I met this morning were from the football team."

"Mmm. Everyone good?"

"Yeah." I took a deep breath. "I'm gonna join back up."

His eyebrows jumped. "Really?"

"They need a kicker, and I'm the only game in town."

Dad scratched at his beard and looked off into the distance. "I'm assuming you've thought about all the ways that this might be hard for someone like you?"

I almost laughed. "Plenty."

"And this is still what you want?"

"Yeah. Yeah, I think so."

That was all it took to satisfy him. "Alright. It'll be nice to have something to do on Friday nights again. If you need anything from me, let me know, okay?"

After Dad retired to the house, I stood outside in my muddy clothes just long enough for a few fat raindrops to hit my head and shoulders. By the time I went inside and peeled off my work clothes, the rain was coming down again.

Before—Nine Years Ago

"What's this one called, Grandma?"

When she doesn't answer you right away, you run back to the porch. "Grandma!"

She puts down her newspaper and drags on her cigarette. She can see the entire yard from her rocking chair on the porch, but she doesn't exactly watch you like a hawk. "What is it? I'm busy."

"I saw a cool flower," you say, "but I dunno what kind it is."

She sighs. "What did it look like?"

"I dunno. Can you come look?"

She sighs, ashes her cigarette, and lets you pull her to her feet. "I'm coming," she says, coughing. "Grandma's knees aren't what they used to be, Jay-Jay."

You run ahead of her back out to the garden, which takes up most of the yard anyway. Grandma babysits you in the summer because Dad's working and there's no school, and it's *boring*. Your video games are all at home and there aren't any kids on Grandma and Grandpa's block. Sometimes you're so bored you have to *read*. It's the worst.

You like the flowers a lot, though, except for the girly ones. They're all so *different*—shapes, colors, smells. The one that caught your eye today is *really* cool: A bunch of little blue flowers that grow off a long stem, so tightly packed together it kinda looks like a baseball bat.

"This one, Grandma. What is it?"

When she reaches you, her expression softens. "That one's called larkspur."

You run your finger along the petals and try the name out. "*Larkspur*. Cool."

"Jay-Jay, I've been meaning to talk to you," Grandma says, kneeling down so she's at your level. She smells like coffee, cigarettes, and potpourri; bitter as motor oil. After she dies on your fifteenth birthday, you'll realize how much you miss that smell.

You shrug. "Okay."

"And you can't tell your father I said this."

"Why?"

She looks at the flower (*lark-spur*), then back at you. "I don't think it's right," she says, "for a little boy to like flowers."

"But this one's *blue*," you say, confused. "And Dad likes flowers!"

She pats your shoulder. "That Zach What's-His-Name called you a not-nice word at the end of the school year, right?"

You nod hesitantly. It's the summer, so you haven't thought about that in a while. "I guess."

"The way you act sometimes," she says, "it can make those kids think you're ... different. And once they start thinking that, they won't leave you alone."

"But I'm not different."

"Other little boys don't try on their grandma's lipstick, Jay-Jay."

You look away and start to cry. You cleaned everything up and put it right back where it belonged. How did she know about that? Did she tell Dad?

"It's okay," she said softly, giving you a hug. You sob into her shoulder. "It's okay. I know you didn't know any better."

You don't know what to say, so you cry and cry and cry.

"It's okay," she says again. "You're just a little confused, that's all."

Nine

After the final bell on Monday, I took a deep breath, steeled myself, and met up with Coach Rhoads outside the school gym.

"Hey there, kid," he greeted me, leaning on his cane. He grinned like a mad scientist; if his hip permitted it, he'd probably be bouncing on his toes. "How ya feeling?"

All I could do was sigh. I'd barely slept the night before, my focus in class was nonexistent, and neither Riley's attempts to distract me at lunch (Tab spent the period pointedly ignoring any and all Sports Talk) nor last-minute groupchat reassurances from the captains had been enough to make me relax. "Better once I'm on the field, probably."

I followed him outside, squinting against the blinding late-summer sun. He led me along the side of the building, past the door to the football locker room to another door I'd never really taken note of before. "We used to stash extra gear here," he explained, pulling out a ring of keys, "but it got decommissioned last year. S'just sitting here for the taking."

He opened it and flipped a switch, throwing fluorescent light onto the cluttered room. Pushed against the left wall was a treasure trove of unused football gear: a leaning tower of neglected shoulder pads, a big plastic tote on wheels full of loose knee pads and thigh pads yellowed with age, a cardboard box overflowing with old green practice jerseys. The room had that musty smell of decades—generations, even—of accumulated sweat, the kind that never goes away, no matter how hard you scrub.

On the right side of the room, Rhoads had cleared space for an aluminum bench, a small wooden cubby that my gear could fit in, and a spare coat rack. There was an old sink and mirror, thankfully, though I'd have to run into the school for a full bathroom. He'd even scrawled *Woodhouse* on a piece of tape and stuck it above the bench, like the rest of the players had on their lockers next door.

"You might wanna get some air fresheners," he said, cracking a smile, "but I figure this ought to do for now."

I nodded, still looking the room over. "You did all this yesterday?"

"And this morning. Pageland's a public school, sumbitches never throw anything away. All this crap was just lying around." He slipped a key off his keyring and tossed it to me. "This is all off the books. You also have a locker in the big room with your name on it, and you're *officially* using that. I made a copy of that key just to be safe, but don't lose it. Understand?"

I slipped it into my pocket, feeling immensely grateful. "Thanks, Rhoady."

"Pleasure's all mine, kid. C'mon now, let's get you some gear."

We slipped through the mostly empty locker room (the two seniors there gave me Boy Nods, which I returned) and into the supply room, which was close enough to Rut's office that loud metal music seeped through the walls. I gathered the basics: helmet, knee pads, shoulder pads, practice pants. I still had my old girdle, thankfully, so I didn't have to borrow *that*.

I hesitated when it came time to pick my gameday gear, staring at the cardboard box full of emerald home jerseys. "Someone nabbed your old number," Rhoads said. "Booker, I think. But I don't imagine that's a problem for you."

I'd never been diehard superstitious about numbers—not like Prez and his precious nine in honor of Joe Burrow (yuck) or Dray and thirteen, the same number his dad wore at Shelburne A&M—but I'd always opted for twenty-three if I could get it. I'm not gonna spell out why I used to wear that number, since I'm sure you can put two and two together, but I *definitely* wanted a change. I dug through the box, desperate to find anything that meant something to me. My go-to fallback was my birthday (March 1), but thirty-one was gone, too. Everything left was ugly, unconventional, bad luck, or a combination of all three. So where did that leave me?

After a minute of consideration, I pulled out forty-seven—the ugliest football number I could possibly imagine—and held it up to Rhoads. I'd stick out like a sore thumb on the field anyway, so why not embrace the weird? "What do we think?"

He chuckled. "Well, it's certainly unique. You can make it your own."

As he led me back through the (now much fuller) locker room, one of the guys wolf-whistled. "We got a *'lady'* in the locker room, everyone!" came the voice of Casey McReynolds, this big goon of a defensive tackle. He was always going for the Scary Tough Guy thing, but it was hard for me to be intimidated by a junior. "Best behavior!"

Ahmed's eyes found mine as the room broke into snickers. His silent question: *Want me to step in?*

I shook my head *no*, since it wasn't worth escalating things over a dumb joke. Just before I passed through the locker room door, McReynolds decided it was a good idea to carry on. "You're not changing with us, Woodhouse?"

Over my shoulder, I called: "You *wish*, dude!"

When the locker room erupted in a chorus of *oh, shit!*s and *got eem!*s, I couldn't help but grin. Yeah, I could hang. I could *definitely* hang.

Back in my personal locker room, I finally got ready. Thanks to eligibility rules, I couldn't wear full pads in practice or dress for a game until next week, so I didn't have to don my armor just yet. I slipped on one of my new sports bras and threw a baggy green practice jersey over that. Athletic shorts. Cleats.

I scrubbed my face, sending makeup down the drain in a swirl of cloudy water, and pulled my helmet on. When I looked in the mirror, a football player stared back at me; a football player with red hair trailing out of her helmet, sure, but a football player all the same.

I gripped the sink tightly and took a deep breath. *You're ready.*

When Rhoads and I took the field, I really did start to feel better.

With the rest of the team still inside watching film, we took sole ownership of the "Big Field" (the gameday field, since the practice field didn't have goalposts) and fell into a familiar groove. Rhoads razzed me about this week's Bills loss as he settled into his folding chair, I razzed him about the general state of the Atlanta Falcons while I set up my kicking stand. Even the little things I *hadn't* missed—the stale sweat smell of the practice jersey, the nauseous ache I always felt the first time I wore a helmet after an offseason—felt like old friends.

"Take it slow, now," Rhoads said, grimacing as he adjusted in his folding chair. Given his bad hip, he tried to stay off his feet whenever he could; for kicking sessions like this, he'd always set it up on the field to watch me up close. "I just wanna see your process. Make sure you're the same Grace Woodhouse I remember from the good ol' days."

My first attempt from the ten-yard line sailed cleanly through the uprights, and I was so relieved I could cry. "Y'ain't totally soft just yet," Rhoads joked. "One more, then let's back it up."

It definitely wasn't my best day of kicking—I made more mistakes than I normally would, which I chalked up to shaking the rust off—but overall, it wasn't bad. The guys started filing out of the locker room by the time I'd worked back to the twenty-five-yard line, and a few of them hung around to watch.

"*Bomb it, Woodhouse!*"

"*Let's see the leg!*"

"*Put it in Lake Erie!*"

Rhoads chuckled, shaking his head. "Wouldn't be polite to disappoint the sumbitches, now, would it?"

I moved the ball back to the thirty (the furthest Rhoads would permit on my first day back), calmly paced out my steps, and took a deep breath. The ball felt good leaving my foot, but the velocity just wasn't there. For a terrifying moment I thought I'd miss the kick *short*—missing short from forty would be mortifying for me, especially without pads on—but the ball cleared the crossbar by a few feet.

While the guys cheered, Rhoads and I made eye contact. He was thinking the same thing I was. He rose to his feet with the help of his cane. "You're in good shape overall. Technique's still great. We just need work in—"

"The weight room," I filled in, feeling my face redden. Leg strength had never, *ever* been one of my problems, but that's what an offseason free of football (and full of estrogen) will do to you. "I know."

He tapped the side of my helmet. "Don't sweat it, it's your first goddamn day back. We got lots of time to get you ready."

He followed my eyes over to the practice field where Ahmed led the guys through stretches. Even though they were only a couple hundred yards away, I'd never felt further from them.

"We'll make tomorrow count," Rhoads said, reading my mind. "Don't worry."

Ten

"Lemme see that beautiful belly, Ahmed! *Stretch!*"

From my spot fifty yards away, Prez's voice at the front was hardly more than a whisper. I'd gone through warmups a million times, and that Tuesday—my first day with the rest of the team—was maddeningly familiar. Prez led us through stationary stretches, chirping the guys relentlessly as he went. The assistant coaches stalked up and down the rows, doing some ribbing of their own. It was easy, comfortable in the way a group of fifty can only be if they spent their summer giving each other brain damage in ninety-degree heat.

The difference, of course: I hadn't been there with them, so that comfort didn't extend to me anymore. I thought about what Rhoads said yesterday, about making today count.

From my spot in the very last row, that was starting to look optimistic.

I couldn't hide as easily once we bunched up for dynamic stretches, all eyes falling on me as we worked our way through lunges. "Careful, Woodhouse!" There was McReynolds again, because he clearly hadn't learned his lesson yesterday. "Don't want your tampon to fall out!"

There were more hissed *shut up*s than laughs, but I didn't dignify it with a response. The guys in my line gave me looks that ranged from Skeptical to Sympathetic as I rejoined them. Tobe Okoro, the six-six tight end who stood before me in line, had clearly been filled in by someone else on what happened. "You good?"

God, I had no idea. Word that I was playing again had traveled through school in a flash, and suddenly, everybody's interest in pretending not to stare at me had come back with force. The only thing more confusing than a football player transitioning, I guess, was that same girl deciding she still wanted to play football.

"You're gonna be *famous*, Grace," Riley had informed me that day at lunch. I rolled my eyes and threw a pretzel at her.

"Really, though," Imani said. "You're a badass bitch, you know that?"

Nothing says *badass bitch* like not saying a word when Casey McReynolds busts out his middle school–level misogyny on you. Nothing says *badass bitch* like hearing the thumping bass from the locker room speaker through the wall while you change alone.

I signed back to Tobe that I was okay, which was basically the extent of my sign vocabulary. He usually got by alright thanks to lip reading and his cochlear implant, but he had trouble hearing in crowds. A bunch of us (including Tobe, who wasn't fluent) learned some basic ASL last year to help keep things running smoothly on the sideline, in huddles, stuff like that. Plus, it opened up a whole new frontier of cursing for us.

I remembered just enough to sign *six-three*—McReynolds's number—followed by the hilariously literal sign for *asshole*. Tobe grinned, then shook his head. "Course it's him."

High knees were next, and McReynolds couldn't help himself. "Nice legs, Woodhouse!"

"Mind your fucking business, dude," I snapped before I could think better of it. "Grow up."

Rut, who'd been glowering nearby, finally stepped in. "I hear another word, you're all running!"

So, of course, *I* was the one who got cold looks from people. *Great*.

When I got back in line, Tobe flashed me my favorite sign: *Bullshit*. Again, very literal. I grinned and signed it back, trying my best to loosen up. This would be a long season if I couldn't take a joke.

When it was time to break off for position drills, I found Rhoads waiting for me on the sideline. "Same plan as yesterday?"

"Not exactly." He cupped his hands around his mouth. "Nguyen! Katsaros!"

Truck and Ash. Their names were both Conner, but out of necessity the various Conners, Connors, and Conors in our class all had nicknames. Ash, our rugby-playing punter/holder, got stuck with it because of an *extreme* obsession with Pokémon in first grade. Truck, our left guard/long snapper who wore hunting jackets year-round and planned to enlist after graduation, got his nickname in high school because he was big as hell. Simple, clever, elegant.

Truck dutifully jogged over, but Ash was nowhere to be found. "Katsaros! What're you doing? Get your ass over here!"

That's when I found him: with the defensive backs, hands on his hips, staring at me. After he got chewed out by another assistant coach, Ash took his time walking over, hands on hips, pointedly not looking at me. "I'm not doing it, Rhoady."

Oh. *Oh.*

From the first day of training camp last year, Ash and I always stuck together; the punter and the kicker basically *have* to hang out, especially if the punter's pulling double duty as a holder. We got along well, laughed at the same dumb jokes. I never would've called him my *best* friend, but he was definitely a friend.

"I'm not asking," Rhoads said sternly. "Get your ass over to the Big Field. We're running field goal op."

Ash finally looked in my direction, and I really, *truly* wanted to die. "Yeah," he said dryly. "I'm not gonna hold for him. Sorry, 'her.'"

"C'mon," Truck growled. "I know it's weird. Suck it up."

Ash glared at him. "He was *such* a dick to you last year, and you're siding with him now? Really?"

"If you have something to say to me, dude, say it to my fucking face," I snapped, finally remembering how to speak. "I'm right here."

"*Grace!*" Rhoads barked. "Calm your ass down."

"But he—"

Rhoads shushed me, then pointed in the direction of the defensive backs with his cane. "You're off special teams, Katsaros. Head on back to the DBs now."

Ash's eyes went wide. "But—"

"You don't wanna cooperate with special teams, we'll take you off special teams," Rhoads said. "I'm sure Coach needs his third-string strong safety back. *Urgently*. Go on, now! Hustle!"

Ash gave me one more piercing look, shook his head, then jogged off. *Asshole*. "Well, I guess we *aren't* working on our operation today, then," Rhoads sighed. "You can head back to the linemen, Nguyen."

Before Truck took off, I put a hand on his shoulder pad. "I appreciate it, man."

Without looking back at me, he shrugged. "Yeah."

"Are we . . . cool?"

He hacked at the dirt with his cleat. "I'll do what I'm told. But we're not cool."

Then he was off again, back to the lineman, leaving me alone with Rhoads. For a few heavy moments, I watched the linemen work their way through their kick slides and thought about all the ways I was a terrible, *terrible* friend.

"Had a kicker back in the aughts when I was at Piedmont State," Rhoads finally said. "James, his name was."

I groaned. Rhoads's experience was invaluable—it was a miracle a coach like him was in Pageland at all, and even then it was only because he wanted to be close to his grandkids—but I thought he'd have the decency to wait a week before breaking out a certified Rhoady Story. "Did James have to deal with transphobic teammates too? Or did he have some other valuable life lesson to teach me?"

He side-eyed me. "He was a smartass, matter of fact, just like you. This kid, he transfers in from South Carolina, and he's a cocky sumbitch. He's got God-given talent, and he knows it. To him, we were just a stepstone back to the SEC. Then—get this—he tears his ACL taking out the goddamn garbage in the offseason." Rhoads shook his head. "Unluckiest sumbitch in the world. We worked with him through his recovery, but he wasn't ever the same. Didn't want to put in the work, didn't know how to ask his teammates for help when he needed it. Last I heard he's got a nice little dental practice in Spartanburg."

I didn't say anything. I *couldn't* say anything.

"I know for a *fact* that you're a better kid than James," he said, crossing his arms. "And given your circumstances, I'm sure things haven't been easy for you between the ears. But I'm also sure we can agree that your behavior last year wasn't your best, yeah?"

I felt my face go red. "Yessir."

"I'm glad you recognize that." He gestured in the direction of the practice field with his cane. "Now, I won't make excuses for Katsaros. If he's not gonna respect you, he's not gonna be on special teams. Nguyen, on the other hand? That's on you. And it's gonna take some work on your end."

I swallowed a lump in my throat. "I wanna make things better with him. If he's willing."

"I think he will be. Boy's got a bigger heart than he lets on. Now"—he rapped his knuckles on his folding chair—"get set up on the Big Field. Take this with you. We'll worry about our operation tomorrow, okay? Don't sweat it."

I hustled towards the goalposts, chair clutched under my arm, and tried *very* hard to believe him.

⬩

After the end of team practice that day, Coach Rut blew his whistle. "Goal line, everyone! Goal line! Let's hustle!"

The collective groan that went up was so familiar that it made me queasy. Lining up at the goal line could only mean one thing:

gassers. Formerly called "suicides" in football's pre-woke era. The most dreaded conditioning drill of the summer, one not usually run mid-season. Rut must've been *pissed*.

I reluctantly took my place on the goal line, gravitating towards Dray and Prez, each of whom tapped my helmet. "You ready?" Dray asked.

Given that the rest of the guys had been conditioning since June and I'd been on the team for forty-eight hours? No. I was very much *not* ready.

"Ten and back, boys!" Rut cried. "Linemen first! On my whistle!"

It was simple: Run to the ten-yard line, touch it, run back. The first sprint was always easy, especially since I was typically the least-exhausted player on the field. When I finished at the back of my pack, I bit down hard on my mouthguard. *Shit.*

Rut backed up to the twenty and shook his head. "Sloppy. All of you. Sloppy in stretch, sloppy in team drills, sloppy in scrimmage. Sloppy on the goddamn field last week. Nut the fuck up! Twenty and back!"

I stumbled on the start of the second sprint, and I could feel the entire coaching staff's eyes on me. "PUSH, WOODHOUSE!" Rut bellowed. "Move it!"

I finished last, my heart hammering in my chest. Kaeden, barely out of breath, slapped my hand while we waited for the linemen. "Push through, dude. You got this!"

He didn't mean anything by *dude*. I knew he didn't. I couldn't let it bother me.

Thirty-and-back. Forty-and-back. Rut was *screaming*, going off on a lineman who got beat in one-on-ones. Then Scotty Bowen, who half-assed a tackling drill. Then a junior whose name I would've known if I'd had the energy to remember mine.

Fifty-and-back. "Think Ken West is gonna roll over for you 'cause you're the section favorites?" barked an assistant coach. "After *that* showing against Seabass? I know you can push harder, Prez! Set the goddamn tone!"

I was last again on sixty-and-back, and when I crossed the goal line it took all of my willpower not to crumple to the turf. My calves screamed. All I could hear was the distant shriek of the whistle and my own heartbeat. I wanted to be anywhere else but this stupid football field, stuck with this idiot caveman of a head coach.

I felt an arm around my shoulders; it belonged to Prez, of all people. "Hang in there, okay?" he said in my ear. "He's trying to make your ass quit. But you're not gonna quit."

I felt myself nod. "Yeah. Okay."

Seventy-and-back. At the end of his sprint, a lineman hobbled off the field to toss up his lunch on the sideline. Eighty-and-back. My head felt fuzzy, the cries of the coaching staff melting into an indecipherable soup between my ears. Ninety-and-back. More lunch-tossing.

After one-hundred-and-back, Coach Rut finally seemed satisfied. He took his time jogging back to us, settling at the ten-yard line as we rebuilt ourselves. Hands on knees, hands on heads. Heavy breathing everywhere. Fifty pounding heartbeats.

"No goddamn distractions," Rut finally barked, his words bouncing around my brain like a pinball. "All that matters are the people on this field right now and the game we play. If we do our job—if we *execute*—we can beat any team we face. I know that. You know that?"

Several dozen weak *yes, coach*es filled the air.

"That was good work we just put in," he said, his tone lightening a bit. "*Great* work. Take it easy tonight, show up tomorrow focused and ready to go. Break us down, Nassar."

We circled tight around Ahmed, leaning on each other for support. Dray had an arm around Prez's neck, whispered something in his ear. Somewhere behind me, a lineman consoled his quietly sobbing teammate. I rested my helmet on Kaeden's shoulder pad and took deep breaths. A hand was on my back; I'm not sure who it belonged to.

Ahmed, who was just as gassed as the rest of us, was quieter than usual. "Good practice, boys and girls. Way to gut it out at the end. Nothing we can't fight through, right?"

"Yessir!" said Dray. *Woo*s rippled through the crowd.

"I wanna address something," Ahmed said, "right the fuck now. Grace Woodhouse is a part of this team." If I wasn't dead tired, I would've snapped to attention; instead, it took me a second to register he was talking about me. A few nearby hands tapped my helmet. "If you have a problem with that, take it up with *me*. Or the rest of the captains. No more bullshit."

I heard a few murmurs from the back of the huddle, but there were also a lot of nods. A few *hell yeah*s. Not bad, all things considered.

"Not that she needs me to defend her," Ahmed said, smirking at me, "since I'm sure she'll kick your ass herself."

"I did taekwondo in third grade," I said weakly. "Watch out."

That broke the tension, thankfully, with half the huddle coughing up exhausted laughs. "Alright! 'Work' on three! One, two, three–"

"WORK!"

The comedown after a practice like that is gradual.

That volatile *buzz* under my skin faded while I was changing, and by the time I shrugged back into my school clothes, my body was stiff as a board. My lungs felt like they'd been scrubbed with sandpaper. My hair was a rat's nest. I tied it up in a messy bun at the top of my head, trying hard not to think about how much I looked like Old Me without makeup.

I found Prez chilling outside the locker room by himself when I finally ventured outside. He raised his hand in greeting. "Trial by fire, huh?"

I couldn't stop thinking about what he said in my ear earlier: that Rut was trying to make me quit. Would he *really* run the entire team just to put pressure on me?

The longer I sat with it, the more I believed it.

I groaned. "I'm gonna go lay in bed for three weeks now."

"You did great," Prez said, glancing over his shoulder like he was waiting for someone. *Or* like he was making sure he was alone. "Hey, so, I wanted to say–"

Just then, a dozen guys rolled out of the locker room in a pack, all cackling over some dumb joke. It was Casey McReynolds and the rest of his goofballs, all camo sweatshirts and jeans that practically billowed in the wind. A few of them held spitters. *So cool.*

These were the Wannabe Rednecks: kids from the suburbs who had family out in the sticks, had an uncle who was really into hunting, or just liked the aesthetic of it because it lined up with their politics. Guys who grew up in my neighborhood (or, in McReynolds's case, in a big-ass McMansion in South Pageland) but pretended they were country. Of the factions the average football locker room divided itself into—cool kids, meatheads, nerds, assorted weirdos—Wannabe Rednecks were always well represented. There was Ash, right in the middle of the throng, and Truck, who awkwardly hung around on the fringes.

"Don't worry about them, Woody," Prez said, reading my mind. "They're harmless."

"Not Woody," I mumbled, tired enough that I couldn't summon the grace to ignore it. "Woody's a dude's name."

Prez flinched. "Sorry. I—look, I wanted to feelingsball real quick. I'm sorry I didn't, like, reach out when you first came out, but—"

I *really* didn't have the energy for a Straight Ally talk right now. "It's fine, okay? You don't have to make a big deal out of it."

"Well—that's—" Prez looked like he was short-circuiting. "Just, with what McReynolds was saying, I-I've got your back. Okay?"

I told him I appreciated that—because I really did, even if I was being cranky—and strode off for the parking lot, where I collapsed into Lorraine's lumpy driver's seat with a *thud*. This would be a *long* season.

BALLBAGS 4 CHRIST
(SCOTTY'S VERSION) 🏈🙏💩

Today 8:12 PM

AHMED: Welcome back Ms. Woodhouse

Congratulations on being the first female ever added to ballbags

GRACE: wow honored

when did ballbags become dedicated to christ i was only gone for like 4 months

KAEDEN: Turns out Scotty has a birthmark on his ass that looks like Jesus

GRACE: wait. in what way

SCOTTY: well i'm not gonna post a pic of my ass now that ur here

that's ungentlemany

AHMED: It's different if it's your bros seeing your ass. That's normal. Can't have girls seeing your ass that's embarrassing

TOBE: facts

CALVIN: Facts

TINO: facts

GRACE: i have literally seen most of you naked before

why tf is the football groupchat named after a birthmark on scotty's ass anyway

DRAY: It was all anyone talked about the whole second week of practice girl. They were sending his cheeks in here all August. It was brutal

GRACE: i forgot how fuckin gay you all are

im quitting again

Before—Three Years Ago

You *will not* cry, no matter how much it hurts.

One of the other boys pulls you to your feet while Coach screams at you. "Ball security, Woodhouse! Goddamn!"

"You good?" the boy—Dray—asks. Another freshman running back.

You nod, even though your neck's killing you. "I fuckin' suck."

It's your second week of football, and you're already thinking about quitting. You thought you knew what you signed up for, but nobody *really* knows until a linebacker puts you in the dirt in your first all-pads practice and it feels like you've been hit by a car.

"Don't say that, Woody," Dray says. It's only been a few weeks, but it's clear he's *way* better than you. Still, he's the closest thing you have to a friend right now. "You're quick, we just gotta get you used to the contact."

Coach blows his whistle, calling for a new pair of players to step in. Oklahoma drill is simple: there's a ballcarrier, and there's a tackler. They line up on opposite sides of a tiny corridor outlined by pads, maybe six yards long by two yards wide, and the entire team circles up around them. The tackler tries to bring down the ballcarrier, the ballcarrier's job is to not go down. It's a fistfight in a phone booth. It's illegal in some states. It is *not* mentioned in the sign-up meeting.

Two volunteers step up: sophomores, a tight end and a safety. When Coach blows the whistle, the tight end dashes forward, lowers his shoulder, and bounces off the safety with a sickening *crunch*. The team loses its mind while the safety struggles to his feet.

You try your best to stay out of this drill when you can, and Coach has noticed. He's started calling you out specifically. Football coaches, you've realized, are like dogs: they can smell fear.

After a few more reps that end in bone-crushing hits, Dray steps in. He *cooks* the sophomore they put in front of him, juking him out of his cleats. While the team cheers, Coach blows his whistle.

"The point of the drill is *contact*, Fulton! If you're running between the tackles, you gotta be able to lower that shoulder. Run it again. Woodhouse! You're in on defense."

Crap. If you hate this drill from the offensive side, it's even worse flipped. You barely even know how to *tackle*. While you dutifully take your place, you and Dray make eye contact. There's a silent understanding: what's about to happen is business.

Coach blows his whistle and Dray crashes through you, effortlessly putting you on your back. The team whoops and cheers for him, but a moment later, he's helping you up. "Sorry, bro," he whispers.

"Grow a pair, Woodhouse!" a sophomore lineman calls. "This isn't soccer anymore, foot fairy!"

The calls of *foot fairy* build while you shuffle back out of the drill, your face beet red. *Foot fairy. Twinkle toes.* As soon as you showed up for summer practice, they pounced on you. For being weak, for being the weirdo who played soccer and always seemed a little gay, even though you're *not*. You picked this sport so you could prove that, and you're failing. *Foot fairy. Twinkle toes.*

Your hands work themselves into fists. After the next rep, you stomp back onto the field and take the ball from a freshman receiver. "Alright, Woodhouse!" Coach cries. "Let's see some energy!"

A sophomore linebacker lines up across from you with a crooked smile. "C'mon, foot fairy. Let's see what you got."

Your vision's red. When Coach blows his whistle, you strike like a snake.

You get as low as possible—low man wins—and crash your shoulder into the linebacker's chest. Unlike every other time this has happened, you don't immediately crumple; after first contact, you're at a stalemate. He's stronger than you, but you have leverage. You keep your feet churning, because the second you stop moving, you're dead.

"Attaboy, Woodhouse! Finish the drill!"

His grasp on your jersey weakens, and you use his momentum against him to wrench him to the dirt, hard on his side. When you stand over him, he looks shell-shocked. "Talk about me again, pussy," you hiss in his face. "See what happens."

The team around you *explodes*, everyone clapping you up while you hand the ball off to the next kid. "That's good shit, boy!" Dray says, slapping your helmet when you get back to the sideline. "You run that angry on every play? *Sheesh*. They're not gonna know what to do with you."

You're so drained you can't even summon the words to reply.

Eleven

"You're messing with us, Grace," Tab concluded. "There's no way."

"I'm not!" I insisted, hugging myself to ward off the September night air. "The thing football players wear that holds their lower pads is called a 'girdle.' Look it up!"

The Pageland Lady Druids were hosting Orchard Park at Whitney Field under the lights on Thursday, and the non-soccer delegation at our lunch table decided to show up in support. The bleachers weren't quite as full as they got for football games, naturally, but the crowd still jumped when Riley ripped a shot that the OP keeper was lucky to get a hand on and punch out of bounds. Thirty minutes in, the game remained nil–nil.

"Wow," Jamie Navarro said, squinting at his phone. "She's not lying. Look: 'football girdles for sale.' 'Football girdles *near me*.' Weird auto-fill, but okay."

"The homoeroticism of football is inherent," Tarot Card Robin said, her vocal fry deadpan making it sound like an ancient proverb. She'd spent most of the first half trying to cajole Jamie into helping her construct his birth chart; he'd declined. "It's boys in tight pants wrestling. Why are you surprised?"

Naturally, they'd been asking me about football, and I'd spent most of the night trying to convince them that the boys were good to me (not mentioning McReynolds). Tab had thawed a *bit* on the whole concept, maybe, but she wasn't moved. The others seemed merely skeptical.

"Football's always seemed fascist to me, not homoerotic," Jamie Navarro said, scratching at his wispy beard. "Like, I sell bud to Ahmed, and he's chill. But the rest of 'em? Nah."

"*C'mon*," I protested. "They're good guys!"

Tab huffed. "It looks like Nate Bowen showers once a month."

"*Scotty*. And he'll talk your ear off about his haircare regimen if you let him!"

"I heard Conner Nguyen listens to the same song for, like, weeks at a time," Houseplant Jade mused. "Everyone knows Valentino Russo cheated on his last girlfriend."

"Calvin Reagor's DMed every girl in the school by now," Tarot Card Robin said. "Except me, but that's only 'cause we're cousins."

"And," Tab concluded, crossing her arms, "I don't know why Aundray Fulton is too cool to hang out with the gays."

"It's not that he's too *cool*," I protested. "Football players run with other football players. That's how they are."

"*You're* here!"

"I'm also wearing mascara," I countered. "The rules don't apply to me."

"Look," Tab said, undeterred, "even if some of the guys *are* nice, they're still football players. Your fancy shoulder pads are the reason we don't have a costume budget, you know!"

I tuned out the girls as they started dissecting the latest Theater Drama, focusing back on the field. The Lady Druids finally broke Orchard Park's attack, pushing the ball back to midfield. Riley, from her position at center mid, dribbled the ball into OP territory, and—

"Oh, wow," Houseplant Jade said. "Look at Zoe Ferragamo's hair!"

I snapped to attention in an instant (embarrassing, I know), and it only took me a moment to spot her talking to one of her student council friends by the fence. Her face was mostly obscured in shadow, but her *hair*...

The entire time we dated, she had this gorgeous hair: brown, wavy, settling into curls at the ends. Since mine was a thin, frizzy mess, I'd always been silently jealous. It was nearly to her waist the last time I'd seen her, but there she was, hair chopped off just below her chin. It framed her face well.

"That's . . . different," I breathed. "Jeez."

"It looks nice," Tab said, her earlier hostility gone. She flashed me a quick look of concern, like, *do you want me to change the subject?* I had no idea how to respond.

"My money's on a sexuality crisis," Tarot Card Robin deadpanned.

Yeah, I wouldn't bet on that.

Tab cleared her throat. "Do we maybe wanna talk about something else?"

"Ooh, I totally forgot about all that." Houseplant Jade spun in her seat, turning to face me. "Do we hate her ass, Grace?"

"I don't—"

"Cause she always rubbed me the wrong way. Little Miss Perfect, you know. She's so Type A they should come up with a new letter for it."

I swallowed my initial response—that she wasn't like that once you got to know her—because I wanted this conversation to end as quickly as possible. "Nah, there's no beef. We've, like, talked. It's all good."

Houseplant Jade frowned. "Blegh. I hate it when cool kids are nice."

"Wait," Jamie said slowly, his face scrunched up like he was trying to solve an algebra problem. "Why would you hate Zoe?"

"Jamie," Tab said slowly, "they dated. For over a year."

His eyes went wide. "*Ohhhh.* Okay, yeah, that tracks."

While he looked back at the field like nothing had happened, everyone else was busy staring at him. "What?" He shrugged. "I used to think Grace was straight. I don't pay attention to straights."

While Tarot Card Robin (our resident heterosexual) defended the honor of her people, Riley led the Lady Druids on another attack. After a quick back-and-forth with the left mid, she nutmegged a pesky midfielder and pushed the ball into open space. I leapt to my feet. *"Finish!"*

Riley sent a gorgeous pass to Imani that threaded the needle between two OP defenders and gave her a clear shot on goal. Imani cut left, drawing the goalkeeper towards her, then sent the ball back across the box to Riley, who hammered in the easiest goal of her life.

The bleachers exploded, and I gave every single one of my friends a dozen high fives. *"Let's fucking gooooo!"* I cried until my voice went hoarse, Tab laughing at me the entire time.

When things calmed back down, I quietly opened my texts and scrolled down to June to find Zoe's name, the heart emoji she'd texted me when I came out on Instagram. Before I could think better of it, I tapped out *your hair is really cool* and hit send.

It was the friendly thing to do, you know. No big deal.

"Stay still." Tab's eyes flickered between Riley and her sketch. *"Really still."*

"I am staying still."

"You're talking," Tab said through clenched teeth, "so your jaw is moving. *Stop.*"

"Whatever."

"Riley!"

We were in the library in fourth period the next day, which had become our B-day ritual. Officially, we called this "studying." Really, Riley cracked jokes, Tab tested the limits of how loudly she could listen to musical soundtracks (specifically, I think, in an effort to torture Riley), and all of us got stern glares from the librarian. Today, though, Tab came through with fancy pencils, a sketch pad, and an assignment from art class to sketch someone. Art kids baffled me; I mean, who signs up for *extra* homework?

I had zero interest in being the subject, so Riley was up. She was wearing *my* Buffalo Beauts hoodie—she'd stolen it last week without my permission—that was two sizes too big on her, which didn't strike me as particularly model-esque. Neither did the engine grease under her fingernails, a holdover from when she'd tooled around under Lorraine's hood that morning before school to figure out why my check engine light had turned on. Still, she leaned forward in her chair and rested her chin on her fist like Tab told her to, looking bored out of her mind. *Nobody* was worse at sitting still than her.

I leaned over and checked on Tab's sketch, which was still just bendy lines. I could squint and see Riley in them, though: her lanky frame, her angular face, her slender fingers. "Not sure if you got her jaw quite right. She's clearly grimacing."

"*Eat my ass, Grace,*" Riley said, keeping as still as possible.

"Not helping," Tab huffed.

While Riley shut up and Tab concentrated on smoothing out her shoulders, I checked my phone, where I'd gotten a handful of *good luck* messages from civilians who didn't realize I wasn't playing tonight. The trans girl wearing her football jersey to class on gameday had gotten everyone's attention, believe it or not. Miss Quinn, my English teacher, called me up to her desk at the end of class to tell me I was brave, which just about killed me. It's not like this was my *fourth* season on the team or anything.

I also had a text from Zoe, who'd replied to a TikTok I sent her that morning. It was something dumb, this thirty-second clip of a guy talking to his pet bunny that I knew would make her laugh.

ZOE:	*Omg this man should not be allowed to have a bunn!! It's impolite to swear around animals* 🐰 🐰 🐰
GRACE:	*why? it's not like they can UNDERSTAND what your saying*
ZOE:	*Well would you swear around a baby?? Same principle*
GRACE:	*only baby ive ever been near is kaeden's and im a saint around that thing so maybe youre right*
ZOE:	*There you go!*

"*Look at this*," Riley said, barely moving her jaw. "*Look at this dope* grin."

"Riley—" Tab pinched the bridge of her nose. "Whatever. What's going on?"

"*Look at Grace!*"

I locked my phone and set it down, shrugging like nothing happened. "Dunno what she's talking about."

"You're *still* smiling," Tab said, sounding amused. "Well?"

"Just a meme," I deflected, waving my hand. "Just Instagram."

"Instagram doesn't make *anyone* happy."

I sighed dramatically. "Fine, you caught me. My secret Australian lover sent me a photo of him lounging on the beach. Our affair has been revealed."

"Give me his number," Tab said, returning her eyes to the sketch. "I'll ruin our friendship over an Aussie."

With the girls distracted, I mentally breathed a sigh of relief and tried to play it cool. That was, of course, until my phone buzzed again and my hand shot out to check it so fast I sent it clattering to the ground. It landed face-up, the text notification from Zoe out in the open.

Riley, who followed the noise, managed to peep the screen before I shoved it back in my pocket. "*No!*" she yelped, bolting forward and completely breaking her pose.

"*Riley!*" Tab protested. "What the hell?!?"

"This bitch is texting Zo—"

"*Shh!*" I hissed. "There's *other people* in the library!"

While Tab sulked, Riley shook her head in disbelief. "Grace, my sweet baby gay daughter, I knew this day would come. I just didn't think it would be so *soon*. It's time we had The Talk."

Oh my god. "Ri—"

"No! Straight! Girls!" Riley clapped after every word for emphasis. "No crushing on straight girls! That's the first rule of lesbianism! And let's add in the fact that she is your *ex-girlfriend!*"

"We're just texting! We're, like, trying to be friends again, you know? It's *adult* of us!"

After I complimented her hair last night—a *perfectly innocent* compliment—we'd texted a little. TikToks. Memes. We knew what made each other laugh. Was that such a bad thing?

Riley rolled her eyes. "That's a slippery slope. What happens when you catch feelings again and she's busy patting herself on the back for being progressive enough to be friends with you?"

"Grace," Tab said warily, "Riley may actually have a point here."

I looked between the two of them, genuinely baffled. "I'm *serious*! Feelings won't be caught. Feelings were fumbled months ago. On *both sides*."

Riley glared at me, like she was trying to see through my skull and into whatever lovesick machinations were at work in there, but she ended up shaking her head again. "Just be *careful*. She dumped you, remember? I'm allowed to hold a grudge over that. I get protective over my friends."

I flinched. "She didn't dump me. It was mutual."

Riley turned to Tab like she was a doctor delivering a grim prognosis. "I'm afraid I have bad news, ma'am. She has a fatal case of Down-Bad-itis."

Tab shook her head solemnly. "She was so young."

Twelve

After a blowout win at home against Kenmore West, the Pageland Druids were back on track.

Even though I'd spent Friday's game filling water bottles and giving Kaeden kicking tips, I still sat with the team in film review on Monday. Coach Rut ran down a laundry list of things we had to do better, chewed guys out for bad reps. Ultimately, though, a forty-point blowout is a forty-point blowout; nobody took it that seriously.

When Rut switched gears and put on tape of our next opponent—Wake East's recent demolition of Orchard Park—the room got *real* quiet. Since Pageland High got bumped up to Class AA a decade ago, we'd *never* beaten Wake East. Not once. Our only regular season loss last year was a massacre they'd committed on our home turf. They'd pulled their starters at halftime and everything. Everyone in the locker room was still sore over it.

After a particularly beautiful run fit by the Wake East defense, the entire room groaned. "*Fuck* these dudes," Dray grumbled, which broke the tension a bit.

"Just another team, folks," said Rhoads, rapping the ground with his cane to quiet us. "Just another team. Leave the feelings out of it."

Then it was out to the field for my first practice in full pads, my first step towards actually playing on Friday night. After warmups,

Rhoads pried Dray—Ash's replacement at holder—and Truck away from the first-team offense for a few minutes and stole a corner of the practice field to drill our operation.

"Let's just get the snap and hold down for now," Rhoads said, settling into his chair. "Hang tight, Grace."

Dray eased into a kneeling position about seven yards behind Truck, who'd hardly glanced at me all day. Yeah, things were *great*. "Alright, Trucky. Ready as I'll ever be. *Set!*"

Truck rocketed the ball between his legs with an easy flick of the wrist. Even though the snap was near-perfect, it bounced off Dray's fingertips. He swore, scrambled to recover the ball, and slammed it to the turf in frustration. "God*damn*, Truck. You got howitzer arms."

Dray's job as the holder was *hard*: he had to catch the snap, rotate the ball to make sure the laces were facing the goalposts, and put it on an exact predetermined spot on the field. If any of that went wrong, the rhythm of my kick was ruined. Truck and Ash had functioned like a machine last year; our operation time—from the snap to the time I kicked the ball—had been a rock-solid 1.4 seconds. I didn't need to look at Rhoady's stopwatch to know that we were a few tenths of a second off last year's pace.

After Dray started to show some improvement, Rhoads was satisfied enough to call it. "We'll get there. Don't beat yourself up, Fulton, we're still learning."

The wide receiver rose to his feet and unfastened his chin strap, shaking his head. "This special teams shit is serious business."

"We're the only real football players on the field," I agreed. "Welcome to the big leagues, kid."

"Don't get cocky, now!"

A moment later, Rut called for a water break. Just before I turned to jog for the sideline, Truck put his hand up. "Wait."

"Uh—"

"What the hell's up with you?"

My stomach did a cartwheel. "What do you mean?"

Truck crossed his arms and looked down. "You used to be one of my best friends, even if you're kind of an asshole," he mumbled. "I don't really get what your whole deal is now. I did some googling, but I think I'm more confused now than I was before. So: explain it."

Honestly, with how everyone else around me was tripping over themselves to pretend nothing was different, I respected Truck's stubborn insistence that I spell it out for him. "Uh, okay. What confuses you in particular?"

"Well . . . I dunno." He scratched the back of his neck. "You always seemed pretty normal. Like one of us, I guess. You're into girls, at least I think. You're dressing like a girl and stuff, but you still *sound* the same. And now you're on the football team again? I don't get it."

I swallowed my initial negative reaction and led him to the sideline, trying to compose myself. "I get what you mean," I said, picking my words carefully. "About sounding the same, looking the same. Not everything can change overnight, though. You gotta trust the process."

He shrugged and followed me. "Sure. Okay."

"I guess . . . I've always felt different." We weaved over way through the crowd, through the writhing mass of sweaty teenage boys. "Like, since I was little. I dunno if you remember, but I got bullied in elementary school."

It was never *physical*. But some of the other boys—a few of whom ended up on the football team—got pretty verbally nasty with me. It's not like I was a super feminine kid or anything, but I guess they smelled the Different on me. Compared to a lot of queer people, I probably got off easy.

Truck shrugged. "Sure, I guess."

"Well, that fucking sucked," I said, summing up a whole lot of feelings as best I could. "I tried *really* hard to not be different. So yeah, you thought I was *one of you*. That's what I wanted you to see."

Truck had his own experience with this stuff, given that he'd always been the quiet Vietnamese dude who kept to himself. He was *definitely* not an athlete until he hit puberty in ninth grade. "I guess that makes sense. Hand me a bottle?"

When I did, he launched a jet of water through his facemask, and I had to keep myself from laughing at the beads of water stuck in his beard. He looked like a very burly pirate. "I still don't really get what you mean when you say *different*," he said, handing it back to me. "That you *feel* like a girl. What do you mean?"

"Jeez. Big question, dude. I dunno if I can explain gender dysphoria over a water break."

He stared at me, like, *go ahead*.

"I've felt . . . I dunno," I said, struggling for the right words. "I've felt, as basically as long as I can remember, that I *belonged* with the girls. That I should've been one. Like, being a girl would've come naturally, but instead I had to learn how to be a boy. It's hard to describe if you don't, you know, feel the same way."

That was an oversimplification, really, but I was still learning how to put those feelings into words for *myself*, much less Truck. He was silent for a few seconds, then he gave me this skeptical look. "I'm not sure I get it, still."

"I doubt you'll ever really *get it*. I'm just asking you to not be a dick to me."

He scrunched up his face like he was offended. "Why would I be a dick to you?"

Was he *really* asking that? I mean, this was Conner Nguyen, the guy who'd been planning to enlist in the Army since fifth grade. The same Conner Nguyen who once showed up to school in a Lynyrd Skynyrd shirt with a Confederate flag on it before Dray took him aside and told him it wasn't cool to do that. To his credit, I guess, that shirt never saw the light of day again.

Rut blew his whistle before I could come up with an answer; time to get back to practice. "Hey," I said, forcing the words out. "I know I've said it before, but I feel terrible about last year. The end of the season. It wasn't your fault."

Truck, again, just stared at me.

"I was going through a lot," I said in a single breath. "I shouldn't have taken it out on you. I was an asshole. I'm trying to not suck anymore. I'm sorry."

After a second, he nodded. "I know. I'm sorry about last week, too. We're cool."

Before—Last December

You're holding up a dress in front of the bathroom mirror.

You don't know enough about dresses to know the style, but it's cute. It has a flared skirt that ends around the knee, short sleeves. It's flowy and loose, which is why you were drawn to it. You've only seen Zoe wear it once or twice; she probably wears it to church more than anything.

You know taking clothes from your girlfriend is wrong. Over the summer you nabbed a black-and-white skirt, a few weeks ago it was a floral blouse. You know it's bad, but it's not like you can just walk into a store, and you'd rather die than ask for your dad's credit card over *this*. What if he saw the package? What if he asked questions? You're just doing what you have to do, nothing more. It's not really stealing if you're gonna return it anyway.

While you peel off your shirt and boxers, you wonder what exact brand of freak this makes you. You're not trans, obviously; you'd already know if you were. There are dudes who get off by wearing women's clothes, but you're not like that. Nothing about this gets you off. It grabs your heart and squeezes it until it pops. This is just something you *have* to do, and the less you think about it, the better.

You pull the dress on like a T-shirt and smooth it out, keeping your eyes off the mirror. It fits weird, since Zoe has boobs and you don't, but you try not to let that bother you. The material is soft like butter, so different from anything you usually wear. The skirt falls a few inches above your knees, which are prickly with leg hair. That ruins the picture a little, but still, you feel good. You do a quick twirl, letting the skirt *whoosh* around you. A smile tugs at your lips.

When your eyes finally do hit the mirror, it makes you ill. Your body does *not* wear this well. Your shoulders are wide, the material straining to contain them. Your torso looks bloated and gross. This isn't natural. This isn't *right*. What were you expecting to see? You're a football player who put on a dress. You're *disgusting*.

You peel off the dress you stole from your girlfriend and toss it to the ground in a heap. It takes all your willpower not to shatter that stupid mirror.

Thirteen

Being a kicker is lonely work.

I warmed up with the rest of the team, sure, but that's almost always where it began and ended. A typical practice for me was thirty minutes of work one-on-one with Rhoady, maybe some time with Truck and Dray to work on field goal op, and then a bunch of standing around while the offense and defense scrimmaged. It'd been like that last year, too, even when I wasn't an outsider by default.

Pros: I had my own specialized coach, an entire field to myself (usually), and I was almost always the least exhausted player on the team by the end of practice.

Cons: My usual drills were repetitive and monotonous, I spent the back half of practice bored as hell, and that field all to myself felt a *lot* bigger than 120 by 53 and one-third yards when I was alone on it.

So when Coach Rut finally blocked out a half hour of full-team special teams scrimmage that Wednesday, I was stoked. After the punt team got a few quick looks, he bellowed: *"Kickoff!"*

I ran onto the field without a second thought, but Rut put his hand on my shoulder before I could join the huddle. "Woah, woah. Park! Where's Park?"

Kaeden, who was minding his own business on the sideline, buckled his chinstrap and jogged onto the field, looking confused. "Coach?"

"You're in first," he said. "Woodhouse, I'll call for you when you're up."

Kaeden and I shared a bewildered look. "Coach, I thought–"

"You're here to *compete*," he said, fire creeping into his voice. "I was clear about that. And you said you understood it."

I balked. "But–"

"You here to play football or be a diva? If it's the latter, head back to the locker room. If you're here for football, wait on the sideline for your snaps."

Kaeden gave me another apologetic look before joining the huddle, and I had to literally bite my tongue to keep from saying something I'd regret. I hustled back to the sideline with my head down.

"Hang in there, G," Ahmed said, slapping my helmet. "Make it count when you get out there."

When it was my turn to tag in, there was no doubt in my mind that I outperformed Kaeden. We each ran through a few onside kicks before we transitioned to regular kickoffs. I was still missing last year's distance, but I easily cleared Kaeden's wobbly line drives, even notching a pair of touchbacks that bounced into the end zone. If it was a "competition," I easily won.

Still, even after Rut blew his whistle and wrapped practice, I was *pissed*. I managed to put feelingsball aside on the jog back to the locker room, formulating a quick plan: I'd get changed, duck into the main locker room, and ask Rhoads about special teams snaps going forward. He'd be on my side, surely.

My plan was interrupted by a *very* strange sight: an old dude with a notebook posted up by the locker room.

"Dale?" Rut barked. "What the hell are you doing here on a Thursday?"

Dale Weingarten was a local reporter who covered high school sports, one of those guys you'll see at anything from football to softball to rifle. While the captains spoke to reporters like him every week, I'd only ever been in demand twice last year: after my forty-eight-yarder, and then again after my miss. Kickers were only ever newsworthy if they did something exceptional, be it positive or negative.

Transitioning, I realized, might be one of those things. *Crap.*

Dale waved Rut over so the two of them could talk. I only caught a few snippets—Rut wasn't pleased, so I heard more of his side than Dale's—but I distinctly heard the reporter say *Jordan.* I swallowed a lump in my throat, balled my fists, and fought the urge to bolt for my little locker room. If this was about me, I needed to deal with it head-on.

After another minute of bartering, Rut sent Dale packing. Then the coach spun around, pointed at me, and narrowed his eyes. "My office. Now."

I dutifully followed Rut through the big locker room, praying I wasn't about to get screamed at for pulling reporters to practice, only for McReynolds to wolf-whistle at me *again.* Jeez, dude, get some new material. Rut slammed his door shut before I could hear anyone chew his ass out over it.

"Dale saw you at the game on Friday," Rut said as he eased into his chair. His office was a total printer explosion: scouting reports, notes, and plays that caught his eye were taped to the walls all around him. Stacks of paper were piled everywhere—on chairs, on the floor, on the small couch pushed against the far wall. "Did some digging. Found out you're *that* Woodhouse, and that you're, you know, transgendered."

I didn't correct him on the terminology. I just nodded.

"We agree that you're not gonna be a distraction?"

"Of course."

"So you haven't spoken to Dale?"

My eyes went wide. "*No.* Definitely not. Local sports media are the last people on earth I wanna talk to."

I meant it, too. But Rut crossed his arms and kept on glaring at me, my palms started sweating, and I felt the need to say more. "I'm just here to kick and help the team win games. That's it."

After a moment, Rut rapped his knuckles on his desk. "Good. When the reporters start coming for you—I mean, *really* coming for you—that's what you'll say. I'll make sure the rest of the team gets the memo, too. Understood?"

"Understood," I echoed, biting back a grimace. I knew he was right about this, but I didn't feel great about being in alignment with Rut on anything.

He leaned back in his chair, closed his eyes, and sighed. "You can go."

After *that*, all I wanted to do was get back through the locker room without another incident. I lingered in the hallway for an opportune moment, put my head down, and marched for the door.

Naturally, I wasn't that lucky.

"Woodhouse!" It was McReynolds, of course, sitting by his locker in the far corner with his fellow Wannabe Rednecks. Ash sat a few lockers down, looking amused by all of this. "Why aren't you changing with us? I mean, *really*."

I should've just ignored him. McReynolds was never gonna be worth it, and I knew that, logically. But I was tired, in my feelings, and more than a little rattled. "Think about it for two seconds, you fucking moron."

The locker room got quiet in a hurry. I heard a few people nervously laugh. "McReynolds," Ahmed warned, his voice sharp.

McReynolds's eyes flicked down, lingering on my chest, and the fire in my gut roared. "You already get the surgery or something? 'Cause, I mean, *I've* got bigger tits than you, otherwise there's nothing to see."

I only managed to take my first step towards him through the collective uproar before a pair of hands grabbed me, only gripping tighter when I struggled. "Come on," Dray said in my ear as the rest of the captains rose to my defense, getting in McReynolds's face. "The boys'll handle it. Let's go."

After a few seconds of resistance, I let Dray lead me out of the locker room. Once he deposited me outside, I let myself breathe for a minute. *God*, I'd wanted to break that idiot's nose. If Dray hadn't been there to pull me out, I wouldn't have hesitated.

The fire in me was already dying; since starting hormones, I'd gotten worse at holding anger in my chest. "*Fuck*," I muttered, pawing at my prickling eyes, trying to forestall the inevitable. "Thanks, man."

"No problem." Dray ran a hand through his twists and sighed. "Feelingsball?"

"Course," I said, grateful for a distraction.

"You remember Travis Bell?"

I nodded. Travis was the quarterback before Prez, back when we were sophomores. He was five-nine, tops, but he wore number seventeen and ran around behind the line of scrimmage like Josh Allen. Last I heard, he was playing JuCo ball somewhere in Kentucky.

Dray closed his eyes and took a deep breath. "You remember I came out before sophomore year, right? So, Bell, he's the QB that year. And he just spends all season fucking with me."

"Wait, *what*?"

"It was little things," Dray said, sucking on his teeth. He looked away. "All summer, he threw me terrible passes, never let me show off what I could do. One day in September, I get back to the locker room after a practice where Coach kept me late, and my backpack is soaked. Must've been a whole bottle of red Gatorade dumped in there. All my stuff was trashed. That's not all of it, either."

I stared at him, wide-eyed. "Wait—you—*Travis Bell*? Really? How do you know it was all him?"

"He told me himself," he said coolly. "Said he'd get me booted off varsity if I told anyone. Probably wasn't all him, but it was him and his boys."

"Why didn't you ever tell anyone?"

The second that left my mouth I realized how stupid the question was. "I was scared! I was embarrassed, and *ashamed*, and . . ." Dray took a deep breath. "It was a bad time."

I couldn't believe he'd been holding all of that in for years, that I'd gone on remembering Travis as a nice guy when he'd done *this*. "I just wish I could've known, or done something, or—"

"Nothing to apologize for, girl," he said, clapping my shoulder. "I just wanted to let you know that I'm not gonna let this shit fly any longer. Neither will Ock, or Zach, or Kaeden. We got your back. Swear on it."

Obviously, knowing Dray was on the team made coming back a lot easier, but I didn't realize until then just how much it mattered. Without Dray in my corner, I couldn't do this at all. And he'd done it *without* that help.

"Thanks," I said, giving him a quick hug. "Really. You're the best."

He squeezed my shoulders. "Wear that jersey proudly on Friday, okay? You're one of us. Don't let anyone tell you different."

Kaeden was waiting for me when I ducked out of my locker room the next day, ready for Thursday walkthrough.

"Did you hear the news yet?"

"Uh. News?"

His shoulders slumped. "Come with me."

As he led me to the big locker room, my heart sank. "Wait. Is—"

"Soon as I saw it, I tried to change Rut's mind," he said over his shoulder. "Rhoady won't talk to me about it either."

He led me to the bulletin board where the coaches posted the depth chart every week. "This is such bullshit, Grace. I'm sorry, I-I don't know what to do."

Next to "K," for kicker, was *Kaeden Park-Campbell Sr.* Listed as the backup: *Grace Woodhouse.*

Fourteen

> **TRIG 11R SUPPORT GROUP**
>
> *Today 7:18 AM*
>
> **RILEY:** YOOOOO IT'S THE BIG FUCKIN DAY
> **RILEY:** ARE YOU READY???
> **TAB:** it is entirely too early for that many caps
> **RILEY:** SUPPORT YOUR FRIEND
> **RILEY:** . . . YOU BETTER BE AWAKE GRACE
> **GRACE:** i got 2 hours sleep last night. max
>   i feel like how i imagine jerky does. im in the little plastic bag. its me in there with the fuckin silica packet
> **RILEY:** AT LEAST YOU GOT A SILICA PACKET!!!

"Grace," Tab said cautiously, "did you hear me? Are you *sure* you're not sick?"

I blinked and rubbed my eyes. I'd been tempted to have Dad call me in sick, actually, but there wasn't anything wrong with me. I just didn't want to wear my jersey to class or hear my friends tell me how excited they were to see me play. "I'm fine," I mumbled automatically. "Just slept bad."

I hadn't told anyone I was benched. Not Tab or Riley, not Zoe. I couldn't even tell Dad.

Jamie nudged an unopened can of Diet Coke across the cafeteria table. "You need this more than me."

I thanked him and cracked it, so exhausted I didn't even care that Diet Coke tastes like robot sweat. "Take a nap before kickoff," Imani suggested. "We need you balling out tonight."

"Are you actually gonna play like this?" Tab asked, looking horrified. "You look like you'd keel over if I breathed on you."

"I'm fine," I said again, eager to change the subject. "Tab, what were you asking me? Before, I mean."

Tab pursed her lips. Her outright opposition to me playing had morphed into fierce protectiveness, but I could tell she wasn't going to dig her heels in. "I was just wondering what you're gonna do with your hair. Under your helmet, I mean."

"Uh. I'm gonna wear it down?"

"You're just gonna let it spill out all crazy? It's gonna be a *mess* for your post-game interview!"

Riley snorted. "Yeah, Tab, I don't think she's gonna get interviewed."

"You don't think they're gonna try and interview the first trans girl to play high school football, like, maybe ever?"

A trans girl who's not going to play a snap.

"Journalists aren't gonna talk to me," I said, waving her off. "I'm sure everyone would rather act like I don't exist."

"You know that meme that's like, *I pretend I do not see it*?" Riley asked. "That's sports media with female athletes that aren't Caitlin Clark."

Tab huffed. "Quit jocksplaining! Grace, seriously, braid your hair. Cute *and* practical. That way you'll look hot when you grab the mic and passionately advocate for trans athletes after the game."

The thought of doing something like that—my stupid clocky face plastered on TV, centering *myself* after a football game, putting a target on my back—wasn't helping the Diet Coke settle in my stomach. "A braid wouldn't work," I said, trying to distract myself. "Football helmets are too tight on your head."

"Well, what about two French braids?"

While the table descended into a debate about the pros and cons of different hairstyles, I silently prayed Riley and I were right.

I sat alone on the bus ride to Wake East, minding my own business while the guys roughhoused and played gay chicken in the aisle. I pressed my face against the cool glass of the window and listened to music loud enough to rattle my fillings (*Good Kid, M.A.A.D City* was an old standby of mine), trying my hardest to find some zen.

When I pulled away from the window, I caught a glimpse of my reflection in the glass. A genderless spider with split ends and a jaw sharp enough to cut glass looked back at me.

So this is *the dumbass that signed up for all of this just to ride the bench.*

CRUNCH TABLE

Today 5:21 PM

TAB: *we just got here!*

JAMIE: *This is my first ever football game Grace. No pressure or anything but Imma need you to score like nine touchdowns. I assume you're the quarterback?*

IMANI: *dont worry woodhouse i'll explain ball to him just focus on you*

TAB: *still time for me to braid your hair if you change your mind!*

RILEY: *She prolly doesn't even have her phone dumbasses*

When we finally got there, the sun was low in the sky, everything cast in orange and pink. The Wake East Pirates, in those ugly yellow jerseys they'd been wearing since the nineties, barely looked at us as we worked through stretches. I expected one or two of them to drift over and chirp me, maybe notice a few staring, but nope. So far, I was invisible.

I was pretty sure I was okay with being invisible.

When we brought it in before kickoff, Prez took center stage. "History, guys. *History*. Pageland's oh-for-eleven against Wake East. And it's not gonna be us, right?"

"Not us!" Ahmed cried, which everyone echoed.

"Not lil' ol' Pageland. Not the Druids. They're overrated. They already have an L, they're nothing. That QB? Noodle arm. That loudmouth receiver? He's all talk. That defense is *Charmin* soft."

"*Charmin soft!*" Kaeden hooted.

"We're gonna hear it all night, guys, but they don't know shit about us. We go out there and we play our game, all night long, and we dominate their asses. 'Dominate' on three! One, two, three—"

"*Dominate!*"

When the captains took the field for the coin toss, I tried to let myself enjoy it: the lights, the infectious energy, the roar of the crowd. I tried to make myself believe I belonged here.

Everything came crashing down before the end of the first quarter.

The game looked like a shootout early on, with the Druids and Pirates trading touchdowns on their first possessions. A long run from Scotty Bowen put us up 14–7, but we broke the game open when Kaeden intercepted Wake East's quarterback on their next possession. In a game like this, the Pirates couldn't afford mistakes like that. Momentum was shifting our way. We just had to make it count.

The play that changed everything was a read option: Prez put the ball in Scotty's chest before pulling it away at the last second, faking out half the defense in the process. Ahmed and Truck had given him enough room to drive an eighteen-wheeler down the near side of the field, and in an instant, our sideline sprang to life. I jumped and screamed with the rest of the mob, pushing my way to the edge of the field to see it up close. Prez had *nothing* but green grass ahead of him.

The problem: he wasn't the fastest guy alive. He was thirty yards downfield by the time a defensive back caught up to him from his right. Prez tried to juke him. If everything had gone perfectly, he'd have planted his left foot, made a sharp jump cut to the right, and left the defender lunging at air while he motored upfield.

Since he was running along our sideline, I saw it all up close.

When Prez dug his left cleat into the turf, his leg gave out. He crumpled to the ground in a heap of limbs as the Wake defender fell on him, trapping Prez's leg between his body and the turf. From how loud and horrifying the *crack* was, I thought for a second that he'd been shot. While most people on our sideline gasped and looked away, I couldn't take my eyes off him. Prez sat up like nothing had happened, looked down at his leg, and froze. His left foot pointed to the right, nearly ninety degrees out of whack. His tibia jutted out at an unnatural angle, bulging against his sock.

I remember the crowd going silent, quiet enough that everyone could hear Prez scream when his brain caught up to reality. I remember Dray saying something in his ear while medical personnel loaded him onto the cart. I remember Prez's face as he waved to the crowd on the way to the parked ambulance by the field: bright red, streaming tears, in absolute agony.

It was stupid, but I couldn't help but remember something Prez mentioned before the game: Ithaca College had sent their QB coach to watch him play tonight in-person. Would he stay for the rest of the game as a courtesy? Or would he shake his head, cross *Zach Przezdziecki* off his recruiting board, and get an early start home?

When the ambulance left and everyone returned to their feet, our sideline felt like a crime scene. People shuffled around listlessly, not saying a word. When play resumed, our backup quarterback, a skinny junior named Steinmetz, fumbled his very first snap. The defense, completely depleted, got picked apart by Wake East's rushing attack. A quick touchdown made it 14–14; after the offense stalled out again (a sequence which included an ugly overthrow by Steinmetz), the away crowd started *booing*.

The score at halftime: Wake East 28, Pageland 14.

While the rest of the guys packed into Wake East's minuscule visitor's locker room, I chose to linger on the periphery, standing by the door. It gave me a great view of the worst night of everyone's life.

The room didn't have nearly enough bench space for fifty football asses, so guys stood in little clusters, spoke in whispers. *Have you heard anything about Prez? You were closer, how did it look? Did you hear it too?* Rut and his assistants had an animated argument over something Rut was scribbling on a clipboard. Ahmed and Kaeden tried to keep Steinmetz's morale up, but the poor guy looked like he was drowning. Dray was inconsolable, hammering away at his phone, trying to get an update on his best friend from someone, somehow.

"*Alright!*" Rut bellowed. "Listen up!"

A dozen voices demanded answers about Prez at once. Rut took off his visor, ran a hand through his buzzcut, and shook his head. "We're still waiting to hear from his parents. As soon as we hear something, you will too."

The entire team exhaled at once, all murmurs and cursing, and Rut's control of the locker room was gone as soon as he had it. Everyone looked like they'd rather wait at the hospital than go out there for a half we couldn't win, and I felt the exact same way. The coaches exchanged nervous glances, and for just a second, I couldn't help but wonder if we *wouldn't* go out there for the second half.

"Hey!" Someone snapped, and I couldn't figure out who said it until he banged on the side of a locker. "HEY!"

The booming voice belonged to Dray, who'd popped to his feet. "I know we're all hurting. Zach is—" His voice broke. "Zach's our brother.

But we have to focus up, alright? We can sit here and feel bad for ourselves, or we can leave it all on the field for *him*."

Finally, the room fell silent. After a few seconds, Scotty Bowen clapped once. "We got you, Cap." The rest of the room mumbled agreement.

"Good," Rut said, "because we have some adjustments to make." He held up the quarterback's wristband. "Steiner, son, that was some gutsy work. You're a warrior for hanging in there. Clap it up for Steiner."

The guys half-heartedly cheered and thumped on Steinmetz, but the obvious didn't have to be stated. The guy wasn't remotely ready, and we didn't have much of a shot with him at quarterback. Whatever "adjustments" Rut had in mind, there was no way around that fact.

Rut turned to the right side of the locker room and held up the wristband again, and in an instant, the world flipped on its head. "Fulton, this is for you."

Dray caught the wristband and stared at it in disbelief while the rest of the team *freaked* out. "Sir?"

"We're gonna keep it *real* simple," Rut said. "Passing ain't working, so we'll run the option with you and Bowen. We'll keep the playbook small. They load the box, we'll call a screen. We're gonna punch 'em in the mouth."

As far as I knew, Dray had *never* played quarterback before, not even in peewee. He used to be a running back, obviously, so running between the tackles wouldn't be totally new to him, but *still*. Against all odds, he looked calm and collected. "Gotchu, Rutty."

"I know you can handle it, son." Rut took a deep breath and turned to face his assistants. "Rhoady?"

My heart pounded as Rhoads carefully rose to his feet, leaning heavily on his cane, and stepped forward. "Well," he said, evil genius glint in his eye, "we're kicking off to start the second half. But, erm, we're gonna be keeping the ball. Grace Woodhouse?"

I nodded, feeling light-headed. "Coach?"

"You're up. Time for an onside kick."

Fifteen

For how complicated football can be, kickoffs are pretty intuitive. Almost every time, they look something like this: the kicker boots the ball as far as they possibly can downfield, and the other team fields the ball and runs it back as far as *they* can. They're a lot less predictable and routine at the high school level, but still, it's rare for anything too exciting to happen on a kickoff. Unless you're a kicker, it's easy to forget they exist at all.

The thing is, a kicker can *also* kick the ball deliberately poorly—ideally with as many random bounces as possible—to give their teammates a chance to recover it themselves. As long as the ball goes ten yards downfield—or the other team touches it first—it's all completely legal.

Pros of the onside kick: it lets you steal a possession, it can bail you out of desperate late-game situations, and it usually swings the momentum and energy to the kicking team if they can pull it off.

Cons of the onside kick: the other team has great field position if they recover it, the bounce of a football is entirely dumb luck, and it's nearly impossible for the kicking team to recover if the receiving team knows it's coming.

Hopefully, Wake East didn't.

When the referee blew his whistle to signal the start of the half, Dray grabbed me and slapped my helmet. "You're a star, Grace," he said, adjusting his new wristband. "Get my offense on the field."

I tried to give him a confident smile, which was total bullshit. My mouth tasted like pennies; I was *just* barely warding off a panic attack. "Gotchu, QB1."

When I jogged onto the field rather than Kaeden, the Pageland student section lit up. "*Number forty-seven, Grace Woodhouse, is on for the kickoff,*" called Wake East's announcer, and my heart pounded even harder.

"Let's steal one, guys," I said in the huddle, my voice shaky. We'd gone over the plan in an impromptu special teams meeting before we took the field, but we'd never practiced a surprise onside kick before. This was uncharted territory. "If you can't fall on the ball, fuckin' hit somebody. Make it hurt."

Scotty Bowen, who never needed to be told to hit somebody, cackled. "Let's *go!*"

Tobe Okoro clapped. "Behind you, four-seven."

When the referee handed me the ball, I could breathe again. The leather in my hands, seeing my guys on either side of me—this was *natural*. I placed the ball on the tee and counted off my kickoff steps: nine back, four to the left. I made sure everyone was set, then raised my right hand.

The referee blew his whistle.

On a normal kickoff, I would approach the ball slowly, gradually accelerate through my steps, and hit the ball just below its midpoint for maximum distance. On this play, though, a few steps before I made contact with the ball, I opened my hips early, letting me kick the ball across my body to the left. Just as I hoped, the ball struck the ground a few yards away at an awkward angle and took a *ridiculous* bounce— footballs tend to do that—that sent it hopping across the turf with all the jittery unpredictability of a housecat on speed.

Wake East was *sleeping*.

The *Onside!* call didn't arrive from their sideline until the ball was off my foot, and by then it was too late. The ball took *another* cursed bounce and caromed off the facemask of a Wake East linebacker, which put it right in Tobe Okoro's lap.

A scrum formed in an instant—Druids diving on top of Tobe to keep the ball secure, Pirates desperate to knock the ball free—and it took the referees an eternity to get to the bottom of the pile. Finally—*finally*—the head referee pointed towards the Wake East end zone. *Our ball.*

Holy shit.

Our teammates mobbed us when we returned to the sideline, all of their energy and enthusiasm back in an instant. "That was a *beauty!*" Ahmed said, catching me while he jogged on the field with the offense. "She's the secret weapon!"

"Clutch gene!" cried Tino Russo.

"You still got that dawg in you," said Scotty, shaking me by my shoulder pads and laughing like a maniac.

When Rhoads found me helping myself to some water (I know I was only out there for one play, gimme a break), he tapped my helmet. "Knew you had it in you, Grace."

I shrugged. "I got lucky."

"With how talented you are, kid? All you need is a little luck."

Just when he started to turn away, I cleared my throat. "Coach—"

"You're full-time again," Rhoads said, twinkle in his eye. "I think the shock of the first half made Coach see some sense. Stay warm; if the offense works, we're gonna need you for extra points."

I nodded, bouncing on my toes. "I know Dray can do it. I just . . . I can't stop thinking about Prez."

He patted my shoulder and dialed up a classic Rhoadsism. "You can only focus on what's in front of you. It's horrible, I know, but you've got to keep your head right here. That's what Zach would want."

I knew he was right, logically. But that didn't it make it any easier.

When Dray took the field as the quarterback, the Pageland bleachers cheered (probably with a healthy bit of confusion) and the Wake East defense looked completely lost. On the very first play from scrimmage—inverted veer—Dray kept the ball and gashed the middle of Wake East's defense for seventeen yards. It was *gorgeous*. Our offensive line coach was so excited he jumped a foot in the air.

We didn't pass a single time in the third quarter. Dray and Scotty picked up yardage in chunks, mixing in normal rushing plays with options and QB keepers. Dray punched in the first touchdown, taking a sweep into the end zone from eleven yards out. After Wake East responded with a touchdown of their own, Scotty capped off a methodical drive by following Ahmed and Truck into the end zone on a goal line plunge. Just like that, we'd narrowed the gap to 34–28 at the start of the fourth.

The two extra points I had to kick were incident-free, thank god. The Wake East special teams unit *definitely* figured out who I was; it didn't take long for everyone to realize I wasn't Deadname Woodhouse's secret twin sister or whatever. I got some pretty lame heckling from the sideline on my first kick, someone screaming *don't hit the upright again*, that kinda stuff. I could handle that all day. The kick was good.

On my second attempt, this goofy-looking Pirate, number thirty-two, wandered my way after I split the uprights. "You get a sex change or what?"

Without a second thought, I snapped: "Ask your mom."

Dray grabbed my arm and pulled me away while Three-Two complained to the closest official. Stripes hadn't heard the exchange, thankfully, so he wasn't moved. "You gotta *chill*," Dray said, chuckling. "Get your ass back to the sideline."

"I didn't start anything!"

"Yeah, and what do you think Rut'll do if his kicker catches a personal foul?"

After a quick Pirate punt set up *another* touchdown drive for Pageland early in the fourth, I was called on yet again. This extra point was crucial; with the game tied 34-34 now, there was a chance this one single stupid kick could decide the game. When we broke the huddle, I glanced in the direction of Three-Two, who was rushing off the edge. *Big* mistake. He knew he was in my head now. "Let's see that legendary leg, Jordan!"

I froze. It's not that I wasn't expecting it—of *course* I was—but that didn't make it any easier to hear.

"You're good, Grace," Dray said, putting his hand on my shoulder pad. "Let's get it done, okay?"

After a moment, I nodded. "Yeah. Yeah, okay."

For the third time in a row, the snap and the hold were phenomenal, and my kick sailed true. Three-Two came around the edge with a full head of steam, and even though he didn't get close to blocking the kick, he ended up in my personal space yet again.

So I took advantage of it.

I let my follow-through take me further to the left than it normally would, just far enough that I put my body in his path. He realized what I was doing a second too late; he tried to avoid contact, but his knee harmlessly clipped me.

I threw myself dramatically to the ground like he'd just taken a baseball bat to my leg.

The referees furiously blew their whistles as I collapsed, and I didn't have to see the flags to know they'd been thrown. While Truck pulled me to my feet (he didn't bother to ask if I was okay, because he knew me too well), I could hear Three-Two scream at the officials that it was all garbage, that I was flopping, that *I* should be getting an unsportsmanlike conduct. He made a fatal error while pleading his case: when he tried to point in my general direction, his gesture accidentally glanced the line judge in the shoulder.

That, in case you didn't know, is how you turn a relatively harmless roughing the kicker penalty into a full-blown game ejection.

While I took my time strolling back to the sideline, Dray draped an arm around my shoulders. "You need to go to the medical tent?" he asked, laughing.

"I think I can make it," I said, biting my lip to keep a grin off my face. "I think I'll be okay."

If my time as a soccer player taught me *anything*, it was how to flop and get away with it.

When the final gun sounded, the scoreboard read *Visitors 49, Wake East 40*, and I'm not sure anybody knew how to feel.

We rode the manic high of a comeback victory through post-game handshakes, but once the coaches led us back into the visitors' locker room, it was *total* feelingsball. Tears, hugs, mumbled *I love you, bro*s. Rut finally had news to share, even if it wasn't surprising: Prez was being prepped for surgery. The room went quiet. Ahmed wrapped a beefy arm around Dray and held him while the poor guy sobbed.

"Keep him your prayers," Rut said. "This is bigger than football."

The first game ball went to Steinmetz, the very definition of a participation trophy, but the guys clapped him up anyway. The second game ball went to Dray, who accepted it with as much bravado as he could muster. "I'm giving this to Zach when I see him next," he said, the team mumbling in agreement. Prez deserved it.

Between all the feelingsball and the cramped quarters of the locker room, I needed fresh air badly. While the guys collected themselves for the ride home, I took the opportunity to duck out the door. My first step outside was glorious; the relative quiet, the cool night air, the earthy smell of early fall.

Then: "Excuse me, Grace, could I get a word?"

Before me, to my horror, were a small pack of journalists. They always hovered around the edges of high school football games, working for local blogs or newspapers, but Ahmed being such a big recruit had amplified the situation. *Maybe* half of them looked familiar to me.

A young woman was the one who had spoken up, one I didn't recognize. "Uh," I said, flailing, "everyone'll be out in a minute. Captains. Coaches. People you wanna talk to."

"We'd love to hear from you," said a guy who might've written for *The Buffalo News*, I couldn't remember. "About your decision to come back, everything that's happened since last year."

"I . . ." I realized how I must've looked right then, with my helmet clutched in my hand, my hair loose and messy around my shoulders. Probably not very Football Girlboss or Kicker Barbie. Maybe Tab had the right idea. Mercifully, there wasn't a camera in sight.

"What prompted you to return to the team?" the young woman asked.

When I didn't immediately answer, Guy Who Might Be From *The News* asked: "What's it like being the first transgender football player in Section VI history?"

"Would you like to comment on transgendered women who compete in women's sports?"

The questions wrapped around me, choking me like ivy, until someone asked: "What was going through your head the first time you set foot on a field after last year's miss in Brockport?"

That's what made me snap.

"Aren't you gonna ask about, you know, what actually happened in the game tonight?" I asked. "I mean, my friend broke his leg, and– and god knows *what* else, and you're asking me about *this* stuff?"

For a moment: blissful silence. "Apologies, Grace," said Dale, the guy Rut had to shoo away from practice. "Of course we'd like to speak to you about the game. It's just–"

"Your story is bigger than the game," the young woman filled in.

"No, it isn't," I said, shaking my head. "I'm here to help my team win games. I'm here to kick. That's it. Publish *that*."

When I left them to rejoin my teammates, I "accidentally" slammed the door behind me.

◆

The bus dropped us off back at Pageland High after eleven, and by then whatever nervous energy animating us had dissipated. We were sluggish, stiff, and quiet filing off the bus. I dipped into my sad little locker room and threw on an old hoodie and joggers, since I no longer had the capacity to care about how I looked. My friends would be waiting for me in the parking lot: Riley, Tab, the other queers who showed up, all of them eager to crush me in hugs. Dad would pat me on the back and tell me I handled myself well. I'd pass out the second I hit mattress that night, so exhausted I'd forget to shower.

Before all that, though, I left my locker room to find Rhoads waiting for me. He handed over his phone, mischievous glint in his eye. "I'm talking to a friend, Grace," he said, winking. "Here, why don't you bend his ear for a minute?"

Honestly, I was too tired to question it. "Uh, hello?"

"Miss Woodhouse," came a voice I *swore* sounded familiar. "I heard the weirdest thing from my old pal Howard today. Sounds like a kicker I thought had retired made her season debut tonight. *And* she hit an onside kick that helped swing the game her team's way. Care to enlighten me on the situation?"

I thought I knew the answer, but I made myself ask: "Sorry, but it's late, and I'm beat. Who is this?"

The voice on the other end laughed, smooth as butter. "I imagine it's been a long day. My name is Jerome Metellus. You served me burnt coffee a few weeks back."

"Of course," I said, my head starting to spin. "Of course."

"I wanted to see how you felt about the Saxon Valley football program."

PART II

October

"Don't wanna live without teeth
Don't wanna die without bite
I never wanna say that I regret it."

—*Laura Jane Grace,*
"FUCKMYLIFE666" by Against Me!

ARTICLE EXCERPT. *Published by* Out of Bounds: Queer Stories in Sports. *October 15. Written by Oliver Muncie.*

At Pageland High School, Queer Football Players Shine

The suburbs of Buffalo probably aren't the first setting that comes to mind when you think of high school football.

While the lights here aren't quite as bright as they are in Texas, Pageland, a suburb just a short drive from the home of the Buffalo Bills, is home to a football juggernaut. The Pageland High Druids are 4–1 (3–0 in league play) and have firmly established themselves as the favorite to represent the New York State Public High School Athletic Association's (NYSPHSAA) Section VI in the Class AA state playoffs.

What makes them unique? Two of their key seniors, receiver-turned-quarterback Aundray Fulton and kicker Grace Woodhouse, are both openly queer.

[. . .]

While Fulton, who currently leads NYSPHSAA's Section VI in rushing touchdowns, has spoken publicly about the unique challenges of competing as an openly gay man, Grace Woodhouse has preferred to remain private. While she is believed to be the only out transgender woman in American football, she's chosen to avoid the spotlight thus far. She declined to comment on this story.

The only quote to the media she's ever given—"I'm here to kick. That's it."—has made Woodhouse, who recruiting database

FightSong ranked as the eighteenth-best kicker in her class before she withdrew from football to begin her transition, something of a folk hero online. She returned to the Druids in September, where she is four-for-five on her field goals and perfect on her extra points at time of publication.

"Grace is a great teammate," said Pageland tackle Ahmed Nassar, listed as a four-star prospect by national recruiting database FightSong. "And I respect her privacy, so that's all I'll say."

"Well, [Woodhouse] is certainly a heck of a kicker," said Adam Friesen, head coach of Mauldin High, whose team lost to Pageland 41–14 on Oct. 3rd. "It takes guts to do what she does, week in and week out. I respect her for it."

Sixteen

No one in Pageland was under delusions of Homecoming grandeur.

I *used* to be, maybe. Movies always made it seem like a big deal: elaborate floats, a capital-*r* Romantic dance, a Homecoming king and queen. So when Zoe dragged me to my first Pageland HoCo last year, it was a wakeup call. The dance was pitch-dark, held in the school gym that reeked of old sweat. The dance's vaguely nautical theme was expressed via a hastily painted mural of a pirate ship hung outside the gym and a few "treasure chests" pushed against the walls. If there was a Homecoming court at all, not a single person cared. "Catering" consisted of individual bags of chips laid out on folding tables in the cafeteria across the hall.

The dance itself wasn't even the most hyped social event of the week for the football team. Next Thursday was Bonfire Night, when the school would burn a towering stack of pallets in the empty field behind the gym and students enjoyed both school-sanctioned activities (the Semi-Ironic Bounce House, janky carnival games, and a local band that played heinous pop covers) and extracurriculars (slugging lukewarm vodka out of water bottles and surreptitiously hitting vapes). Afterwards, Ahmed was planning a massive party back at his place.

Still, the grand tradition of Float Day endured.

"Grace," Zoe wheezed, setting down two paint cans with a *clunk*, "can you get the linemen? These are *heavy*."

I side-stepped a soccer player knelt over a poster and squinted out at the parking lot full of kids hard at work. "Ahmed! Truck!"

While the boys dutifully marched over to take their orders, I turned back to her. "Need anything else?"

She *hmm*ed for a sec before digging into her purse and tossing me her car keys. "Could you be a doll and bring me my hoodie?"

"Seriously?"

She dramatically clasped her hands together. "Please. I'm freezing!"

I sighed, rolled my eyes, and ventured back out into the parking lot. A group of tiny freshmen crowded around a pickup truck, trying to figure out the best way to turn it into a dinosaur with nothing but construction paper and glitter glue. The sophomores' "superhero" theming was even less inspired, with the half the class abandoning the project to organize a four square tournament. The only real competition we faced were the juniors, who were going for a *Dungeons & Dragons*-type thing, but I trusted Zoe's attention to detail would put us over the top.

I'd always loved Float Day, the Thursday afternoon before Homecoming Week when Student Council herded Pageland's restless jocks into the parking lot with the promise of free pizza in exchange for their help on HoCo decorations. In reality, it was lightly supervised anarchy, with a handful of Student Council kids and teachers desperately trying to keep order. I didn't envy them; it'd be easier to herd buffalo than dozens of starving post-practice athletes.

And instead of enjoying all that anarchy, I'd been roped into running errands for my ex. *Wonderful.*

Zoe's Kia *chirped* when I hit the unlock button on the key fob (what high school senior drives a car that *chirps*?). I opened the back door, grabbed a lump of fabric on the backseat, and held it up. My stomach dropped.

I was holding The Hoodie.

Last October, when I was still a hot college football prospect, an interested program sent their special teams coordinator to visit my school. I won't say where he was from—I'm no narc—but the school was *big*. Out of every coach I'd ever spoken to, this one fed me the most bullshit: I could win the kicking job in my true freshman season, I was the only kicker on their board, that kinda stuff. It was a real full-court press. They wanted me *bad*.

While the meeting wound down, the guy mentioned that Coach Rut's office was a little stuffy, so he peeled his official Anonymous University hoodie off. He balled it up and clutched it in his lap, and, at some point, let it fall to the floor.

Soon, the meeting was over—shaken hands all around, *you're a really bright young man, we'd love to have you*, the usual shtick—and the coach was off to catch a plane that would take him to his next victim. After practice that day, though, Rut called me into his office.

"Your pal left this on the floor," he said, tossing the hoodie to me. "Make sure he gets that back."

I stuffed it in my backpack and forgot about it until I got home that night. Then, when I pulled it out of my bag in my room, I noticed he'd left something in the pocket.

I pulled out a wad of cash and stared at it for a solid minute in disbelief, unsure if I should even be *touching* it, lest the recruiting cops immediately descend on my house. Eventually, I counted it: two hundred bucks in tens and twenties. In the pocket of a hoodie that had been left for me to find.

I had three options in front of me:

One: I could report the school for a recruiting violation. Like I said before, though, I'm no narc. I crossed it off immediately.

Two: I could send the hoodie, money in the pocket and all, back to the coach. Maybe this was a test of character, not an illegal gift, and that's what they were expecting me to do.

Three: I could pocket the money, keep the hoodie, and never speak of it again.

Being in my fuckboy phase, I picked Three.

I shoved the money in my sock drawer and didn't touch it until I started hormones and needed the cash. The very next week, though, I strategically left the hoodie at Zoe's house, knowing she would pull a classic girlfriend maneuver and claim it as her own. Worked like a charm. She never even asked me where I got it.

So, yeah, holding The Hoodie again was more than a little surreal. I hadn't thought about it after the breakup, but Zoe still had a few of my other hoodies, maybe a T-shirt or two. It's not that I wanted them back, but it felt bizarre to know that this girl I was trying to be friends with still held onto pieces of Boy Me, this person that never really existed at all.

I finally shut her car door and locked it, since it occurred to me that standing around holding a sweatshirt like it was radioactive must've looked pretty weird. I found Zoe sitting on the steps to the back entrance of the school, taking a bite from a lemon poppyseed muffin.

"Mmmph. Thank you." She pulled the hoodie over her head, her torso now sporting the logo of a school that was *still* paying for my monthly HRT prescription. "Seriously."

My stomach rumbled. One thing I hadn't missed about football was my mid-season appetite. "You don't happen to have another muffin, do you?"

She rolled her eyes, holding out a Tim Hortons bag. "Pizza's *literally* on the way, but sure. You're lucky I'm so nice."

"Thanks." I took the bag, then decided to go for it. "Still wearing my old hoodies, huh?"

She looked down at her chest, then back at me. Her eyes were wide. "I-I wasn't even thinking about it. Is it weird? Be honest."

"It's okay," I said, furiously unwrapping a blueberry muffin. "I don't need them back. My wardrobe's pretty different these days, y'know."

"Well, sure. But I could . . . I dunno. Now I feel bad."

Zoe and I were still figuring out the whole *friends* thing, and we kept ending up in awkward apology deadlocks. Usually, since Zoe was Zoe, it was my job to bail us out. "Only thing you should feel bad about is how badly the juniors are gonna beat our asses if you don't get on your feet."

She flipped me off. "I'm tired, okay? I need a sec."

Deciding she had things under control, I wandered back to the football players. Under Ahmed and Kaeden's supervision, the guys painted decorations to be hung in the gym. The theme of this year's Homecoming was A Night in Paris, and their artwork was . . . *interesting*. I saw a half dozen Eiffel towers, a café scene. A group of linemen worked on a barely recognizable spoof of the *Mona Lisa* where she wore a Pageland football jersey. Scotty Bowen, who wore a beret over his freshly trimmed mullet for the occasion, painted what looked like a Mardi Gras parade, which, hey, at least he had the spirit.

Ahmed saw me approach and waved. "Hop in wherever you want, AK."

"I *told* you not to call me that!"

"It's a dope nickname," Scotty said. "You're automatic. You wear forty-seven. I mean, *c'mon*."

"It *sucks*," I groaned. "Also, it's horrifically problematic."

Ahmed pouted. "Whatever, fun-hater. Like I said, hop in wherever you want. Assuming *Zoe* doesn't need you for anything else."

A few of the guys snickered while I rolled my eyes. "Uh-huh."

"Still holding a candle?" he asked innocently.

I threw my crumpled-up muffin wrapper at him. "Some people are mature enough to be friends with their exes, Ock. When was the last time McKenna Haden even *looked* at you?"

The boys cracked up while Ahmed lobbed the wrapper back at me. "Alright, alright. You can't blame a guy for putting two and two together, you know?"

"I heard Zoe's going to HoCo with a Seabass guy anyway," Kaeden said, bouncing KJ on his knee from his nearby perch on the tailgate of his mama's pickup truck.

"That true?" Ahmed asked me, eyebrow raised.

I shrugged. She was going with this guy, Nick Akers, who lived on her street. They grew up together, went to the same church, that kinda thing. Zoe told me her parents had more to do with arranging it than she or Nick did, because they just *couldn't* stand to see their precious daughter without a date for Homecoming.

There were worse dates you could have, I guess. Nick was always chill, and even I could tell the guy was good-looking. So at least I could be happy for my friend while I laid in bed and imagined all the fun everyone was having.

"Think so," I said, trying to keep my tone light. "I'm not going, anyway."

"Yo, Woody," Calvin Reagor interjected, looking up from his group of receivers. "If you *did* go, like, would you wear a suit or a dress? What's the deal?"

That was *far* from the most out-of-pocket thing someone had asked me since I came out, but still, my walls went up immediately. "Reags," Ahmed said, "c'mon. She identifies as a female. Why would she wear a suit?"

I winced. Ahmed was trying to help, but I didn't "identify" as anything.

"But–" Calvin squinted at me. "Woodhouse, don't you still have a . . . ?" His face went red. "Wouldn't that make wearing a dress kinda–"

"*Reags!*"

"Nah," I answered, swallowing the lump that had formed in my throat. "After a few months on hormones, everything down there shrivels up and dries out. You know how tumbleweeds work? Well, last week, there was this real strong breeze out on the practice field, and . . ."

The horrified look on Calvin Reagor's face–and the dozen guys who burst out laughing at his expense–was *absolutely* worth it. "She's *fucking with you*, dumbass," Ahmed informed him. Then he frowned. "I think she is, anyway."

The boys kept on razzing Calvin, thankfully, giving me a chance to breathe. I'd gotten pretty good at playing the bizarre questions off, making jokes at my own expense. If I got the guys to crack up, it was easier to pretend nothing weird had just happened. I was already forgetting Calvin Reagor (and, probably, most of the team) had thoughts about my junk. See? Foolproof system.

I was about to offer Scotty a hand with his Mardi Gras parade when I heard someone call: "*Grace!*"

I looked up to find Tab, to my surprise, getting out of a car across the lot. She held up a pastel-colored drink. "*Boba!*"

I jogged across the lot to greet them, grinning. "I didn't know you were coming!"

"We decided to be spontaneous after rehearsal," she said. By then, the rest of her friends had piled out of the car too: there was Tarot Card Robin, Houseplant Jade, and two other girls I won't even pretend I remembered the names of.

It was good to see Tab. It wasn't on purpose or anything, but as I became more and more busy with football, I'd been spending less time with her.

"School spirit, rah-rah, all that stuff," she said, passing a pink beverage my way. "I don't know what you like, so I figured strawberry milk tea was a safe bet."

I looked at the cup skeptically. "So . . . there's stuff in there you have to . . . chew?"

The other theater girls giggled at my ignorance. "You've never had *boba?*"

I certainly had not, and now I felt like a huge idiot for it. My face went red. "Never mind. You guys should go talk to Zoe, she'll give you something to do."

"Oh," Tab said, sounding put-off. "I thought we'd, you know, hang out with you?"

I looked over my shoulder at the football team, a few of whom were watching us, and suddenly felt *very* self-conscious. "Look–Tab, I'm sorry, but it's kind of a tradition that sports teams stick together for this stuff. Riley's with her teammates too, you know? It's just how it's done. It'd be weird for me to ditch the guys."

I hoped she understood the subtext there, that the last thing I needed was guys like Calvin Reagor thinking I was *different*. But her face fell. "Oh. Are you sure?"

"I'm sorry," I said again. "We're still on for the haunted house next week, though. You don't think I'm a bitch, do you?"

My joke could've gone over better. Tab's face turned wooden, like it had a *lot* over these last few weeks, and she shook her head. "Of course I don't. You're welcome for the tea, by the way."

As she and her friends marched to Zoe for their orders, I looked at the sweating plastic cup in my hand. Yeah, I probably deserved some Bad Friend Tea.

Before—January

"Come check the chart," Ms. Switzer says, "for your new assigned seats."

Your trig class, fresh off yesterday's midterm, groans in unison. Assigned seats are unnecessary cruelty in a class that's cruel enough already. You only survived the last couple months because you got to sit with Reagor and Powell from the team, even if they're still pissed at you over the miss in Brockport.

You elbow your way to the chart she's taped to the whiteboard, feeling your stomach sink. She's done it alphabetically, broken the class into little islands of three desks each. Finally, you find yours:

Rolón, Tabitha

Vandeberg, Riley

Woodhouse, Jordan

Your life is a never-ending series of tiny humiliations.

You shuffle to your desk and keep your head down, exchanging Boy Nods with Vandeberg when she sits across from you. You kinda know her—you're both jocks—but she's not your friend. You're *friendly* with girls; you're not friends with them.

Tabitha walks in next, and you have even less in common with her. She's a theater kid with a dozen buttons on her backpack, an activist type. She doesn't say a word to either you or Vandeberg, but she gives you a wary look. *Football player*, she probably thinks. *Neanderthal.*

When the bell rings, Ms. Switzer says: "Introduce yourself to your neighbors! We're gonna be working in groups a lot this semester, so let's get caught up."

The three of you shift uneasily, with Vandeberg eventually taking the lead. "Riley," she says flatly. "I play soccer and softball. I like to work on cars. I think icebreakers should be classified as a crime against humanity under the Geneva Convention."

You and Tabitha both cough out laughs. "Oh my *god*," she says, "I know, right? So awkward. Uh, I'm Tab. I do theater."

"Woodhouse," you say eventually, keeping your eyes glued to your desk. "Jordan, I guess."

"Used to play soccer, right?" Vandeberg asks.

"Yeah, a few years back."

"My mom made me play soccer," Tabitha says, lazily spinning a purple pen between her fingers. "I was *not* good at sports. I think I quit by age five."

"You should try out next year," Vandeberg suggests jokingly. "Can always use a benchwarmer."

"Mmm. Might cut into my theater schedule. Plus, I'm bi. Thought you guys only took lesbians."

"You could blaze a trail!" Vandeberg says, her smile crooked. "It would be *so* brave of you."

You're minding your business. You're inspecting the surface of your new desk like it's your job.

"I think we're scaring Jordan," Vandeberg says. "Come back, buddy! We'll act straight around you."

You laugh nervously. "It's cool," you say, sitting up. "I'm, like, I'm cool with it."

"*So* progressive of you," she replies, and Tabitha slaps a hand over her mouth to conceal her laughter. "See? We'll have fun here at End-of-the-Alphabet Island."

You almost want to believe her.

Seventeen

The text came in that night while I was trying to teach myself how to do eyeliner.

> **JEROME:** *Hey, Grace. You available to talk?*

I scowled at my reflection in the cheap desk mirror I'd bought off the internet and admitted defeat. I'd gotten okay at makeup in the months since I'd come out (YouTube tutorials were a godsend), but eyeliner eluded me. My eyes twitched, my hand shook. I could barely get the pen to the edge of my eyelids, much less figure out *wings*.

Since autumn was in full swing and it was pleasantly cool outside, I decided to head out. I washed off my sad eyeliner in the bathroom sink, threw on one of my old XXL Dysphoria Hoodies that hung off me like a dress, and creaked my way down our ancient wooden stairs.

"Going out, Grace?" asked Dad, who was reading a book about submarines in his big comfy recliner.

"Just a quick walk."

"Gotcha," he said, setting his book down. "You working on your college applications?"

I told him I'd started my Common App, which was true. I was applying to a few local schools, still holding out hope that one of them would make me feel something. Without a scholarship, college would be hard to afford, and it wasn't like my GPA or SAT score were anything to write home about. I still hadn't told him about the one college I *had* been seriously looking into. Right now, that stayed between me, Coach Rhoads, and Jerome Metellus.

"Excellent." Just like that, he went back to his book. A first-ballot inductee to the Pro Feelingsball Hall of Fame, he was. Since I didn't see Dad most mornings and he'd throw himself into a home maintenance project nearly every day after work, this might be our single check-in of the week. One thing Dad and I have always had in common: the need to stay busy.

I slipped out into the night without another word, the crisp air perfect for a jog. I settled back into a walk after a mile, dug out my phone, and called Jerome.

"Hey there, Grace," he said warmly. "I just wanted to touch base, see how you were doing."

I told him I was hanging in there, and after we small-talked for a minute about the Bills game this weekend (which is how I found out Jerome grew up a *Dolphins fan*, to my horror), he cleared his throat. "So, you said you've looked more into Saxon Valley. What are you thinking?"

I'd spent the better part of a few hours on the school's website the other night and came out of it feeling as neutral as I did about, like, every other school on earth. Once you've seen one school website you've seen them all. Photos of kids studying in the quad, athletes working out in expensive-looking facilities, and a bunch of cattle in a picturesque meadow that advertised the ag program. *It's not all dairy farms*, Jerome assured me on our first recruiting call. *I'm from Miami, so that scared the shit out of me at first.*

I'd done my research on the football program, too. The team had only been around for five years, the newest member (and current bottom-feeder) of the Mid-American Conference. The MAC was mostly

Ohio and Michigan schools, but since SUNY Buffalo was a member, too, it was the closest thing to a "local" college conference we had around here. The MAC wasn't a power conference or anything, but it was still Division I. Still better than the vast majority of high school football players could hope for.

"I don't have... much to say about the school," I said, before realizing how bad that sounded. "I'm not sure what I would major in, I mean. The thing that's making it hard is... everything else."

Like, you know, being the first trans football recruit in NCAA history? Moving to a state I'd never been to in my entire life, separated by hours from everyone I'd ever known, while I broke a major sports barrier and threw myself under the microscope for the entire country?

"Sorry, I didn't mean to put you on the spot," he said. "I understand why there's hesitation on your part, but we wouldn't be talking if I didn't think you were worth going out on a limb for. Which is why I wanted to circle back to the topic of you making an official visit."

I started to walk again, the process of putting one foot in front of the other helping me gather my thoughts. "Right."

Jerome stressed that a campus visit was *not* a commitment. "We just wanna get you in the building so you can meet Coach Oestreicher and the rest of our staff. We can talk logistics—how we'd break the news and handle the media scrutiny, your medical needs, that kinda stuff." He paused. "I'm not trying to rush you here, Grace, but we should really hammer this out sooner rather than later. Could you have a decision on the visit by, say, next Friday?"

"Umm... sorry, one sec."

I muted my mic and took a deep breath. Around me, North Pageland's old houses leaned precariously like they always did, the wind rattling their shutters. Silly lawn ornaments, quaint *bless this mess*-type window decorations. Nearly all of them had Bills flags, Bills signs, Bills anything. I loved Western New York, especially this time of year. It could be painfully corny, sure, but it was home.

Did I want to leave it?

It'd always been hard for me to see a future for myself. How could you imagine yourself in five or ten years if you couldn't imagine yourself *now*? Obviously, realizing I was trans helped, but it still felt like everyone else was following a set of instructions I never got. And that was before I started playing football again. My old instructions might've gotten lost in the mail, but there *were* no instructions for the path I was on.

I did the only thing I could: I unmuted my mic, told Jerome I'd have a decision by the end of next week, and ended the call.

I opened my messages app and thought long and hard about who I could talk to. Tab wasn't happy with me at the moment. Riley was hosting team bonding at her mom's house, where the soccer girls were probably playing *FIFA* and angrily throwing controllers at the TV. Out of the football guys, the only one I trusted to understand the situation was Dray, but he already had a ton on his plate. It felt selfish to offload my problems on him.

My thumb hovered over Zoe's name for a second. Then I locked my phone and jogged back home.

Eighteen

The game on Saturday was another blowout.

"Good half, boys," Rut said at halftime, the scoreboard reading *Visitors 28, RedWolves 6*. After our win against Wake East, he'd made the no-brainer decision to keep Dray at quarterback. We rolled out our new run-always playbook against Niagara Falls the week after and won 52–0 on their turf, which was when I realized that we might have gotten *better*, somehow, despite it all. "But there are still some mistakes we need to clean up."

Paderborn Central was up in the farm country where Buffalo ends and New Yorkabama begins, a school so broke their field didn't have lights. After Dray's third touchdown of the day early in the third quarter, Rut took mercy on the poor RedWolves and pulled our starters, sending out Steinmetz and the backups for mop-up duty. The sideline was deeply unserious, loose even by our standards, with as much talk about Ahmed's Bonfire Night party next week as there was about the game. Tino Russo and Scotty Bowen debated which of their HoCo dates had a better ass. Calvin Reagor and DeSean Kirkland joked about a mildly sexist TikTok that was making the rounds. I wandered over to Rhoads's spot by the water cooler, hoping to escape the worst of it.

"You going to Homecoming, Grace?" he asked, shifting on the bench. He preferred to watch the game on the sideline with everyone else, but his bad hip kept him back here more often than not. "I got volunteered for chaperone duty, so I'm getting a headcount. Someone's gotta keep you kids outta trouble."

I crossed my arms. "You're worrying about the dance during a *game*?"

The old guy shrugged. "Central's just gonna run the clock and get out of here. Coach said as much to us at halftime. It's over."

I caught a glimpse of the current play by hopping up onto the bench next to Rhoads, my soccer cleats loudly scraping the aluminum. Tobe Okoro, pulling double-duty as a defensive end, completely wrecked the right side of their line and dropped the running back in the backfield for the umpteenth time today. Rhoads was right: it was *so* over.

"Anyway, I'm not going," I muttered, half hoping he wouldn't hear me.

"Is there any par*tic*ular reason why?" he asked, leaning into his drawl.

I sucked on my mouthguard while the teams huddled for second down. This sounded suspiciously like feelingsball, and I wasn't eager to go there with him. "What's this got to do with the game?"

"It doesn't," he said, sounding a little taken aback. "But it's good to let off a little steam once in a while. You kids never have fun anymore."

I groaned. Didn't he know how much pressure we were under? I mean, the crazy high expectations for the football team were only the tip of the iceberg. Unlike Ahmed or Dray, most guys wouldn't be playing college ball; Tobe was a surefire D1 basketball recruit, sure, and a handful would go to local DIII or NAIA schools just because they loved the game, but most were balancing football with regular-ass college applications. Truck was enlisting, and I knew he wouldn't be the only guy who did. Kaeden was balancing school, football, *and* being a father all at the same time. I was so deep in my own bullshit I could barely keep my head above water.

"We still have *fun*, Rhoady," I said. "But it's not like it was when you were a kid. College costs way more, and we're all expected to be perfect. We have less space to fuck up. You were pretty lucky back then, you know."

I expected him to go Old Man Mode and tell me I was entitled, spoiled, and soft, which was how adults always reacted when you told them the truth. Instead, he sighed. "You're right. Just sad to see, I guess."

Central dialed up mesh on second down, but their poor quarterback was under pressure from McReynolds (ugh) within seconds. He lofted a wobbly pass to his tight end, who got leveled by a junior linebacker. I clambered back down from the bench; I'd seen enough.

"Everything going well with Saxon Valley?"

I clenched my jaw. "I dunno. Sure."

"Coach Metellus been respectful of you and your situation?"

"Is it cool if we just focus on the game right now?" I snapped. My life was easier to handle if I cordoned off little chunks of it and only let myself face one thing at a time: *Football. My friends. Saxon Valley. Being trans.* Start mixing them together, instant headache.

Rhoads held up his hands in surrender. "No problem."

Central's running back fumbled on the next play.

When it was time for the post-game handshake, I took my spot at the back of the line and dutifully passed out *good game*s, even if half the Central players pulled their hand back when they got to me. The RedWolves had been quiet all day; I expected worse from farm boys, but I guess it's hard to talk that much when you're getting your ass kicked.

"Faggot," a RedWolf mumbled under his breath when he passed me, refusing to extend his hand. I wondered if he'd done the same for Dray.

When I got to the end of the line, their head coach gripped my hand in a real-deal handshake. "Good game," he said, patting my shoulder. "You know, you're still the best kicker in the section."

"Thanks, Coach."

"I just wanted to say," he said, his grip tightening, "that I admire the way you've handled this situation. These days, you know, everything's political. I saw that quote of yours—'I'm here to kick. That's it.'—and I thought: 'There's someone who's doing this for the right reasons.'"

Of course, there were reporters. They swarmed along the fence and by the locker room like locusts. The worst of it had already passed; dozens of reporters from across the state had turned up for my second game back, all believing *they* would be the one to finally coax a story out of me. They'd invaded my Instagram comments too, though I'd quickly learned in a hurry to never, *ever* check my mentions.

I stonewalled every single one of them. After a few weeks, most of the attention beyond Western New York itself had died down, though I knew the occasional post still made the rounds. I couldn't control that, but I *could* control my own words.

"Got time for a few questions, Grace?" Dale Weingarten, persistent as ever, asked me while we shuffled back to the bus.

I gave him a tight grin. "You know the answer, Dale!"

"Can't blame a man for trying," he said, begrudging smile on his face. "Good game out there."

I lingered in my locker room when we got back to Pageland. I wasn't *strictly* waiting for everyone else to leave, but I needed peace and quiet to help me switch back out of Football Mode, and it was always easier to get there alone. Eager to kill time, I checked my phone.

> **RILEY:** *tab and I are gonna hit thessaloniki after 6 if youre down*

> **RILEY:** *be there or beware*

I could run home, shower, and make it there in plenty of time. A quiet night with the girls sounded nice. And maybe it'd help smooth things out between Tab and me.

Or it could be horrifically awkward if Tab was still mad at me. Whatever. I'd figure it out when I got home. I waited another few minutes before heading out to my car, finding the lot mostly abandoned. Key word: mostly.

"Yo, AK!"

There was Dray, jogging towards me from across the lot. "Of all people, *you're* calling me that?"

"It's a dope nickname," he said, smirking. "You should wear it proudly."

"Sure thing, *DI Dray*."

"Girl, fuck you," he laughed, giving me a playful shove. Ahmed started calling him that when the first few FCS coaches hit Dray's DMs a few weeks ago, and he was still pretending to hate it. "I was gonna ask if you wanted to chill, but you came with the spice."

"What's up?"

Dray put his hands in his pockets. "Zach's back in the hospital, so me and the rest of the captains are gonna go watch some ball with him. I know you haven't had a chance to see him yet, so you should come through."

"Oh. Uh."

"If you're busy, that's cool," he said with a shrug. "But you got time to shower and all that. Kaeden's grabbing his son, and you know Ahmed's gonna make him take his ass to McDonald's. You got plenty of time."

Since I didn't know what else to do—and I really did want to see Prez, despite his leg being . . . *messed up*—I shrugged. "Sure. Wanna scoop me in half an hour?"

He saluted and grinned. "I'll be there, AK."

I didn't even remember that I was ditching the girls until I was in the shower.

Nineteen

Prez was checked into a hospital in Amherst, all the way on the other side of the city, so it wasn't exactly a short ride.

Dray and I had fun, though. He blasted his go-to playlist with the windows down as we glided down the Skyway, the two of us screaming the words to "Still Tippin'" while the city flew by us below, neon lights slowly flickering to life. Tiny people streamed towards the Key-Bank Center for an early-season Buffalo Sabres game, all full of delusional hope and optimism that *this* year would be different. The setting sun painted Lake Erie orange and pink.

Add *this* to the list of things I'd miss about Buffalo.

"Quick game of feelingsball?"

Dray had taken me off guard, so it took me a sec to notice he'd uncharacteristically turned the music down and everything. "Feelingsball's in your court, bro."

"Do you . . ." He hesitated. "You ever done, like, a support group or something?"

Huh. I shook my head *no*. "Why, what's up?"

He shrugged. "I just . . . I think it's cool you have queer friends. I'm jealous, lowkey. I was just thinking about, like, trying to connect with people. Sometimes I feel like I'm missing out on something important, you know?"

"*Oh.*" The thought of sitting with a bunch of strangers and talking feelingsball made me feel itchy, sure, but I could see the appeal for him. "Sorry, man. Jamie Navarro mentioned he goes to one, but that might just be for trans stuff. I can ask, though."

"Nah, it's all good. S'just curious."

I considered inviting him to hang out with me and the girls sometime, but for some reason, I couldn't get the words out. Tab barely tolerated *my* football-playing tendencies; I was sure she'd draw the line at me adding another jock into the mix.

I cleared my throat and changed the subject. "Who're you taking to Homecoming, by the way? Dallas?"

He shook his head. "Nah, I'm flying solo."

I groaned. Dallas was the dude from Orchard Park Dray had brought to a few parties last year, and I'd really liked him. "I was rooting for you two! What happened?"

"I'm, uh, actually talking to someone new. Or . . . I dunno. We've messed around a little, if that counts as talking. But he's not ready to be out like that."

I stared at him in disbelief. "You have a new guy, and you didn't tell the *only other* queer on the team?"

"Nosy ass," he said, chuckling. "But yeah, he's still figuring his shit out, won't commit to anything."

"You're telling me the *illustrious* Dray Fulton, star quarterback of the Pageland High Druids, has a secret boyfriend? And this secret boyfriend *doesn't* want to associate with him in public?"

He flipped me off. "It's complicated! I don't see *you* with a girl, either, you know."

Part of me wanted to press him on it, but it's not like I wasn't keeping secrets from *him*, too. Plus, he'd hit me with the Uno reverse card, and my main priority was keeping this conversation *far* away from Zoe Ferragamo.

"No interest right now," I said. "Ball is life."

"Married to the game?" he asked with a grin.

"The game and I are in love, okay? It's the twenty-first century."

"Love that for you! You're *so* valid, queen."

"*Thank* you. It's getting pretty serious, you know. The game got me pregnant and everything."

"Wow. I hope you got your baby names picked out."

A surprise guest was waiting for us in the hospital lobby.

"The hell you doing here, Trucky?" Dray asked, his tone clearly showing he was joking.

Truck, who looked like he was trying to disappear into his trademark hunting jacket, just shook his head and glowered. "He's my quarterback. I need to see him too."

While most of the boys were trying to stay light after Prez's injury, Truck *definitely* wasn't. His job as an offensive lineman was to protect Prez, and even though he had nothing to do with the injury he still took it as a personal failure. Ahmed tried to talk sense into him, but when Conner Nguyen wanted to brood, he brooded *hard*.

"Hi, KJ," I said, waving at the little guy. He was strapped to Kaeden's chest in one of those tactical camo baby carriers they market to men. "You excited to see Uncle Prez?"

KJ squinted at me for a few seconds before hiccuping and looking away.

"He's in a weird mood today," Kaeden explained. "Don't take it personally."

While the captains debated the cause of KJ's bad vibes—Ahmed suggested he was worried about tomorrow's Bills game, as reasonable an explanation as any other—I fell in line with Truck. "You doing alright, big guy?"

He grunted. "Sure."

Pulling a conversation out of Truck when he wasn't interested was nearly impossible, but I took another crack at it. "Have you, uh, been to see Prez yet?"

"No."

"Me neither."

"Yeah, I figured." *Good talk.* I gave up, deciding it was best to let Truck be Truck.

It took some exploring and a helpful nurse, but we eventually found the right room. Prez's face lit up when we started filing in through the door. "My boys! My beautiful fuckin' *boys*! And *Woodhouse*!"

Our former quarterback looked exhausted and gaunt, his normal comic-book handsomeness muted. A few droopy balloons were tied to a chair next to the bed. A bunch of get-well cards decorated the windowsill, along with a photo of Dray and Prez celebrating a touchdown and a group shot from junior prom (one that, mercifully, didn't include me). Next to it: a game ball signed by the entire team, the one that Dray received after the win over Wake East.

While Prez slapped up his fellow captains, I let myself take a peek at the reason he was still in the hospital. His leg was set in an external fixator that ran from his foot to his calf, inserting over a dozen metal rods into his tibia to keep it in place. Bruising and stitches were the gruesome reminder that it'd been a *compound* fracture. Just in case all that wasn't enough, he'd dislocated his ankle and torn a few ligaments for good measure.

"You still in pain?" Truck was asking him, fully in Mama Bear Mode. "They giving you the right meds? Do you need anything?"

"It's alright, Trucky," Prez said, laughing. "They get paid to take care of me. You don't need to—"

"Seriously," Truck said, like it was a matter of life and death. "I don't care if it's a hospital. I *will* bust heads."

Finally, after Dray handed his friend a binder full of assignments and class notes (to much eye-rolling and cursing from Prez) it was my turn for a slap. "It's good to see you, Woodhouse," he said, his smile warm. "Glad to see you're holding it down."

"You too, dude. Getting out of here soon?"

"Think so. Surgery number three was Thursday night, which is hopefully gonna be the last one. No signs of infection so far. Should be back home tomorrow."

His first surgery had gone poorly, prompting a second one almost immediately. He'd gotten to go home for a couple of weeks before *another* round of complications dragged him back in for more torture. I wondered if he'd made the choice to set up his get-well-soon shrine again or if his parents went and did it for him. Either way, this whole thing had gone on long enough that the cards were collecting dust.

"It's fine, though," he said. "Looking at a six-month recovery time, probably, which gives me plenty of time to get ready for next fall. Ithaca is out, but I'll go the junior college route. I've looked at some programs. If I ball out at a JuCo, I can transfer up to a four-year school later. Guys do it all the time."

Kaeden exhaled sharply. Dray glued his eyes to the floor.

Ahmed was the first to break the ice. "Yeah, bro. Sounds like a plan."

Everyone else in that room knew it was bullshit. Prez's leg was currently being held together by a contraption from *Saw*, and he wasn't ever gonna play at Georgia anyway. Pre-injury, he was a marginal player at the college level; post-injury, he was done.

For as long as I could remember, Prez's only passion was football. He wasn't a brilliant athlete, but he worked harder than anyone else. He hadn't even done anything wrong: he planted his foot exactly like he'd done a billion other times, and that *one time* it betrayed him. What kind of ridiculously cruel sport does that to you?

"Enough of that crap, though," Prez said with a crooked grin. "Let's get some football on. Did you bring . . ." He pantomimed cracking open a can.

I stared at him. "Did you ask them to—"

"He *did* ask for brews," Ahmed said, "but *Dray* didn't want us getting in trouble."

"And if we got banned from seeing Zach over some room temperature beers," Dray said slowly, "you'd be okay with that?"

Prez pouted. "You brought me *homework* and *no beer*. You're the worst."

We settled in to watch Clemson mount a methodical scoring drive on the fuzzy hospital TV, competing to see who could name the most ACC schools without getting one wrong (I was out first; damn you, Maryland). As the conversation passed lazily from football to school to video games, I tried to summon the willpower to bring up Saxon Valley. Most of them had dealt with recruiters before. I trusted them to keep the secret. They all wanted the best for me.

The problem was that none of them knew what it was like to *be* me, couldn't fathom how hard it would be for a trans person to play college football. Even in Dray's case, there'd been openly gay players in Division I before; it wasn't common, but it wasn't unheard of either. There was a path, even if it was remote and dangerous.

Cutting your own path is another thing entirely.

Twenty

Monday brought the beginning of Homecoming Week, which plowed through the monotony of October like a drunk elephant.

Our regular season finale against Hutch Tech on Friday was a pushover, even by our standards, so our eyes had already shifted to the playoffs. Our long march to Syracuse for the state championship was only just beginning. We'd have to fight our way through Section VI playoffs, Regionals, State Semifinals, and then, finally, if we made it: the Carrier Dome in Syracuse on the first weekend of December. Monday film study was all hushed playoff speculation, running through the various scenarios (assuming we clinched the 1-seed against Hutch Tech) in between Rutkowski's cries for us to shut the hell up. We stayed loose through Monday practice, and when we met up at Kaeden's for team bonding that night, it was *on*.

Besides Ahmed, Kaeden was everyone's favorite team bonding host. He lived out on the edge of the school district, where the exurbs melt into farm country, and his backyard was *massive*. His moms were legends to both Pageland's jocks and queers: badass lesbians, the most country people I knew. I mean, seriously, his mama owned a barbecue joint and drove the biggest truck I'd ever seen in my life. I always wondered how the Wannabe Rednecks reckoned with the fact that these two queer women were cooler than they'd ever be.

Unfortunately, among the twenty who'd shown up, McReynolds and a few of his boys were among them. I hung on the periphery while everyone talked Bonfire Night and HoCo plans before festivities migrated outside, where we ate hot dogs off the grill and the guys organized a game of touch football under fluorescent lights. While they picked teams and argued over house rules, I settled into a lawn chair on the patio, content to enjoy the chaos at a distance. I was getting more comfortable being around guys like McReynolds, sure, but progress was gradual. Like slowly wading into a cold pool, letting your body acclimate inch by inch.

"You not joining them, Ms. Woodhouse?" a gruff voice from behind me said. "Or are they too afraid you'll whup them?"

I grinned at Mama Park-Campbell, looking as incredible as ever with her hair up in a red bandana. Even *Tab* thought she was a gay icon. "Don't wanna bruise their egos."

"Course not. D'you mind grabbing my son? We're having trouble getting KJ to sleep."

I popped to my feet, standing on the periphery of the game while Ahmed barked out an over-long cadence, clearly relishing the chance to be a quarterback. "Blue forty-two! Omaha! Lizzo, Lizzo!"

"Snap the ball, Ock!" Tobe Okoro cried, laughing.

When he finally called *hike*, he dropped back, evading an imaginary blitzer. "*Four!*" counted McReynolds, waiting for his chance to rush. "*Five!*"

Ahmed let it fly a moment later, a wobbly spiral floating towards the end zone marked by DeSean Kirkland's slides. Dray, who had a step on Scotty Bowen, motored to his right to catch the ball. *Then*: streaking across the field like a bat out of hell, Kaeden swooped in to knock the ball to the ground. Dray collapsed in despair while everyone else lost their minds. "On his Ed Reed shit!"

"Man looked like the Asian Micah Hyde!"

"That's just Taylor Rapp, dumbass," Kaeden laughed, brushing grass off his cargo shorts. A moment later, when he looked up, I met his eyes and gave him a quick nod.

He told the guys to run the next play without him and jogged over to me. "What's up?"

I felt the eyes of the team on us while I relayed his mama's message. He left for the house without another word. "Everything good?" Ahmed asked.

I told them that Kaeden was helping his moms with the dishes, but DeSean Kirkland smirked and shook his head. "Nah, that's cap. That man's changing diapers."

One of the Wannabe Rednecks cackled. "S'what he gets for not wrapping it."

I crossed my arms but didn't say anything, not wanting to push it. While a few more of the guys made digs about Kaeden's pull-out game, I saw Ahmed and Dray exchange glances.

The thing about hanging out with boys is: if the group's larger than five or six, there are *always* gonna be dudes on the fringes you can't stand. You have your close friends, but there's also an ever-expanding network of Guys You Have To Tolerate, too, spiraling out in all directions forever. In my experience, boys don't really do drama, not the way girls do. When someone's out of line, it's always easier to let it go, to not say a thing.

If the guys were letting Kaeden have it behind his back like this—in his backyard, even—what were they saying about *me* when I wasn't there?

When the father in question emerged from his house a moment later, the boys mock-cheered. "Here comes Philip Rivers!"

"Ol' Iron Balls himself!"

Kaeden rolled his eyes and laughed along with the jokes, but I couldn't help but notice the strain in his smile.

> ## TRIG 11R SUPPORT GROUP
>
> *Today 12:18 PM*
>
> **RILEY:** Yoooooo Grace wya
>
> **GRACE:** crap sorry i forget to say something
>
> i'm sitting with the guys today. kaeden brought his switch in, impromptu mario kart tournament
>
> **TAB:** wtf? are you allowed to do that?? i swear ppl get in trouble for that all the time
>
> **GRACE:** rhoadys the lunch monitor over here lol. we can do whatever we want
>
> **TAB:** seriously?? these guys get away with so much shit
>
> **GRACE:** i know lol it rules
>
> **TAB:** 😑😑😑
>
> **GRACE:** oh cmon. its not that deep
>
> **TAB:** ok

"Make sure it's straight!" Zoe called from the ground.

I huffed, offended, as I stuck Scotty's beautiful Mardi Gras art to the wall of the gym with tape. "Did you think I would hang them crooked on purpose?"

"Just be *careful*!"

I leaned back a bit to examine my handiwork, eliciting an ominous *groan* from the decades-old ladder supporting my weight. "You're trying to kill me," I concluded. "You're trying to send me to Catholic God."

"I am *not*," she protested. "I just can't do it myself."

Zoe had roped me into Homecoming prep again, pulling me out of my eighth period study hall on Tuesday so I could help her decorate the gym. She wouldn't be able to get any work done after school thanks to a doctor's appointment, and I was the "best candidate" she had for the job. Presumably, I was the only one stupid enough to trust a ladder that was probably old when my *dad* went here.

"You *could* do it yourself," I teased, easing my way to the ground. "You're just scared of heights."

When I skipped the last few rungs and leapt down to the hardwood floor with a *thud*, Zoe's eyes went wide. "Jeez, are you okay? That would've killed me."

I laughed. "C'mon. You know I'm fine."

Zoe had always been painfully clumsy. She had a lot of things going for her, but physical coordination was not one of them. "How you're doing all this in skinny jeans is a mystery to me," she said.

Doing it tucked is harder, I thought, but I would truly rather die than say those words aloud to my ex. "I'm a natural. What can I say?"

And then it was back up the ladder with the next priceless work of art, this one a particularly sloppy Eiffel Tower the soccer boys turned in. "I don't think any of us are making it to the Louvre," I mused as I taped.

"The Louvre is a museum," she said, laughing. "You don't make it *to* the Louvre. You make it *in* the Louvre."

"You're in APs! We get it!"

We joked back and forth for most of the period, slowly getting work done, until Zoe got around to the plans she and her friends made for Homecoming. "We're all meeting up at Leah's house for pictures," she told me as I balanced on top of the ladder. "Are you gonna do pictures with your friends? Riley and Tabitha, I mean."

"Oh, I'm not going." I squinted, making sure the *Mona Lisa à la Pageland* looked somewhat level.

"*What?*"

"I told you already!"

"You said you were *thinking* about it," Zoe said, "but you weren't sure."

Oh. Yeah, I probably had. Specifically to avoid this conversation. "Well," I said, looking over my shoulder and giving her a tight smile, "I'm not going."

She was waiting for me with wide eyes when I finished descending the ladder. "But it's your senior Homecoming! You *have* to go."

I took a deep breath and leafed through the beautiful pieces of art on the floor before me. I didn't trust myself to look her in the eyes right now. "I don't want to."

"Why not?"

"School dances are *patriarchal*, you know. It's all just an excuse to throw ass on school property anyway."

"Be serious," she said, and I could hear the hurt in her voice. *Shit.* "Really, Grace. What's going on?"

I picked up another sloppy Eiffel Tower and finally turned back to her. "You really wanna know?"

She didn't flinch.

"I can't wear a dress," I said, the words spilling out of me fast. "I mean, you know what my body's like. Girl clothes are already hit or miss for my shoulders, my chest. So the idea of wearing a formal dress?" I shook my head. "No way. Everyone would . . . *see me.* See my body, I mean. That's terrifying. And I'm not gonna show up *not* wearing a dress, 'cause then everyone will know *why* I'm not wearing a dress." I swallowed a lump in my throat and looked away, unable to meet her eyes. "So, that's why I can't go. Hope that satisfies your curiosity."

I hurried back to the ladder, trying my hardest not to cry while I climbed to the top. God, estradiol was a pain sometimes. While I fumbled with the roll of tape, I heard the squeak of Zoe's sneakers on the hardwood.

"Grace?"

I guess I taped one corner of the poster a little *too* forcefully, because the ladder shuddered. I yelped involuntarily.

"Just come down, okay? Please."

Her voice hit me like a ton of bricks. I froze, the Eiffel Tower half-taped, and blinked hard. After I clambered back down the ladder, she enveloped me in a hug.

I melted into it. It was a combination of a lot of things—the topic at hand, the nostalgia of the smell of her shampoo, everything else happening in my clown car of a life—that made me cry. The tears came hard, and it took me a full minute to realize I was crying about a *lot* more than just Homecoming.

I'm not sure how long we stood there like that before I started feeling self-conscious; I mean, what if someone else saw me like this? I stepped back, keeping my head down. "Sorry," I whispered.

"You don't have to apologize," she said, giving my arm a reassuring squeeze. "*I'm* sorry. I can't even imagine what all this has been like for you. I just . . . you can talk to me, okay?"

There it was again: the apology. She talked to me because she felt bad for me. She thought I was *sad*.

"For the record," she said, "I think you'd look nice if you dressed up. You're a winter, so something, like, *cool*. Deep green, maybe. Or a cobalt blue."

I couldn't stifle the laugh that burst out of my chest. "You don't have to say that."

She furrowed her brow. "What do you mean?"

"I know you're trying to be nice and all, but you don't have to lie to make me feel better."

She stomped her foot self-righteously. "I'm not lying! And *you*"—she jabbed my sternum with her index finger—"need to learn how to *take a compliment*."

"Only when I'm dead in the ground and don't owe anybody anything."

"You're so dramatic it makes me sick."

That night, I came home to a rare sight: Dad making dinner. He raised his hand in greeting without turning away from the stove.

"What's cooking?"

"Spaghetti and meatballs. Traditional Irish recipe. Your grandma handed it down to me."

That was an old joke, but one I always smiled at. A box of pasta, a jar of Ragú, and frozen meatballs from Wegmans was about as chef-y as he got. "The food of our people."

"The Emerald Isle in a pot," he said, giving me a tight smile over his shoulder. "Practice okay?"

I pulled a Gatorade (lemon-lime, because I have good taste) from the fridge and took a long drink. "Not too bad. Everyone's talking HoCo." I paused, faced with a thought I'd never had before. "What'd you do for *your* Homecoming, Dad?"

He stirred the pasta for a moment and said nothing. With him, you couldn't tell if he was taking his time formulating an answer or he simply decided he didn't need to give you one. "I went with this friend of mine," he finally said, "named Anna Leland."

I perked up. He'd never mentioned an *Anna Leland* before. "Who was she?"

"Nice girl who lived down the street. We grew up together, you know? It wasn't serious, but we had fun. Think she got married to some doctor up in Williamsville."

There was a question on the tip of my tongue, since there were always questions about *her* on the tip of my tongue. "Did you know my mom in high school?"

Dad froze for a moment, then clicked off the burner. "Could you grab the strainer?"

I dug our ancient plastic colander out of the cabinet above the fridge and kept quiet while Dad strained the pasta. I breathed in the steam that curled out of the sink.

Here was everything I knew about my mom:

Gretchen had been a waitress at the diner my dad and his old friends used to hang out at all the time. She started getting friendly with them, going to their parties, et cetera. I was the result of that *friendliness*, gruesome details thankfully omitted. They tried to make it work for a couple of years before Gretchen ditched us when I was two. Based on late-night Facebook searches I did sometimes when I couldn't sleep, she and her husband lived in Ohio. Her parents never got along with Dad, so they weren't in my life. I didn't have, like, sepia-toned early memories of her or anything. I had no memories at all. She hadn't left a mark.

I don't remember how old I was when I figured out it was weird that I didn't have a mom, but it never affected us much. Dad didn't like to talk about her, and I was mostly content to know that yes, I had a mother floating around out there somewhere, but she didn't give a fuck about me, so I didn't need to give a fuck about her.

Finally, Dad sighed. "Gretchen went to Pageland High, yeah. But we didn't know each other in school. Why the sudden curiosity?"

"No reason."

Dad clearly didn't buy it, but he hesitated, like he wasn't sure if he should press me on it or not. As he transferred the pasta back to the pot, he pressed his lips into a line. "If you wanna talk to me," he offered, slowly and deliberately, "you can."

I felt that familiar prickling behind my eyes, and I knew I was about to spill. "I'm . . ." I took a deep breath. "A school in Wisconsin wants me to play football for them, Dad."

I gave it to him from the top: how Jerome and I met, what the deal with Saxon Valley was, that they wanted me to visit. He tossed the pasta in the sauce and listened intently, not saying a word until I was done.

"I guess . . . whenever I have to make big decisions, I think about her. I think about what she would say. I wonder what . . ."

I wonder what she would say about me being a girl.

"I'm sorry," he said, his voice quiet, "that you don't have her around right now. I'll never forgive her for that. But you've got me. And I wish you'd told me about this sooner."

I cleared my throat and rubbed my eyes. "You know me," I said, trying to deflect, "always turning in assignments last-minute."

He didn't seem to think that was particularly funny.

"So, you know I didn't go to college," he said. "My policy has always been: if you want to go, I'll support you however I can. But it helps if you keep me in the loop. That's all I ask. Okay?"

I nodded sheepishly. "Sorry."

"So"–he handed me a bowl of pasta–"what do you think about this coach? This school?"

Wish I knew, Dad. "The coach seems great, but the school..." I groaned. "I feel like I need more information."

"Maybe it'd be worth visiting, then?"

"Maybe," I said, my voice tiny.

After we ate, I pulled on a denim jacket that I'd thrifted with Riley and Tab a few weeks ago and headed out into the yard. Dad's fall flowers were still kicking: mums, goldenrod (a newcomer; Dad complained about their spread, so they probably wouldn't be coming back next year), Russian sage. I reached for a rusty orange marigold, running my thumb along its petals. Marigolds didn't have long lives, even for annual flowers; they grew, withered, and died in a hurry. I dug my thumbnail into the stem and decapitated the poor thing, holding the flower up to the light. They weren't my favorite *smelling* flower, but they were gorgeous.

I slipped the marigold behind my ear and headed back inside, checking my reflection in the bathroom mirror. I wasn't sure the flowery thing really worked for me, fashion-wise; I was no one's cottagecore dream girl. Tough Jock looked a lot better on me than Flower Queen.

But I liked it. Sue me.

Twenty-one

"Top five if you were straight, Ri," Tab said, lazily twirling a pencil between her fingers. "Go."

I came into Wednesday's study hall hoping to grind through a scene of *Hamlet* I was supposed to read for English, but I'd admitted defeat almost instantly. Focusing on anything with these two around was near impossible, of course, but I'd barely seen them all week and I couldn't bring myself to bail on them. I needed a breather from everything stressful going on in my life, and *Hamlet* was certainly one of them.

"Impossible," Riley countered. "I'm a Kinsey 6."

Tab shook her head. "*No one* is a Kinsey 0 or a Kinsey 6."

"What's a Kinsey?" I asked, completely lost.

"It's a sliding scale of sexuality," Riley explained, to which Tab was already rolling her eyes. "Zero means you're all-the-way straight, six means you're all-the-way gay."

"Which assumes a gender binary, first of all," Tab said in her Speaking-to-Children voice. "And second of all, it assumes that sexuality is a single point you can plot on a graph, rather than a complicated jumble of emotions that is constantly changing. It's patriarchal nonsense."

"My sexuality is *not* complicated, Tab. My sexuality is *girls*, preferably naked ones. I couldn't even give you *one* if I was straight."

I rolled my eyes. "Even I could do that."

"You go, then."

I had to think about it for a second. "Caleb Williams. He's pretty."

Tab gave me a blank look. "Should I know who that is?"

"Quarterback for the Bears. Just google him." I turned back to Riley. "C'mon! Not even one?"

She huffed. "Whatever. It'd have to be someone, like, big and scary. Like André the Giant in *The Princess Bride*."

"He's not scary. He's downright cuddly!"

"He could take me in a fight. That's, like, the first barrier a guy would need to clear for me."

"Oh," Tab said, raising her eyebrows as Caleb Williams filled her phone screen. "This guy is *fine*!"

"Told you!"

Riley sighed. "He's literally just *some guy*."

"I could show you a male supermodel and you'd say 'it's just *some guy*.'"

"Would I be wrong?"

"Whatever, André the Giant," Tab said, rolling her eyes. "Hey, have we figured out when exactly we're gonna meet up for FrightZone tomorrow?"

We'd had these plans for a couple of weeks now. Tab *loved* haunted houses; every October she tried to hit all the big ones in the county. I'd never been to one (I was a massive wimp) and Riley thought they were boring, but we all agreed that going together would be fun.

"We said it would be at eight, I think," Riley replied. "But we should factor in traffic. There's always a ton of people out on Bonfire Night."

Shit. *Shit*. "Wait, guys," I said, my mouth feeling dry. "Can we delay until next week?"

"Why?" Tab asked.

"I didn't realize—" How was I supposed to explain myself? I couldn't even figure out how I'd double-booked myself this badly, like the two halves of my brain that housed Football and Everything Else had failed to communicate. "Bonfire Night is—I mean, it's required attendance for the team."

"It literally isn't required attendance," she said, her face souring. "You're not getting *graded* on how many parties thrown by douchebags you go to."

I was getting *really* tired of her calling my friends "douchebags" every chance she got, but I didn't bring it up. "Bonfire Night is different," I explained. "It's *the* football team event. I'm just—I have a lot going on, and I fucked up, and I'm sorry. We could reschedule, right? We could make time next week?"

"FrightZone closes for the season on Sunday," Tab says stiffly, "and there's no way I can get out of family dinner."

"Well, we could go somewhere else, right? There's other haunted houses. There's that one, umm, it's up in North Buffalo? The building that used to be a Kmart?"

Silence from both of them. *Shit.*

"It's not *just* tomorrow," Tab said, crossing her arms. "You *always* put the team first."

"Football is a big part of my life!"

"So you never have time to hang out with us anymore? You're always with them! During school, after school—"

"This is over who I *hang out* with? What are you, twelve?"

I've certainly said smarter things in my life.

Tab looked like she could breathe fire. "This is over you being too cool to hang out with the queers now that you're a football star again! You're so busy trying to convince them you're '*one of the boys*' that you're losing everything that actually makes you cool!"

I felt like I'd been punched in the face, far too stunned to summon a reply. "Tab," Riley said, her voice even-keeled, "*lay off.*"

"Why's it so hard for you to imagine I actually *like* my teammates?" I asked, anger swelling in my chest. "It's not any deeper than that."

"Because football is the official fucking sport of toxic masculinity! And you're better than that!"

"Come on," Riley said, rolling her eyes. "What's Grace supposed to do? Lecture them on feminism in the huddle? Start a pronoun circle in the locker room?"

"That's not what I'm saying and you *know* it!"

"You don't know what you're talking about," Riley said, crossing her arms. "You're not an athlete, okay? You don't get it. Not everyone in the real world's a perfect little theater kid, you know."

Tab blinked hard, took a deep breath, then rose to her feet. "I'll fuck off, then."

"Wait," I said. "Tab—"

"I don't even remember why we hang out anymore," she said icily. "I mean, you guys don't care about anything I have going on. Fall play's in a few weeks, and you haven't asked me about it *once*."

"But—"

"It's fine," she said, sounding tired. "You're jocks. I'm not. It's whatever."

Riley rolled her eyes and chuckled dismissively while Tab stormed off. "Classic Rolón," she said, trying *very* hard to sound confident. "You know how she is. She heats up, she cools off. She'll be back to her normal peachy self tomorrow."

"Yeah," I said, trying to speak it into existence. "You're probably right."

She was wrong.

Before—March

"Jordan? Is that you?"

You're so lost in your own head that you barely register her voice until she repeats herself. "Jordan!"

You finally look up to find Tab sitting on a porch a dozen yards away. She's safe from the downpour; you, meanwhile, are soaked to the bone. Rain and tears burn your cheeks, your hair's a rat's nest. You're a total wreck.

"Yeah," you say. "Just going for a walk."

"It's *freezing*! Get your ass over here! Out of the rain!"

You oblige, feeling your cheeks go red. You've been friendly with Tab since you started sitting together in trig, but you're not, like, *friends*. You don't know much about her, and she doesn't know *anything* about you.

She gives you this concerned look when you join her on the porch. "Why are you on a walk? It's pouring!"

"I—" You consider lying, then settle on a half-truth. "I walk when I need to clear my head. Why are you sitting outside, anyway?"

"I like to watch the rain," she says with a shrug. She's curled up in a chair with a big shaggy blanket; you concede that she looks cozy. "It's relaxing."

"Cool," you say, your mouth dry. "Uh. Have fun? I should probably get home."

She gives you a skeptical look. "I'm sure my parents would give you a ride home. Or, you know, you could hang out for a little bit and wait out the storm."

"It's okay. Really. I should get going."

"I–" She shakes her head. "Okay. Sure."

Your heart hits the floor. "Sorry, I didn't mean to–I appreciate it, I just can't."

You're in a hurry to leave because being around Tab makes you feel feelings you like to keep buried, but she probably thinks you're some asshole jock who's embarrassed to be seen in public with a theater kid–a queer one, at that. "It's not–" You stop, because there's no way you can finish that sentence. "Never mind."

"What?" she asks, burrowing under her blanket. There's curiosity on her face.

"I think you're cool," you say quickly, "I'm not just trying to ditch you, I promise. I just–I'm sorry."

Despite it all, she looks amused. "I know you're not trying to ditch me. You apologize more than any boy I've ever met, you know."

That sends you reeling. Your ears ring, your chest feels tight. "Are you okay?" she asks. "I didn't–I don't know what I said, but–"

"I don't think I'm a boy."

The words leave your mouth before you can think them over, and as soon as they do, you feel like you might die. Your heart's beating faster than it ever has. What's wrong with you?

"Wait," Tab says, her eyes wide, "you mean you're . . . ?"

You can't bring yourself to speak, but you manage a nod.

"Okay . . . umm, wow."

You look at your feet and cross your arms. You know the words were gonna force their way to the surface eventually, but you never guessed *Tab* would be the first to hear them.

Now your secret's in the air, and you know you can't take it back.

"Sorry," you mumble. "I didn't mean to . . . I wasn't planning on saying anything. I've never told anyone, actually. I just–I know you're bi, and–"

She excavates herself out from under her blanket, bouncing to her feet. "You have *nothing* to be sorry about!" she says. "I don't wanna pry, but... you can talk to me. About this stuff. And I support you, obviously."

"Thanks." You finally have the courage to glance at her; she's smiling. "Are you surprised?"

"Well, you're a jock and you're not a *complete* dick, so maybe that should've been a clue."

"Hurtful."

"Seriously," Tab says, "I'm glad you told me. If you need anything, let me know, okay? And, uh... pronouns and name are staying the same for now?"

"Definitely." You've barely even begun thinking about that stuff, and it scares the shit out of you. Even if you can accept that you're... *like that*, you don't know if you could ever come out. That sounds impossible to you. "She/her, though." It comes out like a whisper. "Someday? Maybe?"

"Okay," she says, her smile wide. "Are you a hug person? Can I give you a hug?"

You have to admit: she's a great hugger. She looks down at the water stain on her sweatshirt once you've disentangled and laughs. "You're *soaked*. Look, if you're gonna walk home, just–just wait a second."

She emerges from the front door a moment later, black umbrella in hand. "There. Don't stress about getting it back to me, it's my spare."

For some reason, *this* is what makes you choke up. You take the handle from her, heave a deep breath, and smile weakly. "Thanks for being cool."

She gives you another hug, and that's when you realize: *I have a non-football friend now.*

Twenty-two

Ahmed's house wasn't *quite* a mansion, but it was in the ballpark. South Pageland was where the rich people lived. It was home to doctors, doctors, and more doctors, its plazas full of chiropractors, dermatologists, any specialist you could ever possibly need. It was nothing like my neighborhood, North Pageland, which used to serve the long-shuttered Druid Steel plant on the western edge of town. That's where the mascot comes from, if you were wondering.

Ahmed's house was nice even by South Pageland standards, so new it practically sparkled. His parents were from Cairo; his dad was a neurosurgeon who liked silk smoking jackets, expensive cigars, and Russian literature, while his mom was a famous historian of French (or was it Spanish?) history. They were eternally busy, always out of town on Fancy-Smart-People work trips.

That meant Ahmed, who loved to throw parties, was home alone a *lot*.

I parked Lorraine halfway down the block, took a deep breath, and flipped the visor mirror down to scrutinize my makeup. I'd run home after the school bonfire to clean up, and I'd opted for a basic look: understated red lip, a flannel shirt under my denim jacket, my favorite jeans. Knock-off Doc Martens (I'd started calling them Doc-Offs) with an inch heel. I'd wanted to get a little crazier, honestly, but I also didn't want to stick out like a sore thumb among the guys.

For a passing moment on my walk down the street, I wondered what Tab would say about that. *Whatever.* Besides, I was a lesbian who played football. No one expected me to wear miniskirts every day of the week.

I opened Ahmed's front door to find his living room *full*. A lucky few had claimed bits of furniture on the edges of the room, but most either sat in groups on the floor or stood in bunches. Red Solo cups, canned cocktails. Empty White Claws decorated Ahmed's fancy hardwood floor. If this was the living room, there must've been over a hundred kids here, probably from all over the southtowns. I hadn't been to a party like this in a *long* time.

I waved and smiled at the few people who called to me and elbowed my way into the kitchen, where I found the host himself. Ahmed didn't drink—religion, you know—so he ran his parties *very* efficiently. He and his fellow linemen worked security, making sure nobody got too rowdy. Someone was *always* watching the alcohol, including a keg that called my name from its place on the island.

When Ahmed saw me enter the kitchen, he broke into a wide grin and crushed me in a bear hug. "I was worried you weren't gonna show, AK!"

"Couldn't miss tonight!" Say whatever you want about Ahmed Nassar, but his hug game was unassailable. "Keeping everything under control?"

"So far. Beer pong in the parlor got a little heated, but Truck broke it up. Our boys are staying out of trouble. You find them yet?"

I shook my head *no*.

"I think most of 'em are out back. Patio." He nudged me with his elbow. "Good to see you let your hair down, forreal. You're so damn serious these days."

While most of the yard was empty thanks to the drizzle, the football team had claimed the deck. Guys were laid out on chairs, sitting on the damp wood itself, leaning against the house. There were a million little conversations. Smoke and laughter hung in the air.

To my relief, my arrival was greeted with cheers.

"Grace!" a shirtless Dray said, sloppily raising a red cup in toast. Did he lose a bet? Did I even wanna know? "You made it!"

"Look what the cat dragged in!" called Scotty Bowen, who seemed to be enjoying himself. His shirt was wet, either from rain or a spilled drink.

Someone said: "Do you have a beer? Jesus, you didn't grab a beer?"

"Someone get this kid a beer!"

A red cup materialized in my hand a moment after I settled into a chair relinquished by Kaeden, who assured me it was fine. "It's good to have you back," said Scotty, who nudged me with his elbow. "I think I speak for everyone when I say we missed Wildcard Woody."

I groaned while the boys cheered at my expense. I earned that nickname last year when I celebrated my forty-eight-yard field goal against Seabass by getting so trashed I lit Frankie Mannino's shirt on fire (long story). The next week, a similar evening ended in me puking on Tino Russo's TV. That was back when I was *really* going through it, when the gender feelings I'd been outrunning for years started gaining ground and I coped by drinking my ass off. That person didn't feel like *me* anymore, not really, but how many people still saw *Wildcard Woody* when they looked at me? Did I really wanna know the answer?

"I'm gonna take it easy tonight!" I insisted, taking a cautious sip. I'd negotiated a hard two-drink limit with myself earlier in the day, and the thin, empty taste of light beer wasn't doing much to change my mind. "Those days are behind me. I'm washed."

"AK's *grown up* now," Dray complained. "This sucks."

"C'mon now. I didn't say *that*."

Soon, the conversation left me and went everywhere else. I settled into my chair and picked up the little fragments I could, fading into the background. I laughed when everyone else did. The low thud of trap music from someone's Bluetooth speaker vibrated in my chest.

This was what I missed about parties: feeling warm and alive, happily fading into the background while the chaos unfolded around me. I finished my beer and another one appeared. The rain picked up.

Twenty-three

"Ladies and gentlemen," Ahmed boomed in his best ring promoter voice, "welcome to Pageland Wrestling Entertainment!"

The massive trampoline in Ahmed's backyard was the stuff of Pageland legend, practically the eighth wonder of the world. Before he was Ahmed Nassar: Football Prodigy, he'd been Ahmed Nassar: Trampoline Guy. When you're a kid, you've gotta be friends with at least one Trampoline Guy, so he'd always been popular. These days, it doubled as a great place to lie on your back, smoke, and imagine how nice it would be if you could see the stars.

A crowd had formed around the trampoline, maybe fifty of us, with more watching from the deck. I'd had enough to drink that I no longer cared about the rain. My hair clung to the side of my face, my neck. I barely felt the cold at all.

Kaeden, who joined me on the edge of the crowd by the fence, looked like he was *definitely* feeling the rain. "This is dumb," he said. "What if someone gets hurt?"

"Loosen up, K," I replied, my tongue heavy with Labatt. "Have some fun."

"In this corner," Ahmed cried, "we've got the boy wonder himself, the kid from Florence Street... *The Rooooooooooose!* Roose is loose! Roose is loose!"

The crowd thundered *Roooooose* while Tino Russo flexed and showboated around the edge of the trampoline, pumping up an imaginary arena.

"And the challenger! He's from the swamps of North Pageland! He was raised by wolves! He eats raw bear meat for breakfast! He once defeated a gorilla in single combat!"

"It's true!" called someone in the crowd. "I saw him do it!"

"Give it up for *Scotty* . . . *'The Hottie'* . . . *Boooooooweeeeeeen*!"

The crowd cheered as Scotty leapt around the Octagon, mullet flying majestically, and then completely lost it when he started shaking his ass along to the Ice Spice song blaring over the speaker. "My god!" Ahmed shouted in between bouts of laughter. "How can a man *be* this sexy?"

As two boys started faux-grappling, I raised my fourth beer to my lips only to find it dry. "Ugh," I grumbled. "Gotta head inside. Can you record this match for me?"

Kaeden looked at me warily. "You've been drinking water, right?"

"Yes, *Dad*." He must've known I was lying, since he'd been around me most of the night. "C'mon, record this while I'm gone."

I left for the house before he could say anything, nearly tripping when I stuck one of my Doc-Offs in a particularly thick patch of mud by the patio steps. I got a sarcastic cheer from the others as I regained my balance. "Graceful, lady," laughed some boy I didn't recognize. He wasn't a Pageland kid, I knew that much.

"That's what they call me."

The boy helped me up the steps, which was a little unnecessary. It wasn't like I couldn't *walk*. "Thanks," I said, scraping the mud off my boot onto the top step. Not very ladylike, but I was too drunk to care.

"No problem." The boy smiled. He was a few inches shorter than me and funny looking: scruffy hair, ears too big for his head. "You okay?"

I squinted at him. Why was this guy treating me like a baby? "Of course."

"I'm Brian, by the way," he said, raising his cup in greeting. "I go to Frontier."

It felt like we were having two entirely different conversations. "Ooh-*kay*. Thanks, Brian from Frontier."

I left him out there on the porch, vaguely aware that a handful of kids around us snickered as I went. I squeezed past a pair of juniors in the throes of a makeout session and into the kitchen, where I got ambushed in a hug.

"Ohmygodohmygodohmygod—*Grace!*"

The girl squeezing me half-to-death was Leah Shoemark, Zoe's best friend. She broke off her hug and held me by the shoulders. "I have been *dying* to talk to you! You look *so* good!"

"*Le*ah," Zoe whined from the other side of the island, "can you not be extra for, like, five seconds?"

"S'okay," I said, grinning. She was a total sweetheart, but *extra* was an apt word to describe Leah. "You look great yourself, girl. Eyeliner's on point, as always."

Leah squealed and squeezed me by the shoulders again. She was *allegedly* five foot zero (that always seemed a little optimistic to me), so she practically had to look straight up to meet my eyes. "You were always *so* sweet. I, like, love and support you more than you could ever know, okay? One million percent. Ride or die."

I thanked her and excused myself from her death grip so I could fill my cup, appreciating the Aggressive Drunk Allyship. "You guys been here for a while?"

Zoe sipped her can. Knowing her, a single vodka seltzer was probably her limit for the evening. "For a little bit. How 'bout you?"

"Been with the football boys," I said through a hiccup. "They're wrestling now."

"Oh my gosh, they're gonna break their necks!"

"It's *fine*." I took a long swig of my beer and leaned against the counter next to Leah. "Ock is refereeing. But yeah, it's been, like, a chill night. Good to relax, you know?"

I was about to ask her who else she came with when a deep voice from the hallway answered the question for me. "Zoe! I was wondering where you went!"

A *huge* guy—broad, all of six foot three—traipsed into the kitchen. He was a lot bigger now, but I still recognized his shaggy blond hair and wide smile from the second-grade class we'd been in together: Nick Akers, Zoe's HoCo date.

"Oh, hey!" Zoe smiled wide. "Gosh, this is—"

"Jordan Woodhouse!" he said, grinning from ear to ear. "We knew each other when we were, like, seven. Ms. Freeman's class! I read all about your gender change on Instagram, man! Pretty cool stuff."

I wasn't sure I'd ever get used to that. My chest felt tight, like it was being squeezed by a vise. My head ached.

"It's *Grace*!" Leah cried, though her voice sounded distant to me.

"Oh. Right, sorry." He clapped me on the shoulder. "Really, I am. Zoe always told me what a good boyf—"

"Nicky," Zoe hissed. Despite it all, I smirked; I'd heard that tone before. "You should go check out the backyard. I heard the boys are wrestling."

He lit up. "Sick. Hey, Grace, it was dope to see you! Seriously!"

While he bounded off on his merry way, I couldn't help but crack up. "I'm sorry," Zoe said, sounding mortified.

"He's a human golden retriever. It's uncanny."

"He's...a sweet guy. Really, though, I promise he didn't mean anything by that."

"I know he didn't." Did that really make me feel better? Not much, no. I still felt breathless. "I've heard worse."

"*Ohmygod*," Leah said, gripping my arm. "Does anyone need their ass kicked? 'Cause I will go apeshit on them. I fight dirty, you know. I pull hair."

I assured her she didn't need to pull anyone's hair. "Tonight's been fine. This one guy was kinda weird to me a little bit ago, but—"

"Where is he? Do you need me to kill him?"

"No!" Another swig of beer. I wanted to be a *lot* drunker, ideally as soon as possible. "I dunno. I, like, almost tripped, and this guy helped me, and then he was weirdly patronizing? And nice? And he told me his name? I dunno. Maybe he's Mormon or something."

Leah's eyes went wide. "Girl, he was trying to *talk* to you!"

I scoffed. "Yeah, right."

"He was totally flirting with you," Zoe said, pinching the bridge of her nose.

A brief wave of nausea rolled over me. "But—no way. Boys don't do that. I don't pass."

Leah punched my shoulder, looking offended. "*Excuse* me! You're pretty!"

"You are," Zoe added, her cheeks reddening. "You do the—you know—the cool jock girl thing well."

"See? You're pretty, boys wanna talk to you. Welcome to womanhood!" Leah cocked an eyebrow. "Was he cute?"

It took me a few seconds to figure out what she was getting at—the beer made everything slower—but when it finally hit me, I made a face. "*Gross.* I'm not into guys. Like, at *all.*"

"Oh!" Leah's face shifted rapidly from Surprised to Confused to Embarrassed before defaulting back to her normal grin. "Jealous, honestly. So you know how I was talking to Tyler Watts last year? Well . . ."

While she told me all about her most recent romantic expeditions and I very politely nodded along, my brain tried to play catch-up. A *boy* tried to talk to me *like that*, because he thought I was . . . *pretty?*

Some part of me was flattered, maybe, but it also scared the hell out of me. I didn't want attention from boys *like that*. I liked that most of my football friends didn't see me that way, didn't start suddenly treating me like an undercover cop when I came out. It was easy. Whatever happened with that boy was the opposite of easy.

If I was gonna play football at Saxon Valley, I needed to learn how to handle that attention. Or, I guess, go *very* far out of my way to avoid it.

There was Tab in my head again: *one of the boys.*

I needed more beer.

Twenty-four

"I'm gonna text him," Dray said, leaning on the pad of Ahmed's trampoline. "Feelingsball time, man. I'm gonna tell this dude how I feel."

After Scotty "beat" Tino on an impressive-looking spear, the backyard had devolved into an Ahmed-moderated free-for-all: ten people on the trampoline at a time, total chaos. Soccer boys took turns throwing one another against the mat, cross country boys competed to see who could do the most backflips without getting sick. Golden Retriever Nick Akers clotheslined Calvin Reagor, who slammed to the trampoline in a fit of giggles.

"Who *is* this dude, anyway?" Tino asked Dray. "Why didn't you invite him to the party?"

"He . . . was busy."

"Well, are you just tryna smash or what?"

Dray groaned. "I dunno. I don't . . . *think* so?"

"You're a *stud*, man!" Scotty, whose Hawaiian shirt got unbuttoned long ago, clapped him on the shoulder. "Shoot your shot. If this guy's worth it, he'll drop everything."

"Bowen's right," I said. "Full send, Dray. Let 'em know."

He sighed. "Screw it." We hooted in excitement as he pulled out his phone. "It's y'all's fault if he's weird about it."

While Dray tapped out his text, taking note to shield his phone from prying eyes, Kaeden shuffled uncomfortably. "How much longer till someone calls the cops?"

"Give it a while," Scotty said with a sloppy wave. "It's Bonfire Night. They'll only come if we don't shut down by midnight."

What I would have said if I was sober: *We should probably get out of here soon, then.*

What I actually said: "I'll fuckin' swing if they come. I could take a cop, easy."

Dray, who always got touchy-feely when he was drunk, put his arm around my shoulders and laughed. "Girl, that's a bad idea." He whispered in my ear: "Remind me to tell you about this dude. There've been *developments.*"

Before I could ask him what he meant, Scotty heaved a dramatic sigh. "Y'know, I could go for another round. I wish there was something we could jump off of onto the trampoline."

Dray snorted. "Like those idiots who jump off RVs through folding tables at Bills tailgate."

"Abso-fucking-*lutely*. You ever done that, bro?"

"I've jumped through a table," Dray said, "but never *off an RV*. That's insane. That's white people shit."

"Well, sure. What Bills fan hasn't jumped through a table?"

"Me," I said, without a second thought.

In an instant, a dozen pairs of eyes were on me. "You're messing with us," Tino said. "You *definitely* jumped through a table last year."

Table-jumping's self-explanatory: set up a cheap folding table, leap from high ground, gracefully crash through it while dozens of strangers cheer. The higher the jump, the greater the drama. It'd become the go-to activity for restless Bills fans looking to go viral before kickoff, because it really only sounds like a good idea if you're drunk in a parking lot at ten in the morning. Or drunk *anywhere*, really.

I shook my head. "Never have."

That was my last chance to avoid my now-inevitable fate, and I flew right by it.

"Yo, Ahmed!" Dray called. "Ock! You got any extra folding tables lying around?"

It only took a few minutes for a junior lineman to procure a gray folding table from Ahmed's basement, and from there, I just rode the wave. In the blink of an eye, the crowd parted, the trampoline cleared, and the table was set.

That's how I ended up standing on the edge of Ahmed's trampoline, drunk off my ass, sizing up a goddamn table while a hundred kids screamed at me.

"Wait! Grace, here!"

Dray tossed me one beer, then another. "Stone Cold!" he cried. "Stone Cold!"

Soon, the entire backyard was echoing him, and I had no choice but to oblige. I cracked both cans, held them up like ancient relics of great power, and crashed them together over my head in a shower of cheap Canadian beer. In my mind, it was *very* badass, but you could see from Scotty's Snapchat story that most of the beer ended up on me and the trampoline, not in my mouth.

After my beer bath, I made the jump. It was a miracle I didn't slip on the slick plastic frame pad, but against all odds my liftoff was clean. After a majestic soar through the air, I led with my left side and crashed through the table, which buckled under my weight and sent me spilling out onto the wet grass. The yard *exploded* in excitement.

While the boys helped me to my feet and got a *Woodhouse* chant going, I started laughing. Dray squeezed me in a big-ass hug, laughing right back. "What's so funny?"

I don't remember what I said back.

I ended up in Zoe's car that night, and I don't quite know how.

My best guess: Kaeden or Ahmed handed me off around midnight when things started winding down, since I was obviously in no condition to drive home. Nick sat up front, so Leah and I stuffed ourselves into the backseat and screamed along to "Industry Baby" at the top of our lungs. She grabbed me and said: "You are *literally* a goddess." I rolled my eyes, laughed, and tried not to cry about it.

Once Zoe dropped both Leah and Nick off, she glanced at me in the mirror. "Hop up front. Can't have you blowing chunks back there."

"*So* thoughtful of you," I said, clumsily climbing over the hump. "I can't believe you remembered my motion sickness."

She sighed. "I just don't wanna clean up your mess."

We drove most of the way without saying a word, coasting back across the train tracks into North Pageland. I shivered, my soaked clothing clinging to my skin. "I was out in the rain for a long time, huh?"

Zoe snorted. "You think?"

Out of morbid curiosity, I smelled my hair: smoke from the bonfire, malt from my impromptu beer theatrics, rainwater. "Jeez, I'm a mess. I must look like I got hit by a bus."

After a second, she said: "You look like a girl that made some questionable decisions."

That made me feel warm and fuzzy even though it was a dig. "So," I said, trying to make my mouth obey my brain through the fog of Canadian beer, "you think I'm a . . . what did you say? A *'cool jock girl'*?"

She groaned. "I can't have this conversation with you while you're drunk."

"Why not?"

Without answering, she parked on the street in front of my house. "You gonna be able to get inside by yourself? Up the stairs and everything?"

"Of *course*. I'm not *that* messed up."

"Okay. I'll, uh, see you tomorrow, probably?"

"I think so."

I didn't move. We kept on making eye contact.

"Grace," she said softly. Her eyes caught the light from a nearby porch. "It's been really good. Spending time with you again, I mean."

My chest buzzed. "I think so too."

"And I meant what I said." She looked down at her lap. "About, uh. About you being, you know. Pretty."

After another half minute of this—a game of chicken where both of us were too scared to move a muscle—she blinked first. She held out her hand and cupped my cheek, her touch warming me from head to toe. "That okay?"

I nodded.

"So . . ." She struggled for words. It was brave of her to try and say anything at all, because I knew I couldn't. "Whatever. Fuck this."

When she kissed me, it was soft and hesitant and sweet. I'd never been kissed like this: like I was delicate, like I might break. After a moment, she pulled back. "Okay?"

I nodded again, because I was too drunk and too deliriously horny to question the wisdom of it. "But, like, for real this time, okay?"

She kissed me again, for real this time. She tasted like cherry seltzer.

Twenty-five

On Saturday night, while everyone else was at Homecoming, I texted Jerome Metellus three words:
Schedule the visit.

PART III

November

"Football is the sport that asks you to believe that there is an acceptable and controllable amount of being on fire."

—Spencer Hall,
"Buffalo"

Twenty-six

My quads burned. My hamstrings burned. Everything burned.

"I need all you got, Grace!" Ahmed cried. "Everything you got!"

The boys hyped me up as I lowered myself into the squat, but I tuned out the noise. I let the pain focus me: the bar digging into my callused hands, my upper back. Dray's hands were on my waist, sure, but he was only there to ensure I didn't die. It was just me and my weak garbage legs against the world.

I tasted fire as I reached the bottom of my squat, hesitating there just a second too long. I felt Dray grab me, about to tell Tobe and Scotty to bail on the rep, but I grunted in refusal. *No way.* Slowly, steadily, I pushed myself up out of the hole. Everything in my midsection felt like battery acid, but I never stalled. *Everything you got.*

When I locked my knees back out, Ahmed lost it. "*Fucking beast!* She's a *fucking beast!*"

I racked the bar with the help of my teammates and inhaled for the first time in forever, letting the ambient BO smell of the student weight room pummel my sinuses. Half a dozen hands clapped my back. Dray passed me my water bottle. "New season record, right?"

I nodded, taking a long drink. These little morning lifts were organized by Ahmed, who'd been given a key to the gym by Rut;

unsupervised access to the weight room was a superpower only conferred to you by football stardom. I went as often as I could, running through my usual routine: oblique exercises, time on the leg press, a few squats and deadlifts.

"Just getting back to where I used to be," I told Dray. The lift clocked in at 245; by no means a bad number for a kicker of my weight, but I'd squatted 275 last year. And I had to work *up* to this weight. "Missing summer workouts was tough."

"*Plus*," Ahmed said, "the estrogen makes it even more impressive."

By invoking the E-Word, I could feel the entire conversation flipping. Scotty's face fell, just a little. "What's that got to do with anything?"

Everyone looked at me, expectantly. *Thanks, Ahmed.* "It decreases muscle mass," I said quickly. "Like, over time. So I'm swimming against the current here."

"Crazy," Tobe said. "I never knew that."

"Wait." Truck, who was leaning against the wall nearby, frowned. "So, if you're trans, you get weaker."

"Assuming you take hormones, yeah."

"So then what was the problem with that swimmer? If she got weaker and all that?"

"Well, that's not the same thing, Trucky," Tino Russo said. "Even Caitlyn Jenner said that wasn't fair."

Kill me. Strike me down now.

"Woodhouse ain't doing anything like that," DeSean Kirkland added.

I would like to fall into a pile of angry scissors.

"I dunno," Scotty said. "Since Woodhouse started being a girl, I'm like ... understanding the stuff in the news more now. Like, you see stories, and you're like, damn, our world is fucked up to trans people, you know? I mean, Grace is just out here doing her dance. We should just let people do their dance."

Ahmed patted his shoulder. "Bowen, my brother, congratulations! You're woke now!"

His face scrunched up. "No way. I'm just not a total dick."

I took the break in conversation to slip away to the tiny weight room bathroom—the door was unlabeled, making it one of three gender neutral bathrooms in the entire school—for a quick breather. I splashed cold water on my face and grimaced at my reflection in the stained mirror. Ill-fitting gym clothes. No makeup. Hair in a messy bun. I was ready to be back in jeans, back in a big sweater. Back to forgetting how my body looked for a few blissful hours.

A day and a half from now, my teammates and I would play for the Section VI championship against Bennett at Highmark Stadium, home of the Buffalo Bills. Then, just a few hours later, Dad and I would hop on a red-eye flight bound for Madison, Wisconsin. Saxon Valley awaited.

I checked my notifications to try and get my mind off of everything: a meme from Riley about a recent Premier League transfer that made me laugh, a message from Dad asking me if I'd watered the garden before leaving for school (of course I had), a mountain of unread texts from the all-out brawl that had raged in the football groupchat last night over whether Popeyes or KFC had better sides.

Just then, my phone buzzed again:

> **ZOE:** *I've got a killer headache. Hopefully I'll feel better tonight* 🤕
>
> *We're still on, right?*

Before I could tap out a response, the door to the bathroom swung open. There, in all his sweaty tobacco-stained glory, was Casey McReynolds.

I didn't turn to look at him, but he filled the mirror behind me anyway. The corners of his big idiot mouth flickered with amusement. "You're a gym rat now, huh?"

I snatched my phone up from the rim of the sink and kept my eyes on my own reflection. He'd mostly left me alone since September, but

I wasn't stupid enough to believe he'd suddenly had a change of heart. If he'd wanted to pull a reaction out of me, I wouldn't let him.

"It was a sick lift," he said, holding up his hands in surrender. "Really. That's all I wanted to say."

When he ducked into the nearest stall, I closed my eyes and focused on my breathing. Get through today, then you can get through tomorrow. Then you can get through Saxon Valley. *Focus on what's in front of you.*

"So," Jamie mused, "let's say you won an all-expenses-paid trip to Europe. You can go anywhere you want for an entire month."

"Does *all expenses* include food?" Imani asked. She twirled Riley's vape between her fingers absentmindedly.

Jamie tapped his finger against his chin. "It's not covering *gourmet*. Just, you know, an average meal in whatever country you're in. If you wanna hit up a fancy restaurant in Paris and eat snails for a month, it's coming out of your own pocket."

Imani took a drag from the skinny gray pen, vapor curling up to the cloudy sky as she exhaled. Considering how deep the Lady Druids were in the playoffs—a win tomorrow would land them in next week's State Semifinals—she and Riley were doing an admirable job of staying loose. "Ri, you go first. I'm blanking."

Riley shrugged nonchalantly. "Europe's overrated. Most of it, anyway. I'm spending the whole month in Spain. Spain and Portugal. At least the food's good."

"Real," Jamie said, nodding thoughtfully. "I think I'd do England. London seems like my kinda scene. Some great places to skate there, too."

"You wanna go to TERF Island?" I scoffed. "You've hit that vape too many times, man."

"It is a *dab pen*." He held it out to me like a wizard's wand. "Sure you don't want some?"

I shook my head *no*. Weed was alright, sure, but not at noon on a Thursday. Not when I could get hit with a random football drug test any day of the week. "I'm all good."

"You could use it." Without explanation, he pulled his arms into the torso of his hoodie like a turtle. His sleeves hung limp at his sides. "You've looked so stressed lately."

In the weeks since Tab and her friends ditched the rest of us for greener pastures with the art dorks (like, kids who voluntarily went to the *Pageland High Book Club*—it was bone-chilling) the lunch table had fractured. Still, Riley went out of her way to hang with Jamie—thereby staking him out as Her Territory—and usually invited me along. Jamie's backyard wasn't my favorite place to kill a lunch period, but it was nice to see the kid. After all, he *was* the only other trans person I knew, even if he was a sentient drug rug.

"I'm fine," I replied woodenly. "Anyway, I don't wanna go to Europe. I already live *here*." I gestured at the oppressively overcast autumn sky. "I wanna go somewhere warm. Get some sun."

"Grace Woodhouse, Cali girl?" Riley asked, smirking. "I can't imagine you with a tan."

I let that thought wash over me. After graduation, I could ghost *everyone*. I could drive Lorraine cross-country and end up in some small city in the Central Valley, somewhere it didn't cost a billion dollars to live. From there, I could start over from scratch, for real this time. A place where I wasn't The Trans Girl Who Played Football, where nobody knew my deadname. A place where I could be anybody.

It all kind of appealed to me before I wrangled those thoughts back into oblivion.

"I could learn how to surf, you know," I said, elbowing her. "I'm a fast learner."

"Suuuuuure. Did you even visit a single school west of the Mississippi on your grand football tour last year?"

"Is Bloomington west of the Mississippi?"

Imani snorted. "*No.* That's dope, though. Where else did you visit? Anywhere fun?"

"For campus visits?" I had to think about that for a second. "Penn State, Indiana, Pitt, and Maryland. I think. It's gotta be on my old FightSong profile."

Riley grinned and patted my shoulder. "And now she's normal like the rest of us. You get that application into ECC yet, girl?"

I swear, I'd *tried* to tell Riley about Saxon Valley a few times, but it never came up naturally. And I wasn't gonna tell her *now*. I'd text her when I landed in Wisconsin, maybe. Or when I got back. No big deal.

"Course I have," I said, plastering on a smile. "I'm on top of shit."

I don't remember when I started lying all the time.

Twenty-seven

Zoe picked me up that night a little after ten.

"Hey," she said as I sunk into the passenger seat of her Kia. "Is that a new lipstick?"

I fidgeted in my seat, feeling very Seen. I was still figuring out the whole *compliments* thing. "Just something I got at Target. I know the lighting in here is bad, but—"

"It looks good." She cleared her throat. "How was your day?"

I mumbled a token "fine" and bounced the conversation back to her, letting her ramble about student council drama (the mistakes the last treasurer made with his bookkeeping that made her job harder, that kinda thing) as she drove us to the edge of town. I knew our destination before we got there: this plaza out by the highway. A Home Depot, an Ollie's, a Mighty Taco. This time of night, it was almost always abandoned. She pulled into a secluded parking spot by the garden sheds and turned her headlights off.

"I found this, umm—I found this playlist on Spotify," Zoe said, fumbling with her phone. "It's, like, all queer, so, I thought . . ."

I tried my *very* best not to laugh at her awkwardness. "Sounds good."

As we moved to the backseat, I had to ask The Question. "Have you . . . given more thought? To what you might identify as?"

I'd been trying *really hard* not to push it, but I'd obviously been wondering about it. It was clear that Zoe liked *me*, the current me, not just the version she'd dated. For the past few weeks, though, we'd been operating in the gray area: sneaking around late at night, never spending time together in public. We hadn't talked about whether we were dating or not, or if either of us was thinking about it, or if that was something we even wanted. We just happened to be exes that made out sometimes, you know? Nothing complicated about it at all.

"I'm—I dunno." She tucked her hair behind her ears and took her glasses off. "Let's just . . ."

Then she pushed me against the door, and things spiraled from there. Nothing we'd done lately was *serious*: makeout seshes, light over-the-clothes stuff. After a few minutes like that, I felt her hands move from my shoulders to my chest. She paused when she felt me inhale. "Is that okay?"

"Definitely," I breathed. *This* was new. "Just go slow. They're . . . pretty sensitive right now."

"It feels good," she said, looking up at me with those ridiculous eyes. "I promise."

Her touch struck me like lightning, something so new and *different* and *incredible* I felt dizzy. The back of my head hit the glass, and when she snaked her hand in my hair and grabbed a handful, I mentally thanked Catholic God for making this girl. Another lightning bolt; I made sure to thank Catholic God for making estradiol, too.

When she *really* started to go at it, this sound I didn't even know I could make escaped my throat, halfway between a goose honk and an eighteen-wheeler horn. I was *mortified*, so much that the mood broke for me. A moment later, Zoe broke off the kiss and grinned. "I guess you liked that?"

I buried my face in my hands. "Shut up!"

"It was cute!"

"I'm gonna go lay down in front of your car," I said, "so you can run me over. And then roast the hell out of me at my funeral."

"Not sure Father Tom would approve of me discussing nipple-related misadventures in a house of God."

"My funeral won't be in a church. It'll be somewhere cool. Like a skatepark."

We settled into a familiar shape: Zoe laying on her back, her head in my lap. We sat like that for a while. Just us, the soft *whir* of the engine, the gay-ass music she'd put on. Distant streetlights lit everything in a soft orange glow. I stroked her hair and hummed along to a Chappell Roan track.

It was stupid, maybe, but I found myself wishing we could switch roles sometimes. It'd pose logistical difficulties—I was taller than her by, like, a lot—but I wondered what it'd be like to be small, to be held.

"So..." Zoe closed her eyes. "I'm pretty sure I'm not straight."

"Really? I hadn't noticed."

"*Stop*," she said, throwing an elbow in my general direction that didn't land in my area code. "This hasn't been easy for me."

I curled a wave of her hair around my finger. "When did you know?"

She sighed and draped her arm over her eyes. "I dunno. In hindsight—you're gonna make fun of me for this—some of the thoughts I had when I watched *Twilight* make a little more sense now?"

"Hell yes. Kristen Stewart?"

"Dakota Fanning," she groaned. "Jane. All day, every day."

"I don't even know who that is."

"Good." She drew back her arm dramatically and looked up at me, about as shyly as I'd ever seen her. "I guess I started thinking maybe I'm ... *not straight* ... sometime in the spring. Before we broke up. And then, uh, *definitely* over the summer."

"Wait, summer? Say more."

Zoe gave me a wary look. "Promise you won't make fun of me?"

"Promise."

She took a deep breath. "Camp."

As soon as I understood her meaning, my eyes went wide. "You messed around with girls at *summer debate camp*?"

"You said you wouldn't make fun of me!"

"That's before I knew it was *summer debate camp*! Did you charm some girl out of her pants with sparkling rhetoric?"

"Fuck you," she said, giggling. "I don't kiss and tell." After a moment of contented silence, she cleared her throat. "When did *you* know?"

I looked out the window and tried to figure out how I wanted to answer it. "I guess it was there for a long time. Like, if you're six, and you think *I wish I was a girl*—you don't know what that means. I didn't, anyway. I really started having inklings last fall, though." I finally looked back at her; her expression was serious, thoughtful. "By spring, I knew."

"Wow," she said, her voice sounding distant. "I mean, I guess I figured *something* was going on, but..."

God, it felt weird talking about this with her. How do you tell your ex-girlfriend that you were miserable, you were stealing her clothes, that everything she thought she knew about you was fake? You can't. If she *really* knew how bad our last year together had been for me, it'd crush her. Better to keep it in, limit the hurt to just myself if I could.

"Grace," she said, snapping me out of my head, "I like you the way you are, okay? Wouldn't change it for anything."

"Then why are we sneaking around in the dark?"

The words fell out of me before I had a chance to consider them, and I could tell immediately that I'd messed everything up. Her face fell. Her eyes went glassy.

"It isn't that easy anymore, okay?" She closed her eyes and hugged her arms to her chest. "I mean, you're *you* now. I'd have to come out to the whole school, which means I'd have to come out to my family, and Mom and Dad, and there's church, and..." She took a shaky breath. "And I don't even know what I *am*. Whether I'm bi or pan or something else."

I knew what she was saying made sense, logically. But it was *very* hard for me to not think about her perfect life—her stellar grades, her loving family with more money than I could fathom, her predestined successful future—and not think about every single way that my complicated transgender ass didn't fit into the picture in the slightest. I wasn't compatible with her world anymore. I never would be.

"It's not you, okay?" she said softly. "I promise."

"Sure. Okay."

"My family wouldn't be like your dad, okay?" she snapped. "I have no idea how they'd react to . . . to *any* of this, Jordan." She froze and slapped her hand over her mouth, eyes wide. "Oh my gosh, I'm *so* sorry, I–"

"It's okay," I said, even though I felt like I'd been punched in the throat.

"It was a mistake, I promise." She bolted upright and sat next to me, putting her hand on my leg. Without thinking, I jerked away from the touch. "I'm so sorry, I just–I didn't mean to. I was worked up, and I wasn't thinking, and it was just instinct–well, not *instinct*, just, you know, I've just said it so many times that–"

"I said it was okay." My voice was flat and distant, hitting my ears like it barely belonged to me. "I get it."

"It's not okay," she insisted, "and I'm really, *really* sorry. Okay? I mean it. I–"

"Stop apologizing!" My voice was louder this time, deeper, and I felt my eyes prickle. "Just fucking *stop*. Please."

For a few minutes, we sat on opposite ends of the backseat and said nothing. Tears fell silently–I refused let her hear me sob–as I stared out at the Home Depot parking lot. How many times in my life would I see this parking lot if I never left town? How many of the same people would I see, week in and week out? How many times would someone call me *that* name?

Two days. *Two days*, and I'd be in Saxon Valley. I'd spent all week so nervous I could hurl, but now I couldn't wait to get away from this place.

"You wanna get something to eat?" she asked softly, like she was afraid to breathe.

"Yeah," I said, trying to pretend like it was all behind us, like there was something different ahead of us. "Yeah, that sounds good."

Before—Last October

"You're a fucking asshole, you know that?"

Your girlfriend's following you out of some senior's backyard and out onto the street because she doesn't know when to give up. You barely pay her any mind. You're so mad you can hardly think straight.

"Hey! Where are you going?"

You wheel around to face her. "*Home*. Why're you starting shit with me?"

"What did that guy even *say* to you?"

You wipe a trail of blood off your lip. You're so drunk you can hardly feel it, but you will in the morning. Busted nose, black eye. War wounds. You spit out a glob of blood, and Zoe recoils.

It all happened at some stupid house party you went to after tonight's game. Some Seabass asshole—a senior—said he thought kickers weren't real football players. It would've slid off your back if you weren't drunk, but you couldn't help yourself.

"Say it to my face," you told him.

The big guy scoffed. "I'm not afraid of you. Fuckin' foot fairy."

So you made him afraid of you. It's not like you broke his jaw or anything. The blood would wash out of his Vineyard Vines shirt if he scrubbed hard enough.

"Called me a faggot," you say, which isn't true, but it *feels* true. "So I messed him up."

"You can walk away, you know! What the hell is wrong with you?"

"He started it! Get off my case, Zoe. Jeez."

She looks like she might cry, and even though some part of you wants to comfort her, you don't. You need to stay strong. You're a fucking man. Sometimes men get in fights. It happens.

"You need to get yourself together, J," she says, her voice cold. Her eyes are glassy. "You never used to be like this."

Well, you think, *shit changes.* You're a real football recruit now. Whatever part of you that's still soft needs to be killed, or you won't make it.

You say: "You don't know me."

Zoe looks at you, blinks, then storms off before she can say anything else.

Whatever. You cough up more blood and shiver in the cold. You're a few blocks from home. You can hoof it.

Twenty-eight

At the eastern edge of Saxon Valley's campus, there was an archway.

River, my tour guide, explained that it dated all the way back to the founding of the college, and it looked the part. It was wrought iron; beautiful in its own way, even if I wasn't really an art person. Heavy letters snaked with ivy spelled out *Saxon Valley Normal School*, the original name of the college.

"Back in the day," River said, placing their hand on the brick pillar that supported one end of the arch, "students would arrive at the train station in town, and they'd all walk through *this* beefy boy"—they patted the brick and smiled—"onto campus. So it became a tradition!"

On the last day of freshman orientation, they herded all the incoming freshmen into this long line and walked them in through the archway, because Symbolism Something Something, you get it. Then, after graduation, they'd line you up and walk you back out the way you came.

I tried my best to listen respectfully while I sipped lukewarm coffee from a paper cup and tried to feel somewhat human. Dad was the more tactful person for a change, throwing in the occasional *hmm* and *well how about that* and *isn't that interesting* when the conversation necessitated it. Between the flight from Buffalo to Madison that took off at six, the car ride up to Saxon Valley that lasted over an hour, and carry-over fatigue from last night's win in Sectionals, I was *dead*.

River, a blue-haired ball of energy, had done a good job showing us around. Both the campus and surrounding area were beautiful in the fall: endless dairy farms rolling northward, maples burning red and orange along the Wisconsin River. The quad had a *very* impressive flower garden that Dad and I were itching to investigate. I'd toured a few campuses last year, but none of them felt this cozy; everything here was smaller, quieter, closer together.

"Now"—River made a show of checking their watch—"I'd imagine the athletic department probably wants you. So I get to take you to Somerset Athletic Center."

I sighed. "Showtime already?"

While River was already off like a rocket, I looked warily up at the iron archway again. *Saxon Valley Normal School.* It was stupid; River had already taken us through it once on our tour of the grounds, after all. Still, I couldn't help but hesitate.

"Grace?" Dad said wearily.

I snapped out of it, and when I stepped through the archway, I was not, in fact, immediately bound to Saxon Valley by a terrible curse. "Sorry. Just need more coffee."

"We can swing by the Dunkin' in the library on the way," River offered. "Caffeine comes first."

I mumbled a *thank you* and fell into step next to them, enjoying the crunch of leaves under my Doc-Offs. You're supposed to dress nicely for these things; last year I'd worn stiff button-ups, billowy khakis, typical menswear garbage. Since I didn't have formal women's clothes yet (and I didn't want to stick out), I rolled the dice on my usual flannel and jeans. If this was the kind of program that would dismiss me out of hand for not wearing a polo, I didn't want to be here anyway.

"Not to be extra or anything, but I was *so* excited when they told me about you," River said. "I don't normally get athletes, you know, *especially* not trans ones."

River was a sweetheart, really, even if they were a *lot*. I'd been waiting for them to say something ever since I noticed the *they/she* button pinned next to their nametag. I figured it wasn't a coincidence they'd been stuck with me.

"Thanks," I said, giving them a smile. "I'm excited to be here."

"Great! And, just so you know, the queer community on campus is beautiful," River said, picking up their pace. "We have a *really* supportive pride club that meets every week. Lots of great events too: dances, drag shows, all that. There's even an adjacent organizing committee that's *just* for gender stuff, and they run, like, trans-specific support groups and everything."

Part of me cringed at their enthusiasm. I knew it would be a big deal if I went for this, obviously, but it hadn't clicked until then that everyone on campus would automatically know who I was, just like they did back in Pageland. And that felt *suffocating*.

"Cool," I said, knowing that football meant I'd never get to go to a club meeting even if I wanted to. "That sounds really cool."

RILEY

Today 11:21 AM

RILEY: Yooooooo do you wanna chill tonight? Jamie's having ppl over to smoke

GRACE: hey! im actually busy

like all weekend

RILEY: Damn. Everything okay?

GRACE: yeah

dad had a work trip out to wisconsin so im going with him

RILEY: Uhhhh you didn't mention that before??

GRACE: oh! sorry. i thought i did

i'll tell you about it monday

A twenty-something wearing a lanyard ambushed us the moment we entered the athletic center. "Football visit?"

Of course, somehow, we were late. Once he checked me in, Lanyard rushed us from hallway to hallway until he opened the door to the locker room and waved me through. Before I could blink, a room full of recruits and parents and coaches were staring at me. I'd interrupted Coach Oestreicher's opening address, but thankfully, he didn't miss a beat. He composed a Football Speak masterpiece: he was *so excited* to have us on campus, they were building a winning culture here in Saxon Valley, et cetera.

It was hard to focus on his speech anyway when the locker room was so gaudy. Everything was charcoal gray and gold, so new it still had that uncannily clean New Car Smell. Digital nameplates hung above spacious lockers, all of it built to impress kids like me who'd spent their entire lives changing in humid concrete boxes that smelled like BO. It didn't compare to Penn State, of course, but I was sure whatever accommodations they'd scrape together for me would beat the hell out of my little storage room back home.

As Oestreicher finished up the motivational portion of his speech, it turned to logistics: official weigh-in, meetings with coaches and position groups, tours of the building, the usual stuff. The talk finally wrapped, giving us a brief moment to relax before the circus got underway.

Jerome made his way to us when he could, raising his hand in a greeting. "Mr. Woodhouse, I take it? Coach Jerome Metellus."

"Patrick," Dad said. "Please."

"Nice to meet you, Patrick. You raised a special young woman."

While the adults hit it off, I eyed up the other recruits. Including me, I counted nine. Save for a pair of linemen, it was hard for me to scope out who played which position. No other kickers, hopefully.

When one of the recruits made eye contact with me, I instinctively looked away.

While I was trying very hard to look like I was listening to Jerome, I felt a tap on my shoulder. I wheeled around to find a familiar-looking muscular dude with dreadlocks behind me. "Woodhouse, right?" he asked. "Coach Metellus told me I wasn't gonna be the only Buffalo kid on this visit."

That was when it clicked: Kendall Cleavers, the linebacker from Seabass who scored the game-winning touchdown against us in Week One. He was from Hamburg, not Pageland, but we kinda knew each other the way all athletes from the same county kinda know each other. I was just happy for a familiar face.

"Came all the way to Wisconsin to gloat about that win?" I asked, flashing him a cocky smile. "Makes sense, considering your season's already over."

He smirked, shook his head. "You can make it all the way to state, *and* you can win that bitch, too. But you'll always be the Pageland team that lost to Sebastian's."

"I don't really care," I lied. "I wasn't even on the team then."

"Oh, I know. Kick wouldn't have been blocked if you were."

I let myself soak in that particular compliment while I looked past Kendall to the rest of the recruits. "Does everyone know my deal?"

Kendall shrugged. "I mean, they know a kicker named *Grace* is showing up. Dunno if they got all the details."

"And you're . . ." Maybe it wasn't fair of me, but he was a Seabass guy, and I generally didn't trust Catholic school kids as far as I could throw them.

Kendall crossed his arms. "My cousin's trans, you know. She's cool. I respect whatever you gotta do."

"Thanks," I said, meaning it. Then, for some reason: "But I'm a football player first, you know. I'm not, like, here for special treatment."

Before he could reply, Jerome nudged his way into the conversation. "Y'all keeping it civil? I know we got rivals in the building today."

"Just keep me on the other side of the room from him," I joked. "Maybe I'll be able to control myself."

Kendall smiled weakly. "Oh, yeah. Can't stand this kid."

"This," Jerome said, squeezing my shoulder, "is Coach Oestreicher."

The head coach of the Saxon Valley Outlaws gave me a firm handshake. "It's good to finally meet you, Grace. We've been hearing a lot about you."

His office was College Coach Chic: huge desk with a fancy *Coach Brennan Oestreicher* nameplate, shelves full of photos, trophies, assorted trinkets meant to emphasize his many accomplishments. A big window behind his desk gave a view of the practice field, everything golden in the autumn sun.

Jerome ducked out of the room to give us some space, and before I sat down across from him, a glass case on the corner of his desk caught my eyes. "Wait," I said, "is that—"

Oestreicher grinned. "That's the ring. Wanna have a look?"

I was *way* too taken in by the gaudiness of it to say no. The Super Bowl ring was all diamonds—more diamonds than I'd ever seen in my life, probably—surrounding a Los Angeles Rams logo. *Rams 23, Bengals 20* was inscribed on the side.

I'd done my research, naturally, so I knew all about this. Oestreicher was one of those young white coaches who got hit with the Prodigy tag due to proximity to other Prodigies, since football logic says genius is contagious. He'd been an offensive assistant for the Rams before Saxon Valley lured him away with the chance to be a head coach in his home state (and, presumably, a big check).

"Coach Metellus has one too," he said, which was news to me. "You should ask him about it. But, anyway: tell me what you're feeling!"

The visit had been what I expected: they took our height and weight (my medical file was marked *special concern*, meaning I had to talk about my transition with medical personnel tomorrow, which I was *thrilled* about), showed us the weight room, all that stuff. While the rest of the guys suited up in Saxon Valley gear and took glamor shots for Instagram, I was here. Not that I was complaining.

Jerome had introduced me to the specialists, of which there were just enough that I couldn't remember all their names. The starting kicker, this Aussie sophomore named Lachlan, was nice enough, but the others hadn't said much to me. The offensive line coach gave me dirty looks every time he had the chance, the strength and conditioning coach misgendered me, and I could've sworn the other recruits whispered about me behind my back, but everything was *fine*. Nothing I couldn't handle, at least, and I knew I'd win people over with time. "Everything's been great so far," I told him. "Really."

"That's great to hear," Oestreicher said, smiling. "Great to hear."

He started going on about *culture* and *identity*. "Our program motto here? It's *Outlaw Life*. What that means to me is: we're looking for players with a chip on their shoulder, something to prove. Because we're a young program, and *we* have something to prove. We're looking for guys cut from a different cloth, who are willing to buy into a program that'll grow with them. Based on what I know about the adversity you've overcome, that sounds like you."

I bit back a grimace. Of *course* a football coach would cram gender transition into the Adversity bucket. Too predictable.

"We're building something special here," he continued, "and it'd be a real statement for the Saxon Valley football program to add a player like you, someone who isn't afraid to be themselves. *That* is Outlaw Life."

I let the gears turn in my head for a moment. That sounded a *lot* like he wanted me to be a sideshow, something that could get the program press attention. "If I come here," I said, "I'm coming here to play football."

"Of course!" he said, holding up his hands. "We're just aware of the impact your commitment might have. I'll leave it to you and the SID to work out the details on how we'd break the news, all that stuff. But, right now..." He retrieved a bundle of fabric from under his desk. "I figured you wouldn't be doing the shoot, 'cause we're trying to keep this whole thing under wraps, but I still had the equipment department throw this together for you. I wanted you to see it."

I took the jersey gingerly and unfolded it. Their home uniform was gray with gold accents and lettering; weird, but I could get down with it. *WOODHOUSE,* read the nameplate. The number: forty-seven.

I'd seen this trick before. Hell, I posed in Penn State gear last year, and they had one of the most iconic looks in the country. But that was last year, and that was a different number. Forty-seven had come to mean a lot to me. It was weird, it was ugly, it was *different*. It belonged to me in a way that twenty-three never had.

Oestreicher said something about how he hoped I'd feel at home here, but I barely heard him.

Twenty-nine

At the game that night, I sat a few rows behind the rest of the recruits. The goal was to avoid drawing attention to myself, so I kept my head down, quietly chatted with Dad, and mostly focused on the game. UConn took a 17–10 lead into the half, but a pair of Saxon Valley touchdowns in the fourth quarter gave the Outlaws their second win of the season. The program was as advertised: new to FBS and building, struggling through growing pains. The kicker, Lachlan, looked competent enough, but beating him out in a year or two looked pretty plausible if my strength didn't completely fail me.

After the final whistle, it was down to the locker room with the rest of the recruits, where everyone was buzzing about the win. Jerome chest-bumped the linebacker that forced a crucial fumble in the fourth quarter and then spent a solid five minutes taking a lap around the room, slapping everyone up. Us recruits were annexed in the corner, where a few of the guys on the team joked with us like we were teammates already. The quarterback, this junior transfer from Louisville named Fuentes, personally introduced himself and shook all of our hands. "Come to the Valley," he said, flashing that same All-American Smile I'd seen Prez use before, "and you'll have a lot more nights like this one."

Finally, Coach Oestreicher took the floor, blinking back Football Tears. "I'm *damn* proud of you," he said, "*damn* proud of how hard you've worked. I know you're capable of this every week. Every damn week. And we're gonna get there."

After the breakdown, I felt a hand on my shoulder. "Tinker Bell," said Lachlan Horner, his face flushed and sweaty. The other specialists—mostly fellow underclassmen—were at his back. "What'd you think of the show?"

"Tinker Bell?" I mean, jeez, I'd barely spent an *hour* with the specialists before the game. At least it was better than *AK*.

"We give out nicknames *early* in the Valley," he said, grinning. "Anyway, second bloody win of the year, we *celebrate*. It's my honor to invite you to the football house for the party."

I blinked. "Uh—"

"Attendance not compulsory," he clarified. "But recruits always get invited."

"We gotta show you how we do it up here in the Valley," Mark, one of the other kickers, added.

Did I *want* to go to a college party where I barely knew anyone? No idea. But the specialists were going out of their way to include me in something when they could've easily blown me off. Plus, if I *did* end up playing ball here, the boys had to know I could hang with them. I had to prove I belonged.

Which was why I said: "Hell yeah."

BALLBAGS 4 CHRIST (SCOTTY'S VERSION) 🏈💩

Today 9:56 PM

AHMED: *These locker rooms at Tennessee are NICE*

SCOTTY: *fuckkkkkk bro if you start sending photos imma shit myself*

AND throw up. AND cry. the three piece combo meal

i'm so jealous

> **DRAY:** *I had pics taken in Furman gear if it'll make you feel better* ☺
>
> **SCOTTY:** *it doesn't!!!!*
>
> *i need to be a senior so bad. fuck*
>
> *yo @kaeden @reagor @woodhouse @whoever isn't on a college visit hop on warzone*
>
> **CALVIN:** *Gimme a kiss and I'll consider it pretty boy*
>
> **SCOTTY:** *bet*
>
> **DRAY:** *I swear I'm the straightest one in here man*
>
> **SCOTTY:** *wait why tf is woodhouse's location in Wisconsin rn*
>
> **GRACE:** *family stuff. ill tell yall when i get home*
>
> **SCOTTY:** 😐😕😐
>
> **CALVIN:** *Still waitin on those lips, Bowen*

The Saxon Valley football house was just off campus in a neighborhood full of other college party houses, and it was straight out of *Blue Mountain State*. There was a bouncer, a fully stocked bar right as you walked in, and rooms upstairs designated for "extracurricular activities." The Outlaws, it seemed, ran a tight ship. Still, if I was at home at Ahmed's, I might as well have been on Mars here.

The specialists, an insular clique on any football team, ran in a pack. I hung around on the edge of the group and kept to myself while they laughed at in-jokes I didn't get and chatted about girls they were working up the nerve to talk to. "I dunno, man," the starting punter—was it Tucker or Tanner?—said. "I can never tell if girls are into me."

"You've just got to be *confident*," Lachlan insisted. "It's all about aura."

"I don't wanna hear it from *you*," Mark said, rolling his eyes. "It's not fair. You turn on the accent, go all Hemsworth on 'em."

"Don't need a sexy accent, mate. All girls care about is confidence." He gestured to me with his drink. "Right, Tinker Bell?"

My cheeks burned red while the specialists turned their gaze on me. "I'm a lesbian," I mumbled. "I dunno."

Tucker-Tanner, who was standing closest to me, visibly relaxed. "Dope. See anyone here you like?"

Yeah, because girls at a football party were interested in what *I* had going on, and I was *desperate* to engage in Guy Talk with college boys. "Not really," I said. "I'm, uh, gonna go get a drink. Be right back."

I kept my eyes to the floor on the way to the bar, hoping I wouldn't draw any unwanted attention. I grabbed a beer, something cheap and light. I closed my eyes and took a long swig, trying very hard to calm myself down in this room full of people I didn't know hundreds of miles away from home.

That's when someone grabbed my ass.

Not *brushed*; anyone can accidentally brush your ass at a party. I was certain it'd been a full squeeze. I whipped around immediately only to find dozens of bodies in a crowd with no obvious suspect. Whoever did it had vanished just as quickly.

I felt my lip quiver. No. *No.* I must've imagined it. Someone *had* just brushed up against me. I had to be wrong. Stuff like this didn't happen to me.

I must've looked *pathetic*, because a nearby group of girls pounced on me. "Are you okay?" one of them asked. She had short red hair, an eyebrow piercing, and a concerned look on her face. "You look lost."

"Umm . . ." My voice came out lower than I wanted. She totally clocked me. "I'm okay. I'm just . . . I guess I'm a little lost? I've never been here before."

"Oh my gosh," one of the others said to the first girl. "I don't recognize them. What's your name?"

I tried not to let "them" stick in my craw, because it was the least of my concerns right now. I made myself say: "Grace."

A couple of the other girls swapped glances. "So, like, what do you identify as?" the first girl asked.

I don't identify as anything, I wanted to snap. *I'm a fucking girl.*
I told them I was a girl.

"Of course," the first girl said. "Obviously. Listen, Grace, what're the names of your friends? Maybe we can help you find them."

"Do you know Lachlan Horner?"

They all giggled. "Yeah, we know Lach," she said. "I just saw him and his posse go into another room. Lemme take you there."

I was desperate to believe her, to get out of there, so I didn't think twice about it. I left my beer on the counter while the girl with an eyebrow piercing led me through the crowd by hand.

"They're right through here," she said, gesturing to a door maybe ten feet ahead of us. "C'mon."

When I opened it, I froze in confusion. The door didn't open to another room; it opened to an alleyway next to the house. "Go," she hissed in my ear. "Get out."

"Wha—"

I couldn't even get the word out of my mouth before she shoved me. The tip of my boot caught on the edge of the door frame and sent me flying into the alley, where I landed hard on my left knee in a pile of slick, wet leaves. I cried out in pain, my voice deep and rough. "Why—"

"Don't try to come back in. I'll tell the bouncer you're a creep if you do."

I forced myself to my feet, ignoring the leaves clinging to my jacket and the pain throbbing in my knee, and looked up at her. "What the fuck is wrong with you?"

"Are you stupid?" Her nose wrinkled in disgust. "Take a fucking hint and go home, *bro*. You're not fooling anyone dressed like that."

She slammed the door shut, leaving me alone in the alley, and I didn't fight it when the tears fell. Through my blurry vision, I kicked the door *hard*, yelped in pain, then lost the will to stand any longer. I sank to the ground against the side of the house, pulled my knees to my chest, and let myself unravel.

I don't know how long I sat there berating myself—for putting myself in a bad situation, for not being strong enough to shake it off—but I sat in the dark and shook until I heard a group of boys round the corner from the front yard. "*Shit*," I heard one of them say. "Is that a girl? What do we—"

"Woodhouse?"

It took a second for me to realize I'd heard my name spoken. I looked up to find Kendall Cleavers, of all people, staring at me with wide eyes. A moment later, he was helping me to my feet. "What happened? What's going on?"

I didn't even know where to start, so I didn't say anything. I wiped the tears off my cheeks and sniffed. "I need to leave. I need to . . . go somewhere."

"Yeah." He nodded. "Yeah, okay. Let's get you somewhere, then."

"Aww, Cleave, you're so *sensitive*." It was one of the other boys, a recruit I recognized from the visit. "You're babysitting!"

"If you don't shut the fuck up," I growled, my voice scratchy, "I'll—"

"Parker, stop," Kendall said sternly. "Grace, leave it."

"But—"

"Come *on*."

I followed him past the boys and out into the front yard, the streetlights temporarily blinding. Seeing the front of the house made it all rush back: the hand in the crowd, that girl's hands on my back.

You're not fooling anybody dressed like that.

I shoved my hands in my jacket pockets, closed my eyes, and took a deep breath. I wanted *nothing* more than to retreat to the relative safety of my hotel room, but I knew I needed to do something first. "Wait, Kendall."

He looked at me expectantly.

"There's someone on campus I need to see."

I didn't have to think twice about whether or not Jerome would be on campus at midnight. I knew he would be. All football coaches are insane.

When he opened the door to his office, his eyebrows jumped in surprise. "Grace. Cleave. What's going on?"

"Woodhouse wanted to talk to you," the linebacker said stiffly. "I'm just her bodyguard."

Jerome looked me over: my red eyes, dirt on my clothes, the tiny bits of leaf I wasn't able to get out of my hair. "Come on in, then. Cleave, there's coffee and hot cocoa in the lounge you're welcome to."

Jerome's office was small, barely more than a desk opposite a couch. I could see paused game film on his laptop beside a Miami Dolphins mug (I was trying *very hard* not to judge). The shelf behind him was cluttered with family photographs, mementos, books on teaching.

"Sit down," he said, gesturing to the couch. "You alright?"

I didn't know how to answer that question. "You don't have to say anything if you don't want to," he said lightly. "I get that."

"Something... not great happened," I mumbled. "At the football house."

He rubbed his temples. "Of course. They love to take recruits to the goddamn football house. I'll ring Horner's neck. What happened? You hurt?"

I winced, thinking about my knee, but shook my head. "Someone said some really ignorant shit to me."

He didn't need to know about the hand in the crowd, about the shove. I wouldn't have been able to get the words out even if I wanted to.

"Well," he said, "for that, I apologize. That's bullcrap."

We sat there in silence for a few minutes while Jerome sipped his drink and scribbled notes onto his legal pad. The scratch of pencil on paper calmed me down, and I let myself sink into the couch. I could've fallen asleep there, probably, though that would've been a real dick move.

"How'd you know?" I asked, the question forming in my mouth before I had time to rethink it. "How'd you know when it was time for you to stop playing?"

"Mmm." He shut his laptop and sat up straight, like he'd been expecting the question. "Well, I'm a Miami guy. Wasn't big, though, so I played at Florida International. Had a decent career there, managed to sign with the Eagles as an undrafted free agent. Grinded my ass off for two years on the practice squad, and then, my third year? I made the 53-man roster." He smiled at the distant memory. "Man, you wouldn't believe how hype we were. My mom and I cried on the phone for hours. My uncles all flew out from Haiti to see me. I was king shit."

"I didn't know you were an Eagle."

He chuckled. "I don't even know if the *Eagles* knew it, Grace. I was inactive the first fifteen games of the season. Week Seventeen, Coach Pederson is resting his starters, so I finally get to dress. Third quarter comes around, Dannell Ellerbe gets his bell rung. He has to sub out, I go in at MIKE. I get one snap—Alfred Morris runs counter to the weak side, I don't have a chance to make the play—and then Dannell checks back in. I come off the field. And that's it."

I stared at him, confused. "Wait. That's *it*?"

"Never got on an NFL field again," he said, sad smile on his face. "I watched us win the damn Super Bowl from the sideline."

"Oestreicher *said* you had a ring!" I cried, my jaw hanging open. "You were on *that* Eagles team?"

Jerome groaned. "I *hate* when he tells people that. Sure, whatever, we won the Super Bowl. But they cut me the next preseason, and that was it for the NFL. I did the Spring League for a season, then the AAF. Had a cup of coffee with the Montreal Alouettes. Next thing I know, Grace, my ass is in *Finland*. I'm playing for the Seinäjoki Crocodiles in front of a dozen bored Finnish rednecks. One game, I led the team in tackles, and afterwards I just drove around all night through the backwoods of Finland, like, *what the hell am I doing here*? I'm a twenty-eight-year-old man playing football in *Finland* and I barely know who I am.

"So *that*," he said, "is when I walked away. Called it quits, moved back home to Miami, and got a gig coaching ball down there. Few years later, here I am." He tapped his desk and smiled. "I'm guessing I know why you asked me."

I didn't see any reason to lie to him. I just nodded.

"Well," he said, "everyone's got their own Finland, and this might be yours. For most people, it is. And that's okay; this game'll take everything from you if you let it. Thing is: no one else can make that call for you, Grace. You've gotta figure it out yourself. And if you *do* decide to commit to this, people are always gonna treat you differently. There's no sugarcoating that."

"I understand," I said, my mouth feeling dry. "Sorry for turning up in the middle of the night, Coach."

"S'alright," he said. "As long as we're not violating recruiting rules, I'm always game to talk."

Even though I knew it was time for me to get out of there, one last thing was bugging me. "Do you still have the ring?" I asked. "Like, here?"

He opened a desk drawer, shuffled some papers around, then pulled out a small black box. "I *do* keep it here, actually," he said. "but I've never worn it."

"Why not?"

He looked at the box like he expected it to answer the question for him. "For a while, it embarrassed me," he said. "It's, like, the ultimate participation trophy, you know? Every time I looked at it, it felt like I was failing to make it all over again. I almost sold it back when I was *really* going through it. But you know what the honest answer is now?" Without breaking eye contact, he shot the small box like a basketball in the direction of a metal wastebasket by the door, where it *clang*ed off the rim and onto the floor. "I just don't give a shit about it anymore."

Because of how exhausted I was, I think I laughed at that for a full five minutes.

Thirty

The bell that signaled the end of third period woke me up.

It wasn't Miss Quinn's fault—she was good at keeping things interesting—but falling asleep in English was too easy. *Hamlet* sounded hypothetically cool when I read the SparkNotes summary, but the play itself bounced right off my brain. Combine that with me sitting alone in the corner, and dozing off was an inevitability.

I tried to play it cool, packing up my notebook—the one I took zero notes in—like nothing had happened. I was almost to the door when Miss Quinn cleared her throat. "Grace, could you come here for a moment?"

I froze. *Crap.* "I'm sorry, Miss Quinn," I mumbled as I approached her desk, keeping my eyes down.

She took her glasses off and pursed her lips. She was my youngest teacher, probably thirty-something, but I'd always respected that she never tried to be The Cool Teacher. I couldn't stand Cool Teachers. "I noticed," she said, her eyes on her computer monitor, "that you didn't submit the writing exercise that was due Friday."

My stomach dropped. As soon as she said it, I remembered it: a two-page assignment we were supposed to turn in online last week about the themes in *Hamlet* Act II. "Shit," I muttered, before remembering I was speaking to an adult. "*Sorry*, I mean. I—could I hand it in this week for half credit?"

She drummed her fingers on her desk before she finally turned back to me, concern written on her face. "Is everything okay?"

I stared at her, confused. "What?"

"You've been struggling with getting things in on time, you haven't been participating in class. And . . . well, I figure there's been a lot on your plate. If there's anything I can do to help, let me know. Okay?"

"Like . . ." I struggled to find my words. "Help *how*?"

"If you've been having trouble with the material, you can stay after school," she suggested. "Or if there's something else going on—"

"What about the assignment?"

She sighed. "Just get it to me when you can, okay? No worries."

"Thanks." I paused, then added: "Not to make excuses, but I had a college visit in Wisconsin over the weekend that was stressing me out last week. We didn't get back to Buffalo till late last night."

"That's great! How did it go?"

I didn't know what my *real* answer was since I'd barely started untangling it, but I made myself say: "Okay, I think. Still pretty stressed about it."

"That could be something to speak to a counselor about," she said. "If you wanted me to refer you."

I swallowed the immediate "fuck no" that rose in my chest, mumbled that I'd think it over, then bolted out the door. I'd never seen my guidance counselor, not since they'd forced us all to meet them as freshmen. I always thought I was too *normal* to need guidance, and then once I realized I was trans I figured my problems were above their paygrade. The thought of sitting in a stranger's office while they pretended to care about me made me feel itchy. Besides, I was *fine*.

Then someone in the hall brushed against my back and I jumped a foot in the air.

"Whoa!" A sophomore girl held up her hands in apology. "I'm *so* sorry, I wasn't watching where I was going."

I barely heard her, though, because every atom in my body told me to run. I ducked into the nearest stairwell and fought to get my breathing under control. *It was just some girl*, I assured myself, but my heart kept on pounding. *This* was new.

I balled my hands into fists to keep them from shaking. *You're losing it.*

In the afternoon, I was excused from class so I could run to a doctor's appointment. It was a long drive to the city, where The Gay Doctor's Office lived, and the experience was always surreal. Everyone here was suspiciously nice, all smiles and undercuts and colorful pronoun pins. While the technician took my blood, I gazed out the window, my eyes on Buffalo City Hall in the distance. Below all that, in a quiet courtyard, two nurses on their break tossed pennies into a koi pond.

"You seem to be adjusting well, Grace," said my doctor, this strikingly beautiful woman in her sixties who smelled like almonds. "Do you have any concerns with your transition at this point?"

Not with the medication, no. Estradiol was an elite skincare routine, even though I was still waiting on everything else. I told her everything was going great between sips of restorative apple juice.

Going from The Gay Doctor's Office—that magical place where pronouns were respected, where everyone was trying their best—back to the real world? That was always jarring. Going from it to football practice was even worse.

I'd hoped I could throw myself back into the Druids and snap out of the funk I was in, but so far it hadn't been working. Film review of our win in Sectionals over Bennett was a slog, since it'd been a sloppy 17-13 affair. Last year, winning Sectionals on the home turf of the Bills felt special, magical, once in a lifetime; this year, it was business as usual. Now we were on to Regionals, where our season ended last year, to meet Bellarmine Jesuit, the team that *beat* us last year. The same team I shanked that kick against, of course, because nothing in my clown car existence is ever easy.

Rhoads and I set up at our usual spot on the Big Field, the old man clearly seeing I wasn't in the mood for chatter. When it was finally time to go, I bit down hard on my mouthguard and tried to focus. Breathe in, breathe out. *You're on a practice field, and you're kicking a football. This is where you belong.* Three steps back, two steps left. *Go.*

The knee of my plant leg screamed when I drove it into the ground. I grunted through the kick, but the pain was enough to lapse my concentration and throw everything out of whack. I pushed the kick wide right. From *twenty yards out.* Useless. I swore and kicked the stand, sending it skittering across the turf.

"Settle down, now, Grace. It's only warmups. Just take it slow."

My head swam as I grimaced through the rest of my kicks, my left knee lighting up in pain every time I planted. A make from twenty-five, misses from thirty and thirty-five. It didn't take long for me to feel sluggish and nauseous, an aftereffect of my blood draw. After a dozen attempts, I trudged down the field to collect the balls I'd scattered behind the goalposts and dumped them in a pile at the twenty-yard line.

Rhoads, who'd been quiet, watched me set up and miss another kick from thirty-five; this one pulled to the left. "Enough," he said. "You're never gonna make a kick with that body language."

That was when I hit my breaking point. I ripped off my helmet, slammed it to the ground with a plastic crunch, and fell to a knee. If I hadn't been so angry at myself—and so exhausted from *everything*—I would've cried. I hung my head and cursed myself out under my breath instead.

I heard Rhoads grunt as he rose to his feet. He tried to hide his chronic pain, but I'd spent enough time around him to know when he was having a bad day. A few seconds later, I felt his hand on my shoulder pad. "What d'you think I'm gonna tell you?"

Of *course* I was getting a classic Rhoady Game when I could barely see straight. "Umm." I filed through the Rhoadsism Rolodex, tried to put together a complete sentence. "You can only fix what's in front of you. Put everything else out of mind."

"Strike one."

I squinted up at him. "The hard work we put in in practice mirrors real life. We are what we practice."

"Strike two."

"When you fall down, you put it behind you and get back up?"

He chuckled. "So you think I'm Coach Rut, is that it?"

I couldn't help but smile at that. He held out his hand. "You're getting a new one from me, Grace," he said, helping me to my feet. "Today's lesson: football ain't shit."

I stared at him, sure I'd heard him wrong. "Is this a test?"

He shook his head. "Football ain't worth much in the grand scheme of things. Attach all the fanfare and the war metaphors to it you like, but at the end of the day, it's just a game. It don't matter. Just be a little better tomorrow."

I let this wisdom wash over me, which certainly *sounded* profound. "It's more than a game for me, though," I pointed out. "It could be my ticket to college. It's . . ."

"Do you like playing football?" he asked me, face completely straight. "Do you have fun? Are you happy?"

I was taken majorly off-guard. "I dunno, Coach," I said, feeling stupid. "Does it matter?"

He gave me a wry smile. "S'pose that's up to you, huh?"

I studied my Nikes and thought about that. I liked the ritual of kicking, of being good at something that gave most people fits. I liked that this was something my body did that I could take pride in, since my body frustrated the hell out of me most days. I liked it when the crowd roared after that onside kick against Wake East. I liked that my teammates were my brothers, even if they weren't always perfect. I thought about Ahmed, Truck, Scotty; guys you'd never imagine would have someone like me's back. That meant something.

So: I liked having a weird talent, I liked it when people cheered for me, and I liked having friends. Was I in love with spending hours in practice every day, in love with how much pressure I was under, in love with the fact that I was a weird misstep and a shredded knee away from everything being over? Of course not.

All I could give him was a shrug. "I dunno if *more* feelingsball is what I need right now, Rhoady."

He sighed. "I hate it when you kids say that. I got news for you, Grace: football's the most damn emotional game on earth. Football *is* feelingsball." He took off his visor, crossed his arms. "Now, I don't wanna pry, but Coach Metellus let me know you had a rough time on the visit. If you ever wanna talk about anything, my door's open." He frowned. "Well, I don't have an office, but metaphorically, that sumbitch is open."

Part of me was annoyed that Jerome told him, but I never would've said anything myself. It's not that I wasn't comfortable telling him stuff; besides Dad, Rhoads was the steadiest adult figure in my life. He had other duties, sure, but we were out on this field alone every single practice. The thing was: I'd never been any good at letting people close to me know what was going on in my head.

And I *definitely* wasn't ready to talk about what had happened at that party. Not yet.

"I hurt my knee," I said, blinking hard. "Plant knee. I don't—I don't think it's why I'm missing my kicks, though. My head's all fucked, and I had blood drawn today, and—"

"Slow down," he said, resting a hand on my shoulder pad. "Let's pack it in for the day, okay? Go see the trainer. Then, if you wanna talk some more, you come find me."

I took a deep breath and nodded. "Sorry for the wasted practice, Rhoady."

"You don't got nothing to apologize for," he said, patting my shoulder. "Go on, now. Ice up."

Thirty-one

After practice, I washed my face, changed into a hoodie and wrinkly joggers, and shuffled out to the parking lot long after most of the boys had already left. Even though my practice had been short, I was bone tired. I needed to go home, shower for a million years, and try to make sense of what the hell I was feeling.

When I rounded the corner of the building, I froze.

Casey McReynolds—all six foot two of him—leaned against Lorraine's back bumper fifty yards away. Phone in one hand, spitter in the other. *Charming.*

I don't know what I would've done (walked home? Called the cops? Crafted a Molotov cocktail out of materials in my backpack?) if he hadn't looked up a moment later. He raised his hands in surrender. "Woodhouse! I wanna talk to you!"

I didn't move from my spot. I just glared at him.

"Seriously!"

I crossed my arms while he approached me, fighting the urge to dart around him to my car. I had to stand my ground, let him know he couldn't get to me. "I'm not in the mood, McReynolds."

"Look," he said, pausing to spit ink-black goo into a Gatorade bottle, "I've been meaning to talk to you. For, like, a few weeks now."

"What makes you think I wanna talk to you?"

"You don't need to be a dick," he said, frowning. "Look. Back in September, I just... I was hard on you because I was worried about the team, you know? I didn't want you to be a distraction, or, like, try to make us PC or whatever. But you aren't like other transgenders."

A choked laugh escaped my throat. Was this what McReynolds thought an *apology* sounded like? "What are 'other transgenders' like?"

He rolled his eyes. "C'mon, you know what I mean. Blue hair and pronouns, that kinda stuff. You're not like that, though. You mind your business, you don't make everything political. You're still one of us, you know? If I'd known all that when you joined back up, I never would have said any of that stuff. So..." He gestured in my general direction with his spitter. "We're cool, right? Is the beef squashed?"

My hands worked themselves into fists. Did he think he was *complimenting* me?

He did. He *definitely* did.

His eyebrows bunched together in confusion. When he reached for my shoulder, I jerked away, physically repulsed by the thought of his hand anywhere on my body. I found my voice, hot and venomous in my throat. "Don't touch me."

"What the hell's wrong with you? I'm trying to be a good guy here."

I had a million things to say, and I wasn't sure McReynolds was smart enough to understand any of them. The loudest one in my head, though, was a question for myself: *Do you want to be the trans girl that Casey McReynolds thinks is cool?*

The rest of my brain answered unanimously.

"Fuck you," I spat. "We are *not* cool. If you ever say some ignorant shit to me like that again, I'll... I'll—"

"You'll what?" Unsurprisingly, his mood had turned on the spot. He puffed out his chest and bared his teeth, because guys like him only know how to get in your face like an animal. I knew what they were like. I spent the first thirteen years of my life fending them off, after all.

I wasn't stupid. McReynolds was bigger than me, and starting a fight would get us both kicked off the team. Swinging on him, as wonderful as it might feel, would only rip open more wounds. So I held my ground, not breaking eye contact for a second. Worst came to worst, I *knew* I was faster than him.

We stared each other down for a few seconds before I heard someone clear their throat behind me. "Mack," came Dray's voice, "what are you doing?"

After a beat, McReynolds raised his hands in surrender and took a step back. "Nothing. We're just having a conversation."

"Grace," Dray said cautiously, "what's—"

"*Nothing* is going on, Fulton." McReynolds set his eyes on me, cold and cruel. "Seeya around, Woody."

While McReynolds turned tail and dipped, I put my head down and bolted for my car. "Wait!" Dray cried. "You okay, Grace?"

God, no, I wasn't okay. I threw open the door to Lorraine and hammered the steering wheel for a solid thirty seconds. I screamed into the rough fabric of my backpack until my throat felt raw and my head ached. When I surfaced a minute later, there was Dray, peering at me through the passenger's side window. He motioned for me to roll the window down.

"How much of that did you see?" I asked, feeling my cheeks redden.

"Barely any," he lied. "Look, if you wanna be alone, I get it. But I can tell you've been going through it lately, and that doesn't sit right with me. You can talk to me, you know? I'm your captain. I'm your brother."

I let out a shaky breath and slumped forward, resting my forehead against the steering wheel. "I'm a terrible friend."

"Knock that shit off right now," Dray said, opening the door and sliding into the passenger's seat next to me. "That settles it. We're getting you right tonight. You wanna smoke? Chill out? Play games?"

As much as I wanted to be alone, I could tell he wouldn't take no for an answer. When Dray knew something was wrong, he locked on and wouldn't let go. One of his annoyingly benevolent qualities. I mulled over my options, realized what needed to happen tonight, and sighed. "There's some stuff I should tell you about."

"Sure. Whatever you gotta do."

"But," I said, "I need to see someone. Like, tonight. I don't think you really know her, so . . . I wouldn't blame you for dipping."

He smiled just as raindrops began to hit the windshield. "Where are we going?"

Thirty-two

Tab opened her front door, took one look at me, and sighed. "Grace."

I gestured at the rain behind me, grinning sheepishly. "This is familiar, huh?"

She rolled her eyes and turned to her other visitor, her expression morphing into something between surprise and amusement. "Aundray."

Dray flashed her his Nuclear Reactor Smile. "Tabitha Rolón. You were great in *A Funny Thing Happened on the Way to the Forum* last year."

She beamed, her guard dropping. "Thanks! I *loved* that show!"

Dray was my Charm Meat Shield as Tab ushered us through the front door, making small talk about the school play he'd inexplicably seen. "I just put the kettle on," Tab said. "I'll make y'all tea."

While the two of us kicked our shoes off, an unseen voice rang out from a room to our right. "Tabitha, who was at the door?"

She groaned. "Just some friends from school, Mami!"

Huh. Tab wasn't much for having people over on account of her "extremely loud and sticky" younger brothers, so I'd never met her mom. "You didn't say you were having friends over!" she called, presumably from the living room. "Better not be any boys!"

Dray and I looked at each other until he burst into laughter. "Y'all want me to wait outside?"

"No—I—you don't have to do that," Tab said, clearly flustered. "I'll just go—"

"I'll talk to her," Dray offered. "Adults love me."

While he disappeared down the hallway, Tab looked mortified. "Ma *loves* your team. She's gonna treat him like a celebrity."

I followed Tab (nearly tripping over a toy truck in the middle of the hallway) to the kitchen, which reminded me of my grandma's old house in the best way. Cookbooks were everywhere, jars and spice containers cluttered the counters. Food bowls were set out for cats that I'd seen countless photos of. I felt safe, like I could breathe for the first time all day.

I lingered, awkwardly, in the entryway. Should I apologize first? Based on the way Tab was hovering near the stove, I could tell she was doing the same mental math.

I said: "So—"

Like clockwork, that was the moment the kettle started screaming. We finally made eye contact and laughed. "Go on, sit down," she said, gesturing to the small table pushed against the wall near me. "Not that it isn't good to meet him, but what's Aundray Fulton doing here?"

I felt my cheeks redden as I slumped into a wooden chair. "He's just worried about me. Sorry I didn't warn you."

"Oh, it's fine. He appreciates musical theater, so he's good in my book." She peered into a cabinet above the sink. "What tea do you like? We've got green tea, chamomile, breakfast tea, uh . . ."

There it was again, that self-conscious pang in my gut when I felt like I was doing Girl wrong. I knew *nothing* about tea. Dad never drank it, and Grandma ran on cigarettes and decaf coffee back when she was around. I knew that green and black tea existed, but I didn't know anything about them.

"Umm," I said, feeling my face go red. "I've never . . . had it."

Surprise rolled across Tab's face. "Well, do you wanna try it?"

"Sure. Just give me whatever you're having, I trust you."

Tab fussed with the teabags for a minute, trying to guess what tea Dray liked, while a massive ball of gray fur strutted into the kitchen like he owned the place. He sniffed apprehensively at my leg. "Wow," I whispered, reaching down to pet the cat's back. "Are you *the* Percy Jackson Rolón? You're even bigger in person than you are in the photos, man!"

Once I passed the vibe check, Percy flopped down on top of my feet and started purring like a radiator. "He likes me more than you. He just told me so."

She turned to me, mugs held aloft, and sighed. "He likes *everyone* more than me, and the twins *terrorize* him. Like I wasn't the one who picked him out and named him! Ungrateful ass."

I had to admit, the mug she put in front of me smelled excellent. "Chamomile," she explained. "Always makes me feel good."

"Cool," I said, blowing on my drink. "I'm a little disappointed I don't get to meet your baby brothers, you know."

"You *just* missed them! Ma sent them to their room for fighting at the dinner table. Supposed to be going to going to bed early."

"No way they're asleep."

"No way," she agreed. "You can't separate Gabriel from his Switch. My parents gave up that fight years ago."

Once I was reasonably sure I wouldn't burn myself, I ventured a sip. It tasted like flowers, which made me feel at home. While I told Tab I feared I might be a tea person now, Dray strutted back into the kitchen. "I thought your mom was gonna ask me for my autograph."

"Ugh," Tab groaned, which I couldn't help but giggle at. "*Mortally* embarrassing. I hope you like chamomile, Aundray."

"I do." He settled into the seat next to mine, thanking Tab as she slid a mug his direction. Somehow, I'd never once seen the guy walk into a room and look uncomfortable, uneasy, or out of place. It was *uncanny*. Reality bent around Dray Fulton. "Y'all are putting on the fall play this weekend, right?"

She nodded. "We're doing *A Midsummer Night's Dream*. You a theater enthusiast?"

"Sure. Mama raised me on August Wilson, but who doesn't fuck with Sondheim, you know? I kinda wanna go out for the spring musical, but it'd mess with my sports schedule." He shrugged. "I've never acted, though. Maybe it's dumb."

"You should try out!" Tab said, lighting up. "Oh my god, dude, we'd *love* to have you, are you kidding?"

It was so bizarre, watching these two get along like old friends. I wasn't sure what I felt more: surprised at how easy it was, or stupid for not introducing them sooner.

After a long sip of her tea, Tab cleared her throat. "So . . . no offense or anything, but, uh, why are you here?"

They both looked at me expectantly. I took a deep breath and forced the words out. "This school in Wisconsin wants me to play football for them."

I spilled everything: how I met Jerome, how he vouched for me to the program, how I'd sat on it for a month without telling anyone. Then the visit: Coach Oestreicher, the other specialists, the way the campus looked in the fall. What that girl did to me at the party. Then, finally, what happened with McReynolds today in the parking lot, and all the other little things the guys had said that hurt me, and the things I'd overheard from opposing players, and—

"Grace," said Tab. "*Grace.* Breathe, okay?"

"And I need to apologize to you," I said, still on a roll. "You were right to be mad at me. I was a bad friend, and I *did* do shitty things, and—"

"*Listen to me.*" When she grabbed my shoulder, I had to fight the impulse to yank away from her touch. "Are you listening to me?"

After a few seconds, the fog that had taken hold of my brain started to clear. I found myself nodding.

"Just breathe, Grace," Dray said. "Slow down for a sec. Everything's cool. Count to three in your head."

I thought it sounded silly at first, but counting to three really did help. My heart stopped hammering in my ears like a machine gun. I took a sip of tea. I pictured Dad's garden in full bloom.

"I'm not mad at you," Tab said. She flicked her eyes to Dray, clearly embarrassed to hash this out in front of him, but she (rightly) judged Dray to be someone who minded his own business. "I've been meaning to apologize to *you*. I thought I was protecting you, but I was way over the line."

"But you were right!"

She shook her head. "About some of it, I guess. But I didn't have to be that mean or dramatic, and I'm sorry. I knew you were going through a lot, I just... didn't know how *much*. Because you didn't tell me."

Feeling pretty called out, I took a moment to reach under the table and give Percy a scratch. "I didn't tell anyone about it, so. It's not like I left you out or anything."

"You could've told me, too," Dray said. He didn't sound offended, just a little disappointed. "Or any of the boys, really. I'm real excited for you, you know? This is a chance to make history."

"I just—" I felt physically sick, like I was gonna throw up. "I *suck* at feelingsball."

Tab looked utterly bewildered. "*What?*"

"Like, I feel everything too much. I always have, but like, even more lately. And it's selfish to make that your guys' problem, you know? I don't want to be a burden. So I just... keep it in. And try to limit the damage to just me if I can."

"Girl," Tab said, "with all due respect, you know that's crazy, right?"

"But—"

"No buts," she insisted. "I mean, first of all, I don't ever think you're a *burden*. Everyone needs help sometimes. That's what friends are for!" She took my hand and gave it a reassuring squeeze. "It's hard enough being a girl in this shitbag world, Grace. You gotta claw and scrape for every little thing. If you don't demand space for yourself, you won't get it."

Dray nodded, like, *obviously.* "She's right. I mean, I dunno about being a woman, but, like, as a gay Black dude? I get it."

"I just..." I exhaled. "I don't know how to 'demand space' for myself without feeling like I'm taking up too much."

Tab crossed her arms. "If I told you that, what would you say?"

I opened my mouth to say something like *but that's so different, because you're you and I'm me* before realizing that was her point. I frowned. "You're Jedi-mind-tricking me."

She rolled her eyes. "Uh-huh."

I stared into the dark surface of my cup, barely making out the rippling reflection of my face in the liquid. You could only see its outline, really: the murky shape of a girl with frizzy hair and a strong jaw. You couldn't see her eyes at all. "I don't wanna be like this forever," I mumbled. "I wanna just . . . feel things normally, then let them go. Like a normal person."

Tab winced. "Let's work on the phrasing later."

"And also . . ." I paused. "Hearing what McReynolds said . . . it really made me feel like shit. I'm not what he thinks I am. Or . . . I don't *wanna* be what he thinks I am. I wish I was a Cool Gay, you know? I *wish* I could make a statement."

"You *are* a Cool Gay," Dray said, sounding offended on my behalf. "The coolest gay I know, matter of fact! Apologies, Tabitha."

"C'mon. You know what I mean."

Tab gave me a pointed look. "You *could* make a statement, you know."

"What are you talking about?"

"Well . . ." She drew the word out and tapped her chin. "Rebelling doesn't have to be big and dramatic. It could be small. Something just for yourself."

An impulsive thought hit me; one I'd had a few times since I'd realized I was trans, one I always dismissed for being too drastic, too disruptive. But the anxiety in my chest was burning out, turning into something that felt like manic spite. I threw myself at it with my whole soul.

"I have an idea," I said. "There's someone we need to rope in, though."

"Oh?"

I practically bounced to my feet from the sudden second wind. "Absolutely. We might need to make a stop at the pharmacy on the way there. And . . . we might be out kinda late. Is that okay? You can say no."

Dray shrugged. "You know I'm in."

Any worry I had that Tab *wouldn't* be down melted away when she grinned mischievously. "I'll cook up an excuse for my mom, don't worry. But who do we need to rope in?"

I pulled my jacket over my shoulders and gave her an apologetic smile. "That might be the tricky part."

Before—April

When the girls stop in front of H&M and you see how busy it is, your blood runs cold. "This is a *bad* idea."

Tab gives you a reassuring arm squeeze. "It'll be *fine*."

The three of you drove all the way up to the outlet mall in Niagara Falls for this, and you know you can't back down now. But seeing the crowd has made it all *very* real for you.

"People don't pay attention to strangers in crowds, like, *ever*," Riley adds. "Plus, there aren't any Pageland kids here. It'll be a piece of cake."

You have no idea where you'd be without these two, honestly. You told Riley after you told Tab, and she was great about it. This whole outing came together last-minute, and while you rode the nervous excitement through the car ride, the reality of what you're about to do has crashed down on you.

"Just look like my disinterested 'boyfriend'"—Tab adds air quotes—"and I'll grab stuff off the rack for you. It'll be fine."

Riley goes off to do her own thing while you and Tab make the rounds, ending up near the sweaters. "How about this one? I think it would look great *on me*," she says, holding up a purplish cable-knit thing that makes your chest vibrate like a strummed guitar. You swallow the lump in your throat and nod.

That's how you go through the store: quietly choosing clothes, approving the occasional Tab suggestion. Once you're satisfied, she throws a few men's polos on your pile for camouflage. She gives you a reassuring smile.

"Now: fitting rooms," she says. "You good with that?"

You wish you could do a shot, something to give you a boost of courage. "Let's do it before I lose my nerve."

The fitting room is tiny, crowding you on all sides like a jail cell. You strip down to your boxers and undo your "man bun," letting your hair fall to your shoulders. You force yourself to look in the mirror. *He*'s there, of course. The goal for today: don't see *him*, even if it's only for a moment.

You step into a black skater skirt, because you might as well go full send if you're doing this. Next, you shimmy into the purple sweater, and once you're done smoothing it out you summon the courage to check the mirror.

Your relationship with this stuff has never been *magic*. You always assumed that trans girls put on a dress, Catholic God descends from Heaven and bellows *your name is Emma now*, and that's that. Catholic God doesn't speak to you, though. You shake your hair out, try to tease it into something vaguely feminine. The sweater bunches in such a way that it's not completely obvious you're flat-chested, and the skirt flares enough that your narrow hips are hidden. It's . . . not bad. What you're looking at is something closer to the *You* that you want to see in the mirror every day, even if you're not there yet.

You end up keeping a few things, putting the rest in a discard pile. Tab and Riley pantomime clapping when they see you emerge. "White smoke!" Riley says, grinning.

"How did it go?"

You find yourself saying: "I think it's a start."

Thirty-three

"Yo," came Riley's voice, rough over Lorraine's speakers. "What's good?"

"You doing anything?" I asked, nervously glancing at Tab in the passenger's seat.

"Not really," Riley replied, and over the line I heard the sound of a toolbox clattering shut. "Working on Scarlett's transmission, but I'm calling it for the night. Why, what's up?"

I laid out the plan for her while I waited at a red light, and I could practically hear her expression light up. "Hell yes," she said, laughing. "Let's *go*. Mom's still at work, you can totally come through."

"Need us to stop somewhere and get supplies?"

"Nah, I've got a few colors on hand. But who's 'us'?"

"Well, I've got Dray Fulton in the car. But also, Tab's with me. I'm on speaker, actually, so she can hear you too." I cleared my throat. "We playing nice?"

Silence from my phone. Silence from the girl sitting next to me. I took a moment to glare at Tab when we hit a stop sign. "I'm sorry for being a bitch," she said, exhaling. "Really."

To my shock, after a few seconds, Riley said: "I'm sorry, too. I should've been a better friend."

Tab and I exchanged bewildered looks. "I don't think I've ever heard you apologize," I marveled.

"Don't get used to it. You'll never hear me say that gay shit ever again."

After the call ended, Dray spoke up from the backseat. "Hey, so, this might be weird, but do you mind picking up someone? I kinda... had plans to see him tonight."

"Shit, Dray, I'm sorry. We can—"

"Nah, it's no big deal," he said. "It's just... well, it's the guy I'm talking to. He needs to get out more, and I know y'all are cool, so I'm dragging his ass with us."

While Dray dictated directions to his house, I felt a suspicion take root in my brain. I kept expecting Dray to prove me wrong and point me down some random side street, but it never happened. He had me park in front of a house I knew well.

"Unbelievable," I muttered. "I'm gonna kill both of you."

Tab's brow furrowed. "Wait, what's going on?"

Dray gave me a sheepish grin and ducked out into the rain to help his mystery man, who hobbled towards us on crutches. When streetlight caught his face a moment later, Tab gasped.

First came the crutches, and then, with the help of Dray, in came Prez, his leg in a heavy boot cast wrapped in plastic. His Golden Boy-ass hair fell in his face in messy, rain-soaked clumps. His face was *cherry* red.

"So," I said, while Dray took his seat, "you know I'm gonna need, like, a full written report on how this happened, right?"

Dray laughed, and even Prez cracked a smile.

When we pulled up to Riley's house a few minutes later, she waved us in like nothing was weird about our little posse of four, or that Dray and Prez kept bumping shoulders. "You picked up a stray quarterback," she finally noted, looking at Prez with the same analytical expression I imagined she wore when she popped the hood of a car with some *very* interesting problems.

Prez, still red, mumbled: "Sorry for showing up uninvited. Blame *him*."

While Riley disappeared upstairs to retrieve her supplies, Dray fussed over Prez, who was struggling to unzip his windbreaker. "Stop being so damn stubborn," Dray said softly, a voice I barely recognized. "Let me help."

As I watched them bicker like a married couple, it all clicked into place: Dray's mystery guy wasn't out. The two of them had always been at each other's side, always had great chemistry on the field. Best *bros*. Such a good *bro*mance. I mean, god, Dray called him *Zach*. How had I missed it?

"Am I allowed to ask how long this has been going on?"

The boys made eye contact, a silent conversation happening between them. Prez glanced at Tab, who was pretending not to watch them while she lounged on the bottom stair. "Okay, first of all, it's a secret," Prez said, trying in vain to fix his hair. "It stays a secret."

"Of course," Tab and I both said at the same time. "In this house, it's queers all the way down," I assured him.

"Okay," he said, still looking a little uncomfortable. "We've kinda been talking since the summer?"

"It's old news," Dray said with a smirk. "The captains have known for months."

My jaw dropped. "*Months?* And the *other* queer on the team is just finding out *now*?"

"That's what you get for skipping two-a-days, girl!"

I barely had time to process that before Riley plodded back down the stairs, her hair kit in hand. While she prepped the bathroom, I studied my reflection in a mirror by the coat rack. When I wore my hair down like this, the ends hung a few inches below my collarbone. I watched my mirror doppelganger touch the ends of her hair like she wasn't sure it was real.

I'd been growing it out for almost three years. The longer hair had been a good look for Old Me, bumping me up from something like a Boy 6 to a Boy 7.5, which was funny to think about in retrospect. While Dad was cranky about it until I came out to him, Zoe had *loved* it. She only asked me when I was getting a haircut once, just a week before we broke up. By May, it had left the domain of Cute-and-Shaggy and entered the awkward genderless in-between.

Riley's head poked out into the nearby hallway. "To your battle station, Commander Woodhouse."

I settled into the chair that Riley dragged into the bathroom and looked at the gangly girl with freckles in the mirror again. My hair was, objectively, kind of a mess. It was shapeless, the ends badly split. I knew from working in the garden my whole life that you need to prune living things to let them grow back healthier, stronger, better. I knew that, logically, but it didn't make this easier to swallow.

I told her a few inches needed to come off. She held up a few of the dyes she had on hand, the others shouting their opinions on which one was best. I nervously pointed to one that made her grin like an imp.

While Riley snapped the nylon cape around the back of my neck, I felt a chill. I couldn't help but inhale sharply when she reached for her scissors. "Are you good?" Riley asked, her voice uncharacteristically soft. "I'm . . . sure this is a lot for you to handle. You don't have to go through with it if you don't want to."

I sat up in my chair, breathed in, and cracked my knuckles. Out in the hallway, Dray, Prez, and Tab were all talking about some Netflix show they'd all seen. The boys sat side-by-side on the floor, and Prez shyly held Dray's hand. I couldn't help but smile at the absurdity of it.

"Full send," I said, putting on a brave face. "Time for a little anarchy."

Riley cackled. "Attagirl!"

When she made her first snip, loud and sharp in my ear, I felt the bundle of nerves in my chest unravel. Riley patted my shoulder. "Just imagine the look on Rutkowski's face when his kicker shows up to practice with pink hair."

OLIVER MUNCIE
@Munce_11

OCT 6 at 2:41 PM

MUNCE_11: Hello, Grace! My name's Oliver Muncie, I'm a features writer at Out of Bounds - you might know us already? We cover LGBTQIA+ stories across the world of sports. We've done a lot of reporting on trans athletes, specifically, and your story caught my eye. I wanted to see if you'd be interested in giving an interview.

MUNCE_11: I respect and understand your reluctance to speak out so far - as a former trans athlete myself, I've lived what you're going through. I want people like us to be able to tell our stories on our own terms, and I'd like to give you the opportunity to do that.

NOV 10 at 11:57 PM

GWOOD301: okay this is definitely 100% out of pocket bc it's the middle of the night and everything BUT: i'm tired of shutting up, and i don't know if I'll have the nerve to do this in the morning

GWOOD301: i think i'm ready to talk. i don't want to do a big long profile or anything, tho. something short

GWOOD301: i saw you guys have a weekly podcast?

Thirty-four

[INTRO: Twenty-second sample from the first verse of "Sports" by the Viagra Boys]

OLIVER MUNCIE: Hello! Welcome back to *Out of Sounds*, brought to you by *Out of Bounds* and Vapor Audio.

LINDY BRAVERMAN: [snorts]

OLIVER: Oh, come on. It's, like, basic podcast etiquette not to speak until you're introduced.

LINDY: I didn't speak! *Out of Sounds* will NEVER not be funny to me, Ollie!

OLIVER: [dramatic sigh] We're never getting that Homefield Apparel money at this rate.

LINDY: [cackling laughter] Call us, Homefield! You know you want to!

OLIVER: Our normal intro's been totally stepped on, but you probably know who we are by now. I'm Oliver Muncie, he/him, a features writer for *Out of Bounds*. And the nightmare creature I'm shackled to for all eternity, for some reason—

LINDY: Lindy Braverman, they/them, social media editor for *Out of Bounds*. You may also know me from *Balls and Dykes*, my baseball podcast.

OLIVER: Great show, by the way! Check it out. But, obviously, if you've clicked on this episode, you know we've got a very special bonus show here for you. We are absolutely *thrilled* to be speaking to Grace Woodhouse, who is—you know what, I'm gonna let Grace tell us herself. Grace, how are you today?

GRACE WOODHOUSE: Hi! I'm, uh, good. Happy to be on. I'm a high school student—a senior—in Pageland, New York, near Buffalo. Also, I guess, I kick footballs.

LINDY: You're pretty damn good at it, by all accounts.

GRACE: [shy laughter] Not *bad* at it, anyway.

OLIVER: So, Grace, you're believed to be one of—if not *the* first—trans woman playing organized football . . . ever? We don't really know. That's incredible, but to take it from the beginning: how the heck did you end up as a kicker in the first place?

[GRACE talks about her history with soccer and the adjustment from kicking a soccer ball to kicking a football. The discussion moves from her early days as a kicker to football more generally.]

OLIVER: I'm curious: do you have a favorite kicker to watch? To take inspiration from?

GRACE: Wow. Umm—that's tough. Obviously, you know, there's Justin Tucker, but picking him almost feels like cheating.

LINDY: It's kinda like saying your favorite musician is Taylor Swift. Like, of *course* she is.

GRACE: [laughing] Totally. There are a few others I really like—Brandon Aubrey is great. Tyler Bass, obviously. But my favorite? It's gotta be Younghoe Koo. He's so cool to watch. Like, his mechanics are great, but he's also the coolest dude doing it right now, I think. That game where he hit, like, three onside kicks? I was losing my mind watching that. Plus, there aren't a lot of Korean players in the game, and the way that everyone wrote him off after his first season, to come back and be as consistent as he is? It's just awesome. I could go on about him from, like, a technical perspective, but—

LINDY: Bringing the people exactly what they wanna hear: that hot and heavy kicking content.

GRACE: [laughing] Of course.

OLIVER: So, I think, maybe, riffing off of Younghoe Koo being unique—this might be a little clumsy—

LINDY: Another *sparkling* segue from award-winning journalist Oliver Muncie.

OLIVER: They call me the King of Transitions—[LINDY laughs]—that was unintentional! But anyway: You're a unique athlete yourself, Grace. Your junior year, you break out as this young kicking star. You're one of the top-ranked kickers in the country, probably looking at the opportunity to get a scholarship from—or at least walk on to—a big football school. Then you chose not to sign up for football after that season to pursue your gender transition. Could you walk me through some of that decision, and then why you decided to come back?

GRACE: Well, I guess... it wasn't an easy decision for me, is what I'll say. I don't wanna get into all the details, but after the football season ended, I realized just how much dysphoria was affecting my life. It felt like... I dunno, like sitting in a car in the winter with the heat cranked up just a *little* too high for too long. Like, a constant feeling of, oh god, I can't breathe, I feel queasy, and I can close the air vents near me for a little bit but that doesn't fix it, I've gotta roll the windows down eventually.

It was hard. I mean, I had to accept that football would be over for me.

OLIVER: And yet, here you are. You joined back up with your team in September, and since then, you've been kind of an internet folk hero, at least for people like us. And I wanted to ask you: what made you come back?

GRACE: Well, what I've said before is totally true: I came back to kick.

[GRACE recounts the captains of her team reaching out to her just before a tough loss, emphasizing their acceptance and support, as well as the tutelage of Coach Howard Rhoads. She slips into Football Speak, seemingly by instinct.]

OLIVER: How would you describe the reaction from your teammates?

GRACE: Well, it's—like I said, the captains had my back, and of course, Coach Rhoads has always been in my corner. So, I mean, it's been an adjustment, naturally, but—

LINDY: What about—sorry for cutting in—what about everyone else? We're talking about dozens of players and probably, what, five or more coaches?

GRACE: Well, sure. But, I would say, on the whole, things have been . . . I mean, overall, it's been good. You can't control how *everyone* is gonna feel, but the majority of the team has been great.

LINDY: The "majority"?

GRACE: Yeah, the majority. Like I said, nobody's . . . nothing's perfect, you know? Of course there's been a little friction here and there. It's never easy to be visibly trans, but like, right now . . .

LINDY: Absolutely. Everything is a *mess* right now, especially in this country. But that "friction" you mentioned—where have you been experiencing it? Teammates? Coaches? Opposing teams?

GRACE: [After a beat of silence] I think—of course, like I said, most of the reaction has been positive or even, you know, neutral, which is fine. I've heard it from a few opposing players, but it's never been anything I can't handle. Some dork throws a few bad words your direction while his team is losing by three touchdowns—it's kinda sad, right? [LINDY laughs] Exactly! That doesn't really get to me. Or if an opposing coach gives me the evil eye or says something out-of-pocket, whatever.

I will say, the team has not . . . it hasn't been unanimous support. Coaches, teammates. That's harder, having it in-house. But you can't force people to change their minds. I'm here to kick and help my team win a state championship, and if nobody is . . . as long as they're not being detrimental to that goal—

LINDY: Sorry—Ollie, can I editorialize here for a second?

OLIVER: Name literally one time I've ever been able to stop you.

LINDY: Point. Grace, you can speak openly here, okay? It's a safe queer space, et cetera. But I understand that there are some things you'll be reluctant to say. So *I* will speak openly real quick: there's no place for transphobia in women's sports, men's sports, whatever. You don't have to make excuses for it here.

GRACE: I mean, I totally agree. Trans athletes should be able to compete against, you know, their actual gender. Obviously, football being what it is, I have to play with the boys, and there'll always be that gap of life experience between me and my teammates. There's a distance that's always gonna be there.

OLIVER: Right. When I was a senior in college and I wanted to start my transition, obviously, I couldn't go on HRT or anything because of softball. So I came out to my teammates privately and stayed closeted publicly. There was support, of course, but like you said, there's always that gap.

GRACE: Exactly. Like I said, I've had so many great teammates: Dray Fulton, Ahmed Nassar, Kaeden Park-Campbell, Conner Nguyen—so many I can't name all of them. So many great dudes. I really want to emphasize that. It's been better than I could've imagined, honestly.

[The conversation moves to a discussion of playing with fellow queer teammate Dray Fulton and then, more broadly, to Pageland's season. GRACE clarifies that they're just a couple of wins from Syracuse now. After that, it's time to wrap things up.]

OLIVER: Now, Grace, I know you have to be out of here at 1:30, so first of all, thank you for joining us today!

LINDY: Ditto. This has been awesome.

OLIVER: This is normally the part of the outro where I ask our guests to plug their work, but I know this is kind of a special circumstance, so I wanted to give you the opportunity to send a message to any kids like you who might be listening to this—trans athletes, queer athletes, queer folks in general. Anything you'd like.

LINDY: Jeez, Ollie, that's not existentially terrifying at *all*.

GRACE: [laughs] No, no—it's okay. I just . . . okay. I think I've got something.

It hasn't been easy for me, not even a little bit. Some of the stuff I've heard since I came out back in June . . . it's been hard. But I wanna say: for a few months there, I assumed that football—sports in general—wouldn't be there for me again. But I was wrong. If you're gay or you're trans and sports make you happy, you belong. If you're a cis girl who wants to play football? You belong.

Even though it's been hard, I would do it again in a heartbeat. And—I'll be honest, I don't follow politics as closely as I should—but I know there are some states where trans kids can't play sports, or even can't access hormones or come out, which is just—

LINDY: Evil. Fuckin' evil.

GRACE: Fuckin' evil. It needs to change. The way I look at it is: if I exist, there's no way I'm the only one. There's gotta be tons of us out there, way more than you'd think. So hang in there.

[GRACE laughs self-consciously] Sorry, that was kind of a mess.

OLIVER: No! No, it was perfect. Thank you again for joining us today, and good luck to you on the rest of the season. Go Druids!

GRACE: Thanks! Go Druids.

"Quit hogging that bottle, Pink," Ahmed said. "Big boys need water."

I tossed the bottle at him and scoffed. "You know, 'Pink' is a *lot* better than AK. I'll take it."

"Mmm. Good point, Barbie."

I rolled my eyes while the guys snickered. Roasting is a way of life on a football team—last week we spent a full practice gunning Tino Russo because his new shoes were a little *too* colorful—so I knew I'd hear it all week. But it wasn't anything I couldn't handle.

"Looks good, Grace. Don't listen to the ugly man," Dray said breezily, shimmying past me to snag a bottle. He'd pretended to be just as surprised as everyone else when I showed up yesterday with pink hair to cover his and Prez's tracks. "I'm the manic pixie dream girl on this team, but there's room for a second."

"You going pink, QB1?" DeSean Kirkland asked, laughing.

"I could rock it! DK Metcalf pulled off the pink twists, and I'm *way* prettier than him."

For a dye job done in my friend's bathroom at midnight, it hadn't turned out bad. This giddy rush of energy hit me when I checked the mirror yesterday morning. Electric, *obnoxiously* pink hair hung to my shoulders, where Riley had cut it surprisingly even. I loved it. The person I was looking at *definitely* wasn't the old me anymore. The boys teased me about it, sure, and Dad gave me a lecture on the dangers of bleaching your hair when I got home from school yesterday, but overall, everything was still good.

For *now*, at least.

There was no telling what would happen once the interview dropped, of course. After we recorded during one of my free periods that afternoon, Oliver told me that the podcast would release tonight, probably an hour or two after practice was out. From there, it was out of our hands, and I had no idea how wide of an audience it would find.

Out of nowhere, a hand shoved me to the side. "Out of the way," a voice grumbled. "You're blocking the water."

I whipped around to find some asshole—a Wannabe Redneck backup lineman—sneering at me. "What's the matter?"

My heart was pounding, my hands had balled into fists. I was overreacting—it wasn't that big of a deal, really—but I was decidedly *not* in the mood to be touched.

"Mayle," Truck said, appearing at my side, "don't be a dick."

"Really? He can't fight his own battles?"

I clenched my jaw and remembered what Dray told me: *count to three.*

One.

"I said: *don't be a dick*. Mind your business. Get your water and go."

Two.

Mayle rolled his eyes. "Whatever, Nguyen."

Three.

He grabbed a water bottle and vanished, off to rejoin his gang of idiots. I caught my breath and slowly unclenched my fists, feeling soreness radiate through my knuckles.

Yeah, I wasn't regretting that interview. Not one bit.

Truck looked at me, silently asking: *You good?* I nodded in reply.

"Can't have you starting fights at practice and getting suspended," he grunted. "Then we've got no goddamn chance."

GOOGLE SEARCH RESULTS. *For search term "Grace Woodhouse."*

Inspiring: Grace Woodhouse speaks out about her experience as a transgender football player

BREAKING: Trans-Identified HS Kicker Slams "Teammates, Coaches" in Interview

Trans Athlete Uses Podcast Appearance to Trash Teammates, Promote Woke Ideology, Urge Children to Transition

Should Grace Woodhouse be considered a pioneer for women in football?

Is Football Ready for an Openly Transgender Player? Former NFL Linebacker Weighs In

TWITTER/X POSTS:

@jswizz518: if i talked nasty about my coaches on a podcast when i was in high school my ass would be running laps EXPEDITIOUSLY

@JamesLancerCFB: Good for Grace Woodhouse. An out trans player was inevitable, and if you haven't listened to the podcast in question, it was excellent. Much respect to @OutofSoundsPod for giving her the platform.

@xx_MelanieGC: If trans activists try to turn Jordan Woodhouse into some kind of feminist icon for choosing to grow his hair out and destroy his body with hormones I will SCREAM. Women aren't even allowed to break their own barriers anymore.

@SapphicRat01: grace woodhouse is an icon for clockable bitches who love drama ... she just like me fr

@WooInRockyTop: I know we all want the Vols to sign Ahmed Nassar but... it's never a good sign when local HS drama is national news. It doesn't reflect well on his leadership skills as a captain. Coach Heupel needs to be careful.

@Logical3Tech: They won't even let us have football anymore. The Left is coming for everything you care about. If you think this is the end of it, I have a bridge to sell you.

Thirty-five

"Grace Woodhouse, please report to Principal Keller's office."

Riley, who sat next to me in pre-calc, whistled. "That didn't take long."

It was *fifteen minutes* into first period, to be exact. Mr. Ryland, who'd been in the middle of a lecture on logarithmic functions, sighed. "Go ahead, Grace."

I took a deep breath and bounced to my feet, crossing my arms. It was the first time I'd ever worn the sweater I'd bought with Tab and Riley back in April, this slouchy eggplant purple thing that showed off my collarbones. Since I usually went to great lengths to make people forget that I had a chest at all, I was pretty self-conscious about it. If I'd looked at my phone this morning and realized just how much I was under the microscope, I never would've worn it.

I fought the urge to google myself for the millionth time on the walk downstairs, but Tab had already shown me enough. The initial reaction to my interview was tepid, but things had *really* taken off last night and continued into the morning. I wasn't sure exactly how bad it was going to get—if I'd come home to reporters on our front lawn, trampling Dad's asters—but today, at least, was going to suck.

I'd been expecting some of it, of course. I wasn't stupid enough to think the worst people on the planet wouldn't twist my words, try to make me into something I wasn't. But it's one thing to *know* you're about to be dissected and another entirely to see your insides on display for the entire internet.

I wasn't sure what to expect from Principal Keller, but I had a feeling this wasn't going to be a handshake and a pat on the back.

BALLBAGS 4 CHRIST (SCOTTY'S VERSION) 💬🏈💩

Today 8:42 AM

AHMED: A grown man DMed ME a threat bro this is insane

It's Wednesday morning bro go take your damn kids to school. Go to work. Do you even have a job

TOBE: yo what

KAEDEN: Check the news Tobe

TOBE: OH

DRAY: Anyone heard from her yet?

AHMED: Nah. Can't blame her. I'd stay off my phone too

CALVIN: do you think we're gonna be famous 👀

PREZ: Shut upppp man

"Sit down, Miss Woodhouse." Principal Keller, a severe silver-haired woman who wore a permanent frown, gestured to a chair opposite her desk.

I missed that, though, because I was busy staring at the man seated to her left. "Sit down," Coach Rutkowski echoed. He crossed his arms over his chest, which he did whenever he wanted to make his biceps pop. "Some stuff we need to talk about."

I set my jaw. "Right."

Principal Keller reminded me that students are to abide by the code of conduct, et cetera et cetera, and we're expected to represent the school and the district well. I suspected it was the same talk Riley got last year when she wore a shirt with the word "dyke" on it to class, or whenever a girl was treated like a felon because her shorts were an inch too short. Righteous anger burned in my chest.

"And the football team, as you *well* know," Rut added, "has a strict policy about outside media. They don't get access to you without our supervision. Do you remember when we spoke about this?"

I told him I did.

"So, then," he said, clearly tempering his anger because he was sitting next to his boss, "what on earth possessed you to trash your team on a podcast? A *political* podcast, even."

My jaw dropped. "Are you serious?"

"Grace," Principal Keller said, straining to smile just a bit, "obviously, we support you. And we support you being yourself. But you have to understand that going on a podcast with a national audience and expressing . . . controversial opinions? Implying negative things about other students, staff members? That's unacceptable."

"What were my 'controversial' political opinions? That I really like Younghoe Koo? I spent most of the time *praising* my teammates!"

"Nobody heard that, and you know it," Rut said. "They heard that Pageland High isn't supporting you enough, which, I'd like to add, is a *crazy* thing to say. We bent over backwards to get you on this team on short notice. I've defended you more than you'll ever know. Do you know how many opposing coaches I've had to justify my decision-making to? How many parents who've called me? How many journalists I've chased off?"

"I'm sorry I've been such an inconvenience," I said coldly.

"See, Barb? She doesn't get it." Rut shook his head. "You know what I think?" He looked at me expectantly, like I was going to read his mind. "I think every idiot talking about you online is *chickenshit.*

They have no right to do that. But you can't just break the rules. That has consequences."

He sighed, rose to his feet, and ran a hand through what remained of his hair. "You're indefinitely suspended from the football team."

I shot to my feet. "You can't—"

"He can," Principal Keller said. "Extracurriculars are a privilege, not a right."

"But—" I sputtered. "Rhoady told you about Saxon Valley, right? You know what getting suspended would look like to them!"

He pinched the bridge of his nose. "Of *course* I know. I can't tell you how many times I've spoken to Coach Oestreicher. But you've got to learn your actions have consequences, Woodhouse. Decision's final. I'm sorry."

⬥

"No," Rhoads said before I could get a word in. He leaned on his cane from his post next to the cafeteria door. "There's nothing I can do about it."

"Nothing?" I glared at him, trying to read his face. I'd found him the first time I knew I could: in his position as a "security guard" in the cafeteria, the job the school gave him so they could sneak a football coach on faculty. Hundreds of eyes were on me. I didn't care.

"Disciplinary actions are handled by the head coach, Grace. I'm not involved."

"Really?" My voice caught in my throat; my eyes felt hot. A knife in the back from Rut hadn't surprised me, but this was too much. "I thought I could trust you."

"Listen—"

"What about the 'metaphorical open door'?"

"You *know* I support you," Rhoads said, tapping the ground with his cane for emphasis. "But you should've been smarter than to talk to that podcast. I don't have any tools in the box that can get you out of this one, kid. I'm real sorry."

"So that's it?" My voice came out low and hard and rough, like it did when my guard wasn't up. I winced at the sound of it. "That's all the fight you're putting up?"

He shook his head, his expression utterly defeated. "There's nothing I can do."

I stormed towards my lunch table, my head a swirling mess. Who else was there? Principal Keller was on his side. I barely knew the other assistant coaches. By the time I got back to friendly territory at our lunch table, I'd already run through every conceivable way out of this mess and come up empty.

"Are you good?" Imani asked me. "You look . . . pale."

"She's always pale," Riley countered.

I slid onto the bench without replying. I was so distracted that I barely got to appreciate the newly reunified lunch table, brought back together once the schism was mended. "Seriously," Jamie said. "Even *I* heard about the interview."

I took a deep breath. "I got suspended."

I relayed the events of that morning to them, leaving out the part about Rhoads, which was still *way* too sore to touch. The soccer girls roared in righteous anger. The theater girls told me how sorry they were. Even the perma-chill Jamie looked pissed.

"This is my own fault," I groaned, putting my head in my hands. "Why the hell did I do that interview?"

"There wasn't anything wrong with it," Riley protested. "You're an *American*. With, you know, rights? Freedom of speech? There's no way they can punish you for this."

"Well, what am I supposed to do?" My voice was scratchy. The wave of anger I'd been riding all morning had crashed; Rhoads was my last hope, and he had nothing for me. "The game's in two days. Who knows, Rutkowski said my suspension was 'indefinite.' Maybe that means I could play next week?"

"You really wanna take that chance?" Imani asked. "Plus, those boys could easily lose without you. Y'all lost to Bellarmine last year, and that was *with* your help."

"I don't know if I'd say I 'helped' last year," I grumbled.

Riley rolled her eyes. "You made a mistake. So what? Everyone makes 'em. They all know they need you to win state in Syracuse, and you'd deserve to be there even if they didn't."

Then, suddenly, there was the telltale *squeak* of sneakers marching into the cafeteria. I looked up to find a fleet of football players headed our way: the captains, Scotty, and a few others walking in formation like the goddamn Avengers. At their head: Prez, rolling in his wheelchair. "Rhoads told us what's going on," he said, coming to a stop before me. "You good?"

I coughed out a laugh. "Oh, I'm *great*. Least I'm not looking at my phone, I guess."

Ahmed nodded. "That's good." He took a second to appraise the lunch table, scratching his chin. "Solid squad we've got here. We plotting our next move?"

I scoffed. "What 'next move'?"

"How we're gonna fight this thing," Dray said, like it was obvious. "You're playing on Saturday, lady. We're not doing it without you."

"But–"

"No buts, Woodhouse," Scotty said with a grin. "We're going full send on this."

"You guys are hardcore," Tab said, her tone betraying begrudging admiration, "but it's *really* hard to organize a protest on short notice. I mean, what could we even–"

"The game tonight," Riley said suddenly. Then her eyes went wide. "The game tonight!"

I'd been so distracted by my own shit that I totally forgot about the Lady Druids' playoff run. Tonight, they traveled out to Rochester to play in the State Semifinals; if they won, they'd play the championship game in Cortland on Sunday.

"We can get, I mean, at *least* the majority of the team on board for something," Imani said as she pulled out her phone. "A pregame or post-game demonstration, maybe. Should I put it in the groupchat?"

Tab practically shot up out of her seat. "*The play!* The first showing of *Midsummer* is tomorrow!"

Just like that, the table was off like a rocket. The theater girls huddled together and started jamming while the soccer girls debated what they could pull together at the last minute, all while football players jumped in where they could. Jamie cleared space so Prez could roll up next to him, complimenting the quarterback on his "sick wheels." Kaeden offered to help coordinate whatever the soccer team did, jotting down notes on his phone. Tobe squeezed in between Jade and Tab so he could better listen in. Scotty and Robin traded notes on mullet maintenance. None of it made an iota of sense.

Dray patted my shoulder. "Pretty cool, huh?"

I nodded, soaking in the chaos unfolding around me. These people were all here for *me*, for some reason. I refused to get my hopes up—none of this would mean anything if the school wasn't willing to listen—but at least I'd go down swinging. A warrior's death. I could get down with that.

"Pretty cool," I echoed, my voice small. Then I banged on the table with my open palm to get everyone's attention. "Listen up, guys! If we wanna do this, we need to get organized."

Riley suggested getting a groupchat going, and a minute later, everyone was passing phones around. "We could really use, like, an official organizer," Tab suggested. "Someone in charge of logistics."

Oh. I swallowed a lump in my throat. "I think I have someone for that."

"Really?" Riley asked, glee in her voice. I hadn't told anyone about the recent . . . *developments*, but Riley had figured it out, or suspected at the very least. Lesbian intuition, I guess. "Who is it, Miss Woodhouse? Share with the class?"

"*Or* I can ask Jamie," I said, sighing dramatically. "You wanna be our chief of staff, Jame-o? Our quartermaster?"

The stoner smiled serenely. "I can bring the bud."

Thirty-six

Jamie did not bring the bud.

The only time we could all meet up again before the soccer girls left for Rochester was right after the final bell at 2:50; since football practice and theater rehearsals never began before 3:30, we had a small (but workable) window. We invaded and occupied the tennis courts, setting up our base of operations at an ancient scoring table that wobbled whenever you put weight on it. Within a few minutes, half the Lady Druids and nearly the entire theater delegation had shown up.

Darren Gossum, president of the Pageland High Drama Club, ambushed me in a hug. "He*ll*o, Grace!" He squeezed my shoulders and beamed. The sunlight glinting off his glasses temporarily blinded me. "I have been *dying* to meet you. Tabitha has been telling us for *months* how lovely you are."

"Oh," I said, blinking. "That's—"

"My goodness, I'm being extra!" He dropped his hands. "I just wanted to say, first of all, you look *radiant* today, and second of all, we are *not* gonna stand for this nonsense. Honestly, Pageland football? You're queer icons at this point. You and Aundray bring the slay. Without you, the team's slay potential drops significantly."

I laughed, unable to keep a smile off my face. "I'll let Dray know he slays."

"Girl, I plan on telling him myself." He paused. "Is he seeing anyone?"

A dozen or so football players joined the melee after I broke the bad news to Darren, followed by a few queer band kids and their friends Tab had roped in. Then a few of Jamie's progressively minded stoner buddies, some of Zoe's student council–type friends. Dozens milled around the tennis court; chatting, laughing, relishing in the opportunity to cause some chaos.

"Grace," Ahmed said, poking his head out of the athlete crowd, "we really don't have all day. We gotta get things started. Are we sure she's coming?"

"She's got to," I said, as much to myself as it was to Ahmed. We hadn't spoken since The Backseat Incident last week, but I told myself she'd come. She *had* to. "She's probably just running—"

The rest of the crowd murmured and then parted, revealing a *very* flustered-looking girl wearing an NCAA recruiting violation of a hoodie. A binder was tucked under her right arm, her left hand clutching a coffee thermos. When she saw me, her cheeks reddened.

"Hey, captain."

Zoe just gave me a tired smile in reply.

"Everything is color-coded," Zoe explained, setting up her Protest Binder—of course she already had a binder—on the scoring table. "*Soccer* is red, *theater* is yellow, and *general* is green."

"Damn, girl," Dray said. "You went full bullet journal on this."

I said "that's what she does" at the exact same time she said "it's what I do," and I thanked Catholic God only a few others were in earshot. Ahmed snorted. Dray and Prez glanced at one another and smiled. Riley pretended to gag.

"I like to keep things organized," she said, pushing her glasses back up her nose. It was *so* annoying how cute she got mid-project.

"Anyway, I think we can pull this off. We'll delegate the details, obviously, but I'll keep everything straight here. Plans, materials, whatever." She pointed at me. "You're on general planning with me, but first, you gotta talk to these people."

I stared at her. "What do you mean?"

She gestured at the mass of humanity around us. "These are *your* troops, Grace. They're here for you. You've gotta say something."

Right. Somehow, in the excitement and chaos of everything, it'd slipped my mind. "Uh ... how do we wanna do this?"

Zoe looked at me, then at the scoring table. "How adventurous do you feel?"

If anyone else had said it, I might've said *no*, but I had an incurable case of Down-Bad-itis. I accepted a hand from Ahmed up onto the table, which expressed its displeasure with a frightening groan. I cleared my throat. "Alright, guys!"

"Everyone, shut it!" Ahmed bellowed in his very best Captain voice, which did the job much better than I ever could.

"Uh, hi, everyone," I said, *really* wishing I'd written an inspiring speech in advance. "Thanks for being here. We're getting organized, so in a few minutes we're gonna start *actually* making plans."

Silence. Some mumbling. My heart started beating faster.

"Umm—" My mouth felt dry. "It's kinda crazy that you're all here for me. So, thank you, again. Really. It means a lot."

"We've got your back, Grace," Imani called.

"All the way, four-seven!" called Kaeden.

The rest of the crowd murmured their agreement, and from my vantage point I could see just how crazy the group was: athletes and queers, stoners and do-gooders. Different worlds, all of them mashed together. All here for me.

I swallowed the lump in my throat and tried not to cry. "I wish we didn't have to do this, but it's great to see everyone here, together. It means a lot to me. I don't even know what to say, I—" The table creaked treacherously, long and low, distinctly fart-like. Everyone cracked up, the tension mercifully cut. "I promise, that *wasn't* me! Lemme get off this thing before I die."

Zoe helped me down, clasping my arm while my sneakers hit the court again. She leaned into my ear and whispered: "You look really good today."

I tucked a loose strand of hair behind my ear. "Pink do it for you?"

"Shut *up*," she said, her smile wide.

It was a challenge, but we managed to behave ourselves all night.

We sat next to each other through the soccer game—the Lady Druids coasted to a 3-1 win thanks to two early goals from Imani—and cheered our heads off when more than half the team showed off their pink-and-blue wristbands and held up a banner with my number on it after the game. We lingered near each other during our late-night sign-making marathon at Riley's house, sipping seltzers when the soccer girls offered them.

"When's your mom getting home tonight, Ri?" I asked *very* casually once things started to wind down.

Riley knew what was up, and even though she didn't quite disapprove, she took the opportunity to throw me a judgmental glare. "She's working an overnight," she said. "There's a couch in the basement. Leave room for the Lord."

That is how Zoe and I ended up in Riley's basement, limbs tangled, her hands running through my hair. "You know," she said in between kisses, "pink hair *does* work for me."

"Never knew rebellion was your thing."

"Neither did I," she said, running her finger along my cheek. "This is new."

A minute later, she peeled her top off, and for the first time in half a year I was looking at a nearly naked Zoe Ferragamo. "You're really pretty," I breathed.

"*You're* really pretty." She reached for the hem of my sweater and then paused. "Is this okay?"

I shivered when the cool air of the basement hit my skin. I didn't bother with a bra when I wasn't working out, but I always wore an undershirt—in this case, a black cami I'd bought somewhere for three bucks. "Do you want that to stay on?" she asked.

I told her I did, and she settled back into my lap. "You're so soft now," she said, running her hands along my shoulders.

I would've been fine with this all night: her hands on my chest, mine on hers, making out at our own pace. It was perfect. We might've been at it for five minutes or five hours, and I savored every second of it.

Then I felt her hand reach down, fumbling with the button of my jeans.

I froze, feeling paralyzed. She giggled self-consciously, finally unclasping the button a moment later. Her fingernails grazed the skin of my hip when she grabbed my jeans by the belt loops, pulling them down just a few inches. She ran her thumb under the waistband of my underwear, and suddenly, I couldn't breathe.

It'd been months, and I never once thought about what I'd do whenever I got back here. The thought of her hands on me *like that*—like it'd been back in the old days—made my blood run cold.

"No," I choked out, feeling like my throat was closing. "No!"

Zoe froze. "What's wrong?"

I pulled my jeans back up, nudged her aside, and shot to my feet. "I can't," I stammered. "I'm sorry, I just . . . I can't."

"Oh!" She went red. "Gosh, I'm sorry! I should've asked, I—"

"It's okay! You stopped when I asked you to, so . . ." I swallowed the lump in my throat. "You didn't do anything wrong."

I *wanted* it to be okay. The second I said something, it was over, and she respected it. But I couldn't shake the feeling that she'd gone there because she wanted us to do what we *used* to do, be who we used to be. I imagined how Zoe must've seen me in my cami: this flat-chested thing with wide shoulders, this person who used to be her boyfriend.

"I'm *really* sorry," she repeated, approaching me hesitantly. When I nodded, she dug her head into the crook of my neck and hugged me tight. "I should've asked. I don't ever wanna make you uncomfortable."

I hugged her back, resting my chin on the top of her head. "I know," I mumbled. "I know."

Before—February

Your relationship is dying.

This realization hits you like a lightning bolt while you and Zoe sit over a tray of hot dogs at Victor's, this tiny place by your house. It's cheap, it's fast, and it tastes the exact same way it did when your grandma took you here as a kid, so it's perfect. The two of you are here all the time.

"J?" Zoe asks suddenly. "J, are you listening?"

You force down a bite of your hot dog to buy yourself time and make something up. Truth is, Zoe's been telling you about family drama and you've been zoning out hardcore. You've been glancing out the window at the foot of gray snow that fell last week, remembering something funny Tab said in trig, thinking about The T-Word Discord server you spent last night poking around in.

In the end, you come up with nothing. "I'm sorry," you say. "I spaced. Just . . . tired."

That's the lightning bolt moment, because you realize something all at once: you had this *exact* conversation last week when you got coffee together after school. Zoe tried to engage with you and your brain refused to be present in the same room. You're doing it again. *Fuck.*

"You've been tired a *lot* lately," she says softly. "Is everything okay?"

You look back down at the tray of food between you, unable to hold her gaze. Shared order of onion rings, shared order of fries, shared loganberry. She's *here*, right in front of you, but she doesn't know the least fucking bit about your late-night google searches, about The T-Word you can't even bring yourself to *think* because it terrifies you so much.

She's right here, sure. But she might as well be a thousand miles away.

"I'm good." You smile, sit up in your chair, and take her left hand in your right. "Really. I just suck at sleeping right now."

Your heart breaks at the skeptical look she gives you. *None* of this is her fault. She signed up to date a fun idiot football player, not... whatever it is you are. Being her boyfriend used to be easy—you think—but now it's harder every time you try.

Eventually, she's gonna figure out something's wrong. She's too smart not to. Right now, though, her look softens. You realize that she wants to believe you as much as you want to believe yourself. "Have you tried melatonin? My mom *swears* by it."

While she starts rattling off a story about her mother, your brain actually stays in the room. For a while, anyway.

Thirty-seven

> **OPERATION FUCK EM ALL 666** 🙂 〰️
>
> *Today 7:10 AM*
>
> **ZOE:** Okay, I got the passes. We're on.
> 8:30. The spot we discussed. We're all ready to go?
>
> **AHMED:** Yes Madam Treasurer 😤
>
> **LEAH:** lets get this bread
>
> **KAEDEN:** Copy copy
>
> **GRACE:** robin prolly rolls out of bed five minutes before class. were locked and loaded

The next morning, I spent the first half of pre-calc staring at the clock.

The plan was good—I mean, I'd trust Zoe to defuse a bomb if she had a few hours to plan for it—but I couldn't sit still. The hallways whispered about last night's soccer game before class; a few kids came up to tell me the suspension was bullshit. Even if we had public opinion on our side, though, this would be a delicate operation.

When it was *finally* time, I raised my hand and asked to go to the bathroom, slyly slipping my backpack over my shoulder. Tab grabbed my wrist and mouthed *good luck*. Riley flashed me a thumbs up. We agreed to send just one kid per class to avoid suspicion, but still, I wished they could come with me.

The rendezvous point was this quiet landing by the band room where Lucy, a tiny queer freshman thrilled to associate with seniors and cause some mayhem, had lent us her locker for the cause. I was the second to arrive (after Zoe, who mumbled *good morning* without making eye contact), but the entire squad assembled within a minute or two. Leah Shoemark, the last to arrive, crushed me in a hug. "Girl, I will *breathe fire* today," she assured me. "They can't do you like this."

They can and they will, I thought. But it was nice to see that her aggressive allyship transcended drunkenness.

"You brought your jerseys, right?" Kaeden asked while Zoe got her supplies together. "Home and away?"

I pulled them out of my backpack while Kaeden shimmied out of his much-beloved number nineteen. "Sorry, Pink." Ahmed patted his belly and grinned. "Your dainty womanly size ain't exactly compatible with the ideal male form."

I scoffed. "Who're you calling *dainty*?"

Kaeden's head popped out of my jersey's collar a second later. He smoothed out the shoulders and looked down at the forty-seven on his chest. "You're lucky I like you, Grace. I wouldn't be caught dead wearing this nasty number if I didn't."

"I like to think it's *unique*."

"What's your sign, Grace?" Tarot Card Robin asked, somehow sounding both intensely interested and completely indifferent at the same time.

"Uh, Pisces? Is that the fish one?"

She nodded sagely. "Four and seven are good numbers for you. You were probably drawn to it subconsciously."

"Well, I don't know about all that," Ahmed said, "but on a sports jersey, it's, like, objectively nasty. Only good thing it gave us was AK."

"Yeah, saying that in a school hallway is a *great idea*." I tossed him my away jersey. "Get that to Dray."

He saluted. "Will do."

Zoe cleared her throat. "Let's roll. Kaeden, Ahmed: first floor. Get the spots by the gym and the cafeteria. Robin and Leah: third. Hit the science wing. Grace, you're with me on the second. If you get spotted"—she pulled out a stack small of hall passes—"you're on student council business. I'll take the heat."

"Where did you get these, anyway?" I asked when she handed me one.

She blushed. "Swiped them from Ms. Riordan's desk."

"Zoe Ferragamo? *Breaking the rules?* Now I've seen everything."

She flipped me off and turned back to Lucy's locker. Ahmed elbowed me and whispered: "Got yourself a real one."

"Oh, *fuck off.*"

Zoe distributed posters and tape, and then we were off. Ideally, we'd have more hands, but we wanted to keep things small, so Zoe and I got to work. We focused on an empty stretch of wall opposite the entrance to the library, where tons of foot traffic moved between periods. We'd kept the posters simple and practical: *LET GRACE PLAY. RESPECT FREEDOM OF SPEECH.* Some well-intentioned theater kid's sign read *PUNT TRANSPHOBIA*; close enough.

"Grace," Zoe whispered, "can you help me? My tape roll's messed up, and—"

I taped the last corner of her *TRANS RIGHTS NOW* poster while she held it steady against the wall. She mouthed a *thank you.* "Have we covered this spot enough?" I asked.

"Think so. I wanna hit the main hall too."

I took a step back to admire our handiwork: a wall of posters, all demanding change. All about *me.*

"You look like you hate it," Zoe said.

"I don't," I said, bouncing on my heels nervously. "Just . . . feeling very *seen.*"

"I get it," she said softly. She gave my hand a reassuring squeeze. "But it's a show of how many people care, right?"

She left without another word, already fixated on the next spots she wanted to hit, but I couldn't take my eyes off the posters. I imagined what four years at Saxon Valley might look like: how many places I'd see my name, my face, the *idea* of me. How could I possibly handle that?

Focus on what's in front of you, I reminded myself. I took a deep breath, counted to three, and joined Zoe down the hall.

Except for Robin and Leah, who nearly got caught when a German teacher took a bathroom break, it all went off without a hitch.

We booked it at the end of first period before Ryland could start asking questions and waded out in the chaos. The school was *buzzing*. People crowded around the posters, gawked at them, took photos. I watched a pair of sophomore girls snap a selfie with *TRANS PEOPLE BELONG* in Jamie Navarro's messy handwriting behind them. Teachers poked their heads out of their rooms and looked at one another, unsure of what to do.

"Goddamn," Riley said, taking in the scene. "Not bad, Ferragamo."

When I checked into my second period study hall, the posters were still up. By the time the bell rang again, they were gone.

OPERATION FUCK EM ALL 666 ☺ ≈

Today 11:04 AM

GRACE: can't believe keller hasnt called me down yet lol

ZOE: Well, we know they have cameras. It's just a matter of time.

AHMED: Thought we would've had a hacker take down cameras or smthng

KAEDEN: Do you know any hackers??? Goofy ass

> **LEAH:** *omfg did you guys see lucy rabinowitz's IG post??*
> **ZOE:** *No?*
> **LEAH:** [embedded post]
>
> @luceeeecakezzzz: This is what Pageland High thinks about queer students. Please share.

The first time I saw the video, I knew the school was screwed.

Lucy, our eager freshman co-conspirator, had filmed the janitor, Mr. Fletcher, tearing down posters and chucking them in a garbage can. *GIRLS BELONG ON THE FIELD?* In the can. *LET GRACE KICK?* In the can. *TRANS EQUALITY NOW?* In the can.

Honestly, my first thought was: *poor Mr. Fletcher, he's just doing his job.* My second: *oh my god, this thing already has hundreds of likes.*

By lunch, it was up to eight thousand. I wasn't sure how it happened—a local reporter, maybe, tipped off by a student—but it left Pageland circles early and found its way to the capital-*i* Internet-at-large. Even if (*when*, more likely) Lucy was forced to delete it, that video was never getting scrubbed from the internet, and everyone knew it.

It wasn't *just* the video, though. Ahmed, whose recruiting status gave him a sizable following, posted a photo of him holding up my away jersey in front of a wall of posters. Captioned: *I'll always ride for my day ones. #LetGracePlay.* It garnered hundreds of comments, and it took all of my willpower not to check them.

"Earth to Grace," Riley said, snapping her fingers. "You remember to pack lunch?"

I set my phone down, checked my backpack, and sighed. "'Course not."

"I brought two sandwiches," Dray said, holding up a brown paper bag. "You like peanut butter and banana?"

I accepted one happily and dug in. "*Mmmph*. You saved my life, dude."

Barely anyone at the table blinked an eye when Dray sat down with us, immediately settling into a conversation with Tab about some show they were both watching. He fit in well. I imagined a world where Prez could hang with us too, comfortable enough to put down the Golden Boy mask. I wondered when—*if*—that could ever happen.

The sandwich was a welcome distraction, but I couldn't relax, not entirely. Any minute now, I'd be called down to the office and suspended, expelled, sent to prison, I dunno. I had no idea what punishment the Pageland High code of conduct prescribed for Poster Criminals.

"You guys all set for tonight?" I asked the theater kids, trying to clear my head.

"I think we'll be fine," Tab said, fiddling with her newest pentagram necklace. "Our sets are a little sad, but we're saving the budget for *Legally Blonde* in the spring. Plus, there's only so much you can do for *A Midsummer Night's Dream*."

"Nah, come on," Dray said, playfully nudging her. "You guys'll ball out. We'll be there, you know, getting loud as hell for the curtain call."

"Does that one have crossdressing?" I asked, since that was one of the only things I knew about Shakespeare plays that don't end with everyone getting murdered.

"Not unless you count the play put on by the mechanicals," Tarot Card Robin replied. I nodded, pretending like that meant anything to me. "But it's high school Shakespeare, so half the roles are gender-bent. I mean, I'm playing Quince and Egeus."

"I'm Puck," Tab preened. "I was put on this planet to play that gay little fairy."

Riley heaved a sigh, shook her head. "I don't even have to roast you. You did it for me."

"Whatever, Ri. We all know you're *actually* nice." She pointed at me. "Protest is a go, by the way. Darlington told us she'll look the other way."

"Damn," I said, my chest buzzing. I'd never even *met* her. "She sounds badass."

"If you think a drama teacher is gonna turn down the chance to give the athletic department a black eye," Houseplant Jade said, "you don't know drama teachers."

I took another bite of my sandwich and tried to think positively. Odds were, by the start of the show, any chance I had of playing tomorrow would be gone. But a black eye didn't sound so bad.

"Let us take the lead," Dray said. "Just like we did back in the diner."

That rainy morning at Thessaloniki felt like a million years ago, but here we were again, about to plead for my reinstatement. I tugged my denim jacket tight around me, tried to keep the wind out. The weather had turned since our planning session out on the tennis courts yesterday; the clouds had come, the temperature plunging under forty. There was a chance it would snow in Brockport by kickoff tomorrow.

I tried not to think about it like I'd be there.

"How long?" I asked.

"A few minutes, maybe," he said. "Just chill in your locker room, 'kay? I'll come get you."

The wait was *agonizing*, giving me plenty of time to replay today's events in my head a million times. I distracted myself by taking one last look in the mirror. My makeup could use a little touching up, sure, but there was Grace Woodhouse, cheap-ass red lipstick and all. Something like the real me, I figured. The guys could take it or leave it.

Bang bang bang. "Ready?" Dray called.

The girl in the mirror looked determined, angry, ready for a fight. "Ready."

Thirty-eight

The chatter in the locker room died when I walked in.

"The fuck is he doing here?" McReynolds asked from the far corner, the Wannabe Rednecks around him echoing the sentiment.

"Players-only meeting," Dray said, crossing his arms. "Watch it, Mack."

"Woodhouse isn't on the team anymore," Ash Katsaros said, and the knife he'd stuck in my back in September dug in deeper. It was hard to look at that little twerp and remember I'd ever considered him a friend. "Can't fight his own battles, not even now. He's gotta hide behind 'our'"–he added air quotes–"captains."

"Shut the *fuck* up, man," Prez snapped. The team mumbled in agreement. "You never even see the field, bro."

"We don't want him here," McReynolds said, "and you don't get to overrule us just 'cause you're captains."

"We *do*, actually," Ahmed said, an edge to his voice. "We're here to talk about how we're gonna fight this garbage."

"Come on," McReynolds said, sneering at me. "This is *exactly* what Woodhouse wanted. A chance to run away and call himself the victim. His name on posters, his face all over the internet. He didn't even have to *earn* any of it. Congrats on your participation trophy, *Jordan*."

The room was silent for a few seconds, so quiet I swore no one breathed. Guys looked down, looked away, pretended this wasn't happening. I read Dray's eyes: *We're here if you need us.*

Finally, I found my voice. "Every *fucking* day since I've rejoined this team, *you* have singled me out. *You* go out of your way to make everyone look at me. Why would I want that? I just wanna be left alone." I took a few steps towards him as the room murmured. "*You* put that spotlight on me, dumbass! *You're* the one who makes a scene every time, because you're a little dick coward who can't stand the thought of someone like me playing the same sport you do!"

The locker room exhaled in a wave of *oh shit*s, nervous laughter, and a handful of *sheeeesh*es. McReynolds tried to play it cool, pretending like I hadn't just stuffed him in a garbage can. "Whatever helps you sleep at night, *bro*."

Finally, the door to Rutkowski's office opened.

I expected to see Rut's Polish Hulk face, the one he pulled out whenever he wanted to scream his way out of a problem. Instead, he strolled out into the locker room and put his hands on his hips. "Woodhouse," he said, his tone unusually placid. "If you wanna clean out your locker, I can let you in some other time."

The rest of the coaches started filing into the room too, and I found Rhoads: expressionless, but with that same glint in his eye I'd seen at Thessaloniki. I glanced at Ahmed. *Now or never.*

"We want Grace to play, Coach," he said. "She has the right to help us finish what we started."

Most of the boys nodded and voiced their agreement in *yessir*s, a few of them clapping. I swallowed a lump in my throat. So far, so good.

I wouldn't say Rut looked *surprised*; he'd seen the posters, he saw Kaeden and Dray wearing my jersey, and he must've heard about Ahmed's Instagram post. He seemed... maybe not *amused*, but something like it.

"*We* don't want anything," McReynolds said, the rest of his punks nodding along. "They don't speak for all of us."

"You know *damn* well that there are more of us who want Grace here than not," Prez said, rolling his wheelchair to the center of the room next to me. "You know how badly I wish I could be out there tomorrow? It's driving me *crazy*, Coach. And you're gonna take this from her for speaking her mind? You gotta let her play."

The room *roared*, and I had to blink to stop myself from crying. I gave Prez a look I hoped conveyed *thank you* and about a million other things. He squeezed my arm and smiled in reply.

"If there's one thing I can appreciate," Rut said over the din, "it's standing up for your teammates. We always talk about football being family, the brotherhood"—I rolled my eyes—"in this room. And it's real. But the fact of the matter is, Woodhouse broke a team rule. If you want me to review your suspension next week, we could have a conversation about that. Now isn't the time."

"There's no guarantee we *get* a next week, Rutty," Dray said, his arms crossed.

"Should've thought about that before playing pronouns on some woke podcast."

I wasn't even sure who said that—one of the Wannabe Rednecks, naturally—and I didn't bother figuring it out, since Scotty was already laying into him. "Coach," I said, not flinching from his eye contact, "let me finish this."

He sighed. "Next week, I said. Now, please, let us—"

"No." Behind me, a boy with a scratchy voice rose to his feet. "Woodhouse plays tomorrow, or I'm done."

"C'mon, Trucky," Ash scoffed. "Be real."

Truck's fists were balled, the glare he fixed on Rutkowski deadly serious. "Woodhouse plays tomorrow," he repeated, "or I'm done. I'll clean out my locker right now."

Truck was *not* one to make idle threats, and the look on Rut's face confirmed he knew it. "Nguyen, let's—"

Tobe Okoro rose to his feet next. "No Grace? I'm gone."

I flashed him a quick *thank you* sign. He replied with a spirited *bullshit*, and I couldn't keep a burst of laughter from escaping my chest.

From there, it was off to the races. Scotty. Tino Russo. A pair of quiet junior linemen who'd never said a word to me. After hemming and hawing, Calvin Reagor stood up. "Free speech, Coach," he said. "I'm out."

Within thirty seconds, another eight players had risen to their feet. "You can count me out too," Dray said. "That's my dawg."

"Ditto for me," Kaeden added.

Ahmed crossed his arms. "Do I even have to say it, Coach? You caught me hanging the posters. You know where I stand on this."

"Fuckin' pathetic," McReynolds whined. "They're *bluffing*, Coach. You know it."

Rut sighed, glanced back at his assistants, then crossed his arms. "No player," he said, "is eligible to suit up if they miss the last practice before gameday. That's New York State rules."

"I–"

"So"–he kept his expression neutral, though that amused smirk fought its way back out–"you'd better get changed in a hurry. Get a move on."

It took me a second to process his words, and by then Ahmed had enveloped me in a bear hug. Around me, a million hands pounded on my back, a million voices yelled in excitement. Finally, Dray's voice cut through the noise: "Alright, alright! Let's get our asses moving! We got walkthrough! Focus on Bellarmine!"

Even as the sea receded back around me, I couldn't keep the grin off my face. The controlled chaos of the locker room, fifty people who (mostly) worked in sync–I hadn't realized how much I'd missed it. How much I *would* miss it next year if I didn't go through with Saxon Valley's offer. But I could practically hear Rhoads's advice: *Focus on what's in front of you.* I stood on my tiptoes and caught a glimpse of him on the edge of the crowd, sly smile on his face.

When I approached him, he tapped his cane on the ground twice. "Knew you could handle this one yourself, kid. Now, go get ready."

Thirty-nine

After practice, I slipped back into the locker room. Most of the team had already dipped; the few stragglers that remained gave me Boy Nods, which I dutifully returned. The guy I was after sat in the corner, bobbing his head to music with his eyes closed.

Truck didn't even notice I was there until I sat down next to him. He finally took out his earbuds, the music so loud that I could hear the song with perfect clarity: "Renegade" by Styx. Tommy Shaw was belting out the bridge.

"*Renegade*." Why was that familiar?

I snapped my fingers in recognition. "You were listening to that the other day, right? After practice. I heard it out of your truck's speakers."

He shrugged. "Yeah."

"You a big Styx fan?"

"Not particularly. Song's alright, though."

"Oh." I wasn't sure what to say to that. "I guess I figured, since—"

"I listen to one song at a time," he explained. Even now, he nodded along to the chorus. "Right now, it's 'Renegade.' Next week it'll be something else."

It took a second for that to sink in. "Wait. You mean you just ... loop the same song? And that's all you listen to?"

"Uh-huh."

"For . . . how long?"

"Never longer than a week, usually."

I stared at him, completely unable to read his face. "Are you messing with me?"

He paused the song on his phone, rolled the cord to his earbuds around his finger into a tight coil and slipped them into his pocket. "Nope. Lets me appreciate every part of a song before I move on to the next."

Truck bent down to lace up his boots, humming the chorus while he did so. He didn't seem to be in a hurry to get me out of his hair or ask why I was depriving him of "Renegade" time, which I appreciated. It'd always been easy to just *exist* around Truck. It was why I used to like hanging out with him.

"So," I said, clearing my throat, "were you really gonna quit if I was suspended?"

He nodded. "Yup."

"It wasn't just a threat?"

"Nope."

"Why?"

"You're my teammate," he mumbled, tying a tight bow on his last boot. He slung his old camo backpack over his shoulder and stood up. "It's not deep."

"Everyone else in this room is my teammate too," I said, "but I don't know if any of them would've stood up if you hadn't."

He shrugged. "Captains would've said something no matter what."

"But–"

"It's not deep," he said again. He held out his hand. "Really."

I took his hand and let him help me up, giving him a friendly cuff on the shoulder. "Thanks, dude." Then, impulsively, I added: "A few of us are going to the play tonight. Wanna come?"

He thought about that, digging his earbuds back out of his pocket. "I don't think I'd like it. But thanks anyway."

Truck ducked out of the locker room without another word, his head bobbing along to music only he could hear.

BALLBAGS 4 CHRIST (SCOTTY'S VERSION) 🩲🙏💩

Today 6:51 PM

DRAY: I can't believe yall really not coming smfh

I'm telling you there's some cool ass kids who do theater

KAEDEN: I gotta watch KJ or I'd be there

AHMED: Niece got a dance thingy

SCOTTY: robin told me not to bother bc im "uncultured" and wouldn't get it but imma pull up at the sunday show

might fuck around and bring her flowers show her i'm nice with it idk

GRACE: consult me before you buy a bouquet please

and since when do you and robin talk???

SCOTTY: 😊😊😊

GRACE: straight mullet4mullet is CRAZY

CALVIN: cmon bro that's my cousin!!!!

SCOTTY: your cousin knows a gentleman when she sees one, reags

TOBE: yo D that theater club president CLEARLY wanna get with you btw

DRAY: Don't worry, I let him off easy

GRACE: lolllll

"So, good night unto you all," Tab-as-Puck said, bowing dramatically. She cast her hand out to the crowd, faux-moonlight glittering off her makeup. "Give me your hands, if we be friends, and Robin shall restore amends."

The lights dimmed, the curtain closed, and the audience gave a spirited round of applause. When the curtain came back up and the cast—a hodgepodge of fairies, toga-wearing nobles, and, for some reason, a lion (I lost the plot, don't ask me)—bowed one at a time, I stood with the crowd and whistled.

"Told you it'd be fun," Dray said, elbowing his boyfriend playfully. I couldn't hear Prez's reply over the noise, but I *did* see a smile spread across Dray's face.

"Wait," Riley said, tapping my shoulder. On stage, Houseplant Jade-as-Helena bowed. "I thought they made a banner, too!"

"I told Tab to call it off," I explained, self-consciously crossing my arms. I'd already been the center of *way* too much attention today. "We already won, y'know. Besides, it's *their* big day, not mine."

Riley glanced over my shoulder and grinned. "You sure about that?"

I whipped around to find that Dray had vanished from his place next to me, leaving behind a sheepish Prez. "Sorry, Grace," he said, his voice barely audible over another round of applause, but the smile on his face betrayed him.

By the time I spotted Dray near the stage, it was far, *far* too late. Tab was the last actor to bow, and while the crowd was still roaring, my no-good traitorous friend tossed her a bundle of white fabric. She caught it, her grin visible even from our spot at the back of the auditorium, and held it up triumphantly: my away jersey, the green number forty-seven gleaming under the stagelights.

We reconnected with Dray once we migrated out into the hallway with the rest of the mob, crowding around the door the actors would eventually emerge from. By the time I finished detailing every single way he was the worst friend of all time, the first few actors were trickling out into the crowd, all bouquets and triumphant laughs and sweaty hugs. The *best* kind of feelingsball.

"This rocks," Prez said, and I couldn't help but agree with him. It reminded me of the football locker room after a big win: joyous, exhausted, relieved. The same scene, really, but with the saturation cranked up.

"You a theater appreciator now?" Dray asked, cocking an eyebrow.

Based on recent revelations, I figured there was a *lot* I didn't know about Zach Przezdziecki. It was still so strange to see him uncomfortable, not at ease in a social setting. He shifted his weight on his crutches. "Do you ever wish you got into"—he waved his arm at the scene around us—"*this* instead of sports? I feel like it's . . . *easier* to be like, you know, *us* over here."

Dray shrugged. "I dunno, maybe. But being a jock doesn't make you any less—" He mouthed the word *gay*. "I like you exactly the way you are, 'kay? Don't stress it, QB1."

The look Prez gave him was so head-over-heels it should've been illegal. Like, so earth-shatteringly gay I had to *look away*. "*Please* get a room."

While Dray and Riley laughed and Prez blushed like a schoolgirl, Tab finally emerged from the dressing room, still decked out in green tulle and pointy latex ears. She immediately flew over to her family, where her little brothers swallowed her in a group hug. Tears. Laughter. Then she was standing in front of us, smiling wide, clutching her roses.

"Was that so bad, Ri?"

"Don't push it, Rolón."

After the two girls finished hugging, Tab enveloped me next. "How fucking dare you!" I cried as she crushed my ribs. The plastic leaves woven into her hair scratched my cheek. "You didn't have to do anything for me!"

"Bitch, I *wanted* to!" she cried, finally releasing me from her death grip. I'd become accustomed to seeing her in all black, but I had to admit, she made an excellent forest sprite. "It *is* nice to see you cheering me on for a change, though."

"Next time," I promised, "I'll pass out foam fingers."

Prez politely declined a hug—crutches didn't exactly make it easy—but Dray accepted one. "Now I *gotta* go out for the musical," he said, laughing. "Y'all have too much fun."

"You were great," Prez said shyly. "I mean, I don't know if I really followed the plot, but you were great."

"Thank you," Tab said with a puckish wink and curtsy. "By the way: theater afterparty. Thessaloniki. You're all invited, and you haven't *lived* until you've gotten pancakes at midnight with the theater kids."

I told her I appreciated it and she waved goodbye, floating off to greet more of her adoring fans. "You guys wanna go?"

Prez looked at Dray, expectantly. He sighed. "I mean, I *want* to. But—"

"Bellarmine."

Dray nodded. "Bellarmine."

I had to remind myself that if everything went well, we'd be right back home celebrating like this tomorrow night. "I can't believe we have a *game* at the end of this long-ass week."

"Neither can I," Dray said. "That's what makes me nervous."

Forty

CRUNCH TABLE 😺

Today 3:41 PM

RILEY: Just hit the road lets gooooooooooo

Check this out Grace: Rolon is wearing a DRUIDS SHIRT

[attached image of Tab crossing her arms, looking very grumpy]

GRACE: AWWWWWWW

WE MADE A SPORTS FAN OUT OF YOUUUU 🏁🏁🏁

TAB: I hate you bitches so much

IMANI: hows the bus ride grace

GRACE: the boys are playing gay chicken in the back, so. morale is high

ROBIN: the ambient homoeroticism is ridiculous.

nate bowen is either the gayest straight man or the straightest gay man i've ever met. i need to figure out which. this is why i need him.

GRACE: scotty*

> **DAD**
>
> Today 4:01 PM
>
> **DAD:** I'm so proud of you Grace. Whatever happens tonight, just have fun out there.
>
> **GRACE:** Thanks pops 🖤
>
> **DAD:** I'm not that old yet. Jeez.

It didn't *really* hit me until we boarded the bus for Brockport.

I knew, rationally, that we could've been eliminated weeks ago. I knew more than anyone that you can't take any playoff game for granted, no matter how sure of a thing it seemed. But I needed to be back in Regionals—back against Bellarmine Jesuit—to realize that this could really be the last time I ever put on pads.

I drank in every last detail of the rest of the night: screaming along to "Dreams and Nightmares" on the bus ride, trudging our equipment across the parking lot, our little pregame rituals in the Brockport locker room: Truck jammed to "Renegade," Dray played *2048*, Scotty watched wrestling compilations. All the loose confidence of our bus ride was gone, last year's disappointment hanging heavy in the air.

Taking the field for stretches made my heart ache even harder. The bleachers full of Pageland parents and students in green who'd made the hour-plus trip to come and see us, clutching hot drinks and burrowing into their coats. Red-faced cheerleaders in green jackets warmed up on the sideline, band kids fussed with their instruments. On the other end of the field, Bellarmine Jesuit, in their white away jerseys with blood red trim, mirrored us. Two-Nine, the linebacker who distracted me on my missed kick last year, led his teammates through stretches with copious hollering and helmet-banging.

The first few jabs from the Centurions came our way when we broke into lines for dynamic stretches, setting up near midfield. "Aww, shit! It's the Pageland Attack Helicopters!"

"Do y'all have to say your pronouns in the huddle?"

"Nineteen! You learn how to use a condom yet?"

"Do it for Allah, Nassar!"

"Keep that energy, boys!" Ahmed called back, cracking his knuckles. "Keep it *all* night long!"

"Hey, Jordan!" called Two-Nine. "Get a haircut, you fucking freak!"

I stuffed my clenched fists into my handwarmer, refusing to let them get to me. My guys fought for me to be here; I couldn't let myself be the reason we went home this year. That, at least, was in my hands.

Just before the coin toss, we circled up around Dray, whose energy was infectious. "I know y'all remember how much that shit hurt last year," he said, fire in his eyes. "Hold that feeling in your chest all night long, because you *know* you're better than them. We've spent a year getting stronger, getting *tougher*. You know why they're talking? They're *scared*. They know we line up and beat every team across from us. We don't talk! We let our play talk for us!"

"Yes*sir*!" Ahmed cried, and the whole team echoed him.

"We're gonna knock their dicks in the dirt from snap to whistle! Offense, defense, special teams—we execute! Make that man across from you fear God tonight!" He raised his fist, showing off his new pink-white-and-blue wristband, and I was ready to run through a brick wall. "*Druids* on three! One-two-three—"

"DRUIDS!"

I rode that wave of energy clear through the coin toss, barely noticing that we'd lost it and Bellarmine elected to receive. Scotty rounded up kickoff team and banged his helmet against mine. "Let's set the tone early, kickoff!" Rut called. "All phases!"

When we set foot on the field, both crowds exploded. *"Number forty-seven, Grace Woodhouse, on for the kickoff. Grace Woodhouse, number forty-seven."*

Our crowd was louder, thank god. I looked in their direction while kickoff team got set and saw the student section on its feet, screaming and stomping on the metal bleachers. I saw *#47* signs and, for just a moment: Riley, Tab, and the rest of Pageland's gays, all of them losing their minds.

Man, I needed that. I took a deep breath, set the ball on the tee, and counted out my steps: nine back, four to the left. I raised my right hand, waited for the referee to blow his whistle, and unloaded.

The ball felt like a rock against my foot—it always did in the cold—but it just kept flying. The Bellarmine returner didn't even field it; it landed in the end zone and bounced out the back for a touchback.

"She's an assassin!" Scotty laughed like a maniac and hammered on my shoulder pads. "All she does is hit nukes!"

I passed Two-Nine while each of us jogged back to our respective sideline, and I couldn't help myself. "How you feeling, big man?" I cried. "You ready for four quarters of that?"

A few of the boys shepherded me off the field, laughing while they did it. "No taunting penalties from you," Kaeden chided me. "Calm your ass down."

Even once I settled into position on the sideline, I couldn't help but bounce on my toes. *I belonged here.* I was ready.

After a quick three-and-out from the Centurions, our offense took over. Dray and Scotty methodically marched us deep into Centurion territory, with Ahmed and Truck mauling the right side of Bellarmine's front. Unfortunately, Two-Nine rallied Bellarmine's defense once we entered the red zone and wrestled us to a standstill. After Dray lofted a wobbly pass to Calvin Reagor that fell incomplete on third down, it left us with a fourth and six at the fourteen-yard line. *My turn.*

The cheering was less enthusiastic for my second voyage onto the field, but still, I felt that energetic buzz in my chest. The wind was at my back, Brockport's field turf was perfect for kicking, and a thirty-one-yarder was more than doable. "Field goal," I called in the huddle. "Let's make this op perfect, boys."

The Pageland crowd hushed as we lined up, meaning that I could hear all the jeers coming from the Bellarmine bleachers. *Faggot.* As

Truck and Dray got set, all I heard was fans pounding on the bleachers, the heckles and slurs that jumbled together and crushed me in an avalanche of noise. *Tranny.* I closed my eyes, counted off my steps, and waited. *You're dead.*

I opened them, and there was Two-Nine thrashing his arms around like he was in a mosh pit. Just like he had last year. *Faggot.* I felt dizzy. *Groomer.* I needed to count to three. *Kill yourself.* I needed to get off the field.

Dray called for the snap.

It was a slow-motion car crash. My plant foot was too far forward, my hips were a mess, and my follow-through was awkward. I watched helplessly as the ball sailed wide right of the goalposts by a few feet. There wasn't a defensive penalty, a timeout, anything that could bail me out.

All I could do was watch the refs wave their arms and hear the announcer call: "*The kick is no good.*" Bellarmine's bleachers roared, their sideline went nuts. Two-Nine ran over to his head coach, flexing the whole way, and the crowd got even *louder.*

A bunch of the guys got in my ear, probably telling me to shake it off, that it was no big deal. I didn't hear a word they said. Instead, I jogged to the sideline alone with my head down and brushed past a glowering Coach Rut.

"Useless piece of shit," McReynolds grumbled, throwing me a shoulder on his way to join the defense. Couldn't even argue with him.

What a catastrophic fucking disaster I was.

I settled on the end of the bench opposite Rhoads and ripped my helmet off, resisting the urge to throw it. I grabbed a bottle and shot a jet of water into my hair, letting the cold liquid sear its way down my back. Grace Fraudhouse, that's who I was. Gripping my facemask white-knuckle hard, I berated myself. *What the hell is wrong with you? Which ancient football spirit did you piss off? Why do you fail every time it matters?*

It was still the first quarter, too. I had a *lot* of time to make more mistakes. Maybe it'd be best if I walked off the field now; the team would be better off without me. Once I was off the field, I could just keep going. I could cross the Canadian border and live with the beavers in solitude. Honestly, I didn't hate that plan.

There was a hand on my shoulder. "What do you think I'm gonna tell you?"

I heaved a sigh. "I'm *really* not in the mood for games right now, Coach."

"Bad news," Rhoads said, "considering you and your teammates are playing one."

"Good one, Rhoady. Clever."

"*I* thought it was a good one." He eased onto the bench next to me and put his left arm around my shoulders, leaning in close to speak. "I'll spare you the guessing game, Grace. I think you're goddamn brave. Braver than any kid should have to be. There's a whole sideline—a whole *bleacher*—full of gutless sumbitches over there. And I think you're gonna prove them wrong."

I dug my heels into the turf, literally and figuratively. "I'm gonna do that by choking?"

"It happens! You ain't gonna wanna hear that right now, but it *happens*. I've coached a lot of ball, now, and I can safely say that out of all the kickers I've been around, you're the one that's hardest on yourself when you miss."

I scoffed. "That supposed to make me feel better?"

"You're also the best, and it's not close," he said. I looked down at my cleats. "But you're only human, Grace. So here's what I want you to do: *breathe*. Have a little goddamn fun. Play some *feelingsball*, as you kids so eloquently put it. There's joy in this game, and I know you know how to find it." He rose to his feet, patting my shoulder pad on the way up. "And: head up, okay? Don't give 'em what they want."

As he hobbled off in the direction of Coach Rut, I counted to three. I thought about Two-Nine, that sideline, those fans on the other side of the field. I thought about the words I heard them scream, the individual voices I could pick out from the crushing sound. I thought about all those idiots on the internet. I pulled my helmet back on.

Once I was back on my feet, I found Dray nearby hunched over the arm of Prez's wheelchair, peering at a whiteboard in his boyfriend's lap. "They walked that strong safety down to the line that entire first drive," Prez said, his marker squeaking as he drew. "I'm telling you, power pop pass is gonna be *there* for you."

"Bet. I'll get in Rut's ear about it." Dray glanced up to see me approach, and his expression went soft. "You good, Grace?"

"Working on it," I said shakily. "Your hold was good, I just—"

He grabbed the side of my helmet and brought us facemask-to-facemask. "It's over, okay? You're a star. Rest of the night, you'll shine."

"Goddamn right," Prez said, reaching up to pat my arm. In his Pageland baseball cap and windbreaker, he looked like the coach I was sure he'd be one day. "We're with you all the way."

I told them they were cornballs, gave each of them one-armed hugs, then surveyed the sideline. I eventually found big number seventy-nine at the very end, alone, intently watching our defense line up on second down.

"The snap was great, Trucky," I said. "That was all me."

"Could've been better," the big guy muttered.

"No," I insisted. "Keep doing exactly what you're doing. That's on me, okay? I'm sorry for letting you down."

Truck hesitated, then shook his head. "You didn't let me down," he said. "You'll get 'em next time."

I settled next to him and enjoyed the easy silence.

Forty-one

The good news: after the defense forced another punt, the offense marched right back down the field. Dray proved Prez right by tossing a pop pass to Tobe Okoro for a touchdown in the opening minutes of the second quarter, and the Druids were finally on the board.

The bad news: during that drive, the wintry mix arrived.

Playing in snow had its downsides: footing was a mess, the game slowed down if it accumulated, and the kicking game became a logistical nightmare. Rain presented a different set of issues: the wetter the ball, the harder it is to catch it, to carry it without fumbling.

So, naturally, a little of both rolled off Lake Ontario.

The first few drops *plink*ed against my helmet around the time the offense crossed midfield and picked up steam as they drove. By the time Tobe (somehow) brought in the slick ball for a touchdown, it was coming down in earnest: a hellish combination of freezing rain and wet snow, melting on impact and forming treacherous puddles of slush everywhere. It soaked you to the bone and froze you for good measure.

"Hoo boy, this is some *football weather*!" Tino Russo hollered, jumping up and down to keep his blood moving on the sideline. "This is what it's all about!"

I was given all of a second to contemplate how I'd kick the extra point in these conditions before I heard Rut bellow "Two! Two!" as he held up two fingers. *Great.*

"It's probably just the sleet," a nearby Kaeden assured me. "I'd go for two with how nasty it is."

I tried to believe him as I watched Dray toss the ball to Calvin Reagor on a jet touch pass, the receiver following Ahmed into the end zone for an easy two-point conversion. I was relieved we made it, but watching Rut jump up and down in excitement made my stomach sink. Of *course* he trusted his offense more than he trusted me. Who could blame him?

It was still my job to trot out for the kickoff, though, whether Rut liked it or not. When my name was announced this time, Bellarmine's bleachers felt twice as loud as they had before. No big deal: I just had to kick on a wet surface while Bellarmine fans were setting a new record for the most transphobic slurs ever screamed during a single football game. Piece of cake.

Still, I booted the ball about as well as I could've hoped for in the slick conditions. It sailed to the right, and the returner, a tiny dude wearing thirteen, fielded it cleanly around his ten-yard line. I watched it happen in slow motion: Scotty, the anchor of our kickoff coverage unit, slipped and tumbled to the turf on the charge downfield. He accidentally collected another Druid on the way down, opening a massive hole in our coverage *directly* in front of Thirteen.

Shit.

My job on kickoffs was (usually) easy: I kicked the thing, hung back, and watched my teammates do the hard job of chasing down the returner. But all it took was Scotty hitting the deck to make this tackle my responsibility.

As Thirteen charged through the gap and sprinted up Pageland's sideline, I took a conservative pursuit angle, aiming to hit him around midfield. My heart pounded in my chest. I tried to reach back to freshman year, back when I'd actually paid attention in tackling drills, trying to remember the best way to take this guy down.

I let my instincts take over instead.

I couldn't tell you exactly what I did or how I did it, but I remembered the basics: *stay low, wrap up, keep your legs moving.* My shoulder slammed into his chest and I drove him *hard* into the turf, which hit us like a freezing wet sledgehammer. Pads crunched. Whistles were blown. The crowd *lit up.* A sea of hands—coaches and players—helped me to my feet, everyone losing their goddamn minds.

Before I turned to any of them, though, I extended my hand to Thirteen. I'd never done this before, but I knew the etiquette from watching my teammates do it a thousand times. He looked up at me, frozen. I panicked, worried I'd hurt him or something, until I realized he was *actually* in his feelings about getting drilled by the pink-hair-and-pronouns kicker. Like, National Feelingsball League MVP–caliber feelings.

Finally, he grabbed my hand and let me pull him to his feet. He nodded, mumbled "good hit," and jogged back to his sideline.

Then I was swallowed by daps, helmet taps, chest bumps, and *hell yeah*s. "You sent that man to God, four-seven!"

"Gave 'em the fuckin' lumber!"

Kaeden gave me a whole-ass hug and then sprinted onto the field with the defense, bouncing with excitement. "Don't let the damn *kicker* have the biggest hit tonight, defense! C'mon!"

After a few minutes, I managed to break free of the melee thanks to McReynolds (ugh) making a play that got everyone's attention. I made my way to the bench in search of the wily old man himself. "Feel any better?" Rhoads asked. The hood of his jacket, pulled low enough to keep out the rain and snow, kept me from seeing his eyes; his grin, however, was wide.

"A little," I admitted. "Never done that before."

"Not so bad, right?"

I found myself nodding. "Yeah. Not so bad."

Wintry mix was the MVP of the second half, hands-down.

The offenses traded drives that went nowhere in the third quarter, with each quarterback putting the ball on the ground at least once.

When Scotty finally scampered for our first big play of the half, he slipped in a slushy puddle, twisted his ankle, and had to be pulled from the game for a few drives. Every step I took on the sideline came with that queasy *squish* of my socks in my cleats, the one that made me want to scream.

The third quarter became the fourth, and I started to believe I'd never see the field again. "Thank god we put together that drive earlier," I said to Rhoads, pacing the sideline for the millionth time. "Nobody's sniffing the end zone again tonight."

"Don't jinx it, now," Rhoads said jokingly.

With a little over five minutes left in the game, the precipitation finally died. I *totally* jinxed it.

Dray and Scotty plodded their way down the field one last time, actually making progress for a change. The longer they held the ball, the better; the clock melted away as Scotty picked up six yards on counter, Dray got four on QB iso. Scoring here would put the game away for good, and it looked like we might do it.

It was all going brilliantly until we entered the red zone, anyway. Two-Nine, for all his obnoxious dancing and shit-talking, flew all over the field. With less than a minute to go, the Centurions dug in and made a few plays, forcing us into a second and long. As it became clear the offense would stall out again, I started drifting towards Rutkowski on the sideline. Just as I feared, Scotty was halted yet again, leaving us at fourth and thirteen. We were stranded at the twenty-two yard line.

"Tell me right now why I shouldn't keep my offense on the field," Rut said plainly, not even particularly red or mad.

Good question, but I had a good answer too. "It's not raining anymore, the offense hasn't been able to finish all game, and you know I can put it away right now."

He glared at me for another few seconds—really piercing my soul with those beady eyes of his—before calling for the field goal unit.

From the second I stepped on the field, I knew things were different. I was cool and confident in the huddle; cool and confident while I counted out three steps back, two steps left.

One.

Two-Nine was there, and he was dancing, but I didn't give a shit. I'd waited years to hit or get hit on a football field, and the fear of it—building it up in my head—had been worse than anything else.

Two.

That night, I'd decleated somebody, and it was *fine*. My circumstances were a little unique, sure, but I was a football player. I could take it.

Three.

When the ball left my foot, I chose to stare Two-Nine down rather than watch it split the uprights.

The score: Pageland 11, Bellarmine Jesuit 0. We'd done it.

With thirty-two seconds left, there was still one last kickoff to get through before we could go home.

Rhoads and Rut agreed that a squib—a short kick designed to keep the ball out of the returner's hands—was our best bet given the situation. Bellarmine needed a miracle to score once, let alone twice, but we knew Thirteen could fly. I'd never been great at squibbing even when the field *wasn't* wet, but I gave it my best shot.

The ball popped off my foot weakly, just as intended, and dribbled through a gap in the right side of Bellarmine's return formation. I watched as they scrambled to react, trying to figure out whether they should scoop it up or just fall on it, and—

The *crunch* of pads was deafening in my ears. I blinked, and I was on my back. I couldn't breathe. All I could hear was my heartbeat. All I could see was the night sky, the lights above the field, and the last few snowflakes from the storm lazily making their way to the ground.

Finally: distant whistles, boys screaming. I tried to claw my way into a sitting position, but my arms gave out; I crumpled back to the turf just in time to see Two-Nine, who'd been standing over me, take a monstrous shot in the back from Scotty Bowen.

I blinked, and Scotty was on top of Two-Nine, ripping his helmet off, getting a good shot in on his jaw. I blinked, and a Centurion was trying to pull Scotty off Two-Nine, but Tobe ripped him away, wrestling him to the ground with a suplex.

I blinked, and a hand was dragging me away from a full-blown brawl. "Trainers!" Truck screamed, his voice sounding far away. "Trainers, now!"

I blinked, and I was in the medical tent. A woman asked if I could tell her what the score of the game had been. Dad was there, hat in his hands, looking terrified.

I blinked, and I was in the hospital. That's when I started feeling the pain.

ARTICLE EXCERPT. Published by Southtown Gazette, November 16. Syndicated in The Buffalo News. Written by Dale Weingarten.

Pageland advances to State Semifinals amidst controversy in win over Bellarmine Jesuit

... The show was ultimately stolen, however, by an incident in the final minute of the game. Bellarmine linebacker Robert McKinnon, a senior, lowered his shoulder into Pageland kicker Grace Woodhouse on the final play of the game. While the referees flagged McKinnon for unnecessary roughness, the bench-clearing brawl that ensued spilled out of control.

"Frankly, it's bush league," said Pageland Coach Dave Rutkowski. "It was clearly a cheap shot. We'll accept whatever discipline is passed down, but, ultimately, you have to protect your own."

Woodhouse, currently being evaluated for a concussion, garnered public attention this week for speaking on behalf of transgender rights on the *Out of Sounds* sports podcast. Several of her teammates felt that she was targeted.

"It's obvious to us that [McKinnon] went after her," said Pageland safety Kaeden Park-Campbell Sr., who recovered a key fumble in the fourth quarter. "It doesn't take a rocket scientist to figure out why. And that didn't sit right with us." ...

PRESS RELEASE. From the New York State Public High School Athletic Association (NYSPHSAA), November 17.

For their part in the November 15th incident, the following Pageland High School students are suspended indefinitely from athletic competition:

    Bowen, Nate
    Fulton, Aundray
    Kirkland, DeSean
    Nassar, Ahmed
    Nguyen, Conner
    Okoro, Tobechukwu
    Park-Campbell Sr., Kaeden
    Reagor, Calvin
    Russo, Valentino

Forty-two

My memory of it all was pretty fucked, naturally.

The first time a nurse came into my room to see how I was doing, I insisted I was fine and told him I could go home. The nurse glanced at my dad. "That's what you said fifteen minutes ago," he said, "the last time I checked up on you."

When they finally released me from the hospital a few hours later, they insisted on rolling me out to Dad's truck in a wheelchair, which I adored. "In my Prez era," I said to myself, grinning. According to Dad, I said this no less than a dozen times.

The drive home is when my perception of linear time and reality started to stabilize, when I was capable of speaking to Dad without my head feeling like it might shatter into a million pieces. "We won, right?"

He pressed his lips into a line. "Yeah. You did. But don't worry about that now."

When we finally got home, I limped into bed, every sound and noise and light and sensation rattling my brain like the bars of a xylophone. I conked out immediately, but didn't stay asleep long.

The way you recover from a concussion is by doing nothing, it turns out. You can't read, you can't listen to music, you can't talk to people, you can't look at your phone, you can't play video games. Every possible way you can use your brain is strictly forbidden. Thoughts must be unthunk. The only approved activity is sleep.

When I *did* manage to sleep, it was in fitful stops and starts, brief moments of peace interrupted by misery. The sun poking in through my curtains hurt, the sound of the garbage truck rolling down our street hurt, using the bathroom hurt. All I could do was lie in the dark and stare at the inside of my eyelids.

I was bored. I was useless. I was *angry*.

It was Tuesday when I felt okay enough to shuffle out of my bedroom and down the stairs for the first time. Miniature lightning bolts of pain came with every step, but I persevered. It was midday—overcast, thankfully—and Dad was home, reading a book at the kitchen table.

"Hey, kiddo," he said, jumping to his feet. "How are you feeling?"

My eyes still weren't cooperating, so I had to squint at him. "Why aren't you at work?"

"Finally using some PTO. Sit down, I'll fix you something to eat."

I did as he instructed. Everything still felt fuzzy, but thinking thoughts was no longer agony. I ran my hands across the wood of our ancient kitchen table, a hand-me-down from my grandmother. I traced a long scratch in its surface with my pointer finger; I'd carved it with a fork at age six. Dad had been *furious*. I couldn't help but giggle at the memory.

A moment later, Dad set a plate of scrambled eggs in front of me, the *clank* of the dish stabbing my ears. "What's so funny?" he asked, sitting down across from me.

"Nothing," I said, shakily bringing a forkful of egg to my mouth. I spoke in whispers, the only thing I could tolerate. "So . . . concussion. A bad one?"

He sighed. "Not sure there's such a thing as a *good* one."

I asked him if it happened on that last kickoff, and he nodded. Two-Nine, it turned out, went berserk and blindsided me. The impact of his shoulder in my chest knocked the wind out of me, but the back of my head slamming into the turf is what did a number on my brain. The hard fall messed up my back, too, which explained the twinges of pain I felt when I moved my left shoulder, but the doctors had assured Dad it wasn't anything ibuprofen couldn't handle.

I inhaled the rest of my eggs, wiping down the plate with toast. I'd forced myself to eat when Dad brought up food yesterday—a sandwich and some water, because I wasn't sure I could stomach anything else—but today, I was starving. "Wait," I said, suddenly struck with a new memory. "There was a fight, right?"

"Yeah," he said, his tone measured. "A fight broke out."

"What happened?"

"I didn't pay much attention. I was a little distracted."

"By what?"

"By *you*," he said, chuckling. "I was hustling down to the field, kid. You gave everyone a heart attack."

"Oh."

He shifted in his chair uncomfortably and closed his eyes. He was preparing a Speech; I knew him too well. "Grace," he said, "you know I'm not really . . . big into talking about feelings."

I couldn't hold in my laughter, which was a big mistake. I cursed and clutched my forehead until the pain receded again. "Don't make me laugh, Dad."

"Sorry," he said, rubbing the back of his neck. "What I'm trying to say is: I've never really been . . . worried about you before. I mean, obviously, as a parent, you're always worried about your kids, but it never felt like you needed my protection. You've always been tough, able to take care of yourself. When you told me you were transgender, I thought, well, I know my kid's tough enough to handle it. She can take care of herself. I trust her. And you *are* tough, and I *still* trust you. I just . . ."

He sipped his mug, mulling the thought over. Something I appreciated about Dad: he wasn't afraid to take his time to say the right thing. I wished *that* particular trait had been passed down to me.

"I guess," he finally said, "I'm still coming to terms with...the ways you're vulnerable now. Being transgender, being a young woman. It first hit me when you didn't come to me about Saxon Valley right away. When you raise a boy, the whole 'rub some dirt on it' thing kinda becomes gospel. That's how my father raised me. But I should've been there for you more, done a better job." He rubbed at his eyes and sniffed. "It shouldn't have taken *this* to make me realize it."

I'd *never* seen my dad come this close to crying before; not after either of his parents died, not for anything. The sight of it made my heart hit the floor. "It's okay, Dad," I said, my words shaky. "Really."

"It's not," he insisted, "and I'm gonna try to be better. Okay?"

My animal brain took over from there: I collapsed into him in a hug and he held me there, in the kitchen, for a long time. I let myself cry, finally. There was *so much* he didn't know: what had happened at that party in Saxon Valley, or the stuff I'd heard from some of the boys. I wasn't sure when (or if) I'd ever be able to talk to him about it.

But knowing he'd be there to listen if I did? That felt nice.

CRUNCH TABLE 😺

Today 9:01 AM

GRACE: *okay i can really only look at my phone for like five minutes at a time without feeling like im gonna barf but hi im alive*

RILEY: *Yoooooooooooo*

She's risen after 3 days like the Lord Herself!

TAB: *It's been 4 days dumbass*

(ily Grace I'm glad to hear you're okay!)

IMANI: *say the word girl and riley and i will drive to rochester to beat that kids ass*

GRACE: *its okay. i hear he already got his ass beat bad enough*

> **ROBIN:** you need to update your homoerotic football friends. nathan has been apoplectic.
>
> **GRACE:** seeing you call scotty "nathan" makes my skin crawl. turning my phone off again

---

> ## BALLBAGS 4 CHRIST
> ## (SCOTTY'S VERSION) 🏈💩
>
> *Today 10:22 PM*
>
> **GRACE:** I Lived Bitch
>
> **DRAY:** AHHHHHHH SHE LIVED BITCH
>
> **SCOTTY:** woodhouse!!!!
>
> **AHMED:** MY QUEEN
>
> **TRUCK:** How are you doing?
>
> **GRACE:** shitty lol
>
> im so bored
>
> **DRAY:** Are you seeing ppl? We can come thru after school
>
> **GRACE:** wait dont you guys have practice
>
> **TOBE:** lol
>
> **AHMED:** Check the news, Grace
>
> **GRACE:** . . . are you FUCKING kidding me

"So that's it?" I asked, still not believing it. "It's over?"

Dray smiled weakly at me from across the garden. "It's over."

It was Wednesday, the first day I'd felt up to seeing people, and the captains (minus Prez, who had physical therapy) appeared on my doorstep after school let out. Ahmed brought me a box of chocolates, Dray held a *Happy Birthday!* balloon (they didn't have any *Get Well* options in stock at the Dollar Tree), and Kaeden brought me the textbooks I'd need when I started making up my schoolwork. I told him I never wanted another present from him again.

A video of the fight had made the rounds, so I finally got to see how it happened: Scotty and Tobe started it, but Ahmed sprinting off the sideline is what made all hell break loose. It took a full minute for the referees to establish order; while assistant coaches on both sides tried to break it up, Rutkowski and Bellarmine's head coach were too busy screaming at each other over the melee to help. The video kicked in after Two-Nine drilled me, thankfully; I wouldn't be able to stomach watching the hit. All you could see was Truck dragging me away and calling for the trainer.

When I saw the list of suspensions handed out, I almost cried. Nine starters suspended, and it was *my* fault.

"There's nothing we can do?" I asked, feeling desperate. "We can't appeal?"

"Even if we *could* get it in front of the state by Saturday, we'd lose," Kaeden said. KJ squirmed in his tactical baby carrier, reaching out a pudgy hand in the direction of the last surviving marigold of the season. "They don't mess around with fighting."

With nine suspended starters, of course, our playoff run was dead in the water. What was left of the team still got to travel to Oswego for State Semifinals on Saturday, but with backups at quarterback, running back, and half of the offensive line, it was all but a formality.

I looked at the three boys sitting in my dad's garden and almost sobbed. They'd stood up for me over and over, vouched for me to belong, and this is what they got for their trouble. "I'm so sorry," I said, putting my head in my hands. "You guys deserved a shot at state, and if I'd just taken my suspension—"

"Stop it," Ahmed said sternly. "We did what was right. You deserved to be there, and you didn't ask that guy to go psycho. You know we couldn't let that stand. You'd do the same for any of us."

As much as I appreciated it, that video still freaked me out. Something about the way Scotty hammered away on Two-Nine, the way Ahmed threw a scrawny Centurion to the ground . . . it scared me. The guys had my back, and that meant they were willing to hurt people on my behalf. Something benevolent backed up by something terrifying.

I guess that was football, too: something beautiful, something violent. I didn't know how to make those two ideas fit together in my head. Maybe I never would.

"Is it gonna affect college for you guys?" I asked.

Ahmed rolled his eyes. "I've got SEC boosters sending my mom Edible Arrangements. The rules don't apply to me."

"Mess around with that sentence structure and you've got a 2 Chainz bar," Dray noted absentmindedly.

"Where the hell are you committing, anyway?" I asked Ahmed.

He smiled slyly. "It's a secret. I'm gonna be such a dick about it. Signing day stream, table with a bunch of hats laid out in front of me, the whole deal. You're all gonna have to wait."

Kaeden clarified that he'd be fine, bouncing KJ on his knee. "I'm taking classes at ECC until this guy's a little older, anyway."

Dray shuffled in his lawn chair, looking sheepish. "I just got offered yesterday, actually. I'm gonna sign this weekend."

Ahmed's jaw dropped. "You're committing, and we're just hearing about it *now*?"

"Spill," I said, sitting forward in my chair. "All the deets."

He got the offer he'd desperately wanted: Shelburne A&M, the HBCU in Georgia his parents met at back in the nineties. "I'm gonna play in the SWAC, just like my pops wanted," he said, his smile a little sad. "I just wish it hadn't taken . . . you know."

I knew what he meant; he *never* would've been on the radar for D1 teams without Prez's injury. "It's okay, buddy," Ahmed said, rubbing his shoulder. "You know Prez doesn't hold it against you. That man's *crazy* about you."

"Yeah," he exhaled, shoving his hands in the pocket of his hoodie. "God's got a plan, and I'm following it. But you, me, Grace—we all get to chase the dream. I just wish Zach had the chance to chase his."

"For sure," Ahmed agreed. Then, a moment later, he sat up straight. "Wait—you mentioned Woodhouse. What are you talking about?"

Dray's eyes went wide. "I'm sorry, Grace! I didn't mean to—"

"It's okay." I took a second to figure out how I wanted to do this, because my brain was nowhere near one hundred percent. "There's some stuff I've been meaning to tell you guys, actually."

"So," Tab said, "what if we did pros and cons?"

I took a break from whisking, my elbow crying out in relief. "That's a good idea." I held up the whisk, letting batter drip down into the bowl for my friends to see. "Think it's mixed enough?"

"Probably," Prez said. "If you overmix cake batter, it'll turn out tough and dense."

Dray mock-gasped from his spot across the kitchen table. "Since when do you know about *baking*, Zachary Przezdziecki?"

Full marks on the pronunciation, by the way. That was how I *knew* Dray was smitten. Prez fiddled with the crutch that leaned against the table next to him. "I contain multitudes," he said with a shy smile.

"Holy *crap*," Riley said, pretending to gag. "I'm fine with you being gay and all, but do you have to do it in *front* of me?"

Tab tagged in for me and my sore elbow, pouring the batter into the only cake pan my father owned. "Riley, you pre-heated the oven when I told you to, right?"

"Yes, ma'am."

"Good." Tab slid the pan into the oven and set the timer. "Concussion Cake is a *go*."

By Friday, I felt good enough to start serious deliberations about Saxon Valley. I called for a meeting of the gays, hoping for a variety of opinions. Once I finished profusely apologizing to Riley that my stupid concussion made me miss the Lady Druids' state championship in Cortland, Tab decided the universe owed me a cake as compensation for my concussion and put us all to work. I certainly wasn't complaining.

"Okay," I cleared my throat. "Pro: I really like the campus. It's pretty, and the football facilities are awesome."

"And you like that coach, right?" Dray asked. "Metellus?"

I nodded. "So that's two pros right away."

"Con would be having to live in Wisconsin," Riley pointed out. "Not exactly a hotbed of progressivism."

Prez stated the obvious and pointed out that the media attention would be hell, while Tab argued that breaking a barrier would be worth it. "This isn't just about Grace," she said. "This is about women in football. This is about trans athletes, like, as a whole."

The thought of being that person made my head hurt, so I changed the subject. "Con: being a student-athlete sucks."

It was hard enough managing school with football in high school; in college, it's your entire life. There would be days where I'd wake up early for a workout, sleepwalk through classes, go to practice for three hours, and then trudge back to my dorm after dark with an essay due the next morning.

"Con," Dray said. "You know how coaches are these days, man. That coach could get fired if the team has *one* bad year, or he'll get hired by a bigger school if y'all ball out. And you don't know who that next coach is gonna be."

We went on like that for a while. Pro: I'd be a national figure, so I could probably sign some endorsement deals and make enough money to set me up after college. Con: making big money as a backup freshman kicker was a surefire way to make my teammates resent me. Pro: most of the players seemed totally chill. Con: there were bound to be a few McReynoldses around. Pro: think about how many idiots I'd piss off. Con: I'd be living hundreds of miles away from everyone I know.

We hit an impasse maybe a half hour later, after the sun went down and Dad got home from work. The list hung at a sixty-forty split; it favored cons.

"Pro," I said. "I'd *really* miss kicking."

The timer on the oven went off, and the sound drilled right through my skull and stabbed my brain like an icepick. "*Shit!*"

"Are you—"

"Can someone pull the cake out?" I asked, slumping onto the table. The coolness of the wood pressed against my forehead felt divine. "*Oww.*"

While Dray popped up to handle it, Tab shifted into Mom Mode. "Are you okay? Is there a medication I can get you?"

"Just . . . shh," I whispered. "Quiet is good."

I don't know how long I sat there—the all-encompassing brain fog will do that—but eventually, when the ringing in my ears stopped and the pain receded from Hellfire to Somewhat Tolerable, I sat back up. "Sorry. That was dramatic."

"Don't sweat it," Dray said. "Remember that concussion I got back in freshman year? I know how it is. Take it easy."

I knew they were right, but that didn't mean I wasn't annoyed about it. It'd been almost an *entire week* by now, and I was going nuts. I closed my eyes, took a deep breath, and counted to three.

"I don't know what to do, guys," I said, looking at the neat list Tab had kept. "It looks *real* even to me."

"You can always wait," Prez suggested. "National Signing Day isn't till February."

He was right, I guess, but it didn't make me feel better. I'd hoped visiting campus would make it all easier, but I felt more divided than ever. If I wasn't rushing to my phone to tell Jerome *yes*, was I really ready to dive into something like this? On the other hand, if I said *no*, I'd have to live with a lifetime of what-ifs.

"Give the cute little mouse that pulls levers in your brain a break," Riley said, nudging me with her elbow. "Think about it more when you *aren't*, you know, literally concussed."

I snorted. "If you were *really* my friend, you'd know it was a hamster on a wheel."

"Nah, it's a mouse. A mouse with pink hair."

"And she wears a little football helmet," Prez suggested.

"Her name is Grace Woodmouse," Tab concluded, "and she's *very* tired."

We all cracked up laughing at Tab's exceptionally stupid joke, and I felt a week's worth of tension leave my shoulders all at once. I was thrilled to be with the four of them, so unbelievably grateful to have people who understood me.

The Concussion Cake turned out pretty damn good, too.

ZOE

Today 10:42 PM

GRACE: hey. i just wanted to let you know that im recovering/doing okay.

sorry it took me so long to say smthg - still cant look at my phone very long

ZOE: That's so good to hear, Grace. I've been wanting to reach out but I figured you were taking things slow

My parents told me to tell you they're praying for you

GRACE: idk if catholic god is looking out for me but I appreciate it lol

ZOE: Father Tom would say he is. I'm more inclined to tell you to take ibuprofen and lie in bed

GRACE: zo im an athlete. over the counter painkillers have always been my god

okay oww. brain hurts. talk more when i feel human

ZOE: Sounds good. Night ✦

Forty-three

On Monday, my first day back at school, I cleaned out my locker room.

Cleanout day was always surreal. The locker room was your second home every single day—for *months*—until, suddenly, it was over, and you had to pack up your life and move on like it never happened. The rest of the team wouldn't get started till the afternoon, but because I was doing half days for the foreseeable future, I went in early.

Improbably, I was certain I'd miss my little storage closet. I said goodbye to the bin full of orphaned knee pads, the leaning tower of shoulder pads, the ever-present stink. Most of my gear had already gone back to the school when they pulled it off me at the hospital: helmet, shoulder pads, my home jersey. When we left the hospital, they gave Dad a bag that held my cleats, my girdle, and my socks. That's all I got to keep.

I gathered up my practice gear and headed for Rutkowski's office. When I knocked on his door, he hollered: "Come in!"

It was dark in the room, an overhead projector throwing game film on the far wall. In the dim light, I saw Rut behind his desk, Rhoads on the sagging couch across from him. It took a moment for me to put it together: this was the State Semifinal that the backups lost in Oswego over the weekend. I watched a grainy Logan Steinmetz drop back, face pressure to his left, then toss a pass incomplete in the direction of a JV call-up.

"You didn't miss much," Rut said, blowing right past *hello*.

"I, uh, heard all about it." I deposited my practice gear on a nearby chair and shifted awkwardly. "I cleaned out my locker room."

"Your father told us you're still healing," Rhoads said. "That true?"

I told him I was improving, slowly but steadily. My focus in first period was all over the place, and my brain was *not* stoked about bright lights or loud noises. Both Dad and Principal Keller agreed that slowly bringing me up to speed was best, thus the half days and plenty of leniency on my assignments. Getting caught up on schoolwork would *suck*, sure, but that was a problem for Future Grace, not me.

"Never seen a cheaper shot in my life," Rut grumbled. "What a joke."

I took a deep breath, swallowed my pride, and said: "I appreciate you standing up for me. After the game, I mean."

"Course," he said. "That's my job. Obviously, you'd prefer *not* to have your captains suspended, but that's what you do. Football's a brotherhood, always will be if a team's culture's worth half a shit." He paused and frowned. "Gender-neutral brotherhood. Whatever."

I snorted. "Thanks, Coach." *Not your coach anymore.* Jeez, what a weird day.

Rhoads insisted that he'd be willing to coach me up in his free time ("If you want to stay in shape for you-know-what," he said with a wink, like Rut didn't know exactly what we were talking about), and I told him I appreciated it. I dug my keys out of my backpack, slipped the old storage room key off the ring, and handed it to him. "I can't believe it's over," I said, exhaling. I hadn't even realized I'd been holding my breath. "Just like *that*."

Coach Rhoads gave me this sad little smile. "Football season comes and goes like any other, Grace." No, it wasn't sad; it was wistful. Hopeful, maybe. "There's always another September waiting for you on the other side."

There's a hole in your life the week after football ends. Your appetite recedes, months of aching muscles start catching up to you. Your body builds up energy that it expects to release at 3:30 every afternoon like clockwork, but instead you're home, it's still light out, and you have no idea what to do with yourself.

Despite it all, life goes on. Everyone was obnoxiously nice to me—being Concussion Girl had its perks, apparently—and it actually felt good for a change. Truck intercepted me in the hall my first day back and doted on me like a mother hen. Tobe and Scotty proudly showed me their bruises and busted lips, pretending to be all tough and badass before accepting hugs. Lucy, our freshman protest sweetheart, even made me cupcakes with little footballs on them. I passed them out in the cafeteria on Tuesday, and we clinked them together like glasses of champagne.

We never got punished for Poster Crimes, to no one's surprise. The heat the school took on social media was more than enough to make them relent; it benefited everyone to pretend like my suspension never happened. I was fine with that, for the most part. I'd have to sit through another six months of school here no matter what, and I'd rather not carry on a cold war through graduation day.

"Good for Ferragamo," Riley mused in pre-calc on Wednesday. "She got to rebel with zero consequences. Batting a thousand."

"Pretty romantic," Tab said, deftly ducking out of the way of my thrown pencil.

On Wednesday night, I finally called Jerome Metellus, who'd been in contact with Rhoads since the concussion. His questions, shockingly, were more feelingsball than football; he asked me about my recovery, how I'd been handling the attention. He complimented me on my interview, which shocked me. "Standing up for what you believe in is important," he said. "I don't care what anyone says. You showed excellent character."

I was the one who brought up Saxon Valley, in the end, when I told him I intended to wait until February to make my decision. He didn't sound surprised, though; he just asked me to keep him in the loop.

"No matter what you decide," he said, "I'm proud to have been involved in your journey, Grace. Keep kicking ass, okay?"

It took me a few months to realize that he probably knew my decision before even I did.

Then school was out, and it was Thanksgiving. Last year, Dad and I caught the invite to Zoe's family dinner, where we had to pretend like we fit in with her very loud Italian family and their mind-boggling food spread. This year, the two of us celebrated the holiday like we had when I was growing up: we ordered Chinese takeout and eschewed the NFL for whatever movies we could find on cable. His choice this year: *The Hunt for Red October.* Dad lectured me about how electrical systems worked in real submarines while I shoveled beef and broccoli in my mouth, just like the good old days. It was the most Normal I'd felt in months, honestly, and there wasn't any other way I'd rather spend my Thanksgiving.

Dad finally turned in around midnight, leaving me alone. I spread out on the coach, threw on an old NFL Films documentary, and let John Facenda's voice lull me to sleep.

Then my phone started buzzing.

"Zoe?" I answered groggily. "It's one in the morning."

"Wait. Did I wake you up?"

I forced myself to a sitting position and stretched, feeling my back ache. "I think so."

"Sorry! I didn't know—"

"S'okay."

We sat there in silence for a bit. My brain was still scrambled from the concussion; add in the sleepiness and the post–MSG haze, and it felt like I was experiencing reality through a dozen layers of plastic wrap. "You called me," I said eventually. "What's up?"

After a few seconds of silence, she said: "I dunno, maybe it's dumb. I was thinking about last Thanksgiving, how you were here with us. And . . . I got to thinking about you, I guess."

"Oh."

"So . . . feel free to say *no*," she said, "but can I come pick you up right now?"

I sniffed my armpit. "I have *not* showered today, Zo, I gotta be real."

She laughed. "Not . . . pick you up like *that*. We just haven't really hung out since everything happened. I've wanted to see you."

I closed my eyes and sighed. "Does it have to be at one in the morning?"

"I have an idea," she said. "A little trip. I think you'll like it."

There it was again: a flare-up of my Down-Bad-itis. I rose to my feet, the *crack* of my knees so loud I wondered if Zoe heard it. "Sure. Yeah. Whatever we're doing, just gimme a sec to wake up."

"Cool. Uh, dress warm, okay?"

Before—May

Your name's not important, because you're changing it soon. Right now, you're trying to give Mr. Ferragamo's camera a convincing smile.

"Excellent," he says, swiping through the photos he took. Mrs. Ferragamo huddles up with Zoe and fusses over her hair, her corsage. Today's junior prom, and you're in Zoe's backyard to take pictures for 1) posterity and 2) the Gram. If everything goes to plan, this is the last time you'll ever have to wear a tuxedo in your life.

"I'm thinking we go for a silly one next," Mr. Ferragamo says. "Sound good?"

You and Zoe settle on posing back-to-back while holding up finger guns; it makes everyone happy, and you admit it's a little fun. Afterwards, Zoe throws her arm around your shoulders and gives you a big theatrical kiss on the cheek. Mr. Ferragamo takes a volley of photos, memorializing this version of you forever.

You've been torn on whether or not to duck out of junior prom for weeks. The suit you're wearing is coarse, baggy, disgustingly hot. It feels like you dressed up for your own funeral, which feels apt. Zoe, meanwhile, gets to wear this gorgeous orange dress, a pretty corsage, a full beat. You're not even ashamed of being jealous anymore.

In the end, you couldn't bring yourself to bail on Zoe. None of this was her fault, after all. Plus, it'll give everyone one last round of good memories before it's all over.

"Hopefully this won't be *too* lame," she says in your ear, not loud enough for her parents to hear. "Sucks that we have to wait an entire year for *real* prom."

A car horn sounds just in time to bail you out of having to promise her a Senior Prom you can't give her. "You mind if I talk alone with Jordan real quick before you go, sweetie?" Mr. Ferragamo asks, and you feel your anxiety surge. He puts a fatherly hand on your shoulder and leads you a few dozen feet away.

"I know you've never been anything but a gentleman," he says, "but that's gonna continue tonight, right?"

"Of course, sir. One a.m. curfew," you say, because you know the script well.

"Good." He glances back at Zoe, who's talking with her mom. "You've always treated her with respect, and that doesn't go unnoticed. But I was a teenage boy myself, if you can believe it, so I know what it's like to make dumb decisions. Think with the head you've got up *here*, not the head you've got down *there*. Capisce?"

Sex is so far from your mind that you almost laugh. "Capisce," you say, your face red.

He laughs and claps you on the shoulder. "You're a good kid. Now, what about this guy from Notre Dame the Bills drafted? How bad's the knee injury?"

Thankfully, the horn blares again, and you're saved from one of the last Man Conversations of your life. "Good talk," Mr. Ferragamo says with a chuckle. "I guess you'd better get going, son."

Then Zoe's there, and her hand slips into yours. In three days, you'll break up; in three weeks, you'll spend a day anxiously pacing in your room before you finally come out to everyone you know. Your life is *so* close to changing forever. It scares the shit out of you. Right now, though, there's a dance, and there's a girl.

When Zoe looks up at you and smiles, your heart aches. "Everything okay, J?"

Not right now, you think. *Someday, though, it could be.*

Forty-four

Twenty minutes later, I opened the passenger door of Zoe's Kia and blinked. "You're gonna be the death of me, Zoe Marie Ferragamo."

She leaned over the passenger seat, holding out a vase of flowers. "You're gonna be the death of *me*, Grace Woodhouse, if you don't take these."

I nearly fumbled the deceptively heavy glass vase. "Where did you even *find* flowers in the middle of the night on Thanksgiving?"

"Bought them a few days ago, actually," she said, looking embarrassed. "But I wanted to wait until the time was right."

It was an arrangement of shrub roses, all this soft apricot color. The inner flower nerd I'd nurtured in the garden over the years took over. "They're pretty," I said, smiling. "I know the cultivar. *Rosa* 'Grace.' You're not slick."

She groaned theatrically. "Damn your flower knowledge."

I ran back into the house and set the vase on the kitchen table, trying not to be The Gayest Bitch Who Ever Lived about it. I'd gotten Zoe flowers a few times while we dated, obviously, because that's what boyfriends do. This was the first time anyone had even gotten me flowers, and she went out of her way to pick *special* ones.

"Even though you're corny as hell," I said when I slumped back into her passenger seat, "I really appreciate it. Means a lot to me."

"I'm glad. After the last couple weeks you've had, you deserve flowers." She threw her car in reverse and backed out of the driveway. "Next stop: Niagara Falls."

"Really?" They're pretty, sure, but living within driving distance made them pretty blasé. "That's like ... forty minutes away."

"Have you ever been at night?"

"No. I think I've gone, like, five times in my entire life."

"You won't regret going at night," Zoe said. "Promise."

She put on an indie playlist and we floated through the Buffalo night, up and over the Skyway. We caught up on the drive: student council drama, which boy Leah was currently blowing up Zoe's phone over. I told her about my recovery, how I'd been bored out of my mind, how the football team handled the end of the season. The conversation carried us clear across Grand Island to the other side, where the industry by the Falls lit up the night sky in a red-orange haze.

"Weird question," Zoe said. "Do you have a middle name?"

"I mean, I did before."

"Well, sure. But do you have a new one?"

I furrowed my brow. "Uh. Should I?"

"I dunno! It doesn't really matter, but you invoked *Marie* earlier, and it doesn't seem fair that I don't have a counterpunch."

"I don't know how you pick a middle name," I admitted, feeling dumb. "I already picked a *first* name. Don't ask me to do any more work."

She was silent for a moment. "I really like your name," she said softly. "I dunno if I ever told you that, but ... yeah. It suits you."

"Cause I'm graceful as fuck?"

"Naturally."

We finally arrived at the American side of the Falls to an empty parking lot, save for the tremendously fat squirrels that bully treats out of guilty tourists. The air was *much* colder up here than it was at home; even layering my Buffalo Beauts hoodie (I used Concussion Sympathy Points to steal it back from Riley, finally) and denim jacket let the air in. I pulled up my hood and shivered.

"I can't believe you've never been here late at night," Zoe said, looking entirely unbothered by the cold. Under her unbuttoned jacket, I caught a glimpse of The Hoodie, and I couldn't help but smile. "You remember Alyssa, right?"

"Your cousin," I said, following her down a path into the park. Zoe was full of energy; I, on the other hand, still felt half-asleep. "The one who goes to Dartmouth?"

"Yeah. We used to come here at night all the time." She turned around and shot finger guns at me. "Keep up!"

"You *could* walk at my pace, you know."

Zoe led us past the closed visitor center and down into the deserted park itself, our path lit by whining streetlamps. Even in the dark, I saw mist rising in the distance. "You know," I said, "it's just water. It's just *big* water. *Loud* water."

"It's pretty! Don't be so grumpy."

We strolled right up to the railing, a group of women speaking Mandarin nearby our only company. The park ran right up to the edge of the Niagara River, where the American Falls crashed down into the rocks below. The falls, always lit by this massive set of lights from the Canadian side of the river, were bright orange. The color danced on Zoe's face, shifting to red as the lights cycled through their pattern.

Way more affecting than that, though, was the sound. Thousands of gallons of water crashed every second, and without the hum of omnipresent tourists, there was nothing to cut the endless churn. It swallowed me in a weighted blanket of noise. Given how tired I was, I could've fallen asleep standing up.

I held up my hands in surrender. "Okay. You got me. This is cool."

Her face silhouetted by the glow of the falls, she smiled at me, warm and sincere. "Glad you like it."

We stood there in silence at the railing for a long time. Eventually, she threw her arm over my shoulder; I burrowed into her side. "It's *freezing*," I complained.

"Let's step back from the rail, then. Don't need you catching a cold on my watch."

We retreated to a nearby bench, but the roar of the river didn't subside. "Do you wanna switch jackets?" Zoe asked. "Mine's a little warmer."

"It's okay." I inched closer to her. "I'm good."

We shared in each other's warmth for a while, our arms around each other, until our faces were an inch apart. We made eye contact. I felt her breath on my lips.

At the exact same moment, both of us said: "I can't."

We stared at each other, frozen in confusion, until the reality of what just happened finally hit us. Then we started laughing.

It began as a giggle, but it quickly cascaded into honest-to-god mania. I laughed until my abdomen ached and my head pounded. It must've looked funny to those poor tourists: two girls tangled in a messy hug on a park bench next to Niagara Falls in the middle of the night, shrieking like banshees.

Once we finally collected ourselves, I scooched over an inch or two. "Room for the Lord."

"Oh, *shut it*."

The next time we made eye contact, it felt steadier, more certain. "Do you . . . wanna talk about it?" I asked hesitantly. God, Grace Woodhouse was initiating *feelingsball*. Maybe that concussion knocked a few screws loose.

Zoe picked a sprig of dead grass and released it, letting the blades fly away in the wind. "I'm guessing we're on the same page, right?"

"That I'm a girl who hasn't grown boobs yet," I suggested, "and you're a disaster bisexual who needs to get her shit together?"

She snorted. "Well, I don't know if I'd put it like *that*."

"How would you, then?"

Zoe considered that, the falls rushing back in to fill the silence. I thought about what Tab told me that night at her house, that my feelings weren't everyone else's burden. I still loved Zoe—maybe I always would—but she *had* hurt me: the night she deadnamed me, the last time we hooked up. I couldn't swallow it and pretend I was invincible, not anymore. I'd spent my entire relationship with Zoe swallowing the hurt, and all it'd ever done was make me miserable.

"I don't know," Zoe finally said, her eyes on the blue-gray rush of the river. "I *do* need to get my shit together. We both do. I mean, someday..." Her voice trailed off, and a moment later, she shook her head. "*Someday* doesn't matter. Right now, *this*"—she gestured between us—"isn't fair. Not for either of us."

The longer we sat there, the more I felt at peace with it. Maybe Zoe and I had a *someday*; maybe we didn't. For now, though? We were just two girls that understood each other. I was stoked to be friends with her.

"This is, like, *so* adult of us," I said, which earned me a playful shove.

"The most adult thing you can do is pat yourself on the back for being adult."

"Whatever." I rose to my feet and held out my hand; she took it. "Are we friends, Zoe Marie Ferragamo?"

She groaned and popped up next to me. "If you insist, Grace Esther Woodhouse."

I clutched my heart, utterly devastated. "You gave me an old lady middle name?"

"Pick one, or I'll give you a new one every time."

We took one last look at the falls (they'd gone green; go Druids) before beginning the trek back to the car. She took the lead again, seemingly by default. "Do you want this sweatshirt back?" she asked, glancing over her shoulder. "Like, for real this time."

"*Absolutely* not," I said. "If you knew how I got it..."

"What? Didn't you just, like, buy it online?"

I shook my head, unable to keep a grin off my face. She frowned. "What's so funny?"

I'd been keeping so much from Zoe. There were the big things, the *current* things—Saxon Valley, what went down on the recruiting trip, how much the thought of my future scared me—but there were a million little lies, too. She didn't know I'd taken her clothes while we dated. She had no idea just how bad things had gotten for me last year. Whatever we were to each other from now on, I knew I owed her the truth.

I had time to get to everything—an entire *senior year*, even—but The Hoodie felt like a good place to start.

"You're never gonna believe me," I warned her. I picked up the pace, fell into step at her side.

"Grace Wilhelmina Woodhouse," she said with a smirk, "you are *full* of surprises. I doubt you've got another one up your sleeve that could faze me."

As I told Zoe the story, I thought about the poor, angry kid that found The Hoodie in the first place, the kid who couldn't begin to imagine where the next year would bring her. I wondered what she'd make of me. I wondered what she'd make of *this*: two girls walking side by side into the night, at ease with one another, laughing like old friends.

She'd have a few questions, probably. But I think she'd be happy.

AFTER

June

"Embrace the endless changes, flames to corners of our pages
There can't be two of us forever."

—Reade Wolcott, "December,"
by We Are the Union

Over the speakers, ScHoolboy Q urged me to shake it one last time. My ankles felt like they might snap at any moment.

"*Man*, DJ's not doing a bad job!" Dray yelled over the outro, squeezing Prez's arm. "Can't remember the last time I heard that song."

"It still goes," I said, my voice scratchy after a long night of screaming pop rap on the dance floor. The next song began, a new track from some pop girlie that made half the hall scream. "I gotta sit down for a sec. You guys good with that?"

The two boys followed me back to our table, giving my aching feet a moment of relief. I'd known my first outing in heels would be an adventure, but nothing could've prepared me for the reality of it. "Kaeden's dancing his *ass* off, bro," Dray said, cracking up. "Good to see him cut loose."

From across the hall, I watched him and Mikayla Gardner spin each other around wildly. KJ was under the watchful eye of his grandmothers back home, and, in a rare moment of feelingsball, Kaeden told us he was excited to feel like a "normal" senior for once while the team posed for pictures. When we all informed him that he was literally the normal-est dude we knew, he beamed.

Pictures had been just another stop in a long, *long* day. A long week, really, if you counted all the bouquets I'd arranged at the shop. Pageland

Prom was always on the first Friday of June, and after breakfast in the cafeteria (when they set out industrial-size troughs of donut holes and passed out yearbooks), seniors were turned loose. Since then, I'd been running around: lunch with the boys, makeup at Tab's house, pictures at the Delaware Park Rose Garden. Prom was at this old event venue in South Pageland with high ceilings and bad AC, and I'd been sweating all night, which was *not* great for my already shaky self-esteem.

I tugged at the neckline of my dress. It was *fine*. I'd be *fine*.

"*There* you are!" Tab shouted, stomping over in very heavy, *very* loud boots. She'd gone full Goth Princess, wearing an elaborate black gown that made her look like a vampire. Waves of teal hair fell to her waist; when she turned eighteen a few weeks back, her parents finally let her dye it. Behind her, hand in hand, trailed Riley and Imani.

Dray pouted. "Grace's dates are here, babe. Fun's over."

"Fun's only just begun," Riley said, rolling their eyes. They'd shed their suit jacket and looked, like, *obnoxiously* good in their dress-shirt-and-suspenders getup. The green of their tie matched the green of Imani's box braids.

The four of us had gone as a unit: Tab and I were the single ones, while Riley finally bit the bullet and asked Imani out a few months back. Between the new pronouns ("they/she, but the 'she' is silent and I'm still a lesbian") and the new girlfriend, Riley was thriving. They'd probably punch me in the kidney if I told them this, but I was proud of them.

The six of us migrated over to the punch bowl, where Dray and Prez joked with the girls and I revived my aching body with syrupy red goodness. Our little gaggle drew more stragglers, like drama president Darren Gossum, who told me my dress was "*ravishing*." Tarot Card Robin joined us with Scotty Bowen on her arm, their whole situation as perplexing and unknowable as it'd been since the winter. Zoe and Leah swept through, giving everyone hugs. "You look incredible," Zoe said in my ear. "*Told you* blue was your color."

I sighed and flipped her off. "No one likes a sore winner."

Like Tab and me, Zoe and Leah flew bachelorette. Zoe vigorously assured her parents that she didn't need them to find her a date this time, a story she told us proudly over coffee a few weeks ago.

"Don't go growing a spine on us now, Ferragamo," Riley joked. "Those rich girls at NYU aren't gonna know what hit them."

Zoe had rolled her eyes, but she couldn't stop smiling.

NYU was new, too. Over Christmas break she'd had a certified Senior Year Crisis and realized she wanted to go chase her dreams in the big city rather than settle for the local school and, after some deliberation, she took the plunge. I was thrilled for her, even though I knew I'd miss her like crazy.

Dray and Prez, who looked incredible in burgundy and navy, respectively, kept bumping elbows. Prez still wasn't out, officially, but he was getting more and more lax; I joked the other day that half the senior class must've known by now. The way he smiled and threw his head back when Dray cracked a joke warmed my cold gay heart.

In the next few months, Ahmed would be off to Tennessee, Dray to Shelburne A&M. Prez officially retired from football and got into Ohio State, where he planned to party first and figure out the rest later. Tab got accepted by a theater program in Boston while Riley started their full-time job at their uncle's auto shop in Cheektowaga next week. Truck (who was *much* too cool for prom) was about to ship out for basic training. Zoe was off to New York. We were scattering to the winds, all of us.

Feelingsball time. I threw an arm over Dray, another over Leah. "I love you guys," I said, wobbling on my heels. "You're the best."

"My girl ain't even *drunk* yet and she's telling the homies she loves 'em," Dray laughed, squeezing me in a side hug. "Long night ahead!"

The DJ called for a slow song, and all of us immediately started egging Dray and Prez on. Dray cocked an eye at his man and held out his hand. "Up to you, QB1."

After a moment that seemed to last a lifetime, Prez took it. "Fuck it. Full send."

We all screamed and lost our minds as the boys migrated to the dance floor, along with just about everyone else. Zoe glanced at me nervously. "Mind if I dance with Leah?"

I'll admit that a tiny part of me—a part I'd long accepted might stick around for a while—was disappointed. Thankfully, the rest of me said: "Of *course* not."

Everyone streamed off to the dance floor in pairs, leaving just me and Tab. "You gonna dance, Grace?"

I shook my head. Even if I *wasn't* in heels, I'd need a few drinks in me before I felt comfortable enough to do it. I told Tab I was fine, encouraged her to go find the band guy she'd been crushing on, and spectated from the sidelines. It was nice, in a way: I watched Dray rest his head on Prez's chest as they swayed, saw Riley swing Imani like a madman. Zoe and Leah goofed around on the edge of it all, both of them having learned high school's darkest secret: there's nothing better than being single, beautiful, and eighteen.

"Fellow introvert?"

A girl I didn't recognize strutted towards me, plastic cup of sparkling juice in hand. She had warm brown eyes, a rusty-orange dress that flowed around her. "Not an introvert," I said, smiling weakly. "Just not a dancer."

She hung around, to my surprise, and we chatted for a bit. She was from Hamburg, it turned out, and she'd come as a favor to some band girl she grew up with. "I don't know anyone here," she complained, sipping her drink, "and I'm making it your problem. Cute tattoo, by the way."

I hadn't realized I was been rubbing it. The ink on my wrist was fresh enough that I probably *shouldn't* have been touching it, really, but the raised skin felt nice under my fingertips. Tab had done the design: A *P* in old-timey script—the logo on Pageland's football helmets—and our graduating year in the same font next to it. Black ink, maybe an inch lengthwise. "Thanks," I said. "My friends and I got it to commemorate . . . something cool we did."

After Dray became the last captain to turn eighteen in May, a whole bunch of seniors from the team rolled out to a tattoo shop and got the same ink. We hadn't won state, sure, but that didn't matter. We were celebrating ourselves.

"That's adorable," Hamburg Girl said, not asking further questions. *Thank god.* "So, I don't mean to be weird or anything, but I wanted to ask you something."

My heart sank. Of *course* she knew who I was; she didn't come up to me because she thought I looked cool or whatever.

Then she surprised me: "Do you work at the flower shop on Gragg and Welles?"

A massive wave of relief crashed over me. "I've been there for a few months now!"

Hamburg Girl explained that she'd come in a few weeks ago to buy a bouquet for her sister's dance recital, and I couldn't keep the grin off my face. "The arrangement you made for me was gorgeous," she said. "You've got skills."

I took a long sip of punch to hide my blush a mumbled a *thank you*.

I'd been making it up as I went along these past seven months, and it was starting to feel like I might actually *get* somewhere. Without football hanging over me, I had time to think about school, about what I actually wanted to do with myself. I got a part-time job working for a florist in town on the weekends, and the extra cash would help me afford tuition at ECC, the local community college. Program: undecided. The plan: pile up credits and see how I felt after a year.

Obviously, all of that meant saying no to Saxon Valley. That wasn't easy, not even a little bit. I'd miss the hell out of football—I mean, I already *did*—and I knew I'd spend forever wondering if I could've made it, if I could've handled the pressure. Did that suck? Sure. Telling Jerome sucked even harder, even if he understood completely.

The thing is: no matter what, at some point, you have to leave the game behind and find out who you really are. I thought about Prez's injury, Jerome's dark night of the soul in the Nordic wilderness.

"Everyone's got their own Finland," he'd said. No matter what, I just kept coming back to that night in Brockport, to that tackle I made, that one last field goal in the slush. *That* was the part of the game I wanted to hold in my heart forever. What I told Jerome was: "That's my Finland."

I'd never felt freer my entire life.

The slow song came to an end, finally, and familiar synthesizer notes lit up the room. Hamburg Girl and I couldn't help but laugh at the sight: hundreds of kids who'd been slow-dancing thirty seconds ago turning back into horny goblins while Flo Rida *mmm-mmm-mmm*ed his way through the intro.

From across the hall: "*Grace!*"

The crowd parted around Ahmed and a few other football boys, all of them waving me over. "Get your skinny ass over here, girl!"

Scotty cupped his hands around his mouth. "We're getting *low*!"

I laughed, apologizing to Hamburg Girl while I set my punch glass aside. "Duty calls."

She raised her glass. "See you at the next slow song, Flower Girl?"

I smiled, told her I'd be there, and hit the dance floor just as T-Pain started belting out the chorus.

Acknowledgements

One of the Boys has always been a hail mary.

For starters, its first draft was written by a horrifically depressed liquor store employee fresh off a virtual college graduation with zero plan for the future, but beyond that, it's about two things young adult fiction usually isn't: trans girls and sports. That this book exists at all is a miracle; that I'm *proud* of it is only possible thanks to the many people I'm about to thank. As a wise man once said, it takes a village to make me look dope, and it's a big, *big* village.

First and foremost, I need to thank the core of Team OOTB: Jordan Hamessley and Irene Vázquez. I was *terrified* before my first phone call with you, Jordan, and you immediately put me at ease with your confidence and kindness. I am eternally, *eternally* grateful that you took a chance on me; I couldn't ask for a better agent in my corner (hook 'em). Irene, your vision and enthusiasm for Grace have stunned me from day one. From rambling emails to texting about Bad Bunny, working with you has been a blast. An outsider story like this needed champions that Got It, and honestly, I think you two Get It even more than I do. Texas forever.

Thank you to the team at Levine Querido for their hard work and belief in me, with special thanks to Antonio Gonzalez Cerna, Kerry Taylor, Danielle Maldonado, and Freesia Blizard. Additional thanks to Jon Stich for bringing Grace to life with a cover that quite literally made me cry, as well as Will Morningstar, Meghan Maria McCullough,

Casey Moses, and Lewelin Polanco. All of you brought this book to life and made it beautiful, and for that, I'm in your debt.

To GiannaMarie Dobson, who read the first four chapters of a meandering story about a transsexual kicker I wrote in February 2021 and encouraged me to keep going: there is no *One of the Boys* without you and your constant belief in me as a writer and friend. "Thank you" is not nearly enough. To Emily, Siobhan, J.R., Katie, Yeardley, Briar, Taylor, and the rest of my early readers: your hands are all on this book, and I hope you approve of where you've helped guide it. Thank you.

To Janet McNally: if you hadn't taken an eggy nineteen-year-old football blogger aside in your Intro to Creative Writing class and told her to consider a major change, I would not be writing fiction right now. I can't thank you enough for getting me through college in one piece, Professor M, but I hope this will suffice. To Professor Eric Gansworth, Dr. Mick Cochrane, and many more professors I could spend all day naming: thank you for making Canisius a place I wanted to be. To Mrs. Carolyn Lee: the Stuff-I've-Been-Reading essays you assigned in AP Lang are what first drew out my writer's voice. Thank you for putting up with sixteen-year-old me. I owe you a beer; let's meet back up at that alley pub in Brixton sometime. (If you're her student and you're reading this: sorry I was assigned reading.)

There have been times in my post-transition life where I feared football wouldn't have a place for me, and I've been thrilled to discover over and over how wrong I was. Thank you to all of my friends working in and around the game, but special thanks to my darling cohost Katie Rose and everyone who made *The Tuck Rule* possible; someday, we'll talk Presbyterian football and Sam Ehlinger again. To Alex, Richard, and Godfrey of *Split Zone Duo*: thank you for keeping me sane in quarantine and inspiring Grace's throwback recruiting violation. To Holly, Spencer, Ryan, and Jason from the *Shutdown Fullcast*: I've been listening to y'all since I was Grace's age, which is beyond surreal to type out. You consistently help me find joy in a cruel game, and for that, I thank you. An especially big thank-you to Jason Kirk, who took me seriously as an Author *far* before I did.

To Mom and Dad: uh, does "thanks" cover it? Mom, I'm honored to have written the first book you've read since *The Fault in Our Stars*; Dad, I hope this gets you off my back. To Cate and Beth: I love you idiots. Next book is about sisters; buckle up. To the real-life male friend group from high school I still share a groupchat with (whose name I'm pretty sure I can't type here): you're the best friends a girl could ask for. You'll never hear me say anything that gay again. I'm sorry/you're welcome.

To Ron: babe, I sleep next to you every night, you already *know* what you mean to me and this story. So, instead I'll say: your talent and thoughtfulness consistently astound me. I can't wait to see what you make next.

Lastly, to all the queer kids holding this book: whether your story looks like Grace's, Zoe's, Dray's, Prez's, or none of the above, this story sees you. You're tougher than every ten-ply soft "adult" that makes it their life's mission to ruin yours. Know this: they *will* lose. Stay strong. Keep your head up. September's waiting for you on the other side.

About the Author

Victoria Zeller is a trans writer born and raised in Buffalo, New York, where she still proudly resides. A former football player and lifelong fan, her initial focus was sports journalism before she made a sharp pivot to writing about queers who can't stay out of trouble. Her sports-writing can be found at Defector, while her manic minute-by-minute sports analysis can be found on Twitter at @dirtbagqueer. *One of the Boys* is her debut novel.

Some Notes on this Book's Production

Art for the jacket was created by Jon Stich using acrylic paints and colored pencils on illustration board. The jacket and case were designed by Casey Moses. The text was set by Westchester Publishing Services, in Danbury, CT, in Richmond Text, by designer Matthew Carter. It is a striking serif family, initially commissioned for a newspaper redesign and has since been expanded with contributions from Jill Pichotta and Richard Lipton of The Type Founders. The display was set in Le Monde Livre Std, by Jean François Porchez, and the sans serif font throughout is Proxima Nova, by Mark Simonson. The book was printed on 78 gsm Yunshidai Ivory uncoated woodfree FSC™-certified paper and bound in China.

Production supervised by Freesia Blizard
Book interiors designed by Lewelin Polanco
Editor: Irene Vázquez
Associate Managing Editor: Danielle Maldonado